ERASE

THE IS THE FIRST BOOK BY J Y BARRIS

ERASE

J Y BARRIS

Copyright © 2017 by Julie Barris

Printed in the United States of America

First Paperback Edition, 2017

ISBN-13: 978-0999277706
ISBN-10: 0999277707

jybarris.wixsite.com/erase

For Sam — my world, my everything.
This book would not have been possible if it weren't for your
constant support and understanding.
I love you with all my heart, always and forever.

CONTENTS

ERASE

PART ONE

RESENTMENT

6 p.m., the sky was already solid black when the two finally went on their way back home. This by no means indicated the end of Daniel's sorrow however. As no one could possibly bring back the dead from their graves, those who loved them that were still alive only continued to suffer. It was a sad fact he had come to realize since the recent passing of his beloved sister — Megan.

Megan was found dead about a week ago, lying bare in her own blood and gore inside the bathtub at her apartment. Her body was cold and stiff, and her skin was already a purple color when the police got to her. The knife used to cut her wrist was still secured in her hand. She had committed suicide, or at least believed by the officials to have been the case. They retrieved a hand-written note from her nightstand that same day they discovered her which just concluded it. Due to sufficient evidence to determine the cause and manner of her death, an autopsy was eventually adjudicated unnecessary and her parents agreed.

Daniel had just gone out of state for business when his mother called to give him the catastrophic news. Immediately, he dropped everything and returned home in support of his folks during this difficult time. Since that day, last Tuesday, time seemed to have stood still for them as they mourned their loss. Just this morning, a small, pri vate memorial service was held for her at the family's church in Blue Port, Megan's hometown, during which Mr. Skala, her pessimist of a father, condemned the dreadful city life for killing his precious little girl:

"She's always been a small town girl, always cheerful and full of life. Never once harmed no thing or raised her voice to nobody... Had I disapproved of her decision to leave home, this would never have happened... For heaven's sake! She was only twenty-eight years old!"

The ancestors of the Skalas originally hailed from Dinkelsbühl, a historic town in Bavaria, Germany, and eventually settled down on the northeastern tip of Minnesota in a remote little farm town called Blue Port. The population of Blue Port had not increased by much since a century ago, from less than a hundred people back then to now just short of five hundred. Shadowing his father's footsteps, Mr. Skala grew up inheriting the family's farm and became a lowly third-generation farmer in his early twenties. Soon married and with a child, life was as good as he had hoped for until Megan was about eight years of age, when his wife suddenly passed away from leukemia.

His wife's death prompted his search for a proper mother figure for their daughter, and as such, through a friend's introduction, he met Denise, a young divorcee at the time with a son named Daniel. Four months after their initial courtship, the two wedded and so their families merged. Living under the same roof, the children naturally became close. Even though they were not linked by blood, growing up, they were like two peas in a pod. The local kids would often tease them for their seemingly unbreakable bond. Although a month younger, Daniel would stand up every time and be a brave, protective brother to his tenderhearted Megan against all sorts of sarcasms thrown at them.

And so, all through childhood to adolescence, the world those two lived in was so different from their peers. It was a world they had created for just the two of them that seemed so perfect and practically impossible to be intruded upon. Well, almost not. It all started to change at the age of eighteen, when Daniel decided to pursue his dream of becoming an aviation engineer. In spite of his earnest persuasion to get Megan to leave home, to go away with him and attend university two hundred miles down in the Twin Cities, she was skeptical. As her mind gradually set on devoting her life to help local children with special needs, in the end, she revoked his idea completely.

The family had a tearful send-off on the day of his departure:

"I promise I will drive home every chance I get," Daniel told his mother, who was already crying at the thought of separation.

"Not if he's busy with school," Megan cut in, standing near the open door of his car.

He moved along to give her a hug right before getting in.

"Promise me you will try harder getting A's than thinking about home," she told him assuredly while hugging, but he did not believe her.

"Is that really what you want instead of seeing me?" he asked her right back.

It took her a few seconds to answer. "Of course."

He let out a soft laugh, and then whispered behind her ear something that made her body shiver. "You liar. Next time I come home, I'm going to take you with me."

Up until that point, Megan had not cried for anyone else other than her own mother when she died on her deathbed, but that night, she cried particularly hard and long behind closed doors, in her bed, and in her sleep.

As sweet as was his parting message that almost sounded like a solemn pledge, it never did come true. Since going on different paths in life, in fact, the two were seldom in touch, and Daniel never did come home as often as he had promised, if at all. Like that, the magical bond between them slowly faded and seemed to have become more of a childhood memory than anything. For a long time they were occupied with their separate way of living, focusing mostly on what was in front of them. It was only natural that, with time, they each met someone special, someone that would take new priority in their new grown-up lives.

Then, a few years went by, a day came when Megan received a wedding invitation in the mail from Daniel. Upon reading it, she set it aside somewhere and never got back to it. From his mother, who, on occasion, drove to see him in the city and brought back news, she had heard of this younger girl he met in college mentioned a couple times. Therefore, his getting married was not really a surprise. Though that might be the case, something about this supposedly blissful event was just too sad for her to feel happy for him and so, as a result, she never attended.

The two only reunited three years later on this last Thanksgiving Day. Shortly afterwards, she decided to move down on her own to seek jobs in the Twin Cities as, incidentally, the organization she worked for back home was forced to shut down due to lack of funding. Life in the metropolis quickly demanded from her. Adapting to it was not easy, especially not for a woman who had spent all her life living and breathing small town customs. Despite hard work, before long, she managed to find herself a cheap apartment and a job at a local welfare center.

Her constructive quality could have been enough to see her through the toughest time, at least everyone who knew her personally believed so, which was why no one — none of her friends or former social work colleagues, and least of all Daniel — would have predicted such a tragedy, a pathetic resolution so to speak, that she had to turn to just ten months following the move. *Perhaps something bad happened on her last days*, they thought, *something that deprived her of all hope, or perhaps it was entirely something else that drove her to the end of her road*... The thing was, nobody really knew the real reason she chose to end her life so brutally and recklessly, but most of them, like her parents, had come to conclude that depression must have somehow found its way to her.

After the memorial service and a reception at the funeral home, the casket in which Megan rested was transported for the burial that followed later in the afternoon, to the family's farm where a headstone was erected next to her mother's, praising her as "One of the Most Kindhearted Persons You'd Ever Meet". The sky that had been crying just started to cry harder when they arrived at the burial ground. In the rain, the parents wept more intensely than ever before. Their moans, at first low and to themselves, became vehement as they watched her casket being lowered into the grave. Strangely, Daniel just stood there the whole time, looking unusually calm and not shedding one single tear, despite the total contrary that everyone had solely expected from him.

2

NOTWITHSTANDING THE FOUR-HOUR drive ahead of them back to their suburban home, Daniel had not spoken since getting into the car. His eyes focused strictly forward, and only on occasion when needing to change lanes did he look out the window to the side for a brief second. His hands held steadily onto the steering wheel the whole time even though, more often than not, he was going down empty, straight roads between either wide-open fields of nothingness or deeply wooded forests.

His wife was not about to be fooled by his stiff appearance however. As good at acting cool and untroubled as he was, Allison had known better — just as his silence proved the opposite — that his mind had long wandered off to misery thinking about Megan. It would seem absurd to be bothered by that, but she was, even just slightly; and she had her reasons to be, good reasons. She also knew now was not the time to make a fuss about the past, so to do him a favor, she just sat in the passenger seat, not muttering a word either and let him be the entire way back.

The minute they walked through the door into the house, Daniel went at once upstairs for a shower. An hour later, the water was still running. Reckoning it as another one of his pitiful attempts to cope with his sister's passing, she intended not to interrupt him. Frankly speaking, she barely pulled through this day herself, but for a completely different rationale.

Having been battling insomnia for two months straight, she mostly felt restless these days. She honestly did not recall the last time she had a good night's sleep nor how that should feel, and abusing over-the-counter sleeping pills only helped build up her tolerance for the drugs, leading to her becoming more reliant for their meager results. Owing to persistent exhaustion, she had come to notice a more easily agitated side of herself that was worse recently than ever before. Sometimes her nerves got so tangled up inside her, to an extent where a simple ringing of the phone could give her the jitters.

Exactly that happened the moment she was shaking pills out from a brand-new bottle. Consequently, it slipped off of her hand and hit the floor, scattering the little tablets all over the kitchen tiles. Meanwhile, her phone continued to ring, and to make matters worse, the caller hung up the second she answered it. Flustered, she tossed it onto the kitchen counter without thinking before squatting down on the floor to clean up the mess.

Having heard the commotion, Daniel showed up at the doorway shortly, half-covered with a towel around his waist. "Who was that?" he asked her regarding the call.

She shot an annoyed look up at him. "Wrong number," she said and then focused back on collecting the pills.

Right then, their conversation ended. As the feeling of awkwardness gradually crept up on them, Daniel responded by retreating upstairs.

This kind of nothing-to-say-to-each-other moment never seemed to leave the couple alone in recent months. As in fact it had gotten more frequent since the day Daniel returned from his business trip, since he learnt of what happened to Megan. Coming up to their fourth wedding anniversary, unlike the previous years, they hardly anticipated this one. Simply put, there had been problems in their marriage that were still up in the air unresolved, and not being able to talk about them openly with one another certainly burdened further their already unstable relationship. Worse yet, every time just when Allison plucked up her courage to try to restore something, fate seemed to have its way to demean her effort.

Right after the cleanup, she sought Daniel out upstairs in their bedroom and found him still in his towel, sitting at the far corner of the bed with his back turned at the door. She went and hugged him from behind, asking in as cheerful of a tone as she could muster, "How are you?"

Having been caught up in thoughts, Daniel was somewhat startled by her notion, yet managed to pull away subtly from her embrace and walked over to his drawer to pick out a pair of boxers and an undershirt.

"Not too bad," he said in the process, "How about you?"

"Same," she muttered back without a change in emotion, even though knowing they were both lying to each other.

Swiftly unwrapping himself, he changed into his undergarments five feet away. Not saying another word, he went on to fluff up his pillow and then lay down underneath the blanket, quietly.

Despite seriously doubting her ability to fall sleep any time soon, she joined him in bed. In that next second, he reached out his hand to pull at the little chain beneath the shade of his nightstand's table lamp, switching it off.

Underneath the dim light from her side of the table lamp that was still gleaming on the walls, they lay there still, both staring aimlessly at the ceiling fan. Their bodies separated from each other as if two magnets with like poles facing one another, creating a natural repellent. There were definitely things to say before they would close their eyes and call it a night.

"I have that appointment tomorrow morning," Allison said out of the blue.

"Oh, right. I said I was gonna look up the address for you... Did you eventually find out how to get there?"

"Yes. I have my GPS all set up for it."

"Good. What time is it at again?"

"Nine o'clock... I told you that like five times this week."

"Right, right..."

Then, there went the agonizing silence again.

Although slightly ruffled by his constant inattentiveness of late, momentarily, she turned her body towards his, leaned in close to his ear and whispered to him: "I love you."

For a moment — even just a brief one — Daniel turned his head sideways to look at her in a way he had not in a long time. There might still be sadness in his weary eyes, but that smile that he flashed her no doubt was every bit genuine and not forced.

"I love you too," he replied, which did her more good than the many pills she had been taking that fixed nothing.

It's okay. Everything's going to be okay from now on. She thought to herself optimistically, but things were not always what they seemed to be on the surface.

3

HOURS INTO THE night, troubles began to visit.

Allison had just dozed off momentarily, dreaming of tossing and turning in the dark and her struggling continuously to find a comfortable position in bed to fall asleep. During the time she heard her cell phone's everlasting siren coming from downstairs. *It's one of the most annoying, infuriating long stretches of sounds known to mankind*, she thought, and no matter how much she tried to ignore it, it was persistent about demanding her attention till it eventually *woke* her.

Her body still ached, and her eyes still felt heavy when she opened them. First thing she saw was the clock on her nightstand that said three o'clock in the morning. She was still very much tired but in a way wild awake. In a moment, she thought she heard a low, tonal tune going off in the distance, thus focusing on her hearing to try and catch it. Then, she heard it again — that same annoying ringtone she was picking up in her dream. It was only then did she realize her supposed "dream" had really been reality. Who knew how long she had actually slept or whether she really did, but so as to not let the ringing wake Daniel too, she had decided to do something about that phone of hers.

When she got to it, it was still ringing from the kitchen counter where she last left it. The screen said "Unknown Caller", and therefore she rejected it without thinking twice. Though as she was carrying it with her back upstairs, it started to ring again in her hand.

She stopped immediately on the steps leading up into the master bedroom to look down at the bright screen that again said "Unknown Caller". This time, she decided to answer it.

"Hello?" she uttered guardedly into the speaker.

"Hi Allie," a distinctively deep male voice, slightly gravelly in its undertone, responded on the other end of the line.

It can't be... "Who is this?" she asked for the sake of certainty.

"It's Adrian," the man said.

Her heart skipped a beat hearing the name that would confirm her speculation. Her mouth opened slightly and then closed, wanting to say something but she was not so sure what to say.

"Hello?" Adrian called out, having not heard her for quite a while.

Turning away from the bedroom door, she sat down on the carpeted step and held her free hand just over her mouth to sort of block out her voice as she continued, "How did you get my number?"

"That's not important —"

"It is to me."

"I want to see you Allie."

She paused to gulp, and then told him bluntly, "It's not possible."

"Don't say no to me before considering it first."

Despite his plea, exactly what she did not allow herself time for was to consider it.

"I'm sorry, but I can't. Please, don't call me again."

"Allie —"

"Good-bye."

"Allie wait!"

She hung up.

DAY 2 | SEPT 7 MONDAY

4

ALLISON WAS NO stranger to psychiatry. She had always hated those much-ado-about-nothing visits to the psychiatrist's office her parents put her through at a young age, but as a child, she really had no power to raise an objection. Owing to many poor experiences in this area, she would surely never seek help from a psychiatrist, and their ilk, if she had a choice today.

Her options were running out fast however. Solely last month, she had attempted numerous home remedies to induce sleep; though from taking long, warm baths to aromatherapies, none thus far had produced a satisfactory result for her. About two weeks ago, her best friend since high school, Sara, mentioned Dr. Lisa Cooke during a causal chat over the phone and recommended her to make an appointment. She certainly doubted the idea at first, but after much struggle with herself, helplessness eventually motivated her to give it a go.

Dr. Cooke's office was located in downtown Minneapolis, inside one of those tall, shiny commercial buildings. There were a variety of registered businesses currently leased in that particular, twenty-story building. A single, locally established e-prescribing corporation that utilized the space as their headquarters occupied the first five floors. Three floors above them were shared by three different medium-sized LLCs offering digital-marketing services to independent enterprises. And then, there was the ninth floor, where a mix of small law firms and specialized medical practitioners cluttered together and often referred their clients to one another when deemed appropriate.

Her office was among those on the ninth floor, no. 910 to be exact, the one with big black letters in alignment that read "LISA M. COOKE, MD OF PSYCHIATRY" hanging on the display wall inside two great glass doors. Allison saw those letters immediately after the elevator door slid open. She had not let the idea of seeing a mental-health professional sink in entirely just yet, and therefore, every little step she took her heart somewhat held back. Upon getting out into the hallway, a sense of apprehension quickly overwhelmed her. She stood there, outside, running her eyes across those letters once more before eventually, hesitantly, proceeding to give the door handle a pull and enter.

Following along that display wall, she took a right when she could, and the reception desk was just around the corner. A young receptionist — no more than twenty years old — was sitting up front, looking very much preoccupied with her phone when Allison initiated a conversation.

"Hi. I have an appointment at nine o'clock."

"Name?"

"Allison Skala."

Seconds later, though unwilling, she broke her concentration to look briefly at the computer screen. "Oh yes, 9 a.m., Mrs. Skala," she said, and then handed Allison a clipboard attached with a two-page survey and a pen placed on top of it. "Here, fill this out and take it with you when you go in to see the doctor."

"What is this?" Allison asked her, flipping through the pages and looking them over.

In turn, the young lady rolled her eyes as if saying "dur". "It's a 'Health Assessment Form' as indicated here," she replied very impatiently, double-tapping on its printed title. Swiftly afterwards, she resumed texting on her phone.

Her less-than-acceptable conduct just so provoked even more negativity than Allison was already feeling about this place, but instead of calling her out for it, she had chosen to turn a blind eye and turned for the empty waiting room behind her. There was a couch against the wall to her left, a coffee table in front of it on which a couple Health Science magazines were strewn about, and a TV mounted on the right wall. She took a deep breath before moving to sit down on the closest end of the couch.

During the time she stressed to fill out the information as requested on the papers, a custodian — middle-aged, bald and wearing a mucky soul patch desperately needing a trim — threw open the door and lurched into the office to take care of some garbage business. He looked to be a fairly curious being. As he went behind the reception desk doing his job, he was paying more attention to his surroundings than what was in his hand.

Meanwhile humming to himself, he had come to empty the small trash bin placed near where Allison was sitting. He was standing close enough for his shadow to be cast onto the sheet of paper to which she was attending. That more or less threw her off and ultimately caused her to lift her head to look up at him. Despite the weird twitching of his eyes that he could not help, he stared back in a snoopy kind of way that made her feel utterly uncomfortable, and, ever so slightly, frightened. Nervously, she smiled back at him, pretending as though nothing was out of the ordinary so as to resist letting her prejudice blow out of proportion.

Just then, a woman, forty-something with long curly red hair partially upswept in a loose bun, emerged from behind a closed door in her white lab coat worn over a purple blouse and dress pants.

"Mrs. Skala?" she called out.

Allison knew right away that had to be Dr. Cooke. Never was she so glad to meet a new face — let alone a doctor — but *thank God*, she thought, and abruptly, jumped from her seat to greet her.

A handshake and a brief introduction later, the two entered the therapy room and thereupon, the door was shut behind them.

5

THE THERAPY ROOM was relatively capacious, with floor-to-ceiling windows letting in the sun that naturally warmed up the space. Though Allison could feel none of that warmth, as in fact her hands had not felt colder since she walked in and went straight for the blue upholstered sofa reckoning it as the "patient's couch" to sit down.

In a leather chair from across her was Dr. Cooke, looking at ease with a notepad on her lap and a pen on top of it. Allison studied her for a minute, *a friendly looking face, and a seemingly confident, competent doctor*, she thought, but really did not care much for any of that as she kept reminding herself at the same time, *prescription, prescription, prescription* — *h*er sole goal for coming here today was to get it and get the hell out.

"I hope it wasn't too bad of a drive for you. Sara told me you live in the suburbs," began Dr. Cooke, whose smile had not dropped since the moment they met.

"It wasn't bad," Allison replied.

"How long did it take you to get here?"

"About thirty minutes."

"Oh that's nothing. Some of my patients live so far away that they can't always make it here on time. It's even harder for them in winter. Where do you live if you don't mind me asking?"

"Arbington. Near Lake Marit."

"I saw some nice houses in that area a few years back. My husband and I were actually planning to settle down there before our first child was born. But then his father passed away, so in the end we decided to stay put in the city so as to take better care of his mother."

Uninterested in making small talk, Allison comment-ed nothing. Her lips sealed tight and pulled back into as much of a near-smile she could muster. Having picked up her notion, Dr. Cooke therefore moved on to look at her Health Assessment Form.

"Okay. Let's see here."

"I haven't quite finished the last portion on the back."

Flipping the form to the other side, she scanned over what she meant and said to her, "That's fine. I tend to pre-fer asking my patients directly regarding that part. So far though, it looks like you don't have a particularly alerting family medical history or any major health concerns be-sides muscle soreness and body aches, which are very common for people suffering from chronic insomnia."

"It's been two months since I've had a decent rest. I've tried many things and taken every brand of over-the-counter sleeping pills available to help me sleep."

"Have you?"

"Yes."

"And did any of them work?"

"Obviously not... Otherwise, why would I be here?"

Just then, Dr. Cooke paused for a moment, leaning forward from her chair to assume a more serious posture. In a calm and respectful manner, she took to start her analysis. "How are you Mrs. Skala? Or may I call you Alli-son?"

"I'm fine. And yes you may."

"Do you feel stressed or worried at the present time?"

Without thinking first, Allison went on to assure her, "No. Like I said I feel fine, just mostly tired. If you could prescribe me some pills, I would much appreciate your help."

"I'm afraid it doesn't work that way Allison."

"What?"

"Drugs can only offer temporary comfort. I can certainly give you pills that work more effectively, but it won't fix the underlying issue that causes the problem in the first place."

"What are you suggesting?"

"To cure your insomnia once and for all, we need to first dig down deeper."

"How do you mean?"

"Well, based on the information you've provided here, it doesn't look to me that it's caused by a known illness or other medication. So let me ask you this, are there any significant life stresses that you are currently facing?"

"No."

This time, Dr. Cooke smiled at her rash answer, all the while encouraging, "Work with me here Allison. I need you to really think. Was there, or were there, perhaps, any unexpected events occurring in the past few months that might have affected your mood whenever you are reminded of them? Events such as moving to a new city, losing or changing your job, or even the death of a family member?"

The death of a family member... Instantly, Allison's heart fluttered at the thought of Megan in a way she could not simply explain.

"Well?"

"My sister-in-law passed away just recently."

"I'm sorry to hear that. Were you close with her?"

"No, not at all. We hardly talked to her in fact, and I've only met her once on last Thanksgiving."

"'We'?"

"Yes, Dan... Dan and I..."

Stupid me. Can't believe I'm dragging Dan into this.

"… I mean my husband and I, we never did keep in touch with her much."

Noting her uncomfortable stammer, Dr. Cooke prompted, "It's okay Allison. Take a deep breath if you want. I know it isn't totally normal for you to talk about your private life with a person you've literally just met, but I'm here to help you…"

Genuine as was her gesture however, Allison ignored it, hurrying to conclude. "All I'm gonna say is, she killed herself a week ago. We had just attended her funeral yesterday and that was the end of that."

"How do you feel about that whole situation?"

"What do you mean?"

"Well, do you feel sad, angry, or possibly relieved?"

"Someone in our family just died, of course I feel sad. So would anyone in the same situation."

"How sad?"

"*How sad*? I don't know. Sad is sad. What kind of question is that?"

It seemed the more Dr. Cooke attempted to get to the specifics, by and by, Allison found her to be incredibly irritating. She could only interpret her tactic of questioning as an aggressive invasion of her privacy and nothing else.

"… To be fair, not even my husband cried, even though everybody expected him to."

"Oh? Were they perhaps close-knit siblings?"

"I suppose they were as little kids."

"How often did he mention her, or does he still?"

"Rarely. Maybe once a year around Christmas time, usually about their childhood together and things that he missed doing as a family back then."

"Does it bother you?"

"Does *what* bother me?"

"Their bond. Did you ever have a problem with that?"

That very question alone might just have pushed her too far. Upon getting asked, her mind debated whether to continue the conversation or should she just get up and stomp off.

Finally, "I don't find this discussion or any of your questions remotely related to my sleeping problem," she snapped.

"You would be surprised how much they relate," Dr. Cooke insisted nonetheless and confidently, going along with her own intuition.

"If something stresses me out, I would know that of all people. Who knows me better than myself?"

"You are right. You should know yourself better than anyone. Although in your case, I sense that it's not a matter of knowing, but rather a matter of facing."

"Facing what?"

"Facing what's bothering you."

"And you think it bothers me that she died?"

"What do you think?"

"For the fact that she died just recently, and I have been suffering insomnia *long* before that, so I'm going to say, *no*."

"Is that your rationale?"

"YES!" Allison shouted back with anger that was perhaps uncalled-for.

"Then — what's really bothering you if that's not it?"

It was as if she had just gotten into an hour-long argument with someone, an argument she could not win no matter how hard she fought. She had come here expecting questions more than anything. Though even knowing she should not take offense so easily when getting asked and especially not at someone who was only trying to be helpful, she had had enough at this point.

"I don't want to answer any more questions. I'm sorry for being rude but to be quite frank, I'm really tired. I would just like my prescription for today."

Dr. Cooke, as it turned out, was not the slightest bit ruffled. "You don't have to apologize," she told her. "I will go ahead and prescribe you some medication for now. Just tell Laura your pharmacy's location on your way out. She will be able to schedule your next appointment as well. I would like to have you come back some other time when you feel more ready to talk —"

"Don't worry about it Doctor."

There went a brief pause before Dr. Cooke would continue again. "I do regret if I have said something to violate your trust."

"It's not that. It's nothing personal really. I just... I just generally don't have a good impression of physicians."

"Well, you might reconsider after —"

"No. I really don't think so."

Since starting to practice medicine ten years ago, she had gone through quite a few patients like Allison who were skeptical about psychiatric remediation at first, but then eventually came around for therapy. Allison might have a more deep-seated antipathy to the idea than the others as far as she could understand, but she was not at all losing hope yet.

"Here, take this as a just-in-case," she said to her, handing her a business card.

Grabbing the card abruptly, Allison stood up simultaneously from the sofa. Her eyes dashed to the door next and her feet followed, all without hesitation to leave.

6

CARRYING HER EDGINESS, Allison exited Dr. Cooke's office back into the hallway. She might have survived her hardest task, but only just. Anxious to leave the building, she pressed the "DOWN" button between two elevator doors multiple times as if that somehow quickened the lift to her floor.

A few seconds passed by, her cell phone started to vibrate through her purse. After digging it out, seeing that it was her friend Sara calling, she picked up.

"How was the appointment?"

"A disaster," she told her, bluntly.

"It couldn't have been that bad."

"Trust me, it was."

"Why? Tell me what happened..."

While still on the phone, suddenly, she perceived a strange vibe from behind, like someone was staring at her. She thought she noticed a person standing in the back earlier from the corner of her eye, so she turned her head slightly to look and there he was, that same weirdo of a custodian with the twitchy eyes.

"Are you there?" asked Sara.

"Yes. I'm here," she replied to her, turning back the other way to try and ignore his existence. "I'll tell you all about it when I see you, so just hang on."

The instant she finished her sentence, she heard the man's distinct gait meandering from left to right and back again at the rear. His feet dragging across the linoleum floor had made the squeak of his rubber soles from the bottom of his sneakers against it unbearable, and as a result, distracted her from listening to her friend's jabbering.

Eventually, "Hello Allie? Are you still there?" Sara called out to her and somehow managed to regain her attention.

"Oh sorry. I'm here."

"Where were you? I was talking to you the whole time and you said nothing."

"I was just... I was just thinking about something."

"There you go again."

"What?"

"Absent-minded that's what. You told me to tell you when you are like this again, remember?"

"Did I? I really don't remember."

"Since when is being scatterbrained *your* thing?"

"I don't know. Maybe it's contagious. I've been chatting with you more often recently."

"Hey! *Don't* tease me like Ed does."

Allison let out a soft titter.

"Anywho — I'm on the highway now, so I'll see you at the pub in a few," concluded Sara, but before she could hang up, Allison stopped her.

"Wait! Stay with me."

"What did you say? You will have to speak louder or I can't hear you. The wind is pushing my car left and right, making loud noises as it goes. I gotta bring this up to my mechanic next time I go in for an oil change..."

As Sara babbled on, for the third time, Allison's mind was held back when she caught a shadow on one of the elevator doors enlarging in a way as if someone was coming up behind and closing in on her. Unable to loosen her nerves, her body literally froze in place momentarily as gradually, she felt warm breath breathing from the top of her head down to her nape. Mystified, she shrieked and dodged away as a matter of course, turning to face the offender. Strangely enough, she saw no one directly there except for the same custodian who was still standing in his original spot, casually leaning against the back wall a fair distance away.

Right then, the elevator door opened and out came a few men in black suits. "Going down?" one of the remaining riders asked her.

"Yes," Allison responded with relief and proceeded onto the cabin promptly. The custodian as well walked in after her and turned his back at her soon as the door closed.

Still holding onto her phone, she spoke over the speaker to see whether Sara was still there: "Hello? Hello?"

Having observed her silly act, an elder male said to her with a grin, "I don't think you can get any signal in here miss. Believe me, I've been there."

She smiled back at him, and then stored away her phone the rest of the way down.

Once reaching the ground level, the atrium, everyone got out and scattered in separate directions. Upon returning to her car parked in a small lot on the back of the building, she sat inside a moment for much-needed, quiet meditation. A few deep breaths later, finding herself ameliorated from the earlier panic attack, she started up the car, shifted the gear to drive and eased her foot off the brake. Just the moment the car began going though, suddenly:

THWACK

It was again that same custodian, who jumped out of nowhere in front of her, smacking his hands concurrently onto the hood to sort of stall it. Instinctively, Allison stomped on the brake just in time to prevent it from ramming into him. The car jerked back and forth before it would come to cease in place. Immediately following the shock, he drew near her window.

She lowered it basically to yell at him, "What is your problem?!" her pulse still racing.

"You, ahem... you dropped this," he said in his croaky voice, holding up the while Dr. Cooke's business card to show her.

Hastily, she snatched it from him.

"Not even a 'thanks'?"

More frightened than she allowed herself to show, she ignored his remark and steered her way swiftly down the main street. When hitting the first traffic light, she double-checked all her mirrors to ensure he was not somehow stalking her, and if he was, she had her phone ready to call the police.

Luckily in the end, that was more a case of her paranoia than anything else.

7

MOONSHINE TAPHOUSE, A pub located next to Metropolitan Mall at the town center, was a place where Allison and Sara used to frequent before either of them were married. Since this morning had been an overall paranoid nightmare, Allison was more than happy to see her friend sitting at the bar waving her over the minute they locked eyes.

"Hey."

"You hung up on me," Sara scolded her jokingly soon as she came to sit down next to her.

"Sorry. I lost reception in the elevator," she told her, and then turned to order a glass of lemonade from the bartender.

"Lemonade? You are not drinking?"

"It would keep me awake all night if I do."

"I thought you do that anyway, with or without alcohol."

Allison flashed her a fed-up look.

"Right. I'm not supposed to kid about that, moving on. So, tell me, how did the meeting *really* go with Lisa?"

"It's like I said, a disaster."

"What do you mean? Did you get your prescription?"

"Yes. I'm picking it up on my way home."

"Then, it's not so bad right?"

"Well... I yelled at her."

Sara's eyes widened for a second. "No way. Did you really?" she said, sympathizing with her, "You are not a yeller. So it really was that bad huh?"

"I was frustrated with her constant snooping, but I did apologize to her after."

"Snooping?"

"She kept asking me all these questions, digging into my personal life. I was uncomfortable the whole time."

"You do know she's a shrink right? I mean that's just what they are supposed to do."

"I know. That is also why I wish I never had to deal with those people. You know how I get whenever I feel intruded on."

"Very defensive. But to be fair, you are naturally reserved. I still remember it took you almost the whole tenth grade to finally warm up to me. Good that one of us is a social butterfly, otherwise we might never have become friends."

"Right. Well, it just didn't work for me. I'm sorry. I know you think very highly of her," said Allison and took a sip of her lemonade.

"Hey, don't be sorry, because I'm not. She worked out great for me. Honestly, if it weren't for her help, I probably would still be down in the dumps today, depressed, blaming myself for Chad's leaving me. But I feel the most carefree these days like I'm ready to party any time I want, well, almost any time..."

Since becoming single again last year, Sara had been seizing every opportunity — whenever her two sons were at daycare or at her parents' — to hook up with all kinds of guys like she did back in her adolescent days. If love was what she was looking for, the sassy blonde should not have to seem so desperate but that was not it. It only took one painful divorce to shatter a woman's complete faith in men, as was the case for her. After a long journey of recovery from depression, she pledged to never waste time again on relationship commitments.

Her first marriage of six months was a total joke. Married to an unemployed drunk at the age of nineteen, she did it merely to get out of her parents' house. Two years later at a bar where she used to work as a waitress, she met the love of her life, Chad Stewart, a married, business attorney ten years her senior with children from three different past relationships. She only found out his marital status after they started going out, but was by then all too taken with him and his sugarcoated tongue to call it quits. As fate would have it, he divorced his wife shortly, and as evinced in his "leaving his former wife and marrying her instead" gesture, Sara gladly gave birth to their twin boys that same year. Though their fairy tale lasted just over two years. Had she not surprised him by showing up at his office one afternoon with a lunch basket in her hands, and walked in the very moment he was holding down, fucking his secretary at his desk, she might still be taken for a fool today, oblivious to her *prince charming's* promiscuous way of living.

"… Men are all the same I tell you. They are all horny and will cheat just to get you into bed with them. I'm only using them before they have a chance to use me," asserted Sara, delightedly.

As assertive as were her words however, Allison disagreed. "That's not true. They aren't all like that."

Sara took a stealthy look at her while drinking from her mojito. Setting it back down on the bar counter, she talked with reduced enthusiasm, "Right. I just feel bad for you is all. Since *that* happened, every time we talked lately you sounded miserable."

Quickly assuming she was referring "that" to Megan's death, Allison informed her, "Well it's all over now. She was buried yesterday. Her whole family was there, Dan and I included."

"Yeah, but I mean, have you gotten over the whole catastrophe yet?"

"What catastrophe?"

"You know, the whole cheating thing with Daniel. How he did it with *her* on the sly while you were with me and Ed in Vegas a few months back."

Allison was unaware of how hard she had been trying to pretend her husband's little affair with his sister did not bother her — or how much she was still in denial of that ever happening — but upon Sara's blunt delivery, her face instantly darkened every bit with shame.

Two months ago, although never a heavy drinker or a bar-crawler of sorts, Daniel came home incredibly drunk and unusually late one night. While she attended to him, suddenly, the levelheaded guy that he was began crying uncontrollably. She was utterly baffled at first until he started talking. It was then did he break it to her:

"Allie, I have to tell you something... something that I've kept to myself for a long time now. It's killing me for hiding it from you so here goes... You know our relationship hasn't been great lately. While you were on vacation with your friends, one night, Meg stopped by the house. We had way too much to drink, and before I knew it... we... we had sex. It was just that one time I swear to you, and it was no more than a mistake..."

His confession of infidelity struck her like an insult, an abuse to their marriage that echoed in her head in a continuum. Right then, she slapped him across the face out of rage and disgust. That following week, they seldom spoke to one another. It was a quiet house until she eventually made up her mind to forgive him. Neither of them had dared to bring up that night since, nor had she asked him further about his relationship with Megan — not that she wanted to know, ever.

She never did answer Sara's question, but her silence just about did.

As a friend, Sara could not resist criticizing her, "I still don't know why you want to stick around. If I were you, I would have left him that very night and told him to go —"

"'Fuck himself'?"

"Yup."

"Do I need to hear this again? It's not helping me. Besides, that's all in the past now, and she came onto him don't forget."

"Only you would believe him."

"Well I do. I trust him. If only you knew what kind of a woman she was, you would understand."

"There you go again."

"What?"

"Defensive."

"Whatever."

In some such way, Allison found it helpful to point her finger solely at Megan for creating this mess, for wreaking havoc on her marriage really, but ultimately doing so did little to heal her scarred heart. Nonetheless however, so long as it continued to diminish the pain of that open wound, she would keep doing it till it stopped hurting, if it ever could.

8

I F THERE WAS one man left standing that Sara approved of, it would have to be her longtime childhood buddy — Ed. As the one mutual friend between him and Allison, she honestly could not have dreamt of a more perfect match than those two. Allison had always been this soft-spoken girl with an elegant edge ever since she got to know her, and Ed, a sensitive, thoughtful guy that was most importantly, loyal. She was there when they first got together; she was there when they drifted apart. She had heard them all, their stories from both sides. She never planned to meddle in their complex relationship drama — anymore — however, provided that Allison was happy in her marriage. Having learned of Daniel's betrayal just recently, in her own wishful way, she had since been ambitious to reunite her two best friends again, despite already been told "not going to happen" twice, straight from Allison's mouth.

As per her tip-off, Ed stopped by the pub during his police shift, looking handsome and confidant in his uniform contouring his brawny chest and biceps. His short, brown hair looked somewhat more neatly groomed than usual. His typical five o'clock shadow was gone, making his strong, square jawline and that slight cleft in his chin stand out. To make certain he consistently smelled nice and fresh, in addition to adding a touch more aftershave before leaving for work this morning, he had just now bothered to put on a dab of cologne behind both of his ears prior to getting out of his patrol car.

As soon as he walked in through the entryway, his eyes locked on Allison sitting at the bar and he headed right over, absolutely ignoring all the fond attention given by the other women, who literally stopped what they were doing for a second to look on at him in admiration of his virility.

The moment Allison saw him coming, she knew right then it was Sara's doing. "What is he doing here?" she asked, but her friend was acting clueless.

"Who knows? Let's ask him shall we? Hey, how's it going Ed? Solved any crimes lately?" Sara teased him the second he got to them.

"I'm a patrol officer Sara, not a detective," Ed corrected her and then turned to look at Allison, asking sincerely, "How are you Allie?"

In response, "Fine," she said, plainly.

"I heard you are still having trouble sleeping. How did that appointment go this morning?"

Upon being asked, Allison shot Sara a quick glare for again being a blabbermouth, except it was cleverly dodged and ultimately ignored.

Finding the need to leave her two friends alone, out of the blue, Sara stood up from her stool and said to them, "I'm gonna go talk to that cute guy over there. He's been gaping at me this whole time. No point in keeping him waiting eh?" Swiftly afterwards, along she went with her drink towards a fresh-faced male sitting by himself at a booth, swaying the while her hips as the two watched her till she successfully got to him.

The awkwardness was just starting to build up back at the bar, more so for Allison than for Ed. Both hoping to smooth the path for the other person, simultaneously they started talking and as such, a little snicker became their initial icebreaker.

"Ladies first," said Ed. One hand over the bar counter, he slipped onto the stool beside her.

Their bodies naturally turned to face one other.

"I was just gonna ask how you've been. I know we haven't spoken much since... um..."

"Since the beginning of August."

"Right. So, how are things?"

"I'm well. Work is same old, same old."

"Good... good."

"What have you been up to?"

"Not much really. Just been trying for a good night's sleep I guess."

"I suppose that's going to take some time. It's not something you can rush, if you know what I mean."

"I know," she said, and smiled lightly at him.

He looked away from her briefly, meanwhile tapping a rhythm with his fingers against the surface of the counter before looking back at her. "So, how is that husband of yours? How are things between you two?"

"Oh he is... good. Busy. It's just as well, we haven't gotten into a fight for a month now."

"That sure counts as a record."

She said nothing.

"Well, aren't you gonna ask about my love life? After all, that's what you really care about."

"Are you seeing someone?" she asked him, curious.

"Her name is Kate. She's a lab assistant working at the university."

"Let me guess? Another blonde."

"She's a brunette actually, very attractive... She's it for me I think." He could barely look her in the eyes when saying that last sentence, by which he tried to elicit amazement from her.

In turn, "You liar," said Allison, who saw right through him straight away.

He gave a laugh at her wit. "But really, we've only gone on two dates and she's already saying we are meant for life."

"Maybe it was love at first sight for her. You know you always make a good first impression."

"You think?"

"I think so. You can be quite the smooth talker on dates."

"Heh. I'm all too familiar with your first point of view, as it has happened to me once too."

"Yeah?"

His eyes that were already sparkling sparkled even more now, as if there were literally tear of joy hidden deep in them the moment he began to speak in reminiscence. "The first time I saw this girl, I will never forget, I was at school playing basketball with my buddies. Suddenly she came walking by the court wearing her long blond hair halfway down her back, and as she went on her way, they flew along with her movement gracefully in the breeze. In a moment, she turned her head in our direction, I was able to give her the once-over before she would turn back away. Those full lips, that perfectly pointy nose and just the way she dressed, everything about her rang sophistication but mostly... mostly it was her eyes, those piercing green eyes of hers — of an angel — that had me mesmerized. She was, and still is, the most gorgeous thing I ever had the luck to come across. I remember distinctly telling myself and the guys right then, 'That girl right there, I'm going to make her my girlfriend.'"

It really did not take much for Allison to recognize herself as that "angel" to which Ed was referring. She tried to play it cool after hearing his entire story, which he told so well, saying to him, "See what I mean? That's the smooth talking I was just telling you about."

Ed was every bit serious after all, insisting back, "I was not doing that just now."

Finally, the moment she wished not to deal with, "Don't do this Ed," she told him, breaking away from his longing gaze.

"I wasn't doing anything, only stating the facts is all. Certainly though, it was more than just physical attraction between us."

"That's all in the past now and we shouldn't linger in the past. It's only natural that things change after ten years and I've been married for four of those —"

"You know what? You are damn right Allie. No man should have to wait forever for a woman. I get that," he concurred so as to please her, but inside him was still filled with unspeakable bitterness.

"Well... in any case, I'm happy that you are dating again."

"Did you say you are happy?"

"Sure."

"Do you really mean that?"

"Of course. Why wouldn't I be?"

Like any young love, their high school romance started out lovestruck and was full-blown infatuation driven. While it was possibly just a coming-of-age process to Allison, to Ed, it had always meant something much deeper. The summer just before college started, she ended it. He took the breakup surprisingly well at first, though later when he discovered about Daniel Skala, a then senior scholar with whom she had become acquainted at the start of her freshman year, he went off the deep end and blew up at her believing rigidly that Daniel had everything to do with their split. His pursue to get her back grew to be relentless after the incident and extended beyond her getting engaged, and then married, constituting a messy falling-out that officially severed their ties. Time and distance might have helped him gain some perspective on that obsessive, one-sided love he had for Allison for so long, but even over the long haul, it had scarcely changed.

An ex-lover like him with such eagerness in time did come in handy for Allison, who had selfishly initiated a conversation with him back in May this year, and had been occasionally seeking his soft words over the phone when she was feeling most troubled in her marriage in the recent months. He was all too willing of course, to be at her beck and call, to be enslaved once more in this hollow — possibly fruitless — relationship so long as doing so kept him hopeful. A part of Allison lately did wonder what life could have been had she married Ed instead, but only a very small part. Perhaps it was never made known to him, cheating or not, she had actually not once allowed herself to ponder the idea of leaving Daniel. Furthermore, since Megan was no longer in the picture, she was ready to focus back on fixing her marriage that was now bearing new hope. Having said that, it was only a matter of time before she would pull the plug on Ed again.

Sara came back just in time to ease their tension but was quick to bid them goodbye. "I gotta go guys. You know, something came up," she said to them both, grabbing her purse and leaving a tip on the counter.

The two turned their heads momentarily towards the exit door, where the same young man, with whom Sara was talking just then, was standing and waiting enthusiastically for her. Immediately, they knew what she was up to.

"Putting out again?" Ed teased her, and simultaneously received a smack on the arm. "I'm just saying don't overdo it. Remember your kids still need you."

"You can bite me Ed," Sara fired back in jest, flicking her hand under her chin at him. Turning to Allison next, she reminded her, "Don't forget about my housewarming on the 27th."

"I haven't."

"Good. Alrighty then. Ciao guys."

After she hurried away, Allison also took the chance to take off. "I'd better get going too. I need to stop by the pharmacy on my way home."

"I should get back to work then. Still have to issue a couple more tickets to fill the quota by Sunday," said Ed.

And so, the two left the pub together. He walked her to the car, which just so gave them a couple more minutes alone.

"Are you planning on going to Sara's party? I heard that she's invited the whole neighborhood. Who knows how many people will actually care enough to show up," he said to her, partly jokingly.

"That's still weeks away. I'll see how things go. Dan might have plans for us that weekend."

"Right... Well, I hope it won't be long till we see each other again. I sure miss getting together, even if you don't feel the same way."

Here we go again.

"You know it's not like that Ed —"

"Hey, I'm a big boy. So, no harm done there," interrupted he assertedly, just so sparing Allison another awkward moment. Right before they parted ways however, he extended his arms towards her for a good old-fashioned goodbye hug. Granted, it seemed like such an innocent request, but still, she was hesitating.

Having noticed that, he asked for it in a playful manner, "Would it be totally awful if I were to give my friend a gentle squeeze?"

Consequently, she smiled and gave in.

As he stood there embracing her, his arms naturally pulled taut till the gap between them was only the narrowest of margins. The fact that he was not much more taller than Allison — about three inches taller at five feet nine — made it easy for him to sniff the top of her head while caressing her soft, shoulder-length blond hair in the process. Meanwhile, in a whisper, "Wow," he exclaimed as if on cloud nine.

"What is it?" asked Allison.

"This. I miss this nice tenderness between us."

She understood what he meant, but she also knew every reason to not surrender to his vulnerability, thus slowly pulling back from him.

"Stay cool Ed, and take it easy," she told him at long last.

Ed could do or say nothing more but silently endure that inner dissatisfaction exclusive to his comprehension, of which he had only been trying his best to obscure this whole time but could no longer. His face dejected as he watched her getting into her car and simply driving off out of there, all in a manner of determination.

9

I T WAS NOT without reasons of course, that absolute devotion Allison had for her husband of almost four years. Surely, with regard to physical appeal, Daniel might not be as athletically built as Ed, but he was too, without question, a handsome young man — dark hair, blue eyes with a lean, fit body of an admiring height at six feet two. There was a distinct, noble subtlety to him like that of Mr. Darcy in *Pride and Prejudice*, despite having been raised in a rural area outside of the metro, in an average family with humble parents. He had always been mature beyond his years, and moreover, a natural-born leader with an immense sense of self-confidence adequately upheld by his intelligence. He was well respected among fellow scholars back in his academic years, and his colleagues now of a world-class airplane-manufacturing corporation called MAG (abbreviation for Mercury Aeronautical Group), for which he had been working since graduating university with honors. All of his superb qualities — having just named a few — fitted every bill in Allison's book, so to speak, as the ideal male upon whom she was so very inclined to bestow her affection. She especially loved him for the gentleman with a hidden wild streak that he was, a man who could rise to the challenge and take charge, a man in which she still very much trusted — or so she kept having to remind herself these days.

Megan might not be a problem anymore, but she would be lying if the idea of Daniel sleeping with yet another woman never crossed her mind. On returning home, she was surprised to see his car parked in the garage at only four o'clock in the afternoon. For he was normally still at work at this time of the day, this had aroused her suspicion. The minute she came through the front door, upon seeing an unknown pair of women's tennis shoes on the doormat, immediately, she was thinking the worst. She nonetheless spent a moment to gather her nerves before going from the foyer, passing by the doorway of the kitchen in stealthy steps and eventually into the living room where he was.

"Are we having company?" she spoke up to him right then, keeping her head held high and her sanity in check.

From the couch, Daniel turned his body around slightly to look at her. "No, why?" he replied without hesitation, seemingly innocent.

"Whose tennis shoes are those then?"

"What tennis shoes?"

"Those white ones by the door. They certainly aren't mine."

Puzzled by her interrogation, he insisted, "I have no idea what you are talking about."

Though just when he finished speaking, a bang emanated directly from above them. They both heard it and looked to the ceiling. Not giving it a second of thought, she rushed upstairs and barged into their bedroom to investigate, but eventually found no one save a bottle of hair conditioner lying on the bathroom floor. It had apparently fallen from the toilet tank where it was originally stored, and most likely what that bang was about. She felt somewhat relieved as opposed to finding a woman in her bed that she was so scared yet determined to catch just minutes ago.

Returning the bottle to its place, she hurried back downstairs to the foyer to ascertain if the mysterious pair of shoes were still there; sure enough, when she got to it, they had since inexplicably disappeared as though they were never there. A similar incident that happened just two days before was now making her wonder whether she was seeing things, again. Instead of a pair of shoes, it was a lady's bathrobe then. She had learned from the Internet about how the lack of sleep could affect a person's perception, but never would she have expected her condition to worsen to this extent and this fast. All she could really do was pray for Dr. Cooke's prescription to work its miracle tonight.

Meanwhile, Daniel had not moved from his spot when she got back to him. Contrary to her anxious state of mind, he appeared calm and collected as usual, sitting at the couch with his ankles crossed, preoccupying himself with some age-old photo albums.

She went to sit next to him, asking him the while, "How was work?"

"Same. Finally finished the aircraft blueprints for the SkyEagle Project. But then a few hours later, Matt received orders from above to move the assembly tasks two weeks sooner. He was ticked off."

"That sounds like more work, and they let you go home early?"

"Is that a problem?" he asked her back, looking right at her.

"No. I just didn't expect to see you home so soon."

He said nothing more, and straightaway focused back on rearranging the few photographs lying before him on the center table.

In an attempt to grab his attention, she moved to climb behind him, squatting down in the gap between his back and the couch cushion to give him a nice shoulder massage. In turn, Daniel closed his eyes for the time being, straining his neck left and right to let the pleasure fully sink in.

Spontaneously, she suggested, "Why don't we go out for dinner tonight? We can go to that Italian restaurant you like, listen to the live music and dance a little. You know, to take a load off. What do you think?"

He gave her idea a moment of thought and then turned to speak to her over his shoulder, "I kinda feel like staying home for the evening. Is that alright with you?"

Despite the obvious disappointment, she managed to disguise it somewhat flawlessly. "Of course. It was just a random suggestion anyway. So, what would you rather do tonight?"

Still very much absorbed in his own activity, Daniel did not respond. As he returned to flipping through the one album lying open in his lap, a specific photo triggering a childhood memory caught his eyes. In remembrance of the particular Fourth of July backyard party that took place in the picture, he could not help a chuckle.

"What is it?" Allison asked him, mainly referring to his laugh but he was unaware of it, or did not care in a sense that he just wanted to tell his story to someone. "This was taken by my mother I believe, in our old back-yard in Blue Port. She came home after shopping for gro-ceries and brought Peter with her. They had been seeing each other for a while, but that was the first time ever both of our families got together to have a barbecue. When he officially introduced Meg to me, I was so totally against the idea of having a sibling. So as a protest, I delib-erately gathered every sparkler there was in the house and would not share them with her. See how I was carry-ing more than my tiny hands could handle? Meanwhile, there she was, little Meggie, crouching down in a corner, frowning enviously on my happiness. Boy, was I selfish as a child..."

His eyes glistened with glee as he went on to tell an-other sibling story brought on by a different photo, and another one after that. Having recognized his effort as mere grief, Allison listened for a while yet made no com-ments whatsoever. Much as she would like to be consist-ently empathetic, each time she heard him say her name in such a sweet, loving way was like provoking a storm, which in time broke out halfway through his speech when she called, "Stop," interjecting in a bit of a harsh tone of voice, "I don't want to hear any more of this."

He was just about stunned by it. "What?"

Coming around from behind, she stood before him and repeated the same sentence to his face, "I said, I don't want to hear it."

"I heard you..." he said, looking up at her. His lips pressed together as if holding back words he feared speaking, and then calmly, he let it go. "Alright."

"Are you really?"

"I don't understand."

"She's gone Dan. *Dead*."

"I know. I just… I just miss her is all."

"'*Miss her*'? Humph. She won't come back to you no matter how many times you dig through those old pictures of yours."

Those spiteful words from his wife, of a jealous type, finally caught his attention. "Did I say something wrong again?"

"Yes. As a matter of fact you did."

"What was it then?" he asked her, slamming shut the photo album and tossing it aside to focus solely on her. "Tell me."

"Everything!!!" she shouted.

"Can you be more specific?"

"How can you be so insensitive —"

"And I really don't think asking my wife for some support in a time of need deserves an outcry."

"'Support?!' Don't even! You don't need me Dan. You need *her*! She is all that there is in your head these days and don't you lie to me!!"

Shaking his head, he told her as rationally as ever, "You've lost your mind. I'm not continuing this conversation until you calm down…"

His calm was her weakness however. "You know what? I don't give a *shit* about your needs. You've been cold and neglectful towards me for a long time now. In the last month, you haven't once had the courtesy to ask about me. It goes both ways Dan." Upon bawling him out, she stormed off before he had a chance to — if he even was going to — justify himself.

10

U P THE STAIRS Allison hastened and shut the door behind her upon entering the bedroom. Right away, she was regretting some of the things she had railed at Daniel back there out of impulse.

Why did I end the fight like that?

Why did I make it seem like I was rejecting him?

I should have given him a chance to defend himself even if what he came up with was likely going to be excuses...

I'm just the worst though; I shouldn't have said all those heartless things to him at a time like this.

His sister did just pass away and he's just grieving; there's nothing more to it... or...

Humph, who am I kidding, she obviously means more than I ever could to him. Otherwise, he would have come after me the second I stomped off.

Even if he was held back by his pride just then, why...

Why isn't he coming up looking for me now?

What is really holding him back?

Does he even love me anymore...?

The deeper she sank into despair, the more her heart was overwhelmed with grim emotions. She threw herself onto the bed, and let her tears run freely into her pillow. Her sobs gradually prolonged and with fewer convulsive gasps in between until she was just crying without pauses. The only reason she stopped a couple minutes later was really because she was out of energy and also, more or less, because her phone had been vibrating on and off in her back pocket since she locked herself in the room.

Sitting up on the bed, she reached to grab it finally and pick up the call. It turned out to be Adrian.

"I told you not to call me again," she told him off straight up, her voice hoarse.

"I need to see you Allie —"

"I've already told you — I can't."

He caught her irritation, thus asking her plainly, "What's the matter?"

"What do you mean?"

"Did something bad happen?"

"No," she lied. "Everything's fine."

Though he was not buying her pretense even slightly. "You can't fool me. I can always tell when something isn't right with you, since you don't lie very well..."

She got quiet, swallowing the rest of her tears. That mild understanding from him somehow helped smooth over her despondent mood.

"Come on Allie, let me see you for half an hour tomorrow."

"I can't."

"Why not? You can't possibly be on your laptop writing all day."

"It's not that. It's just... it's just not a good idea."

"*Please?* What do you have to lose?"

She honestly could not think of anything to lose right that moment. "Um... I... It's just —"

"No more 'um' or 'it's just'. You need to get out of the house to vent your frustration, and you need someone to be there to listen, someone you can trust. Now tell me, who fits that role better than me, your big brother?"

His perseverance was paying off slowly.

"Come on Allie..."

"Where do you want to meet?" she went on to ask him.

"How about our usual place? Say, 10 a.m.?"

I suppose it's only for half an hour. "Okay."

"Did you just say okay?"

"Yes I did."

"Yeeesss!" She heard him cheer in the background and imagined him doing a fist pump. "It's a deal. Until then, just hang on for a bit longer."

After the phone call, she was no longer urging to cry, and was over again vitalized by a sense of hope that she would not have otherwise felt and perhaps should not have, for reasons that were conveyed to her many times in the past.

DAY 3 | SEPT 8 TUESDAY

11

T HE FIRST NOVEL Allison had ever written was a romance fiction about a regular college girl named Alice Reed, her adventure of falling in love and eventually settling down with a egocentric, preppy East Coaster. It took her two years from start to finish, published shortly after her graduating from university with a degree in literature two years ago. Her next novel, also her most recent, was a sequel of the first, involving the same two main characters but this time about their rocky newlywed life. It was put in print in the start of March this year, and since then she had been on a break.

She had wanted to pick up her pen again for some time yet found it all too grueling to actually do so due to her sleep deprivation. But last night, much praise to her new medication, for the first time in forever she slept through the night uninterrupted. Feeling somewhat reenergized, as soon as she rose from her bed this morning, she grabbed her laptop and sat herself down at her desk in the bedroom while still in her sleeping gown, ambitious to put some ideas down for her next book.

Perhaps she was overly optimistic to begin with. An hour into brainstorming, she was still just sitting with her legs up on the chair and her arms wrapped around them, either staring blank at her computer screen or out the big window before her at nothing. The plain white pad of sketch paper she had laid out to use for scribbling notes was still plain white, and the four-thousand-dollar fountain pen her father got her one birthday was still there sitting on top of it, barely touched.

Just then — *9 a.m.*, she thought, staring at the clock.

As time kept ticking, her mind only wandered further from her goal and gradually overloaded itself with anxiety to see Adrian, despite many mental attempts to try overcoming it. Her anxiety after all was reasonable, as meeting up with her brother was generally a daunting task. Aside from the zing of anticipation, there always seemed to be a dark cloud hanging above her head, discouraging their supposedly harmless gathering.

If truth were told, the Crawfords had never been your typical household. Allison's father, Elton Crawford, was an immensely reputable man among his elite circle of friends of high society, and a known political influencer with strong ties to the Republican Party ever since his father was elected senator for the state in 1975. On top of notability, he was also the CEO and chairman of Crawford & MacNeil, a multibillion-dollar pharmaceutical corporation of which he co-founded at the mere age of twenty-five. The enterprise had in the past thirty some years, under his vision and guidance, earned an excellent standing within its competitive market and continued today to flourish through a tremendous network of distributing franchises established throughout the world.

Allison's mother was not any less fortunate, if not more. Perhaps better known as Brenda Becker, she was the daughter of the late Benedict M. Becker the third, a second-generation telecommunication tycoon and historically one of the richest men in Minnesota in the sixties. Coming from a long line of wealth, she had been leading a privileged life pretty much since birth. Due to a strict yet every bit pampered upbringing, she was a well-educated woman with sort of a snotty edge, generally well mannered but only to the people whom she deemed worthwhile of her time. She had never worked for anybody, as there was no need for her to; and like Allison, she was once a novelist in her prime. After her father passed away one year into her marriage, consequently, she was willed part of his estate, money enough to support the most extravagant lifestyle for a lifetime.

Given their enormous fortune and high-ranked social prestige, serious expectations for their children were bound to follow. One of which in particular, they stressed their behaviors in social context to be in a strictly decorous and obedient fashion — meaning doing nothing that could potentially dent the family's name. Though ever since as far back as Allison could remember, Adrian had always been considered — in their parents' eyes — hugely lacking in this area. Due to which, growing up, the discord between him and their mother was especially relentless and at times intense. Allison would frequently find herself, in a sense, trapped between them as she came to know and trust her big brother of a six-year age gap. It was a rare sibling bond that they shared, relying profoundly on their mutual understandings of one another. In return for his selfless, brotherly care, she had even fought back for him many times against their mother's criticism despite her initial instinct — which she was taught — to not.

That support system was not infallible anyhow; because at the same time, Allison had always known her parents' opinions of him were not baseless. After all, Adrian was a neurotic character, lovable but volatile. Of the many legitimately bad incidents that happened beginning at a young age, the one that stood out for her took place when he was around ten years old, where he lit his bedroom on fire solely in the name of thrill seeking. God only knew then it was the first sign of a much bigger issue. During the period that he grew up into a teenager, he had attempted suicide twice and was arrested several times for a long list of offenses by his eighteenth birthday. Later that same year, he was caught breaking and entering their then neighbor's million-dollar house and eventually got sentenced to two years in prison.

The news of his imprisonment, like all other incidents of disgrace that Adrian had brought upon the family over the course of many years, immediately dispersed like seeds in the wind. So as to avoid perpetual gossip that could potentially, catastrophically, destroy the family's reputation, the Crawfords made the decision to move out of Victoria Avenue — practically the 90210 of Minnesota — to a slightly less prosperous town that still mostly belonged to the upper crust. After his release from prison, Adrian no longer lived with the rest of his family and they seldom mentioned him. The only person he remained in touch with was really just Allison, who was by then fourteen years old. For the next four years, the two would meet at least once a month; whether at a park or at a specific restaurant nearby the parents' mansion that she could walk to conveniently, it mattered not. Just one phone call, she would be out the door, sneaking if needed, and vise versa.

Both of them had equally enjoyed those casual gatherings, where they would take turns giving the other person an update on their day-to-day, or from Adrian mostly, about all sorts of troubles he had gotten himself into. It was all going well until one day, something dark and terrible that happened in the fourth year that ultimately forced them apart. Allison could not recall exactly when they began to reconnect again — or for that matter what forced them apart in the first place — but something told her it was just the beginning of this year. He just happened to be reaching out to her when she began to feel vulnerable about her marriage and "boom", just like that, he was back into her life. That incidentally meant she was once again conflicted, stuck in the same position amid the longstanding war between Adrian and their mother. Even if she mentioned nothing of their communicating with each other, their mother always seemed to have her way of finding out. Owing to her ceaseless interference and objection, Allison had been avoiding seeing him for months.

As she knew it however, that was about to change.

12

NNE MARIE BISTRO — a small, mom-and-pop restaurant that Allison and her brother once held dear. The couple that owned the place were at one time close acquaintances of their parents after the family moved to Ship's Haven thirteen years ago. On occasion, Allison used to babysit their son, Chris, in the summer, when he was still in elementary school.

It just so happened that Chris was on his shift when she walked into the restaurant. Having recognized her straightaway, he greeted her with his biggest smile. "Hi Ms. Allie! Long time no see."

"Chris? Is that really you?" she replied, amazed to see him.

"You better believe it."

"Wow. It's been a while. You look… different."

"I hope it's *good* different."

"Of course."

"Heh. Sit anywhere you like. I will bring over some lemonade," he told her and then hurried off to the kitchen.

For a Tuesday morning, business was, as it had always been at this time, slow. With all the empty seats to choose from, Allison aimed for a specific booth by the window, headed towards it and sat down. The last time she visited this place was many years ago, not much of its interior had changed since, nor had the sweet aroma from baking pastries combined with fresh pots of coffee brewing. The red hanging light was still in use, and the tufted-back, upholstered bench on which she was sitting felt to be the same softness. Even the menu booklet that was handy on the table looked to be identical to what she remembered. Perhaps the only change was the floor tiles, instead of the dated, black and white checkers, they had been replaced by brand-new, wood-grain ceramic. A refreshing improvement indeed, as it gave the place a much more modern look.

Speaking of change, the most outstanding of all had to be Chris's appearance. Formerly a chubby boy to whom Allison was once no stranger, he had since grown into a striking young man, with a killer face and height equivalent to that of a male model from fashion magazines. Just then, he stopped over at her table, set down the tall glass of peach lemonade in his hand on a coaster and turned to talk to her with much enthusiasm. "Back when you used to come over for breakfast at our house, you would specifically ask for lemonade every time. My mom would always make sure we had at least one carton in the fridge ready for you the day before. I thought it was strange at first, the concept of drinking anything else besides milk for your first meal, but believe me, once I started to do the same, it drove my parents absolutely crazy."

Allison let out a giggle. "I forgot how old you were when I first babysat you. It seems like such a long time ago."

"I was six and you were twelve. I don't believe I told you, but I had a crush on you for the longest time."

"No you did not. But now that I know, I'm flattered."

"Haha. You don't have to always be so polite towards me. I know I was fat back then and I admit it, proudly."

"You weren't really that fat."

"Come on! A six-year-old boy weighing 59 pounds. I wasn't even tall for my age at the time."

Allison could not help laugh at his self-deprecating sense of humor. In a moment, she continued, "So I assume you are all done with high school. Are you in college now?"

"Nah. Dad is considering having me take over the business in two years. He said Grandma Anne would have loved me to if she were still alive. Plus, it will give him and Mom a good excuse to retire early."

"That sounds like good news, but is that what you want to do?"

"Honestly, I'm not totally against the idea. I know it seems crazy because I'm only nineteen going on twenty, and I definitely still have plenty to learn before I'm really ready for such a big responsibility, but I think I can manage one step at a time. It's better doing this than sticking to a path that I know I will hate. I was never much of a student, I'd really prefer not to step foot into another classroom again."

"Well, I believe in you, always have."

To that, his face lit up with gratitude. "You know what? I'm gonna bring you something on the house. What would you like? Anything on the menu, you got it."

Even though she was not hungry for anything, out of respect, she asked for a blueberry muffin.

Meanwhile, four obese men arrived at the door, most of which could barely squeeze through into the tight entryway. While they stood waiting to be acknowledged, Chris excused himself and headed towards them.

"Hello Jeffrey. Up top," he greeted one of the men, high-fiving him.

"Is your dad in Chris?"

"No, unfortunately. He went early in the morning to the farmer's market, shopping for a few things for the kitchen."

"So he left you in charge again?"

"That's right. He said he would be back by ten…, which is now actually. In that case, I can only assume he's gone home sipping coffee and left me slaving away here all by myself."

"Don't you worry, son," another man told him, "We'll make sure to throw in a big tip or two for you at the end of our meals."

"Heh. Thanks for the support guys. I was partially joking there. I do have Sheryl and two other staff here with me so I'm not totally alone. But I wouldn't mind the big tip, that is, of course, if my service is exceptional."

"This boy's got his old man's tongue I tell you," the third man said, and then everybody laughed. Even Allison smiled at his quick wit, thinking to herself, *looks like he's already got what it takes to become a well-respected restaurateur, good for him.*

One by one, she watched the men follow Chris to their table. Immediately after the last man had moved on along, another man, a rather skinny one at that with tousled, sandy-blond hair, emerged from behind him. Upon her eyes catching him standing there, head down, hands tucked in his pocket, she could not refrain a small gasp. Just as she had been so anxiously expecting, it was Adrian in his usual attire — a baseball cap, a grey long-sleeve Henley he used to wear almost every day, and straight blue jeans. When he eventually looked up, essentially like an automatic reaction, he looked to the booth where she was and his face beamed with joy. Hurriedly, he went to her.

"I had a feeling you were going to pick this booth," he said right when he got there, scooting onto the bench from across her without delay. "We used to sit here like this, face to face, and just talk and laugh about anything and everything that came to our minds. Do you remember?"

Given that there was no time to calm the butterflies in her stomach, she gulped back her nervousness and could only nod her head at him for now.

Adrian continued eagerly. "One of the days it was raining cats and dogs, I sat here by myself for a long time thinking you might not show but then you did, eventually.

As we prattled on, you couldn't stop sneezing. At one point, I swear I saw snot and boogers just fly out of your nose."

"No you did not!" she exclaimed, embarrassingly, barely resisting showing her teeth as a smile formed on her face.

"Alright. I might have over exaggerated there, but then there's this one other time..."

All the while as he talked, Allison was tracing over his pallid complexion, taking a good look at her brother whom she had not seen for a long time and still could not believe seeing. His face might seem paler and cheekbones might be sticking out further than she ever recalled, but those big, bright, green eyes of his were still lively as ever. Just then, he took to browsing through the menu.

"I remember you *always, always* chose their blueberry muffins over their cheesecake. One time I asked you why, you said, or I should say, *insisted*, 'because blueberries are just healthier than cheese.' And you were only serious. Oh man, I laughed so hard at that one." Just when he was mimicking Allison's voice on her part, it so happened that Chris brought over the complimentary blueberry muffin she had previously asked for. Subsequently, when Adrian saw it being placed in front of her on a plate, he just lost it, bursting out laughing, almost close to tears.

Allison was very much put at ease as the coincidence transpired; meanwhile, unaffected by Adrian's sudden outburst, Chris went on to ask her whether she needed anything else. She therefore looked to her brother and asked him, "Do you want something?"

Still very much caught up in his own bout of laughter, Adrian could hardly respond "no".

"I think we are fine here, thank you Chris."

Chris in turn looked strangely at him for a second and then back at her before moving on.

Adrian gradually mustered the strength to calm himself down. As always, the big brother that he was, outright displayed his keen interest in his little sister's problems and intended to console her if not solve them for her. "So, tell me Allie. What happened yesterday?"

Allison's momentary gaiety immediately returned to a serious mood. "It's Daniel. We had a fight."

"Do I even need to guess? It's about that Megan again isn't it?"

She looked away almost shamefully, nodding her head.

"That will pass Allie, trust me, I have no doubt."

"I don't know if I will ever get over what happened between them."

"You will. Like how all wounds will eventually heal, except this one just takes longer. Meanwhile, you must work on your own relationship or it will rot away inch by inch before you even realize it. You can trust me on this one."

"Why? How are things between you and Miranda?"

"We *fucked* two days ago. Forgive my profanity. But honestly, just one Molly was enough to get her rolling through the night."

"I don't mean *that*... but at least it sounds like you guys made up."

"Sorta..."

"Sorta?"

"You know her, she's just as crazy as me. I can barely track down what she does on a daily basis anymore or who she's been hanging out with. I do have my suspicions though."

"What sort of suspicions?"

Suddenly uneasy, he leaned towards the window, his elbow supported on its ledge and his cheek his fist, rubbing his bottom lip with his pinky from left to right and back a few times as though getting an itch. His eyes stared out at the street the whole time as he pondered over something on his mind before he finally let it out. "I think... I think she's secretly sleeping with someone else."

Allison was shocked. "What are you basing this on?"

"One of my buddies saw her at a bar heading to the bathroom with a guy and coming back out together looking all flushed."

"That certainly is a red flag... Are you sure your friend didn't make a mistake somehow?"

"No. Like I said, it's only a suspicion. I might confront her about it later or I might not, but in either case —" he concluded, sitting up straight again, "let's forget about that bitch for now. This is about you. I came to talk to you about you. Speaking of which, how's your sex life going?"

"Adrian!"

"What? What's the big deal? We used to talk about that sort of stuff all the time."

"I know, it's just... can't you bring it down a notch?" she said quietly, slouching into her seat, looking around furtively to make sure no one was overhearing their conversation of the most intimate kind.

Adrian rolled his eyes left to peek at a few of the alerted diners and just chuckled. "Haha, I'm sorry, I should have been more careful with my volume I suppose. Anyway, tell me about it."

"Well... it's stopped."

"Since?"

"Since... a few months ago, maybe."

"That's not saying much."

"I don't really remember. It's not all his fault though. Part of it is because of my insecurity."

"How so?"

"Well, sometimes... sometimes when I think of them together, it makes me feel terrible, like I want to throw up all over again and I don't want him to touch me."

"Did you?"

"Throw up? No, not since that first week after I found out about them, after Dan confessed."

"And by 'together', you mean sexually?"

She nodded. "Their kisses, their body rubs and so forth, everything that happens during sex —"

"Then *don't* think about all of that. You know you tend to overthink things."

"I know, but I can't help it, and it's not like I'm making it all up either."

"Screw them then! I say screw the past!"

"But —"

"Isn't she dead?"

"Yes."

"Has she been buried?"

"Yes, two days ago. But —"

"There's no 'but' here Allie don't you get it? Whatever happened between them is over and done with! She's dead and gone forever but you, you are still here, and that's what counts. You have to let one thing go in order to gain another. Do you understand me?"

Allison did not say anything and just sat with her head low for a while. Hating to see her beating herself up for nothing, Adrian was ready to hammer some sense into her for good, but then —

"Look at me Allie. I said look at me," he demanded her and when she did, he saw two droplets of tears rolling down her cheeks. Right away, he softened up.

Leaning in against the edge of the table, he reached out to give her face an endearing stroke while wiping off her tears with his thumbs. "Don't cry. There's nothing worth crying for here. You are stronger than you think. If only you would believe in yourself more —"

"I have missed you Adrian... a lot," she blurted out, her voice brittle.

He smiled back. "I know you have."

"Mom kept warning me to stay away from you. She said you've gotten yourself into some serious trouble again."

"Pah! What else is new?" he sneered, leaning back, crossing his arms.

"Well? Did you really?"

He gave her a glance and looked out the window for a bit before turning to face her again, replying sort of reluctantly, "Like I said, what else is new?"

"Oh Adrian —"

"But you mustn't listen to her!" he yelled, slamming his fist onto the table. "You have no idea what it has been like for me not being able to see you. Without someone to confide in or someone who truly understands me in my life was essentially like going through hell every day, not knowing you are dead and officially mean nothing to nobody anymore, and I'm not overstating it."

Although his quick flip of emotions was slightly startling, it was nothing Allison had not seen from him before. "I'm sorry... I don't know what to say."

"I'm asking you to please, never dismiss me like you did, again. You need me just as much as I need you Allie, *deep, deep* down you know that."

His anguished plea echoed through her heart and soul. She could not deny but be in sympathy. "You know I never meant to hurt you like that."

"So promise me please, it will make me feel better knowing it's a promise."

Those bright eyes of his that she saw in the beginning had turned sad, changing from green to a slightly grayish color. She wanted to make this right for him and now before any distractions — mainly from their mother — could deter her from doing so.

"Okay." Bumping her fist into his that was still held tightly closed on the table, she poked up her thumb. He followed suit and they touched thumbs together — their secret handshake. It was then she pledged to him solemnly: "I promise."

13

THE HALF-AN-HOUR GATHERING turned out to be an hour long. It could have gone on longer had Adrian not had some unfinished business to attend to regarding his girlfriend. After unloading on him thoughts about her troubled marriage, Allison generally felt better — as she did every time. They both agreed to meet again, not on a set date per se, but soon. Armed with a sense of empowerment, she went home and devoted her time straight back to writing.

Though her fervor had little to no effect on her composition. Much like what happened earlier in the morning, for an hour she sat in her chair waiting for inspiration to strike, her mind was blanked out half the time. Something else seemed to be bothering her, but even she herself could not quite grasp what it was just yet. That alone irritated her to no end. Out of frustration, she crossed out altogether the few scribbles she carelessly jotted down on the paper and started over.

While she could not be more disturbed, her mother, who often gave her a ring once a week just to catch up, called. Taking into account the recent gloom at home brought on by Megan's passing, Allison really had not the slightest interest in listening to her brag about her latest exploration with her father, and in fact had been daringly dodging her calls since last Thursday.

She was seriously considering not answering this call too had her phone not gone on to ring a second and third time. Understanding that her mother was hardly an even-tempered person, she was getting nervous just sitting there looking at its vibrating screen that said "Mom". Just this moment, in thinking that she might very well show up at the door on one random day at a random hour if she was ignored continuously, Allison decided to pick it up and end this unrelenting chase once and for all.

"Hello."

Brenda surely was glad to hear her daughter's voice again, although ever so slightly expressing her anger out of concern. "Your father and I were worried sick! I must have left over twenty voicemails but you never called back!"

"I'm fine Mom, and I did call back, once. I left you a message."

"No excuse! Where have you been these past few days and what have you been up to?!"

Causally leaving Adrian out of the conversation, Allison told her, "I'm not doing a whole lot, staying home mostly. Still dealing with insomnia, but I'm getting better."

"Really? Did you try that massage therapy I recommended?"

"As a matter of fact I did, but it didn't help."

"Then what did?"

"Well — I visited a shrink yesterday. She gave me a prescription which seems to be working out."

Brenda was skeptical at first upon hearing her say that, for she was well aware of her daughter's solemn disapproval of anything psychiatry related. "Are you actually seeing a psychiatrist?" she queried.

"I *saw* a psychiatrist," Allison stressed. "I will not go back again."

"If it's helping you, you should consider going back. In fact, I suggest Dr. Carter, if you will. Do you remember Dr. Carter? He is reputable in his field and he knows your medical history well."

How could I forget him, Allison thought regarding the doctor, who was practically family in her parents' minds. Soon after Adrian got diagnosed with borderline personality disorder following his first attempted suicide, she too was brought in to the mighty man's office for the very first time, which also marked her earliest memory of the vicious cycle of doctor visits.

Dr. Carter was still a relatively young physician at the time, but his radical views on psychiatric treatments pairing with frequent media exposure had already gained him much fame. Most patients of his were young adults coming from affluent backgrounds, whose parents — like Allison's — were usually firm believers in his research studies and would generously endorse him, trusting the man to be doing good for mankind.

Certainly though, not everyone agreed with him.

"That man is a total fraud!" Adrian would argue endlessly about Dr. Carter. "Cunning" and "manipulative" were precisely the two words he used to describe the man many praised, the man he claimed to have made his life hell. Having witnessed her brother's trauma first-hand, Allison, then nine years old, was arranged to see the doctor twice a week for a month as a precaution to ensure her mental stability was unaffected. While innocent and without judgment to begin with, slowly, she came to side with Adrian's opinion about him.

Those wasted hours spent at his office to answer the most ambiguous questions only gave Dr. Carter an opportunity to make a case out of her. There were times her parents sat in on a therapy session, where he would willfully magnify her every response, and more often than not her own words would backfire. After going through that entire month, she was lucky to be able to get out of more sessions as was suggested to her father, but not so at a later time upon Adrian's second suicide attempt.

Years might have come and gone, but Dr. Carter was not any less ambitious than when he was younger. Once a Nobel Prize nominee for his theoretical studies concerning neuroscience, many medical experts today regarded him as one of the most eminent masterminds in modern-day psychiatry. While that might be so, Allison's general impression of him had not changed. There was just something behind that smug grin of his, something wicked and insincere that she wished to *never* see again.

"Don't push it Mom. I can take care of myself," she urged.

"What's the name of the doctor you are seeing?"

"Lisa Cooke. She has an office in Minneapolis."

"I've never heard of her. Is she even qualified?"

"She's fine, but like I said, I don't plan on going back."

"Don't say that so soon. You never know when it comes to medication. It might seem to work one day and then it doesn't the next. Anyway, just mull over what I said before you reject it completely, okay?"

"About what?"

"About Dr. Carter."

"Fine," she concurred just to make happy her mother, who then moved right on to ask about Daniel.

"He's still grieving."

Brenda was quick to ridicule that fact. "What is there to grieve about?"

"Mom, please. Not now."

However tragic, she failed to sympathize with Megan's suicide as she could only see it as a sign of karma well deserved for destroying her daughter's otherwise *perfect* marriage. "Darling, things like that don't just happen without a righteous reason. Out with the evil, in with the good they say. It's evidence that God is watching over you both. You should be thankful for it."

"Thankful for a person's death?"

"Not just any random person of course, but certainly an evil one at that."

There was no question that Allison hated Megan for all the obvious reasons, but she could never wish death upon her, nor upon anyone else. Even so, she was not inclined to argue with her mother about her cold-hearted remark, and therefore saw to end the conversation now.

"Alright Mom, I got to go run some errands. Say hi to Daddy for me."

"Actually, just one more thing before you go darling."

"What is it?"

"Your father and I are going to the Bahamas on the 25th. We would like you and Danny to join us."

"To go on a trip with you guys?"

"Yes."

"How come?"

"How come? We haven't seen you both for so long, your father especially misses his precious little girl. Plus, you kids can probably use a vacation away, you know, to reconnect. It will be a short one, just over the weekend."

Thinking that it might not be such a bad idea, she replied, "Let me talk to Dan about it tonight."

"Tell him to just say yes and don't worry about the tickets or accommodations. Your father will take care of all that, okay?"

"Okay."

14

L ATER IN THE evening, when Allison brought up the mini vacation over dinner, Daniel was not excited about the idea of spending a whole weekend with his in-laws. Previous incidents had proven to him that their boastful nature and callous disregard for others could be, at times, unbearable. Although not at all surprised by his reaction, at the same time, she was unaware of how much she wanted the trip to happen until she went on to fight for it.

"You know my parents mean well."

"I'm sure they do." At a snail's pace, Daniel chewed on the piece of broccoli in his mouth so as to give himself time to compose a decent excuse for saying no. Finally, he swallowed it. "It's been very busy lately at work with all these projects coming due. I might have to work overtime that weekend."

"For the entire time?"

"Probably not, but I can't promise for how long. Besides, I would most likely be a drag if I were to go along with you guys. All the extravaganza your father arranged would be wasted on me."

"Don't be ridiculous. They miss you. If anything, we can really use the vacation to get away for a while."

"What for?" he asked and took a mouthful of his red wine.

"I think you know what for."

"No, I do not," he asserted, setting down the glass. "I feel fine being here for the weekend. If you would rather be away, you are free to go to the Bahamas with your parents while I stay home and focus on work. No one said we must both go."

His blunt rejection was quick to spoil her appetite. She put down her fork and knife and wiped her mouth with a napkin, looking the while across the table at Daniel where he sat curving his back, staring down at the slab of steak on his plate, guiding his knife as it cut into it. His avoidance of her eye contact prompted her to speak out to him: "Don't you want our marriage to work out?"

Taken aback, looking up at her forlorn face, he suddenly felt bad. Right then, he too gave up his unfinished meal and pushed aside his plate.

"Come here," he told her, turning his body sideways and beckoning her over.

She got up and walked on over to him, all along pouting sullenly. Once there, she rested her palm on top of his that was held out for her and asked him again that same question.

"Of course I do," he replied finally, gently stroking her fingers with his thumb. Allison felt a tingle of excitement she had missed for a while, and the sensation got stronger as he pressed his warm lips against them, kissing softly. She was just closing her eyes to properly savor the moment, but then, he let go of her.

One moment he was just showing his wife a bit of tenderness, the next he said to her coldly, "Don't ask me that again okay?"

She noticed his internal conflict. If it was not Megan he was thinking of just then, she did not know whom else. Upset as she was, going along with Adrian's wise words, she had chosen to let it slide.

"Okay," she said; meanwhile turned to sit down on his lap, arms wrapped around his neck. Eyes on the prize, she urged on, flirting a bit, "Let's have a good time together in the Bahamas then. We can chill at the beach, eat some delicious food, and just forget about life for a change. You can bring your work with you if you want, but there's a good chance you won't be attending to it at all." All the while talking, she was eying him yearningly, gradually leaning in for a kiss.

Remaining at odds with himself, Daniel held his head back just when their lips were about to touch. "Let me think about this some more," he told her with guilty eyes, looking her blankly in the face.

"Of... of course," she muttered back, and then withdrew awkwardly and got off him.

The discussion was going nowhere. She knew to put it to rest for now, but she did take his spurning of her affections to heart, and there was only one person in her mind to blame.

Since returning to her seat, Allison gulped down a big mouthful of her red wine and chugged the rest of it from her glass. Soon, she felt a certain rush charging through her, faster than her rational mind could catch up. Partly under the influence, partly not, she causally let slip a rather grudging remark. "You know, it's not your fault that she chose to take her own life. We both agreed not to help when she moved down into the city. It's not like you owe her anything —"

"I know," interrupted Daniel, staring at her with a face straight as an arrow.

She was satisfied then, reaching out for the wine bottle intending to drink some more. At the same instant, he stood up abruptly from his seat and left the table.

Somehow, she knew that would happen.

DAY 12 | SEPT 17 THURSDAY

15

AFTER BIDDING HIS parents farewell, Daniel was to drive back home, but only a few miles down the road he stopped the car. Sitting next to him was Allison, feeling tired and disturbed by his determination to visit Megan's grave again so soon.

"But we've just buried her," she argued with him.

"Well, you can wait here if you want, but I'm going," he said, opening the door and getting out.

She did likewise and followed him to the trunk of the car.

"Aren't you at least going to drive back to the farmhouse first? We are in the middle of nowhere."

"No. I know a quick way from here," he insisted, a flashlight in his hand.

Looking across the road, Allison saw a forest of tall birch trees extending over many miles, and behind her, more trees, and possibly a narrow path leading into what seemed to be unending darkness.

"You are not serious," she said.

"But I am. Like I said, you can wait here in the car and I'll be right back."

Without time for her to formulate a response, off he went into the woods and soon disappeared out of her sight. There was no sign of civilization around her — no lighted houses, and in fact no houses at all that she could see but just a solitary road where their car was parked. All alone underneath the hazy moon, the quietness of the night gave her an unsettling fright.

She dipped her head into the car trunk to check for another flashlight but found none. Despite risk of not being able to see clearly, she decided to go after Daniel anyway. There was no turning back once she stepped foot onto the narrow path leading her deeper into the unknown. A stupid decision it seemed, as she had become lost fairly quickly rushing by tree after tree after tree... Not far along the way, a small flame glowing within reach eventually grew to a great circle of fire as she got to it, burning high up to her knees. Standing near its edge, she felt every bit of the blazing heat rising up to her cheeks.

"Hello? Is anyone out here? Dan?" she called out, wanting a response badly. Suddenly, she sensed a brisk of wind running by her ear. When she turned around to do a one-eighty-degree scan, it had since gone calm. She saw no one at her rear but the immense woodland from which she came. Right the second, totally out of her explanation, she felt a powerful thrust against her chest and consequently, she fell backward into the pit amid the hot ring, a pit so deep that it looked to have no bottom.

Never would she have thought in a million years to be so lucky to have landed safely onto the ground after such a fall, but she did. Right away trembling cold, she wrapped her arms around herself and looked up at the opening appearing far out of reach. Not wasting another minute, she got up and approached the thick, slimy mud wall knowing very well that she ought to climb out of there using her bare hands. It was easier said than done, because time and time again as she attempted to scale, each time she would lose her grip a few feet from ground. The flimsy tree roots out-curved from some spots only helped so much to support her weight, and one by one they snapped, causing her to fall miserably on her back.

As if things were not yet bad enough down in the dark, freezing hole. She was just lounging momentarily on the ground, panting with all the falling, when her palms pressing against the uneven surface felt something strange sticking out beneath her. She moved off of it to kneel and sit back on her heels, leaning so to try and study the object closely. Barely seeing it, she then ran her hands over this bulging *thing* and began to dig around it with her fingers, exerting herself to remove all the soil covering it in chunks until unearthing it entirely. As it turned out, it was a human body with skin frosty to the touch and winkled in every way.

The first time lightning flashed across the sky, the explosive sound of thunder startled her. She looked up and watched the grey clouds flow by the opening for a good few seconds before focusing back onto the body. At that exact time, lightning happened to strike once again and again, lending her a brief moment of clarity. It was then did she see clearly what was really lying in front of her — a female corpse, half decayed, purple with blisters all over. Her eye sockets had been hollowed out by invasive maggots while her other facial features, such as the nose, mouth and ears, remained oddly untouched. *I know this woman*, she thought to herself, and as she came closer to concluding her identity, she became increasingly horrified. Upon spotting a distinctive birthmark on her right cheek just below the cheekbone, there was no denying that she was, in fact, Megan.

As the sudden realization hit her, Allison panicked and scooted backward as far away from the corpse as possible, all the way till her back hit the muddy wall. There, she cowered in terror while the heavy raindrops fell continuously and mercilessly onto her quivering body swamped in cold sweat. After what felt like a long time, the downpour eventually subsided, and all that remained was the everlasting silence and darkness that originally encircled her. With her poor limbs and compromised vision, she took to believe the only way out of this place was from outside help. Therefore, "HEEELP!!! HEEELP!!!" she shouted at the top of her lungs, and then stopped to listen for any sign of assistance coming from up above.

An overwhelming chill flew by her just then, coating her with a fresh layer of iciness enough to almost send her into hypothermia. Her teeth clenched together as her body shivered uncontrollably for a slim chance of warmth. Her ears became the most reliable source in terms of detecting motion at a time like this, where she could scarcely see the white vapor of her own breath every time she exhaled. In the middle of it all, she began to hear something creeping her direction; until she picked out a shadowy figure amidst the dark and felt its rimy hands grab around her neck, then, it was too late to do anything — not that she had any idea what to do. '

"Meg... Megan is dead! She's... dead!" she told herself in a frightened voice, and while struggling to break free from the chokehold, a different voice, distinctively Megan's, responded in a clear whisper directly into her ear: "You should have been the one to die..."

"No...

NOOO...

AhhHHggg...

ggHHHGgRRrrRRGGgg..."

She screamed in pure dread till she was choked out of sound. As those cadaverous fingers around her neck tightened their grip, in due time, she passed out.

16

ALLISON'S FOREHEAD WAS drenched in sweat and her body stuck in a fetal position the second she opened her eyes. "Dan... DAN!" she screamed, flipping over the covers and springing to sit up in bed. Blinded by the ray of sunlight showing through the gap between the curtains, she blinked and looked around the bedroom, immediately feeling a sense of relief having realized her horrific ordeal was just a nightmare.

Ten days since her medication first kicked in, frightening dreams such as that had gradually become more frequent to the point of now happening every night. Sometimes their compositions were so bloody and gory in nature that they would even wake her several times during sleep. She was worried of course. Because, heaven forbid, if the prescription did fail her, she would have to seriously consider going back to Dr. Cooke to ask for a new one. Nonetheless however, for the time being, she had no other option except sticking to it, otherwise her chance of getting even just a bit of rest would be equal to zero.

Soon freshened up and moving on with her day, she went out and completed a few errands. The last thing to do was to pick up Daniel's business suit from the dry-cleaner's down the street. Coming to park outside the shop, she received a call from Adrian. Since their meeting last Tuesday, she had not heard from him till now. Jolly as she was to speak to him, three sentences into their conversation, she began to sense something terribly wrong.

"What's going on Adrian?" she asked with concern, having overheard him whimpering in the background. "Are you alright?"

"Come..." he replied, barely, "Come quickly."

"Come where? Tell me where you are."

Without warning, his voice went from a feeble moan to a harsh yell, commanding her very inarticulately, "To the apartment! Come... come to the apartment I SAID!!"

"What is the address? I have no idea where you want me to go."

He let out a manic growl as if in great, frustrating pain. "Don't pretend bitch! You know the place better than anyone."

"Calm down Adrian. There's no need to resort to anger."

"Then don't *fuck* with me alright."

"I'm not —"

"I SAID DON'T FUCK WITH ME!!!!!"

His increased hostility eventually left her at a loss. For a moment, neither of them said anything. Though she could still hear his anxious teeth chattering and heavy breathing next to the speaker. She only grew more worried.

"Okay... okay," he began to speak again. "We'll do it your way. 770 Crestwood Apartment no. 33. Get here at exactly noon and not a minute late. I can't... I can't guarantee what's going to happen to her... but don't you bother calling the cops! If you want her alive at all, come alone."

"Are you with Miranda? Listen, don't —"

He hung up.

Nothing petrified her more than getting a call like this from Adrian. It was as if he had just flipped a switch and transformed into a violent, malicious person. She could hardly come to terms with what just happened but much as it scared her, she was even more so saddened by his desperate yearning for help. Since his diagnosis, he had been through many treatments that were forced upon him. After repudiating his parents at age twenty, he just left it untreated. His tendency to abuse substances only worsened his condition, encouraging his symptoms to go out of whack and potentially flare up into a psychotic episode.

He might very well be going through one right now. Allison understood him enough to be drawn to that conclusion. Honestly speaking, many times in the past she had been involved, because if anyone could bring him back to sanity, she knew she was the one. Though that might be, she also knew that risk was certain should she decide to show up as demanded. There was always that one percent chance for this to turn out to be something entirely out of her prediction, and further, her control. If worst came to worst, she might even need to call her father for intervention in the middle of it, and this time, he would not hesitate to employ his power to put him away. That was literally the last thing she wanted to happen. So for this sole reason, she was back and forth.

Ed happened to be leaving shortly after picking up his uniforms during his police shift when Allison walked into the dry cleaning shop. Having been so wrapped up in thought, she walked right by him completely unaware of his presence until he greeted her in a delightful manner.

"Hi Allie. It's a good surprise to see you here."

"Oh, hi Ed."

"Picking up something?"

"Uh-huh," she replied in brief and then looked on at the counter, watching the store clerk help the customer ahead of her, clearly not in the mood to chitchat.

While Ed was excited to run into her, he asked her anyhow. "Would you like to grab a bite to eat after this? I can really use a break."

"I'm sorry, but I got something else to do right after."

"I'm sure you do," he muttered back in a bit of a bitter letdown, presuming it to be another one of her excuses to avoid him.

Apprehending his remark, she told him, "I honestly do. I got to go to this place by noon, which hopefully isn't too bad of a drive."

His eyes lit up again. "You've never been there before?"

She shook her head and showed him the address saved on her phone.

"That's all the way west in downtown Blackpool. I've heard many stories coming out of that area and they are not good."

"What sort of stories?"

"You sure you want to hear them? I mean that place is known to have one of the highest crime rates in the metro, home to many crack-heads and lowlifes —"

"That's not funny."

"I'm not joking. I'm just saying that you should avoid going there at all cost."

"But I can't."

"Why not?"

Off the top of her head, she made up something. "I uh... I have to meet up with an old friend. A promise is a promise."

He saw right through her falsehood. Instead of confronting her for the truth however, he urged to offer her a ride there.

"That's okay. I drove here."

He was used to dealing with her rejection. "Does he know about this?"

"Does who?"

"Your husband."

"It's sort of a... spur-of-the-moment kind of thing."

"I see. Look, I don't feel right having you go meet some 'old friend' at this god-awful place all by yourself. Let me come along. I can be your bodyguard."

"I don't know if that's such a good idea."

"What do you have to lose? I will just wait for you in the car once we get there, if that makes you feel more comfortable."

Seeing that she was willing to reconsider, he went that extra mile in an attempt to seal the deal. "Come on. I'll drop you off back here right after. I just want to make sure you will be okay that's all, as a friend."

"I have no idea how long it will take."

"I don't care," he asserted with a face sincere.

Figuring it would only be sensible to accept his help so long as Adrian did not see him, in the end, she agreed, "Alright. Let's get going then."

17

I N ED'S PATROL car, they left the peaceful suburb onto the highway going north and then west. Thirty minutes into their journey, they got off through the exit ramp and headed further west approaching the inner city of Blackpool. The ride came to be bumpier from deep potholes depressed in various spots of rutted roads with wrecked cars parked alongside them. Whether loitering at intersections or entrances of decrepit, graffitied buildings, drunks and addicts became a common sight. Down one particular backstreet, Allison ventured a look and saw what could only be interpreted as open-air drug trade; down another, she spotted a man and a woman doing the dirty deed in a shaded corner, who disengaged frantically seeing their vehicle drive by. The visual devastation of this economically ravaged region called forth speculations of all sorts that gradually took over her mind like para-sites, eating away anything positive. Soon, they took a turn onto Eighteenth Street and eventually came to a halt on the side of the road. "Here we are," said Ed, thankfully breaking her chain of thought. She looked out the window at this grayish, three-story structure standing erect about forty feet away. Its external paint had long faded, and from the distance, some of the windows on the first floor could be seen broken, imaginable as a result of burglaries.

"Are you sure this is it?" she asked to confirm with him.

"That's what that sign said: 770 Crestwood Apart-ment. Besides, my computer's navigation is never wrong."

She looked down at her watch. Seeing it was just ten minutes before the clock would strike twelve, she knew she needed to get moving.

"Are you sure you still want to do this?" he asked her.

"Yes."

"Then, at least let me escort you."

"Um... I don't know." She looked out the window once more, this time at the bleak entryway of the building and her face grimaced as a reaction. She was very much hesitating to go on alone and he sensed it.

"How about I get you up to the floor, and then I will leave, as you wish."

She agreed at last. Therefore, the two got out of the car and marched on.

They could smell something terrible reeking from the overloaded trashcan near the entryway on their way there. A few garbage bags were left to its side untied and unattended to for who knew how long with flies hovering above the spoiled, leftover food spilling over the cemented ground. Plugging her nose, Allison moved ahead to try the buzzer, which was evidently broken. Ed in turn walked up to give the hinged door a hard push only to find the lock defective. So they slipped right through into the tight lobby conveniently. Deciding not to chance their luck, they skipped the elevator and went straight for the stairs going up.

First, second, and finally, they reached the third floor.

"I can walk you to the door if you'd like," he told her.

"It's okay. I'll be fine from here on."

"Are you sure?"

"Yes," she affirmed him.

"Alright then. Give me a ring if you run into any trouble."

"Okay."

"And be extra careful."

"I will."

He gave her an assuring nod and then turned to head back down the stairs.

After parting with Ed, Allison followed the dingy corridor cautiously till she got to unit "no. 33" half way along to her left. Standing facing the wooden door, she checked her watch one last time — it was now one minute past noon. Without further delay, she gave the door a sharp knock.

While she waited, she felt her pulse racing faster, roaring in her ears as the pressure continued to build. Pretty soon, a minute went by unnoticed and then another, but no one had yet come to the door. Pressing her ear against its rough surface, she listened for the slightest movement but heard not a hint of sound coming from the other side. Meanwhile, she raised her fist up to her eye level and gave the door a couple more knocks. What came straight after was the relentless barking of an irritated dog behind the closed door that ended up startling and backing her away. The instant it calmed down, she saw shadows coming near the gap at the bottom of the door.

Slowly but surely, a scruffy, messy-haired, old woman opened it in her long nightgown. Her small, delicate body fidgeted a little as she stood there holding onto the rim of the door, staring back guardedly at Allison who looked just as confused.

"Um... hi. I'm looking for —"

Before Allison could finish her sentence, the old woman had interrupted her with her shaky hand gestures.

"Excuse me, but I can't understand you."

The woman continued gesturing with great intention for her to eventually pick up the meaning.

"Can you speak at all?"

This time, she opened her mouth. Rather than saying actual words however, she tried and only managed to let out a few croaking noises.

Allison gave an awkward smile, taking a moment to look off behind her into her cluttered apartment and notice there were boxes of all sizes occupying virtually the entire living room. "Sorry to bother you," she said after to the old woman, who thereupon shut the door in her face in her slow-motion way.

Not knowing what to think of the whole situation as it unfolded before her, Allison stood feeling deeply bewildered for a minute. Suddenly, here came another canine, a ferocious pit bull, barking at her from three doors down. Its owner, a heavyweight black male, was pulling at its leash, trying to get it under control.

She looked in his direction briefly. The two exchanged eye contact before she would turn to walk the other way back to the stairwell.

"Hey miss!"

Upon his calling, she stopped and turned around. "Are you talking to me?" she asked.

"Yeah. You don' remember me?"

"No. Am I supposed to?"

"Well, yes and no I guess... How's dat mother or sister of yours?"

"What?"

"You know, my dog accidentally bit her in the arm the other day."

"I think —"

WOOF — WOOF —

"SHUT THE FUCK UP ROCKY!" he bawled at his dog to sort of stop it from barking, and then his voice went smooth again. "You was sayin'?"

"I think you've mistaken me for someone else."

"Nah-uh. I don't think so. This brain o' mine don' forget. She was blonde like you. Attractive like you..."

"I'm sorry sir, but I don't think we know each other. I'm going to go now. Good-bye."

"Hey, don' just rush out of here so fast like the las' time. C'mon, I just would like a chat. Pretty girls like you don' come round this shithole very often ya know."

As the man rambled on, he also started to go after her. Frightened, Allison began to pick up her pace and run. Just about getting out of the corridor, she turned her head to get a fleeting glimpse behind her. Not paying attention to where she was going, she literally ran into Ed, who just in time, popped out from around the corner of the stairwell to her rescue. Despite their previous agreement, he had actually come back to the third floor shortly after descending and been guarding there on the quiet since.

"Whoa! Easy, easy," he told her in a soft, assuring tone, catching her by the arms.

"Ed!"

"Yeah it's me. I'll take over from here okay?"

Still quite shaken up, she replied faintly, "O... okay."

Just then, the black man spoke up from a few feet away. "I don' mean to cause no trouble officer."

"You. Get over here," said Ed, beckoning to him

So, he did, along with his dog that was still barking. "I don' mean to cause any trouble officer," he repeated.

"Oh yeah? This young lady here doesn't seem to think so."

He looked briefly at Allison standing in the back. "I was jus'... I thought she was someone else. Sorry."

"Well, don't tell *me* that."

Right away directing at her, he apologized regretfully, "I'm sorry miss. I thought you was someone else."

Looking up at him timidly, Allison replied, "It's okay."

"There officer, I apologized."

"Don't get too cocky," Ed warned him. "You'd better watch your back from here on, because next time, you might not be so lucky."

"*WOOF — WOOF —*"

"Shut-shh!" the man rasped, but his dog would not pick up its ears. "Stupid creature."

"Also a heads-up, put a muzzle on that dog of yours before it will 'accidentally' bite someone again."

"Yes —"

WOOF — WOOF —

"— shhhh... yes sir. I totally hear you."

Ed shook his head at him and then let him go.

Swiftly afterwards, he returned his attention to Allison.

"You okay there?"

"Yeah. I'm fine."

He smiled. "Let's get you out of here."

18

ABOUT THE OLD woman, Ed decided to pay a short visit to the residential office requesting information for Allison while she took a rest in the car. When he returned, together they drove away from the unnerving site.

Proceeding back onto the highway, he enlightened her with his investigation.

"Did you know she's deaf?"

"Not at first, but then it got obvious."

"Right. Well, apparently she had just moved in yesterday. Her children were looking for a cheap alternative to house her, so eventually they settled her into that godforsaken place..."

Half way through his talking, he noticed her sitting zoned out in the backseat. "Still doing okay back there?" he asked her.

"Oh... yes," she replied. "I don't think I've said, but thanks for coming with me."

"It's my pleasure."

Even under this highly unusual circumstance, though he might not show it, Ed was really beyond glad to be of his *angel*'s service. To him, every occasion they met was rare, and therefore every moment they spent alone to-gether felt to be something special. Despite her taciturn mood, he went on to amuse her with a bit of humor hoping to raise her spirits. It worked ever so well, bringing a smile back on her face in no time.

Very soon, they were off the highway onto the road towards the dry cleaning shop. Dreading the upcoming departure, just then stopping at a traffic light, he took a rather long, stealthy look at her through the rearview mirror while she was least aware. One other sly peek and then another later, something inside him started to boil and he became titillated from all the wrong ideas in his head. Helpless at keeping his desire at bay, his mind calcu-lated for a split second. As the light changed from red to green, he took a bold turn into a regional park close by.

Underneath a big oak tree, he pulled up at a well-hidden spot away from the general parking lot and then instinctively, rolled up his windows. Soon as he turned off the ignition, she asked him, "Why are we stopping?" He did not respond, because truly, he hardly knew where he was going with this. Next, he switched off his walkie-talkie and got out, came around the vehicle and climbed into the backseat alongside her.

Instantly, the atmosphere went acutely tense within the tight space, uncomfortable at best. The two sat there, both facing forward for a moment of calm till he eventual-ly began to talk. "I'm sorry that your friend played a prank on you."

"What do you mean?"

"You know, whoever asked you to go to the apart-ment and never showed."

"Oh that... to be honest, everything still feels sort of surreal to me."

"I bet. So, who is this friend that you tried to meet with? Do I know her? Or him?"

"No. It's a childhood friend of mine... Anyway, that's not important now."

"Right. But whoever it was, I got to thank her."

"Why?"

"Because, I wouldn't have been able to spend time with you if it weren't for her."

"That's not true. We spend time together."

"When?"

"In Vegas."

"That was months ago, and it wouldn't have happened if Sara did not insist that I came along."

"We met last week at Moonshine."

"Yeah, but Sara was there, again."

"What's wrong with that?"

"I'm not saying something's wrong, it's just, I'm talking about this... just us."

Allison broke away from his gaze for a second. "I see..." she said, only just managing to move off the subject, "Anyway, thank you again for coming with me today."

"Anytime. Anything for you."

"I mean it. I wouldn't know what to do had that man continued to come after me."

"I meant what I said too."

She looked right at him and smiled. "I know you are good to me Ed, and I'm very thankful for that."

"Now you've officially thanked me one too many times."

Her smile stretched further, but every bit of her remained wary. "So — should we get back on the road?"

"Not so fast." He gulped, suddenly serious. "You know, this might sound a bit mad to you but... I've missed you Allie, I've thought of you a lot over the week."

"Well... here I am!" she cheered, coupling with a few nervous laughs intending to loosen up this so very strained situation in which she was stuck, but it did not work.

"I know... I know... What about you?" he inquired.

"What about me?"

"Did you think of me by any chance?"

Right then, she looked away from him, mildly annoyed. "Don't do this Ed. We've gone through this before."

"I'm not understanding you."

"You know exactly what I'm talking about."

Turning a deaf ear to her forewarning, he reached out to brush away the wisp of hair that had just come untucked from behind her ear and used the opportunity to graze the side of her face. In turn, she drew back, retorting, "This. I mean exactly this. I just want to be friends."

"*Really*."

"Yes!"

"Ha. Friends. I've always admired how you can say that to me so lightly…"

"Can we not turn this into an argument?"

"Then tell me, how can I be just a friend when I know there's still something more between us? Am I supposed to keep lying to myself?"

"It's all just an illusion —"

"*I know it's not!* I still think of that night when you called and we just chatted till the sun came up —"

"I needed a friend four months ago. You were there for me, which I'm thankful, but that was that. Nothing more to it."

"You don't mean that."

"But I do. *Please*. Don't make this difficult —"

"*I'm* making this difficult?!"

"Why are you doing this?"

"*God!* You can be so *blind* sometimes!" he snapped. "Whenever I'm with you… just hearing your voice I… I can't help but fall for you over again. I just… I just can't help myself…" All the while speaking, he was leaning in towards her. His hand cupped over hers that was resting on the bench seat and gently caressed it.

Withdrawing her hand at once, Allison only worked to dishearten him. "This is why I avoid you," she said coldly to him, "If we don't see each other, maybe we can still manage to stay friends."

"Again, 'friends'."

"Yes! We've talked this over countless times, and we have both agreed —"

"Agreed to be friends?"

"YES!"

"I *never* agreed to be your friend, you *make* me your friend."

"So?"

"So?!"

"What's the difference? I don't know what else you expect us to be."

"GOD DAMNIT!" Suddenly he bellowed out in roaring frustration, smacking his fist against the partition. "You just don't get it do you?"

"I guess I really don't."

His face had gradually turned red and eyes looked as though they were about to spill tears. Just then, he took a deep breath and let it out so very candidly. "Whether I see you or not, you... you are constantly in the back of my head. There've been nights that I dreamt of us still going out, making out in the backseat of my old pickup like we used to or even making love... but just as soon as I woke up and realized what we've come to, I... I just feel like ripping my heart out and feeding it to dogs!"

His straightforward honesty, ever so oddly, moved her. She was unable to fire back, and in fact, did not know exactly what to reply to that except for a quiet "sorry".

"Don't. You being sorry doesn't change anything," he told her, pinching away the tears from the corners of his eyes. "Do you really want me to quit? Because if you do, tell it to me right here right now. Tell me to quit chasing this... this hopeless dream, can you? Tell me to go away forever like you did years ago, can you?"

I can, Allison thought to herself, though part of her did not want him to. At least not right now, not yet. Something about Ed's faithfulness was just all too valuable to her to throw away rashly. Even as she looked at him now, seeing his face crooked in obvious pain and sadness, she could not make herself end this, this toxic chase that begot his mental torment. Alternatively, she sought to comfort him in a much-unexpected way.

"Oh Ed." She reached out to stroke him on his face. "The thing is, I can't make that decision for you. Our relationship is complicated as it is. I'm only asking you to not make this even harder for the both of us..."

As if bewitched, he just listened, rubbing his cheek against her palm several times, smelling it as he went. For a moment, he kept his eyes closed to concentrate on the warmth of her soft hand and that inexplicable feeling of excitement when it touched his skin. The second they re-opened, one lecherous gaze at her, his mind twisted. He forwent all of his moral senses and good judgments, making a clutch at her wrist to pull her close. Very quickly, his other hand wrapped around her back, thrusting her body towards his own.

Completely caught off guard by his recklessness, the next thing Allison felt was his tongue inside her mouth. Fiercely, she fought to try to break free from him, but ultimately — like a herculean task — it was no use. During her struggle, he even managed to lower her onto the seat with ease, holding her down by the wrists and forcing himself on her. His lips went smoothly from around her neck down to her chest and bosom when she yelled, "*STOP!!! Stop before you regret it completely!!!*" Which did bring about a brief hesitation, but it was quickly overturned by his deeply ingrained, half-baked self-justification. "Why should I regret? I would never regret loving you the way I've always known how..."

Before he could lay his lips back on her, in the nick of time, she shot him an ultimatum. "I guarantee you won't be able to see me *ever* again if you so choose to continue what you're doing!"

Doubting his own action, Ed stopped midway. Breathing heavily, he watched a drizzle of his sweat dripped onto her chin roll down her neck and come between her collarbones. His eyes, having just noticed her pumping chest then, crept up worriedly to meet with hers.

"I mean what I said... *GASP*... *GASP*..." she persisted, holding her voice steady, "Do you really... really want to put our friendship in peril for this?"

His hands were unwilling at first, but that remaining bit of his rationality finally convinced them to let go.

19

I N THE WAKE of the ridiculous turmoil, Ed got out from the backseat of his patrol car bathed in sweat. Allison remained seated for a minute till her breathing caught up; meanwhile through the windshield, she observed him kicking up dirt and dust at the foot of the big oat tree.

When she too got out of the car, he had since come to his senses, walking back to apologize to her. "I'm sorry... I don't know what came over me. Can you find it in your heart to forgive me?"

Arms crossed over her chest, she cast him a disfavoring look, and only muttered back two seconds later, "Of course."

Right then, he felt somewhat reassured. "Good. Let's get back on the road," he said, reaching around her for the door handle; at the same moment, she wittingly leaned back against the car door and stood there in his way, not moving. He stopped, lifting his face to look at her.

"Don't get me wrong Ed," she started, finding the need to make a few things clear to him. "I appreciate everything you've done for me, really, but I'm married."

He gave her a blank smile. "I know."

"This just can't happen again, *ever*. Things could certainly be different if I weren't with Dan but —"

"But you are. I know." He let out a deep sigh. "I would like to still be friends though."

"That's not what you said back there."

"What? Can't a man change his mind?"

She made no comment.

"Come on Allie. Please."

She stared at his hand extending towards her for a brief moment and eventually gave it a firm grip, shaking it as she affirmed him, "Friends."

Before they would get back into the car, he came to lean up against it beside her, deciding to show her something he had kept on his phone all this time hoping to mellow out her mood. It was a snapshot he took secretly of her, in which she was resting in bed, close-eyed with a blissful smile on her flushed face. Her head slightly turned sideways revealing part of her ear that would have been otherwise covered by her then long, wavy, blond hair. She was wearing a sleeveless, red, A-line dress with a neckline coming down to form an attractive V right at her cleavage.

"I've always liked you in that dress," he told her.

"Was this taken in Vegas?" she asked curiously, and he nodded.

"You were lying there so peacefully. I couldn't help myself... I meant taking the photo."

"I figured."

What came after was his reminiscing about their rare share of privacy like it had just happened yesterday. "You've never been a heavy drinker, but that night was an exception. You were so wasted that I had to literally piggyback you from the bar all the way back to your room and help you to bed. Do you remember any of it?"

"Vaguely."

"I was going to leave you to rest, but then you grabbed me by the hand and told me not to go, to "stay with you" you said. So I did, stay. I watched you slowly drift off before I fell asleep on the armchair near your bed."

"But you weren't there when I woke up the next morning."

"It's because I was up before you. 7 a.m. I believe it was. I went to the store to get you coffee and aspirin. But when I got back, Sara was already there in your room making you tea."

"That's why you walked in with two cups of coffee..."

"Right."

Upon realizing what he selflessly did for her, Allison's heart lightened. "Why didn't you say anything then?"

"What was there to say? I didn't care about much else as long as you were feeling better. Sara was doing such a good job taking care of you, I wasn't gonna stop her."

She shook her head lightly at him. "You are too good to me Ed."

"Nah. That wasn't much, really," he replied, tucking away his phone. "To tell the truth though, lately I've been wondering about that night."

The two exchanged glances.

"Yeah?"

"I've been wondering if... if hypothetically we could go back in time, to that night in your hotel room and redo it, whether or not we would have done something different, you know... something more —"

"It wouldn't have made a difference," she remarked bluntly, rather harshly in his sense. "Still, nothing indecent would have happened between us if that's what you are getting at."

"What makes you so sure?"

"Do you even need to ask?"

Dazed, he looked to her for explanation and she told him, again, bluntly, "Because you are a good guy. Deep down you only want the best for me, and subconsciously, you know not to do what I ultimately don't want happening. Even if, 'hypothetically', I was to come onto you."

Her answer was sharp and to the point. Ed heard it loud and clear but something in him — even just by a small margin — disagreed. "That's a massive responsibility on my shoulders."

"But I trust you, and it shouldn't be a surprise that I do."

"Even with what just happened in the car?"

"I'm not trying to deny our history Ed, as that was never my intent. I was taken aback by what happened I'm not gonna lie, but at the same time, I can be understanding. That little lapse of judgment doesn't change how I think of you."

Feeling a bit of optimism, he smiled at her, warmly, but that smile did not hold for long; by the time she finished her next sentence, it had ceased.

"Come on. Let's get going," said she, coming off the car door and turning to pull at his hand, "I can't stay out for too much longer, still got a bunch of chores to do before Dan gets home."

She had to have noticed his discontent even though he tried in his manful attempt to conceal it, but ultimately, she chose to ignore it for the better.

The "good guy" that Ed was, said nothing more. Swiftly, he moved to open the door for her to get back into the car. Meanwhile, that bitter taste in his mouth only got bitterer. *'Friend', humph. I will be one hell of a friend.*

DAY 18 | SEPT 23 WEDNESDAY

20

I T WAS 10:55 A.M. at Dr. Cooke's office, five minutes before Allison's scheduled appointment. Much like the last visit, she was every bit on edge. When the previous patient left, her name was called next.

Aiming for the therapy room, she took a deep breath before proceeding on. Although outwardly she looked to be everything a desperate insomniac should be, on the inside, she felt like she was betraying herself, knocking on the devil's door once again, dangling her soul in her fingertips in exchange for another pathetic glimpse of normality.

"Come on in," said Dr. Cooke behind the closed door, who spun around in her leather chair just as Allison opened it. As usual, she greeted her with the friendliest smile, gesturing to her, "Please, take a seat."

Allison closed the door behind her, walked over to that familiar couch and sat down.

"How have you been Allison?"

"Could be better," she replied.

"Well, it's good to have you back."

"I wish I could agree with you. Certainly I would much rather have my prescription work out the first time around."

"I can understand your frustration. I do very much have the same hope for all of my patients, but unfortunately, that can't always be the case. You see, every person reacts to pharmaceuticals differently. What works for others doesn't mean it would work just as well for you. To get it right is indeed the tricky part."

Despite the doctor's well-intentioned response, she could merely regard it as a defense mechanism. Though she figured, the eagerer she was to cooperate, the quicker the session would end. After all, she was the one who came asking for help and therefore knew better this time to quiet her negativity from the get-go and go with the flow.

Meanwhile, Dr. Cooke resumed. "Now, I presume the prescription wasn't as helpful as you might have hoped. What seems to be the problem?"

"I've been having terrible dreams pretty much every night since the start of the medication."

"How long has that been?"

"Roughly two weeks. It was working better in the beginning, but then a few days into taking it, the nightmares started to come on and they became more frequent."

"I'm sorry to hear that. That is unfortunately a rather common side effect for this type of drug. Have you tried not taking it?"

"Yes, but then I'd have no luck falling asleep at all."

"It is understandable. Do you still remember some of these dreams by chance?"

"Some, yes."

"What are they like if you were to sum them up?"

"They are dark... gloomy, sometimes very violent. They all take place in the most distressing environments imaginable."

"I see." All the while asking questions, Dr. Cooke took note of the important details for follow-up. "And, among these dreams, do you see a connection?"

"I never really thought about that."

"That's okay. Take your time."

"I'd say no, not really."

"You sure? Are there perhaps similarities, or reappearing elements that you might have noticed?"

There was, indeed, one very enthralling detail that Allison had recognized early on yet was unwilling to bring

up. It seemed almost silly to be frightened by something
as trivial as dreams, but just at the thought of Megan in all
of them instantly gave her the creeps. As much as she
would like to not mention her, eventually, she did.

"You are referring to your late sister-in-law I suppose."

She nodded.

"What is she like?"

"You mean in the dreams?"

"Yes."

"Hostile. Confrontational. Not that she was any nicer
in person."

Dr. Cooke sensed her bitter tone but made no mention as such for the time being and continued with her
analysis. "What does she usually do? In these dreams."

Allison gave it a thought before replying, "Very often
she... in an inarticulate sense, rises from the dead in various messed-up scenarios that my brain manages to crop
up."

"I see." Hoping to finally shed some light on the root
cause of her chronic stress, Dr. Cooke then encouraged
her to recount one of the dreams in detail. "We are in no
hurry. Just try your best."

Projecting her mind on the phantasmagoria of horror
that disrupted her sleep last night, Allison closed her eyes
for a minute to focus her attention as the vivid imagery
gradually pieced back together. Then, she set out to tell
the terrorizing dream like she would a story.

"I remember walking down this dreary corridor. At
its end was a wooden door with an attached sign that read
'no. 33'. When I got to it, I gave it two quick knocks, and
then the old woman who lived there came to let me in.
Her dog would not quit barking from the moment I set
foot into her living room. While she tried calming it down,
I maneuvered my way through the floor of empty boxes to
get to a door left ajar. Peeking in through its gap, I saw an
overflowing bathtub with the faucet still running. I was

just rushing in to switch it off, but then all of a sudden, the door slammed shut behind me.

One moment the room went pitch-black, the next the ceiling light began to flicker on and off. Between the flashes, I noticed submerged in the tub of water, the old woman's body. She was naked and looked to be dead already. Just to be certain, I reached under the water to check her pulse. Right then, she seized my arm in an attempt to drag me under with her. I fought until breaking free from her. My instinct told me to turn for the doorknob, which I did immediately. But despite my relentless twisting, turning, and pulling, the door would not give way as if it was somehow glued into the wall.

Meanwhile, the old woman had gotten up out of the tub and progressed towards me. I caught one quick look of her face and saw that she was actually Megan. Cornered, I shielded myself from her as she launched at me, but then I never felt the presumed attack. When I finally dared a peek, she was gone. The next thing I heard was a splash coming from the bathtub. I looked over and it was now surging blood. The red liquid came jetting over me. In the moment I got swept under, I felt like I couldn't breath. The second I woke myself, I was coughing and spluttering as if I was literally going to choke to death in my sleep…"

While listening attentively to Allison's compelling narrative, Dr. Cooke was impressed by how precisely she remembered everything. As it came to a close, she jumped to ask the few questions she had jotted down.

"Remind me if you will, how long ago did Megan pass away?"

"It's going on four weeks now."

"You've mentioned previously that you were quite distant."

"That's right."

"Allow me to be frank. It seems to me that you were not particularly fond of her."

"What gave you that idea?"

Dr. Cooke gave no answer and just looked at her, awaiting a response.

Allison decided to stop pretending. "You are right. I wasn't. But it was not without reason."

"I'm sure. Which was?"

"She slept with my husband."

Dr. Cooke was disturbed for a second. "Are they not real siblings?"

"She's his stepsister."

Relieved, she nodded in comprehension. "I'm sorry to hear that."

"That's okay. It's in the past."

"Did it happen more than once?"

"As far as I know, it was just that one time... Can we change the subject now?"

"Why? Does it make you feel uncomfortable talking about it?"

"No. I just... I just don't find it very productive."

Dr. Cooke looked at her notes briefly. Intending to slowly acquire Allison's trust, she resorted to come in from a different angle. "This dream of yours, is it a reoccurring one?"

"No."

"Perhaps the number '33' means something to you?"

"It doesn't, except for the apartment I visited last week."

"Oh? Was it the same apartment as in the dream?"

"Yes, but I never went in."

"Why not?"

"Well, I don't really know her personally."

"The old woman?"

"Yes."

"Then — what made you visit her?"

So as to avoid touching on Adrian's issues, Allison did not plan on telling the whole truth. "I was actually there to see my brother. She's an old friend of his that he's staying with. It was just a short meeting, a 'hi and bye' sort of thing. After that, he and I left for lunch."

"I see. Do you guys meet up often?"

"My brother and I?"

"Uh-huh."

"Not as much as I'd like."

"Is he an older brother?"

"Yes, by six years, but we were very close growing up."

"My younger brother and I are also six years apart in age. Technically my parents adopted him when he was eleven, but growing up in our house, he was nicer to me than any of my actual, older siblings. Even now, I receive roses from him every year on my birthday. Dare I say that I sense a similar bond between you guys?"

Allison's lips could not help curl into a smile.

Dr. Cooke noticed it and therefore continued, "So, what kind of a brother is he?"

The mention of Adrian automatically put Allison at ease. Because of his ill-perceived reputation, he was almost never raised as a subject for discussion among her family and friends. This would be her rare chance to talk to someone about him in a good light. "He's a... he's always been sweet and protective of me. Even to this day, he would do pretty much anything for me in my best interest."

"Sounds like he's been there for you."

"He's also the most supportive of whatever I set my heart out to do. I don't tell many people, but he was my inspiration to become a writer."

"Oh? Is he too a writer? Does he have any published work?"

"No. He gave that up very early on, but he could have been a great one for sure. He won the National Juvenile Writer Award for three consecutive years starting from second grade."

"That sounds very impressive."

Allison's eyes twinkled. "It is. And that is only one of the highly regarded composition awards he's won among many others over those few years."

"What happened in that fourth year?"

"I'm not too sure. I was only four years old at the time. I'm guessing something must have distracted him and made him lose interest in writing. That happened to be the same year he lit his bedroom on fire..."

"He lit his bedroom on fire? A ten-year-old?"

"It wasn't as terrible as it sounds. He was just playing with a box of cigars and a lighter one day... Well, to be honest, if anyone were to be blamed, it should have been my father. He really should have stored those things more carefully, really."

"And, you were with him when he did it?"

"Of course. My brother would never let me miss something like that. But like I said, I was too young to remember much. I just know that I ended up crying, and Mrs. Gomez was there shortly —"

"Mrs. Gomez?"

"She used to be my nanny. Anyway, nobody got hurt in the end except for my father's wallet. But that was a minor loss in comparison to what could have been disastrous. Even my father said so himself."

Hardly ever did Allison open up to people she knew scarcely, this was undeniably a breakthrough. While the conversation seemed to be going well, right then, Dr. Cooke made a catastrophic mistake.

"So, what is he up to these days?"

"Who? My father?"

"Adrian," she specified, and then like a bolt from the blue, it hit Allison, who immediately resumed her guard.

"I don't recall ever telling you my brother's name."

Dr. Cooke was disappointed in herself upon her slip of the tongue. Judging by the distrusting look on Allison's face, she knew it was too late for regrets and so opted for coming clean. "Your mother stopped by the office last Friday. She told me about your relationship with Adrian."

"So I see you've gone behind my back to have your little discussion. That's not very professional of you."

"Well, I won't turn away an opportunity to learn about my patient when it is presented to me. If I do that, it wouldn't be very professional of me either now, would it? She also touched on your medical history of depression, which you've deliberately left out mentioning in your health assessment."

Feeling like being ambushed, Allison was plain pissed off. Having sensed her indignation, Dr. Cooke decided to make an effort to vindicate Brenda's action but right away, it backfired.

"Your mother did it out of concern for you."

"You don't know my mother."

"If it weren't such a sensitive topic, I'm sure she wouldn't have had to intervene like she did."

"Our family matters are none of your business, so *stay* out of them."

"It was never my intention to pry Mrs. Skala. Although —"

"Then don't! You could have turned her away instead of doing something so underhanded."

"I can understand your frustration."

"No you don't! You can't begin to understand how I feel."

As Allison's voice got louder in anger, Dr. Cooke purposely stopped talking for a moment for her to calm down.

It hardly worked.

"Forgive me. But with all due respect, it is my job as a psychiatrist to analyze my patients and put forth recommendations where I see fit."

"Humph. If after this pointless chat you were to advise me to stay away from my brother, then don't bother.

I've already had the same counseling too many times in the past thank you very much."

"That's not what I was going to do —"

"Save it!" rasped Allison, her tone cold and as unbendable as a rock. "I know what you're all thinking, but to be frank, I care not about your opinions of him. I love my brother, period. There's no one in the world that can stop me from talking to, or for that matter, seeing him. Not my mother then, and certainly, not you now."

"I am sorry about what happened to Adrian, truly, I am. But I must agree with Mrs. Crawford, I do see a bigger issue that we are dealing with here —"

"I came... I came here today to have my prescription replaced, not chitchat about my family. Can I please just have that, and I will be out of your way."

"That's —"

"*Please!*"

All the tension built up in the room eventually demolished their potential acquaintanceship. Reluctantly, Dr. Cooke put a stop to her analysis and wrote out an alternate prescription as per requested. Even knowing under no circumstance would she be able to get her message across now, she tried one last time. "I cannot stress enough. This is only a temporary solution. In the end, you must address the underlying problems if you are to make a recovery."

Just as she had expected, Allison hurried to snatch the piece of paper from her hand and stormed out.

21

TAKING THE BACKSTAIRS, Allison ran the nine floors down without stopping till she reached the back exit out of the building. All along still grudging about her mother's sneaky, deceitful way, she trod heavily back to her car and shut the door precisely the moment her bottom touched the seat. Inhaling and exhaling slowly, she sat to take a few deep breaths when suddenly a male voice speaking fine Scottish Gaelic broke out from the backseat: "Fàilte air ais."

Instantaneously, she reacted in terror, turning and screaming directly in the man's face. It took her just a bit longer to realize it was only her brother, who immediately burst into laughter upon playing the prank on her.

"HAHAHAHA!"

"What was that!"

"That's 'welcome back' in Scottish. Some guy I talked to the other day taught it to me."

"Don't do that! You totally freaked me out! I seriously thought my heart was going to stop..."

He just laughed harder, barely able to draw breath anymore.

"Yeah, yeah. Very funny."

"I'm sorry, heh... hehe... I will stop. I thought it would have been a pleasant surprise. Didn't mean to scare you like that Allie, really."

Hands over her chest, Allison waited till her beating calmed to ask him, "How did you get in?"

"You left your car unlocked again."

"I did?"

"Yes. You should really be more careful with that. Because who knows, next time it might not be me but some armed robber demanding money from you at gun point."

"Stop that!"

"Am I scaring you again? OoooOOOooo!"

"Come on Adrian. What are you doing here anyway?"

"I came to check up on you of course. Looks like you've decided to listen to Mother after all and turned to the Devil himself for help."

"I didn't see Dr. Carter. It's this female doctor."

"Same difference. In any case — how did it go?"

"You know how it always is."

"Did she ask if you've abused any narcotics lately, or how many people you've slept with in the past week?"

"No. It's not like that."

"I've always thought those were the standard questions. That manipulative son of a bitch used to ask me every time I went for my session... Well, did this one female doctor at least do miracles for you?"

"Her last prescription worked for a little while, but then —"

"But then it failed."

She nodded.

"Ha! Don't they always? Was she at least nice to you?"

"It was a complete disappointment okay? Let's just talk about something else."

"Take it easy. I haven't even asked whether you've told her about me."

Knowing her brother's repugnance at psychiatric practices, she was going to lie to him, but Adrian found her out before she even attempted.

"So you did tell her. I'm assuming Mother put you up to this as well."

"She didn't. It was all me, actually. But it wasn't intentional."

"There's no use mentioning me Allie, that doctor of yours won't understand. Consider it hopeless."

"Then consider it done. I won't be going back to her again so don't worry about it."

Her assurance prompted him to smile.

It was comforting for Allison to see him back to his normal self, taking into account the bizarre incident that occurred just last Thursday. She wanted to ask him many things regarding it, but part of her was hesitating. Though she might not be the one to bring that up, Adrian, on the other hand, knew she deserved the truth and had actually come to tell her just that.

"Remember… remember that I called you last week? I forgot which day exactly but it was some time around noon I believe."

"It was more like 11 a.m., since you asked me to be there by noon."

"To be where?"

"An apartment complex in the west end of Blackpool."

"Right… Well, what else did I say?"

"Not much else, but you insisted that I went, otherwise you would…"

"Yes?"

"You really have no recollection of any of it?"

"Oh man, man, man!" he exclaimed suddenly, rubbing his face nervously, "I screwed up something again didn't I?"

"From what I know, no. Do you at least remember what you were doing or who you were with though?"

"The whole last week was hell for me Allie. I just remember feeling shitty like my world had literally been flipped upside down and crumbled over me. I don't know how to explain everything, but I never meant to cause you any harm."

"You didn't. I was more worried about you than anything. I thought you might have been with Miranda and something terrible happened."

"What gave you that impression?"

"Well, you said… I don't know if I should say."

"Just tell me."

"Well, the reason you wanted me there… you sort of threatened me, saying that if I didn't show up at noon, something was going to happen to her. And you sounded all mad and irritated, I was worried that… that…"

"That I might kill her."

"Not that! I was worried that you might have lost it and took your frustration out on her like that one incident you told me about a while ago."

"Which incident?"

"That one where you... smacked her head against the wall and accidentally knocked her out."

"Oh that. I told you that?"

"Yes you did, among other things."

"At least now she will never have to worry about me getting out of control again."

"What do you mean?"

Just then, a corner of his lips flicked up into a smirk; meanwhile, his eyes narrowed to look evil. In all seriousness, he told her, "I killed her Allie, right that morning. I murdered that deceitful bitch for good."

Allison's jaw just dropped all the way to the floor. Looking at Adrian wide-eyed, she was in total shock.

Then, a moment later — "Ba-HAHAHAHA!" he burst out chortling.

"What! Was that a joke?!" she asked, but there was no stopping him. "It was, wasn't it? That wasn't funny at all!"

"I beg to differ. Ba-hahahaha!"

"Stop laughing! Gosh, I can't believe you sometimes."

"Didn't you think I forgot everything about that day?"

"Well, did you?"

"Honestly? Honestly, that day is like a faraway blur to me. All I remember is calling you and that I was alone the whole time. How is that for comfort?"

"Come on Adrian. I'm being serious."

"Me too. I was intoxicated and my head was spinning, so everything was sort of hazy as it went on. I have no clue what I actually said to you over the phone, I just know that I was really depressed about something."

"About what?"

"That's the irony. I don't really know. It could have been something stupid Miranda said for all I care. As far as I know though, everything is under control now."

"How are you so certain?"

"I'm here now aren't I? And I'm well."

"But —"

"Trust me Allie, I know myself just that much. Everything is fine," he insisted spiritedly, giving her an affirming squeeze on the arm.

Allison knew that her brother had always struggled with handling bad feelings; logic and rationality played only a small role — if at all — in his recovery process. His insistence that "everything is fine" only aroused her suspicion that he had to have done something to unload that melancholy in him beyond the help of drugs and alcohol, and if he did not unload it on his girlfriend, he had to have unloaded it on himself.

A speculation just then occurred to her. She thereupon demanded him, "Show me your arms."

Adrian was a little taken aback. "What? What are you getting at?"

"You know what I'm getting at. Did you?"

"Did I what?"

"Did you cut yourself?"

"Nope."

"Then why can't you show me?"

"I just... I just don't feel the need to prove to you what I know I did not do."

His responses only made her more fearful. She was not about to let him keep up his false front however, and he knew it.

"Fine... fine." Rolling up his sleeve, he revealed his scarred, skeletal right arm and showed it to her throughout. "See? Just some age-old scars is all. Satisfied?"

"No. Show me the other arm too."

"You don't want to do this Allie."

Disregarding his verbal portent, Allison proceeded to grab at his hand, flipped it so his palm faced upward and then pulled up his sleeve herself. Right away, she gasped, not just at his already badly scarred forearm but also — in particular — at this long, deep gash down its center, from the inside of his elbow to his wrist. The wounded area was still very much inflamed with the surrounding skin being red and swollen.

Stirred by his gratuitous self-abuse, her eyes went damp in a flash. She gulped to hold in her tears but only barely.

"Why do you still do this?"

"It's long overdue."

"What is?"

"It's inevitable Allie."

"What is?!"

Retrieving his arm, Adrian continued to speak of his own physical destruction without a hint of regret. "Something's gotta give. No pain, no gain, that's just the way of life. I do feel much better now so it was a fair trade-off after all."

"I don't want to hear the same excuse every time," she retorted.

Seeing him hurt after the fact was certainly less traumatizing than seeing it first-hand, as Allison had experienced numerous times in the past. Though somehow — like all the other times — she ended up crying in front of him while he tried calming her by saying: "Don't cry. There's nothing worth crying for here."

"You don't understand... you just don't."

"You'd be surprised how much I do."

She looked right at him, and he told her, "You are crying because of how much you care for me. You are that one in a million Allie. I honestly cannot ask for a better sister."

His assertion only made her sob harder. Quickly, he moved to get out of the car, came around to the front and into the passenger seat next to her to give her a big, brotherly hug. He rubbed her on the back and rocked her a little till she slowly relaxed, and then worked to steer her focus onto something — supposedly — much more pleasant.

"So, what is your big plan for tomorrow?" he asked her.

Pulling away from him, Allison dried her tears with the back of her hand. "Whatever for?" she asked him back.

"Isn't tomorrow your fourth wedding anniversary? It is something exciting to celebrate," he prompted, which just so brought about more disappointment.

"We don't have any plans."

"Oh? How come?"

"Normally, Dan and I would go out for dinner at a fancy restaurant, but judging by his mood lately, I doubt he's up for it this year."

"You didn't ask?"

"No. It is obvious enough that I don't have to ask."

Adrian shook his head. "Hasn't it been a month already since she died?"

"More or less. He just needs his time to heal and I'm not gonna rush him. Not anymore."

"But you are his best medicine! Are you really willing to let her win even after death?"

"Of course not."

"Then you need to do something about it, and quickly, before a perfectly good chance slips by."

"What are you suggesting that I do? I can't just keep pushing his buttons till he finally decides to get over her."

"That's not what I meant."

"Then what?"

"I'm only telling you to not let Megan or anything else get in your way of getting what you want or doing whatever that you want to do."

"You just sounded like Mom there for a second."

"God, please. Don't start."

Allison in turn let out a snicker, agreeing with him, "Alright. I guess it doesn't hurt to try. I'll go ahead and make a reservation at Pierro for tomorrow night. Even if he was to refuse to go, I'll give him the gift that I bought a while back regardless. It's a watch. He's said he liked it one time when we stopped at a store window to look at it."

"A watch is great, but you've got to do more than just presenting him goods."

"What are your thoughts?"

"When was the last time you surprised him?"

"Um… I don't remember. But I don't think he knows that I got him the watch."

"Again, I'm not talking about material things."

"Then, do you mean… in a seductive way?"

"Well?"

"Well, to tell the truth, it's been a long time since I put on any of my sexy lingerie and did the whole flirty thing in front of him. We only just get along lately, let alone try to have any luck in the bedroom."

"Perhaps it's time to spice things back up then sister. What could be better timing than a wedding anniversary?"

"You really think he would like that?"

"He's a man after all Allie. I have no doubt."

Everything Adrian said to her just now seemed to make perfect sense. She pondered for a moment and suddenly her face brightened with new aspiration. "Okay. I just got an idea."

"That's more like it," he said proudly, smiling. "Glad I can be of help."

DAY 19 | SEPT 24 THURSDAY

22

E ARLY IN THE morning, Allison had worked up a
sweat in the kitchen preparing Daniel's best-loved
breakfast: sausages, bacon strips, and a good old-
fashioned cheese omelet derived from her mother-in-
law's secret family recipe. While dishing up the delicious-
ness onto a large platter, she heard him yelling for her
from their bedroom. In response to what sounded urgent,
she abandoned her task and hustled up the stairs.

"I was gonna bring you breakfast… in bed. What's all
this?" she asked as soon as she walked into the room,
completely thrown off by her husband, half-dressed, sitting on the floor in his woven dress shirt and boxers next
to a pile of clothes.

"I'm looking for a tie. Do you know where the brown-
ish… reddish one is?" inquired Daniel, looking up at her,
seemingly agitated by the overlong search.

"You mean the maroon one?"

"Yup. Can you please tell me where it is?"

"I hung it up together with your suit last night so you
won't miss it," she told him, walking over to the closet to
retrieve a brown garment bag. Swiftly unzipping it, she
took out from within his business suit and laid it out on
the bed.

Relieved at last, he got up and hurried to change into
it. Sensing his urgency, she reminded him, "It's only six-
thirty. Why the rush?"

"I've told you. TPA will be our biggest client yet if
they are to grant us this multibillion-dollar deal. I want to
look my best for the presentation."

"I thought the presentation is in the afternoon?"

"You are correct, but their representatives will arrive in exactly two and a half hours to do an initial meet-and-greet. Every engineer who wishes to become part of the team overseeing this project is attending."

"That means Keith —"

"That means Keith McCoy will be there no doubt," he finished her thought. "And he is presenting right before me."

Notwithstanding the nature of competition among engineers at MAC, the rivalry between Daniel and Keith — two relatively young, promising marvels of the craft of aviation — was particularly cutthroat. Every now and again, big projects like this one would come along raising the pressure amidst them, and then on the day of the official conference with the customer, it would oftentimes be literally dog eat dog.

For the longest time, Daniel had been able to secure pretty much every project on which he set his mind. The tide had apparently turned however during an important project kick-off a month ago at a major customer's office. He had arrived in Virginia the day prior, all pumped up and ready to bring his "A" game until news of Megan's death came crushing down on him like heavy weights an hour before his presentation. It directly degraded his performance in front of the higher-ups of the company, so much so that in the end, he lost to Keith for the first time in two years a project he worked for extremely hard.

"I'm not going to let this one slip through my fingers like the last time, uh-uh, not gonna happen again. I'm going to impress the crap out of these guys," declared Daniel, sounding unequivocally confident. His nervousness still ever so slightly showed as Allison caught him redoing his tie over and over, even though the previous attempt was no better than the last. When he finally found it acceptable, she stepped in to straighten it for him.

"There. Much better. I'm sure you'll do great like you always do," she praised him softly, her hands still pressed against his chest when her eyes slowly shifted upward to lock with his. This tender moment lingered between them for a couple seconds, until he backed away eventually and rather clumsily.

"I gotta get going... still need to prepare a few things at the office before they arrive," he told her, and then moved to hasten down the stairs.

She tagged behind him all the way down to the foyer.

"You should at least have some breakfast before you go."

"No time for breakfast. I want to get there before everybody else does," he insisted, putting on his shiny, leather shoes at the bench. Knowing his strong will, she did not bother to nag and just stood watching him with a face sad. It was only till the moment before he would walk out the door with his briefcase did he spare a glance at her look of disappointment.

"The dinner reservation's at seven, correct?"

She nodded lightly at him.

"I'll be home by six-thirty to pick you up."

"Will you really?"

"Why not?"

"I don't know." She looked away.

Right then, he came right back to her. Lifting her chin gently, he told her firmly, "Of course I will."

Just like that, she felt buoyed up over again.

Not known to Daniel, Allison had in fact a slightly different plan for tonight. After all she reckoned, in order to save their marriage, surprising him with a candlelit dinner was hardly enough, but it sure could be a good way to reignite their lost spark. So, shortly after he left, she as well got to work.

Sitting on the kitchen counter was a shopping list she sorted out yesterday of all the things needed to make this a memorable night. She double-checked it and at the last minute, added on a few ingredients for a special home-made cocktail — one of Daniel's favorite drinks that she only made on rare occasions. On checking for the blender in its storage cabinet, she noticed it missing and right away remembered lending it to Sara months ago for an impromptu party.

First thing, she texted her friend requesting it back. A few seconds later, Sara replied with a simple "okay, I will". Surprised that she was up so early in the morning, Allison decided to give her a ring.

Sara's hoarse voice quickly suggested a lousy hangover. Other than that, she actually sounded notably upbeat. "No worries. I'll bring it over some time around one o'clock. I just need to wash it. Just used it last night for a little intimate get-together."

"Who's the lucky guy this time?"

In a whispering tone, she replied cheerfully, "Oh gosh Allie, I've met the hottest guy in town I swear. He is the quarterback of his high school's football team. His body is soooo gorgeous I wanna cry!"

"Did you say high school?"

"*Shh... shh...*"

Allison waited a second.

"Okay. He just flipped over to his stomach. He's still sleeping next to me by the way."

"I realized that... Anyway, did you say high school?" she repeated.

"Yeah, and I also said quarterback."

"Shouldn't he be up getting ready for school soon?"

"Do *not* tease me like Ed does!"

Allison tittered. "I'm sorry. I got carried away. How did you guys get hooked up?"

"Do you want the long story or a short one?"

"Just tell me the brief version."

"Well, there's this football field not far from my new place. I've already brought Ethan and Reese there a couple times. Don't ask me why, but they love to roll their little

balls in the short grass. Anywho, when we got there yesterday afternoon, his team was halfway through a practice
match. Somehow we got to talking after that, and one
thing led to another, I ended up inviting him and his team
over for a party."

"A party with your sons there?"

"No. I thought ahead and had my mom come pick
them up shortly after getting home. An hour or so later, he
was the only one who showed up. That sort of worked out
for the best as we drank and talked all night just the two
of us. Turns out he lives with his grandparents in the
neighborhood next to mine."

"Sounds convenient. Are you finally falling for this
one?"

"He's real good in bed for his age but heck no! He's
not serious about this and neither am I. He's got a girlfriend."

Allison was mildly shocked and slightly appalled by
the confessed scandal. "What? You knew and you still did
it with him?"

"Chill Allie. I'm more responsible than you and Ed
give me credit for," asserted Sara, clarifying, "I only found
out after the business."

"How? Don't tell me he waited until then to tell you."

"No, he was in the shower when I was grabbing his
clothes off the bed and putting it on the chair next to it.
His wallet somehow fell out of his jacket's pocket during
the transition and landed open on the floor. I picked it up,
took a peek at it and saw a photo of him with this cute
girl."

"Maybe it's his sister."

"They were kissing in it."

"Oh."

"Besides, I asked him about it after he got out and he
came clean. He said he's planned to break up with her for
a while now, but that's his problem not mine."

"Well, I'm glad you had a good time."

"Heck yeah I did. Speaking of which, have you made up your mind yet?"

"About what?"

"Are you coming to my housewarming? It's this Sunday."

"I can't give you an answer yet."

"You said that the last time we talked. If you prefer Daniel to be there too, you can bring him along. I didn't mention that before because I know he's not much of a party person."

"Neither am I," Allison reminded her.

"Well, it's just... he is quite dull in social settings if you know what I mean."

"Says who?"

"You know... people."

"You mean one of your roisterer friends? If Dan's dull then so am I."

"Yeah but you are my best friend! That makes all the difference. But hey, like I said, if that's the only way to get you to come, bring him."

"It's not that. I'm just waiting for him."

"Waiting for him to do what?"

"He's still indecisive about going to the Bahamas for the weekend. I will be sure to bring that up again tonight."

"Isn't today Thursday?"

"Yes?"

"Didn't you tell me your parents are leaving for the trip this Friday?"

"I know that the time is tight, but I won't lose hope just yet."

"Ha. Good luck with that. I hate to burst your bubble but I don't think he will say yes. At least either way you will have a good time, because let me tell you girl, it's going to be one kickass housewarming like no other."

"Right." Though she might seem to agree with Sara, if it were entirely up to her, she would much rather spend the time with Daniel far away from home. That being the case, the success of this evening became exceptionally important.

"Don't forget about the blender. I really need it for tonight. Are you sure you don't want me to just come get it?" Knowing her friend's absent-minded nature, it would be a lie to say she was not a teensy bit worried about her commitment.

Sara was quick to reassure her however. "Nope. You can count on me with this one. I said one o'clock. I won't forget."

"Alright then."

"But I've got to go now. This migraine is killing me. I want to try to fall back asleep for a few more hours before my mom will call and nag me to go pick up my kids."

"Okay. See you in a bit."

"Yup. See ya."

23

AT NINE O'CLOCK, Allison headed out to get her shopping done for the big night. The supermarket was especially quiet at this early hour. Being scarce of customers and all, it just so allowed her to tackle her list one item at a time without the constant yielding and weaving. Strolling along with her cart, she checked off each thing as she removed them from the shelves and very soon, spices were the only things left to pick up. Careful not to miss accidentally the designated aisle, all the while walking, she kept her head up for a sign that read "SEASONINGS".

It was when she was absolutely devoted to her task, something weird happened. As from the corner of her eye, aisle after aisle moving by in a blur, she noticed the existence of one suspicious man, who happened to be wandering along the opposite end of the aisles at precisely the same pace as hers — when she stopped, he stopped; and when she picked up her feet, so did he.

Coming up to an end display just before the "SEASONINGS" aisle, she parked for a brief moment in front of it and slowly leaned her head forward to peek into the aisle with hope to not see him, but there he was. Bizarrely, the man stood in the middle of the lane, did not look to be shopping for anything in particular and only stared back at her. Startled, she panicked and withdrew herself. Her heart quailed despite him posing no immediate threat and quite possibly no threat at all. When finally mentally ready, she took a deep breath prior to moving on into the aisle. By that time, he was already gone. Hurriedly, she picked out what was needed and went straight to check out of the store.

The absurd occurrence could have ended back there, but curiosity had Allison gripped. While all buckled up and ready to drive home, she waited in the car for a couple more minutes, until seeing the same man, empty-handed, walk out into the parking lot and head for a white sedan within her view. Having no basis, she knew pursuing him would be pure madness; but in the moment he steered to pull out of his space, she made a rash decision to do just that.

The roads were free from traffic at the time, making it possible for her to keep track of him while maintaining a reasonable distance all the way into downtown Arbington. Before long, she saw him pull over on one of the side streets, get out and walk up to a nearby telephone booth. She as well parked at a spot about a block away and stayed put observing the booth window keenly. Just then, an anonymous call to her cell phone faltered her concentration. Assuming it was Adrian, she answered it.

"Hello?"

"Hi Allison, having a blast following me around?" a deep, husky voice responded.

Her heart skipped a beat, knowing it was that man. "Who are you?" she asked him.

"I'm an old friend of your brother Adrian, but that's not at all important here. What's important is that I *know* what you are hiding for him."

She was confused. "I have no idea what you are talking about."

"*Really*. And you think I believe that?"

"It is the truth —"

"Oh 'dear sweet Allie.' That's what he used to call you in front of me. As far as I know, he tells you everything. You are the only one he wholly trusts."

"I really don't know anything."

The man guffawed, speaking mightily. "Exactly who do you think you are fooling?! You can't escape from your own conscience any longer Allison. You know it's eating you up, slowly. You can't sleep without your pills now can you?"

"How do you —"

"Things will only get worse from here on if you don't do something about that secret of yours soon."

"I'm... I'm not afraid of you."

"Then why are you stuttering?"

"Stop... stop stalking me you creep!!!" she shouted into the speaker, but the man was not at all intimidated.

"Haha. Who is stalking whom?"

"I will call the cops on you I swear!"

"But I'm on your side. There's absolutely no need to be hostile towards me."

"Whatever it is that you want from me, I don't have it."

"Who said that I want something from you? Because I don't."

"Then why are you telling me all this?"

"I'm afraid you will have to figure that one out your-self, because at the end of the day, you can trust no one, believe no one."

"You are crazy."

"*I am?* Humph. Tell your brother, Justin says hi."

Soon as the man hung up, before he even got out of the phone booth, Allison tossed her phone onto the pas-senger seat, stomped on the gas pedal and left the scene faster than greased lightning.

This Justin guy coming out of nowhere claiming to know her secret even she herself had trouble recollecting was simply baffling. During her way home, it continued to bug her. While she could only rely on her own memories for clues, all that senseless searching for an answer that might not even be there gave her a headache. To distract herself from further absorption in the matter, she turned up the volume of the radio. It just so happened her favor-ite hourly segment was on the air. In the midst of listening in, she let her mind run free...

HOST: Thank you for listening in on KDM1 — your favor-ite radio station in the Twin Cities. The local time is now 11 a.m., let's give it up for our third caller of the day... *CANNED APPLAUSE* Hello?

ALLISON: Hi.

HOST: What is your name? Ms. —"

ALLISON: Allison.

HOST: Ms. Allison! Welcome to *Truth of the Hour*. How is your day going so far?

ALLISON: It's okay.

HOST: You sound a bit down, but don't worry. We've got just the person to cheer you up! Your brother is also on the line. Adrian, say hi to your sister.

ADRIAN: Hi Allie.

ALLISON: Hey.

HOST: I see that you are married Allison.

ALLISON: That's right.

HOST: When we asked you previously "who do you considered to be your closest family", you immediately mentioned your brother. Since I've been doing this segment for so long, I know most contestants would have picked their spouse in your case. Can you tell us briefly just how close you guys are?

ALLISON: Well, my brother means the world to me. I tell him most of everything that goes on in my life. I just feel like I can trust him with anything.

HOST: And, what about you Adrian? How do you feel about your sister saying all that nice stuff about you?

ADRIAN: I feel great, of course. I do pretty much feel the same way about her. I would do just about anything for her, because I love her.

HOST: Haha. Even more than you love your girlfriend?

ADRIAN: Yes, very much so.

HOST: Wow. That's some powerful bond you've got going on. Now, let's put it to the test shall we? Minutes ago, we've asked Adrian to tell us some of the deepest secrets that you two share. Now remember, in order to get these concert tickets, you must tell the truth, the whole truth, and nothing but the truth. Whenever you are ready Ms. Allison, please say our slogan.

ALLISON: 'Cross my heart and hope to die'.

HOST: Alrighty! So, here goes your question, 'tell us the one secret you've been keeping from your husband that you must not tell him regardless of circumstances'. Huh... sounds like a toughie. Allison?

ALLISON: The one thing I mustn't tell Dan... I can't think of anything off the top of my head.

HOST: Are you sure? Nothing pops up at all?

ALLISON: Um... I wish I had a clue but... I don't know, really.

ADRIAN: Come on Allie. Think harder.

ALLISON: The one thing I mustn't tell Dan...

HOST: Would you like a hint?

ALLISON: Yes, please.

HOST: It has something to do with a shoebox.

ALLISON: A shoebox... what shoebox...

ADRIAN: Concentrate on your thoughts Allie. You got this."

ALLISON: A shoebox..."

ADRIAN: Remember I told you to get rid of it? The one that I hid underneath your —"

HOST: Hey-ho! One hint is all that we allow in this game unfortunately. I'm sorry to say this but Allison, you didn't win the tickets. Please continue to tune in every hour, on the hour, for *Truth of the Hour,* where our next winner could be you...

As the applause track rose and faded, Allison cogitated on her own figment of imagination some more.

A shoebox that needed to be gotten rid of...

Could it be...

Finally, something in her clicked. Two weeks back while vacuuming the guest bedroom, she stumbled upon a heavily duct-taped box tucking away underneath the bed. Coming to remember how it originally got there, she only now faintly recalled Adrian pestering her in his most serious tone of voice:

'I'll hide it here for now. When you get a real chance, destroy it. Can I trust that you will do this for me?'

Feeling suddenly obligated to ensure it was taken care of sensibly, on arriving home, she retrieved it from its secret place at long last and decisively moved along with a garden trowel into the backyard. Beneath a big willow tree, she got down on her knees and began digging. Bit by bit, she removed the many layers of soil until a big hole was made deep enough to fit the box in. Before she let go of it however, her stomach twisted. Tempted to find out what was hidden inside, she shook it a little and searched closely for a rupture of sorts; but then on second thought, she ceased her inspection. Knowing better that no good could possibly come from something Adrian intended to keep confidential, in the end, she laid her concern to rest and buried the mystery.

Out of sight, out of mind.

24

BACK INSIDE THE house, Allison put on some jazz music as she began to decorate for the night. She took a few ideas off the Internet about utilizing roses and candles to convey romantic sentiment and acted upon them. Removing the dozens of long-stemmed red roses from their packaging, she trimmed down a great bunch to the appropriate lengths and arranged them thoughtfully in a variety of vases positioned in the living room. As for the remainder, she worked to collect their petals and sprinkled her effort across the entryway floor, over the stairs leading up to the master bedroom and on the bathtub and bed. Votive candles were then placed among the scattered petals, and ones in metallic holders on tables near the vases and in alignment on the cedar railings out in the deck where the dinner was to take place.

After a long period of careful ornamentation, a short break later, she began to cook. She had ambitiously planned for a three-course dinner: coconut shrimp to start, sirloin steak with potato risotto as the main entrée, and chocolate raspberry soufflé to end. Despite having never made any of the dishes before, she followed the preselected recipes step by step, slaved over the hot stove for hours to put together each from scratch and succeeded. The shrimp turned out golden-brown, the steak a perfect pink just how Daniel would like it and the soufflé still baking in the oven added a touch of sweetness to the already appetizing aroma.

Having been so caught up in everything else, she was unaware of Sara's absence until taking off her apron and preparing to blend up some ice and fruits for the cocktail. It was already six o'clock. Just before she would go mad and call her friend up to scold her, someone rang the doorbell. She rushed to answer the door with a face annoyed assuming it was Sara returning the blender at the very last minute. As it happened however, it was actually Ed doing her dirty work.

"She said she's *very, very* sorry."

Retrieving the blender, she spoke with a hint of anger, "I specifically reminded her early this morning."

"You know how she is. She's got a memory like a sieve."

"What has she been doing in the past ten hours?"

He shrugged. "Who knows? When I was just over at her place, she was busy tidying up the bedroom."

"I've honestly not known anyone so forgetful. This is the last time I'm lending her anything."

"Yeah, I had to learn that the hard way too. Exactly why doesn't she use her own? She's the one who's constantly hosting parties."

"It's a long story. Hers broke a couple months ago —"

Just then, the oven timer sounded, prompting Allison to rush for the kitchen to take out the soufflé. On her return, Ed had let himself in.

"What's all this fuss?" he asked her, studying the deliberate arrangement in the living room.

"Tonight's our fourth wedding anniversary."

"And am I lucky to have you as my wife," he kidded, but she was clearly not having it, rejoining, "Not now Ed."

"Relax. It was just a joke."

"I still have so much to do and so little time left."

"What else do you have to do?"

"I still need to make the cocktail and light all these candles."

"Would you like some help?"

She looked at him weird for a second, and he added, "What? It's a genuine offer."

"Thank you, but no. I got everything covered."

"I gotta say though, you must have put lots of thought into this night to make the place look so lovely..."

Seeing him continue to wander in the room with no immediate intention of leaving, she got more anxious. "Listen Ed. Dan will be home very soon —"

"And you want me gone," he cut in halfway through her talking, an envious look on his face. "You know I never planned to ruin your evening."

"I know, but —"

"But dare I say that Daniel Skala is undoubtedly one of the luckiest sons of a bitch in the world."

His rude comment stemmed from pure jealousy stunned her even just for a moment. "Did you drink at Sara's house?" she suspected.

He only let out a scornful snort. "Don't worry Allie. I'll go, and I sincerely hope that you two will have a wonderful night." As soon as he finished speaking, he showed himself out.

She could really do without the drama at a precious time like this, and so she let him leave, secretly thankful, jumping back on track at once.

The time that took to light all those candles proved to exceed her calculation. Eventually, she was forced to scratch the whole homemade cocktail idea, presuming Daniel would be just as pleased. At fifteen minutes to six-thirty, she went swiftly upstairs to take a quick shower, fix up her hair and make-up, and then change into her lacy, tieback, baby-doll lingerie and heels for this particularly special occasion. The sun was just setting when she came back down the stairs. As the colored sky gradually faded, the candlelight shone brighter. The metallic candleholders shimmered in the soft lighting, all at once retaining a charming luster that made the entire house — inside and out — glow.

Any minute now, she thought to herself nervously, barely sitting down on the couch before she heard the garage door opening and Daniel's car going into it. Pretty soon, he came in through the front door with a small bouquet of red roses in one hand and his briefcase in another, both of which he set down onto the entryway bench prior to following the trail of rose petals leading him into the living room.

Faced with the moment of truth, Allison stood with both hands on the hips, greeting him in a seductive manner. "Happy anniversary honey," she spoke up to him softly.

His eyes instantly shifted to her. As she made her way towards him, he looked her over from head to toe, marking her every slinky tread till she stopped right in front of him.

"I made us dinner instead," she said, looking up at him enticingly.

"Is that what that smell is?"

She nodded.

"What's with all the candles and deco?"

"Well... I uh..."

"I like them."

She was beaming with elation then. "Are you —"

Suddenly without warning, he seized her boldly around the waist, lifting her up with one arm and supporting her bottom with the other. Instinctively, she wrapped hers around his neck and legs around his back.

"Am I what?"

"Huh?"

"You were saying something before I interrupted you."

"I... I don't remember what I was gonna say."

He smiled lightly at her and then his lips returned to their normal position. His gazing deep into her eyes was every bit sensual yet self-assured, drawing her closer and closer. Biting her lower lip, she signaled her carnal desire and just as she had wished, he kissed her, tenderly at first and then passionately. She let her mouth be filled with his courageous tongue while being carried out to the awaiting deck. The moist taste of his affection lingered on for the whole time she kept her eyes sealed until eventually, he set her down on a corner of the small, square dining table.

His sexual urge was immediately heightened by the luscious figure presented before him. Positioning himself in between her thighs, he brushed gently his lips against her ear and along her neck as her arms hugged around and fondled his lower back. One moment he pulled back, the next he reached behind her and untied the strip of fabric that was holding her top together, unveiling her full breasts. Her heart was pounding faster then. Legs up on the table, she scooted backward slightly, gripping her hands onto its edges in anticipation of his violation.

Taking his sweet time, he teased her rosy nipples with his fingertips, and on occasion, nibbled on them to stimulate her erotic sensation. The arousal had her moaning away. In a moment, one of his hands went and wrapped around her jawline, tiling her head back just a little bit and maintaining it. "Look at me," he commanded her. Consequently, she shot her yearning eyes at him. Right that instant, she felt his other hand leaving her breast, grazing past her stomach and coming to touch her down there. He rubbed her private part over her lacy thong till her wetness soaked through, and then slid his two fingers underneath it and into her.

In and out they went inside her.

"Tell me. How does this feel?"

She felt her loins melting, like a shot through her trembling body flushing with ecstasy that literally broke down all her guards, although at the time that was happening, she was all too drowned in his arousing foreplay to reply to him. Not that he really needed her to anyway.

"You like that, don't you?"

Her eyes never once left his, just as he never let go of his one hand that grabbed around her jaw to hold her still. In the meantime, he got turned on watching her suck on his forefinger that he casually slipped into her mouth, and her chest rise and fall harder trying to catch her breath due to the brisk movement.

"Please Dan... now," she begged him.

"What now? I want you to say it."

"I want... I want you inside me."

Right then, he pulled his fingers out of her.

"Turn around," he told her, removing his belt and taking off his pants and boxers.

She obeyed, of course, getting off the table and willfully turning her back towards him. Using his one hand, he held steady both her arms behind her back, while the other worked to strip off the tie from around his collar and then bind her wrists together with it. When secured, he bended her over so that her cheek rested sideways against the surface of the table. With her bottom sticking out, he lifted her thong to reveal her vagina and happily make way for his genital.

Excited by her own state of immobility, Allison thirsted for his bestial consumption. Holding her in place, Daniel penetrated her. The thrill of having complete control over her sexual pleasure, in a wicked sense, intensified his lovemaking. Before long, her bare back was spattered with his sweat that had been dripping from his forehead. Her eager responses to his occasional verbal teases, essentially, spurred him further towards his climax.

Her breasts dangled in the evening breeze, swinging back and forth as the sex went on. During the course of all that glory, someone was watching with jaundiced eyes. Directly behind the railing about six feet away from them hid Ed, blending in amongst the bushes, glaring at the intercourse in action. His fingers tightened into fists as anger ran through his core, struggling very much to restraint it. A sharp pang of envy struck him hardest the moment Daniel reached his peak. He looked on at his satisfied face roaring in orgasmic rapture, feeling sick to his stomach. He had to turn away or risk losing himself, forever.

For the thousandth time, and each time more pathetic than before, he vowed inwardly, *that is it... no more.*

DAY 20 | SEPT 25 FRIDAY

25

L ONG STORY SHORT, the candlelit dinner was a re-
markable success. To compensate for his wife's
splendid effort, Daniel eventually agreed to go to
the Bahamas together with his in-laws. Allison was beyond pleased to see his much-improved attitude since last
night, specifically with his taking a half-day off so as to
better accommodate the party, which she fully attributed
to Adrian's brilliant advice. Just so she could officially
thank him, while packing, she kept her phone near at
hand in case he was to call, but he never did.

After a quick grab-and-go lunch, the couple hurried
off to the airport to catch their flight departing at noon.
Making it to the gate at last, they met up with Elton, who
had been watching for them next to two expensive suitcases in a cart.

"There she is! My baby girl."

"Hi Daddy," Allison greeted him with a big smile, and
then the two hugged.

"Well, well, well, let me take a good look at you.
Hmm... something's different."

"It's probably my hair, sort of an awkward length
right now. I've been meaning to let it grow out again."

"No, that's not it. You look thinner. Has Danny been
starving you?"

"I'm not starving."

"Haha!"

"Your father is only teasing Allie," Daniel chimed in.
"How are you doing sir?"

The men in turn shook hands.

"Good. I'm glad you are able to make it."

"I do apologize for the short notice."

"Apology accepted."

"Daddy."

"Yes sweetpea?"

"It's about time to board. Where's Mom?"

"She went to the restroom a couple minutes ago. Ah, here she comes."

Allison and Daniel turned their heads to see Brenda approaching.

"That's all you brought with you? One suitcase?" she said to them.

"Hi Brenda," Daniel greeted her.

"Hey."

"We are only there for two nights. So you guys have two suitcases, big difference," Allison replied to her.

"No, no. Those two are just my stuff, we've had your father's checked."

"Are you planning to stay for more days?"

"I don't think so. El?"

"No. Tom Lee, the chairman of one of our major suppliers, is flying in all the way from China on Monday night. I want to be around when he settles into the hotel..."

Just then, one of the station attendants announced it was ten minutes before the official boarding.

"They said that ten minutes ago," Brenda whined.

"I'm sure it's soon. In any case, we will be the first to board," said Elton in cheering her. In view of this joyous occasion, he had gotten everyone premium tickets, yet more or less could not refrain from boasting about his wealth. "So Danny, have you ever flown first-class before?"

"No sir. I haven't," Daniel replied truthfully.

"Really? Not even once?"

Naturally without delay, Allison jumped to his defense. "Daddy, Dan flies business class all the time for his work which is just as good."

"Well, I suppose it isn't bad for domestic flights, as for international travel, more often than not, the price point can be easily a couple times cheaper that's for sure."

"It's not really about the money. It's paid for every time by his company anyway."

"You are right, comfort is what counts, although, those two things do go hand in hand. And if you want the best in-flight service, you definitely have to go for the best class. That's just how this works. Now I'm not saying I've never flown business before, as in fact I did all the time during the start of my career, but ever since I was able, I've always gone for the best seat available for good reasons."

"I honestly don't see them being that different —"

"Oohh believe me sweetpea, if you fly as much as I do, you will begin to notice all the difference it makes," asserted he, giving his daughter a wink at the end of his sentence.

"Listen to your father Allie. He's the expert on everything remember?" Brenda added to his self-praise and meant it literally. In the next instant, a ground service agent came to inform them it was time to board, which just as well drew to a close the obnoxious chat.

Skipping the long queue, they moved right into their superior cabin. First thing after settling down, Elton took to request for a glass of Scotch. Having overheard him, Allison was quick to express her daughterly concern. "Daddy, didn't the doctor tell you to stay away from liquor?"

"Do not worry, I do this every time I fly. It helps calm me down before takeoff," he explained to her when really it was just an excuse to drink, and then returned his attention to the flight attendant waiting on him. "I'll take a glass of red wine instead just to make my daughter happy." Swiftly, she moved along.

Meanwhile, at the sound of a ringtone, Allison searched frantically her pockets for her cell but could not find it. Seeing her enthusiasm, Daniel, who was sitting next to her, asked, "What's going on?" By that time, the gentleman seated directly behind them had picked up what apparently was his call.

Even after the realization, she was not yet able to sit still. "I think I might have accidentally left my phone back home."

"Are you expecting a call from somebody?"

"No," she replied, "not exactly," sighing with frustration. "I would just like to have it with me is all."

"I'm afraid it's too late to go back. Besides, I thought you wanted to be on vacation. You probably won't need it after all. Unless there is something urgent you must attend to."

"No."

"Very well then," he assured her, patting her on the hand resting on the leather armrest. "All you can do now is sit back and relax for the next few hours, and then we are there."

Finally, she smiled at him in concurrence.

After a brief layover in Atlanta, Georgia, they boarded another short flight and arrived just before dusk at Nassau International Airport. A taxi was prescheduled to pick them up from there straight to their hotel. The transition worked out smoothly. Despite the young couple's last-minute decision to join the trip, Elton was able to arrange for the whole family to stay at Grand Cove, one of the most luxurious, coastal resorts overseeing the North Atlantic Ocean.

"Would you like an upgrade to the Penthouse Suite sir? Complimentary from Mr. Jacob Fenty," the front desk receptionist asked him.

As usual, he did not shy away from gloating about his prime status for knowing personally the president of this hospitality establishment whenever it applied. "See what I'm talking about Allie? There are always benefits for being a VIP wherever you go. Ah, no, thank you, but could you please add a little note for me, attention to Mr. Fenty, expressing my gratitude."

"Certainly."

"Daddy. Why did you say no to the Penthouse Suite?"

"Well..."

Right then, the receptionist shot them a friendly grin, distributing the room keys. "Mr. and Mrs. Crawford, you will be in Suite 304, and Mr. and Mrs. Skala in 306. Would you like assistance with your luggage, sir?"

"Our rooms are next to each other?" Allison cut in suddenly to ask her.

"It is a connecting room as requested."

"What do you mean a connecting room?"

"Umm... is it going to be a problem?"

Before she could say anything more, Brenda had grabbed the set of keys from the counter, pushing her along, replying on her behalf, "No miss. Thank you very much for your help."

The group then moved on up to their rooms. It was only through conversation in the elevator did Allison uncover her mother's insistence on the room arrangement just this morning. When being found out, Brenda tried to rationalize her scheme by stating: "A family that travels together should stick together. It's easier to keep everybody in touch that way."

Knowing it was her mere attempt to keep tabs on Daniel, Allison retorted, "We can keep in touch with our phones in this day and age Mom."

"I know you want your privacy darling, and there will be a door in-between to separate the two suites. How's that for privacy?"

"A door!"

Brenda could really not care less at this point. "It's too late to change anything now and crying won't help. Maybe next time when you guys travel with us again, I might just make sure your room is as far away from ours as possible."

There was no winning with her mother, Allison knew and could do nothing but quit arguing. That however, did not lessen her guilt for dragging Daniel along on promised words that it was going to be a fun and carefree getaway.

"I'm sorry," she apologized to him soon as they got to their room and shut the door.

"What for?" he asked her right back.

"I know this trip isn't exactly what you are hoping for."

"You are right —"

She just got even more depressed.

"— I never expected to have to go on a trip with your parents. If it were up to me, I'd rather come by ourselves at a later time."

"Really? You would want to come here with me?"

"Yeah. But, here we are now, and the weekend has barely started so I'm hopeful."

Grabbing the suitcase from her, he laid it on their fancy, canopy bed for the next two nights and opened it. Her cell phone happened to be tucked in a corner among the clothes.

"And guess what?"

"Yeah?"

"Looks like luck is already on our side," he added encouragingly, holding it upright to show her.

She was immediately all smiles.

26

ONCE EVERYBODY FRESHENED up, the family gathered again on the beach to wait for the sunset. Although the muggy weather would take them some getting used to, their orders of Goombay Smash came punctually to help them adapt and cool off a bit. While the guys stood close by to discuss current affairs, the ladies indulged the remaining hour of daylight in sunbathing on the beach chairs.

"I'm glad that Danny decided to come along with us. We haven't seen you both together in such a long time," said Brenda taking a sip on her drink.

"It feels nice to be away from home," Allison admitted.

"So what changed his mind? I bet *sex* had something to do with it."

"*Mom!*" she exclaimed in a whisper, instantly blushing in embarrassment.

"What? Isn't that what you girls talk about these days?"

"*Nope.*"

"Back then your grandfather was a very conservative man. I wouldn't dare even mentioning the word 'sex' to my few intimates. I was all too worried that he might find out somehow and be disappointed in me —"

"There's no need to mention that now either."

"Looks like someone's embarrassed. But really, he was always manners this, manners that, and much more into finding me an eligible husband than encouraging me to become an independent woman. That was how I met your father actually, through his introduction; and just as he expected, your father's been perfectly reliable and respectful of me all these years. Although, I must agree with the feminists today, there's absolutely no shame for us women to allow ourselves some rough pleasure every now and then beyond the purpose of procreation."

"Where did you learn that?"

"Which part?"

"'Rough pleasure'?"

"Well, nowadays, there's the Internet."

"But you and Daddy are not... young."

"Whoa, I beg your pardon, young lady. What? So you think your father and I no longer make love?"

"I don't really think about that."

"Fifty is the new thirty they say. We are still very much active for your information and picking up some new moves here and there —"

"God. Can we *please* talk about something else?" Allison almost leapt from her chair to beg of her.

"Am I making you that uncomfortable?"

"What do you think?"

All the while laughing at her daughter's reserved bashfulness, Brenda stopped her teasing and began to talk fascinatingly about her last visit to Sweden and the one before it.

"All I'm saying is, you should come with us one of these days, you and Danny both, so you know what a beautiful country it truly is."

"To Sweden?"

"That's what I said."

"Mom, we have no intention to move out of Minnesota, let alone the country. Even if you and Daddy are considering it."

"Did I say that you should?"

"Well, that's what you are getting at isn't it? Why else would you mention that idea to me twice in a matter of weeks?"

Did I?" Just then, having spotted the sparkling, diamond-shaped pendant resting charmingly on Allison's chest, Brenda sat up to look at it more closely. "That's one beautiful necklace you have there."

"This?" said Allison, holding its bottom tip with two fingers to show her.

"Uh-huh. Is that real diamond?"

"I don't think so."

"Still, it looks pretty on you. I suppose that's the anniversary gift from Danny."

"Oh no, this is actually from Adrian for my sixteenth birthday. You don't remember? You and Daddy were there too when he gave it to me..." It was as if she had just said the worst thing possible, when she lifted her head to look at her mother, she saw her usual cheerfulness gone, completely scrubbed off her face as an immediate result of her response.

"Why are you wearing it?" she asked her firmly, almost judgmentally.

"I came across it this morning. I thought it goes well with all my outfits I picked out for this trip, so I figured, why not."

Brenda's expression just got darker. Allison had decided to ignore the obvious nonetheless and attempted to change the subject. "Anyway, Dan's been really busy with work lately, so he wasn't quite as prepared as I was for our anniversary. But he's promised to get me something on this trip and next week. I assume he has something good in —"

"Are you trying to deliberately hurt me?" Brenda cut her off in the middle of her sentence, withholding her anger no longer.

"Hurt you? It has nothing to do with you."

"Hand it over."

"What?"

"Hand the necklace over now I said!"

Like mother like daughter, Allison was not about to give way easily, firing back, "No."

"No?!"

"It's not always about you Mom!"

The guys finally turned their heads.

"Is something wrong?" Elton asked them, and thereupon, Allison turned to reassure him with a forceful smile. "No Daddy. We are just fine." Doubtful as he was, he knew better than to get involved at this state of their quarrel, and so returned to his conversation with Daniel.

The fire was in fact just starting.

"I'm not going to let you ruin this trip Mother, but just so you know, I found out about your visit to Dr. Cooke."

In shock at her disclosure, Brenda's eyes widened, asking her sternly, "What did you tell her?"

"Nothing that you need to know."

"I'm your mother! Tell me what you said to her. Did you talk to her about your brother?"

"That's none of your business."

"I said tell me this instant!" she shouted, grabbing Allison's arm and shaking it.

The guys turned their heads again.

"Let go of me!" Breaking from her grip, Allison got up and stomped off towards the alluring shoreline for some time alone.

During her way down the long stretch of warm pink sand, she came upon a curious little boy building a sand castle. He looked up at her with the most innocent green eyes, which, even just slightly, calmed her in a way Adrian could when she stared into his. Naturally, she was reminded of their childhood together, the time they spent before he got diagnosed, and before all that prejudice prevailed over love and family.

They exchanged smiles, and as she passed him by towards the ocean till it was at her feet, he stayed back and watched agog as the waves hit her above the ankles when they crashed into shore and sprawled over the beach. A minute later, Daniel joined in next to her. He picked up a flat stone somewhere nearby and threw it across the water. They both watched it bounce off the surface thrice before it eventually sank into the water.

"Are you okay?" he asked her in a consoling tone.

"Yes. I'm fine," she replied, thankful that he had come after her.

"If it helps at all, to tell the truth, I don't know how many times in the past I had wished to just storm off in front of your parents like you did back there."

She let out a little laugh. "I don't blame you. I know best what kind of people they are."

Just then, Daniel squatted down to pick up another stone, threw it across the water and stood back up. This time it bounced off the surface four times before it lost its momentum. "Yes!" he yelped quietly to himself, doing a little fist pump while at it.

Allison rolled her eyes sideways to take a peek at his victorious face, smiling on the inside.

Having noticed her looking, he asked her, "What is it?"

"Nothing," she said, but her smile hardly faded.

"Right. Because when a woman says 'nothing', she really means nothing."

She gave a snicker and told him, "I was just thinking about the first time you brought me to that park near the university. You did the same thing there, except that it was a fountain into which you threw rocks and tried to make them skip across the water."

He smiled on reflection of the incident. "You laugh now, but at the time you just stood there next to me, quiet."

"I was nervous."

"So was I. I just didn't look it. That was also when I first started skipping classes. I almost didn't graduate because of you."

"That's not true! Is it?"

"Haha."

Even now, his laughter still made her heart flutter. Slowly, she moved closer towards him till the back of her hand gently touched his, wanting to fold into one. They most certainly would have, had they not been distracted by a shriek of fear coming from the little toddler boy whom she met earlier.

"AAAAAAAHHHHHHHHHHHH!"

Wishing to copy the adults and soak his tiny feet in the massive body of water, he had apparently run for it without parental watch. The peaceful tide turned out to be relatively staggering for his small body of just about three feet. As it came at him, just one effortless push was enough to knock him over. Wave after wave, he tried to stand back up on his own, but each endeavor ended in vain.

Straight away, Daniel rushed to scoop him up from the unforgiving sea before it could — although very unlikely — pull him out further. Luckily, apart from the shock, the boy was well and unharmed. Allison as well hurried to their side and watched in awe as her husband cradled him in his arms. "Shh... shh... you are okay. You will be all right now. No more scares," he said to him in a calm, protective voice. Though still crying, the little one clung against his chest and appeared to be quieting down until his parent's arrival half a minute later.

"Alex! Oh my baby! Thank you! Thank you!" the mother exclaimed out of relief.

Carefully, Daniel turned the boy over to her. "He is fine. Just swallowed a few mouthfuls of seawater is all."

"If it wasn't for you, he could have been much worse. Here, a little gratitude from us," said the father, handing him a hundred-dollar bill.

Daniel kindly declined it. "Please, keep it. Anyone who saw the occurrence would have done the same. I just happened to be close by." Next, turning to little Alex in his mother's arms, he patted him lightly on the head and told him, "Take care now little buddy."

For the brief moment, the boy gulped down his sob. As though parting with a superhero, he was a little timid yet a little unwilling to. Soon as he went on with his parents, the bawling automatically started again. Finding his naive nature exceptionally adorable, Daniel could not suppress a grin watching them leave.

Moving on, the couple coasted along the seaside for some much-needed tranquility, during which time the half-setting sun had gradually painted the sky vibrant red.

Up ahead at a perfect spot, they sat down on the fine beach sand to watch in admiration for its disappearance completely from the horizon.

Having observed her husband taking pleasure in caring for the little boy just moments ago, Allison thought aloud, "I wonder what our life would have been like if we were to have kids."

"Well, I suppose, it might have been more interesting," admitted Daniel.

"You think so?"

"I do. Although I would have been tempted to take them to Burgers n' Bounce every weekend."

She smiled at his remark and rested her head against his shoulder, taking a deep breath and exhaling slowly. "Hmm... What if we adopt a child?"

Stunned by her spontaneous inquiry, he queried back, "Are you serious?"

In turn, she looked up at him, affirming with a wholehearted "yes".

The last time they had this same discussion was two years ago at her gynecologist's office on a Saturday morning — the very morning they found out the result of their infertility evaluation. After being informed of their slim chance of ever conceiving, Daniel brought up the idea of adoption, which led to a heated debate between him and Allison, where she eventually, vehemently, rejected it. "I won't ever feel like the baby's mother. That just won't be fair to either of us." Her assertion then concluded it, and that subject was never raised again till now.

"What has changed?" he asked her, still failing to overlook his wife's own contradiction.

"Well — I just thought you could be a wonderful father, and it would be a shame that you didn't get to be one in your lifetime, don't you agree? I've heard people adopt children from all over the world. I just hope the process isn't too complicated, but I'm sure there are many agencies out there that are more than willing to help us

through it..." Her change of heart, as a consequence, si-
lenced him. He stared into the distance with this faraway
look in his eyes for the good two minutes she took to paint
him an optimistic picture of their future with two endearing children.

Upon catching him lost in thought, she asked him,
"What are you thinking about?"

"Huh? Oh, nothing important."

"Heh. So it's okay when men do it."

"What?"

"You said 'nothing important'. Am I supposed to just
believe that?"

"Yes," he answered, rather soberly.

Even though knowing the contrary was true, Allison
had decided to pretend it was all okay so as to not blemish
a perfectly good time with him; all the while however, her
smile went away.

Abruptly, Daniel moved to stand up and then reached
out his hand to help her get up too. Promptly, she grabbed
onto it, got up and brushed away the sand from her bottom before they headed back.

27

AFTER nightfall, the hotel was a hub of nightlife and
entertainment. According to plans arranged in advance, the family delighted in five-star, outdoor
dining next to the gorgeous, lit-up pool, and then a private
venue where limbo dancing, fire eating acts and live gigs
featuring local artists and bands took place. All of the per-
formances were spectacular, though ever so slightly over-

shadowed by the tension between the ladies, who were still not on speaking terms from the earlier quarrel.

Having gotten up early for work this morning, Daniel felt exhausted just half way through the show, but was too courteous to spoil everyone's fun and so stuck around till the end. By the time they returned to their suites, he crashed out simply touching the end of the bed. Like a devoted wife, Allison attended to him. Meanwhile, her parents' constant mumbling in the next room was piquing her curiosity. In a moment, she snuck over to the adjoining door, leaning just close enough to eavesdrop on them, and caught her mother on the brim of a mental breakdown.

"... If only I knew Adrian would become such a problem, I would never... never have given birth to that child!"

"Darling, no one knew things would turn out this way before they did," said her father.

"What if... what if she still talks to him after all? That stubborn girl has no idea she's playing with fire."

"Honestly, I wouldn't be surprised if she does."

Her mother's sobs just got louder.

"Shh... there, there. Quit crying. You don't want her to accidentally overhear what you're saying and make a fuss now, do you?"

"Maybe it's better that way, since then I could openly talk some sense into her..."

"Don't speak silly now. We don't want to go this far for nothing. And besides, if talking to her is the solution, it would have worked a long time ago."

SNIFFLE "Oh El... what are we going to do?"

"Well — we must find out exactly what she told Lisa Cooke. That's first and foremost."

"That woman's pretty headstrong. I doubt she would actually comply with us."

"We have to at least try, and we must handle this delicately. But you need not worry darling, because I'll get in touch with her this time. I'd better give Carter a call too once we return to the States."

"Is it that serious?"

"It wouldn't hurt to keep him informed and get his opinion on this. If there indeed is something we can do on our end, he will tell us. From now on, for our daughter's sake, we will make sure to check up on her more often..."

Revolted by the elaborate deception of which she had listened just about enough, Allison pulled back. Hand over the doorknob, she thought about telling them off right then and there, but changed her mind in the end knowing very well she had absolutely no control over whatever her parents set their minds on doing.

All the while backing away from the door, she felt her stomach heave, bringing on a bad nausea that she had not experienced in a long time. Feeling like something inside her was going to burst from out of her mouth, she wherefore darted towards the bathroom and threw herself in front of the toilet bowl to try to vomit but nothing whatsoever came out. With each exertion, her chest tightened a little, and she began to feel shortness of breath.

Somebody... help me...

Almost like a telepathic miracle, right that moment, her phone started to buzz. She answered the unnamed call in a heartbeat with a certain confidence that it was her brother, and it was.

She began to sob just hearing him.

"What's wrong?" he asked her, catching her breathing irregularly.

"I... I feel like I... I can't breathe..."

Adrian heard her voice trembling in fear and right away knew how to fix her. "Okay. Listen up Allie. Are you listening?"

"Ye... yes."

"I need you to concentrate all your energy on how you breathe. Follow my rhythm as you go: one... two... three... four —"

COUGH *COUGH* *COUGH* "I... I can't... can't do it."

"Don't tell me you can't. Do I ever tell you to do something you can't do? Come on. Trust me on this and you will feel better in a minute. Again, long, deep breaths: one… two… three… four… five…"

She followed his instruction the best she could, and then gradually, her chest began to loosen up and lungs refreshed themselves, taking in air and expelling it normally as they should.

Sensing she was breathing better, he stopped counting. "Feeling better?"

"Yeah," she replied eventually, and calmly, no longer feeling nauseous either. "Thank you."

"So, what happened? I was just calling to ask you how it went with your anniversary, but now, do I still need to ask?"

"It's not Dan this time. Our anniversary actually went well."

"Oh? Who else could have gotten you this upset?"

She sighed deeply and told him, "It's Mom."

"I should have known that. What did she do? Or say?"

"I just overheard her and Daddy talking in the next room —"

"Wait. Where are you?"

"We are at a hotel in Nassau."

"The Bahamas? What are you doing there with them?"

"Dan's here too, he's just sleeping. Mom invited us both to come along, and I thought it was a good idea for us to get away from home for a few days. It's just over the weekend."

"I get it. Well then, it doesn't really matter what they were talking about."

"Why?"

"Because, like I told you two days ago, don't let any distraction steer you from what you went there to do."

"What I came here to do…"

"Yes. Your one and only goal should be to have a good time with Daniel, to rekindle your relationship. Everything else is not important. At least not right now."

"Right."

"So chin up sister, and try to focus your mind on the bigger picture. The last thing you want is to have this trip go to waste. Do you understand me?"

"I do."

"Good."

"Gosh. I don't know what I would do without you there to constantly back me up."

"That's what I'm here for."

She smiled. "Ah, I've been meaning to ask you something."

"Shoot."

"Is there a way for me to contact you?"

"You mean if I've gotten a cell phone?"

"It would be ideal that you have one."

"My dear sweet Allie finally can't get enough of me! Truly, I'm touched. But ever since my last cell got me in deep shit — excuse my profanity — with the cops, I've grown used to not having one, and I really don't find the need to keep one. You are the only person I call anyway, and payphones are easy enough to find wherever I go."

"What about Miranda?"

"What about her?"

"Don't you call to talk to her too?"

"Since you asked... well, we've broken up."

"Oh no. How did that happen?"

"It's too long of a story to tell over the phone. All I'm gonna say is, despite what a liar and cheat that bitch is, I haven't quite given up on her just yet, not this easily."

"I'm really sorry. I know that you really do love her."

"Pah! As if... I tell you what, I promise I will ring you more often from now on, and I will stop by your house one of the days next week to catch up."

"That sounds like a plan."

"Alrighty!" he cheered. "Until then."

"Actually." She caught him just before he could hang up. "Just one last thing."

"Yeah?"

"Do you happen to have a friend named Justin?"

Suddenly, he got quiet.

"Adrian?"

"Yes."

"So, you do..."

"Sorry, I eh... It's been a while since I heard that name. I'm just surprised that it's coming from you. Did he contact you somehow?"

"He did, yesterday."

"Well, did you tell him anything?"

"No. I would never. I don't trust him."

"Haha. He's harmless."

"Really? He sure didn't sound like it over the phone... In any case, you should be careful, whatever you do."

"Ha! Since when have you started giving me advice? That's my job!"

"I'm being serious. Just be aware."

"I am and I will, so don't worry. Now, go get some beauty sleep. I'm sure it's going to be another long day for you tomorrow when Dad is leading the group."

DAY 21 | SEPT 26 SATURDAY

28

F OLLOWING A LONG night, the four set out on a private yacht into the deep ocean in the morning. Elton, priding himself on being an experienced angler and a big-game fishing enthusiast, was particularly excited for this day because in his opinion, one of the best things to do in this archipelagic state was to fish. "Nothing beats the thrill of catching a creature that outweighs you three times over," he told the others proudly, extending his arms fully to emphasize the massive size of a blue marlin that he caught previously in the area on a different trip. "Although, let me tell you, the hauling in of the five-hundred-pound giant was no picnic even with the help of my four other highly competent fishing buddies."

"How long did it take you?" asked Mr. Campbell, captain of the boat.

"About forty minutes in total from the fish getting hooked. I was actually hoping it would take half the time. So, the next day, I convinced the guys, booked another sailboat and went out to sea again to try and beat that score."

"Phew! I can't imagine doing it over again right the next day after all that backbreaking and muscle cramping work. This sport can be quite physically demanding."

"Tell me about it. But oh well, I am an ambitious man, naturally."

"I can't argue with that."

As ambitious as he was, Elton expected nothing more than an opportunity for family bonding this time around and in particular with Allison, who was only a toddler the first time she went fishing with him.

"Speaking of which, my daughter was really a prodigy of this. Growing up, she used to love being out on big lakes with me, catching walleyes and whatnots. We did that almost every weekend in the summer until she grew tired of me one day."

"I'm not tired of you Daddy."

He just laughed.

"So Allison, have you ever partaken in any offshore fishing events or tourneys?" Mr. Campbell asked her.

"Has she ever. Ha! Many," Elton answered the question for her. "She caught a shark one year that weighted 175 pounds and won the grand prize. She was only fourteen years old."

"Fifteen, actually," Allison set straight the fact. "And it was a team effort. I couldn't have done it if my father weren't there to coach me —"

"She's just being modest. Though she may never quite measure up to her old man in terms of physical strength, in every other way, she's just as proficient at the sport as I am."

Per Elton's insistence, he and Allison worked side by side to set up the equipment and prepare the baits, while the crew stood aside watching in amazement of their speed.

"Believe it or not, many people we meet on the boat are first time anglers wanting to find out what the fuss about this game fishing is. When we do run into enthusiasts, rarely do we see such excellent coordination between two partners," said Mr. Campbell, complimenting their efficient teamwork.

"To be fair, those two have had years of practice," Brenda commented.

"I assume you are also into the sport Mrs. Crawford."

"Oh me? No, not at all. I'm more of a tagalong really. Just watching is enough for me. I would much rather hang loose than get my hands smelling all fishy. Ugh!"

"Haha. I personally understand that frustration. My father was a fisherman all his life. Since I was a little kid, he would often have me help unload his catch from the fishing net and pack them into styrofoam boxes for sale. For my entire childhood, I kid you not, I had to carry that fish stink wherever I went. My friends used to tease and call me the 'fishy boy'. It was quite embarrassing."

"Don't fishermen shower too?"

"Mom."

"What? I only asked because I'm curious."

"Haha, that's okay. You can ask me anything. And to answer your question, yes we do, but after a while, soap no longer helps get rid of that odor."

"Really? You sure don't smell fishy standing next to me."

"Well, I haven't exactly been a fisherman like my father, but I'm glad to hear it. I do hope that you like seafood at the least."

"Oh yes, there's nothing else I eat besides seafood whenever I'm here in Nassau."

"Good. Because Steven here is a superb chef, he will be preparing all of you a complimentary seafood buffet served at noon..."

Two hours into their journey, the boat was then about fifty miles north of Paradise Island from where it originally docked. The sun was warm, and the big, blue sea shimmered underneath it with water so deep that light could only penetrate so far beneath its calm surface. Looking out over the boundless horizon, Mr. Campbell enlightened them, "You guys are in luck. Lately if it wasn't overcast, it would have been raining by now."

"What do you want to catch today Daddy?"

"I've always wanted a sailfish."

"That's generally a rare find in this season," one of the crewmen informed them.

"What are our best bets then?" Allison inquired of him.

"Popular game fish wise, I'd say broadbills. The guys we sailed with yesterday happened to catch one in this exact zone. Of course, groupers and snappers are also common as they are all year round."

"Well, we'll just leave it to chance," Elton concluded, slipping on a pair of gloves and securing his harness. Soon, he made his first cast overboard and then the crewmen starting chumming. Next came the agonizing process of waiting for prey.

"This is going to take a while," said Brenda, taking a rest on the shaded bench.

"Here Daddy, have some water," said Allison, uncapping and handing him a bottle of distilled water.

"Thank you sweetpea. It seems like such a long time ago since we last sailed together."

"It's been over four years."

"Darn! Has it been that long?"

"Uh-huh. The last time was a month before my wedding. We went on that five-day fishing trip together in Costa Rica."

"Oh yeah with Uncle Brad. Gosh, time really flies. It seems like just yesterday when I formally asked him to be your godparent."

"You and him must have gone way back."

"I never told you?"

"Told me what?"

"He saved your father's life once," Brenda filled her in.

"When was this?" she inquired, curious.

"I was in New Jersey at the time, going for my master's degree at Princeton."

"You guys went to college together?"

"No. I don't think Brad got further than high school actually. His folks didn't believe in education. And besides, he had his mind set on the career he wanted ever since he was in middle school anyway, he told me at one point."

"Isn't he a police officer?"

"He was for a long time, but somewhere along the way he became a detective and he's been one ever since."

"So — how exactly did he save your life?"

"It's an ancient tale really."

"Tell it again El. It's a great story."

"Alright. Well, I was about Allie's age when it happened. It was a Friday night, and a long weekend was coming up. I was just heading out to join a few of my boys at a bar downtown after finishing my night class. As I went to my car parked in an alley near the campus, a man, a drug addict, hippie of some kind, came from behind me with a gun, pointing it at my temple. I gave him my wallet straight away but the two twenty-dollar bills in it apparently did not meet his need. He was desperate for more money, and by the way he slurred his words as he made threats at me, I figured he had to be on something. I had never been so scared my entire life. I was so sure he was going to fire his gun and kill me by mistake if not by intention, but in either case, I would have been a dead man."

"But then?" prompted Allison, fascinated to know how it ended.

"But then, in the middle of all that chaos, Brad showed up. Like a hero, he tussled with the man barehandedly and took him down to the ground."

"Isn't that what he was supposed to do though? I mean he was a cop."

"Sure, but he was also off-duty at the time, out of town visiting his family. He didn't have to risk his life for me, he could have just called 911 and have his mates come and handle it all. Plus, he got injured for it."

"How?"

"During the tussle, the man took a shot at him and the bullet hit him in the arm. The injury wasn't life-or-death serious, but still. I very much admired his bravery that night and will perhaps never forget what he did for me. What was more coincidental was later when I found out that he's also from Minnesota. Long story short, we've been close friends since."

"You never told me that story before. I had always thought he was just one of those friends that you shared similar hobbies with."

"You wouldn't have said that had you remembered your earliest childhood," Brenda chimed in.

"How so?"

"For the first three years or so since you were born, Brad used to visit you every Sunday, and he never came without bringing you gifts. They were nothing fancy like what my intimates back then would have brought, just some regular clothes and toys that he thought you might like. I did very much appreciate his thoughtfulness though. And when you were old enough to walk, you grew to love playing chase with him. One time you fell and scraped your knees, I watched him pick you right up off the ground, cradle you in his arms and take care of you, even though I told him to let Mrs. Gomez worry about it."

"That does not surprise me at all," said Elton, praising the man continuously. "Brad is a responsible man and a very loyal friend. I have no doubt that he loves Allie like she is his own daughter."

"I really have no recollection of any of it. But, if he really used to care for me so much, why doesn't he show it now? I mean, he's always quiet around me and he never talks to me much but only to you guys."

"He's probably just being respectful of us, and of you too. After all, we are your birth parents, he isn't. And it's only sensible of him to have some boundaries between you and him, woman and man."

"Is he not married? He's got to be around sixty some-thing."

"Sixty-two to be exact and no. He was married once but then divorced a year later. It was a long time ago, before I even knew him."

"That's just too bad," sighed Brenda. "I mean, he's a decent looking man, healthy and well-built for his age. Maybe we can introduce someone to him."

"I'm not so sure he'd like that. Anyway — enough talk about Brad. How are you all liking this trip so far?"

"You know how I feel about being on a boat. I'm just waiting for lunch time to come around to see what that 'superb chef' of theirs has prepared for us," Brenda said truthfully.

"How about you sweetpea?"

"It's been great. Dan and I are having a good time. Aren't we, honey?" She turned to look at Daniel sitting a few feet away from them near the railing, wearing his baseball cap low to shroud his face from the sun. He had been concentrating on his phone all morning, almost not noticing his wife talking to him just now.

"Pardon me?" he replied, looking up at her.

"Aren't we having a good time being away from home?"

"Oh yes."

His preoccupation had brought attention to Elton early on, who had only been keeping an eye on him since boarding the boat and not saying a word until now. "Hey Danny! Too busy to be on vacation?"

Daniel shifted his eyes at him. "Just checking a couple of emails here."

Of all people, Allison should know that fishing simply was not up his alley, but she nonetheless wished him to be more involved with the family activity and it showed. Elton caught a glimpse of the downhearted look on his daughter's face and decided to call his son-in-law out in front of everybody.

"Well, take a good look at this stunning scenery for a change, or your beautiful wife for that matter. It's only fair to show some respect —"

"Daddy —"

"— don't you think son?"

Right then, everyone, including the two crewmen standing by, all looked on at Daniel, anticipating his response. Under such an intentional compulsion, at last, he put away his phone and just sat there, quietly.

Elton, for one, felt pleased.

Having witnessed this stiff moment, Brenda stepped in intending to taper the edginess. "Danny is a top engineer. Important men are always on their electronics these days."

Hoping to restore harmony quickly, Allison as well joined in to smooth out the situation. "You are right Mom. As a matter of fact, Dan is going to be one of the lead engineers for this multibillion-dollar project kicking off in a few weeks. He's just too humble to say anything. Go ahead honey, tell my parents about it..."

Before Daniel even opened his mouth, Elton caught the heart-stopping sight of a broadbill swordfish crashing after the trolled bait out of the corner of his eye. What immediately followed was the shriek of a reel as the great fish attempted to rip away the line. "ALLIE!" he called out, and all at once, everybody was alerted. His knuckles turned white as he took a firm hold of the rod, all the while applying smooth pressure at opportune moments. "Oh boy! It's a big one! Time to show him who's boss!"

Mr. Campbell began to maneuver the boat so as to keep the great fish astern. As the two crewmen raced to reel in the empty lines, Daniel made room for them by leaving his seat to approach Allison.

"I'm going to be on my laptop. If you need me, I will be in the cabin."

"Are you sure you don't want to stay and watch for a little while?"

"Nah, that's okay," he said plainly, already moving on his way.

There was nothing she could do but watch him go.

Returning to her father, she stood by his side, occasionally gave him verbal cheers as he set in motion an epic fight against the beast. Ten, twenty minutes into the battle noon arrived, where the sun was at its highest and brightest. The monster fish was just beginning to tire, but at the same time, Elton's energy too started to give out. On account of the aggressive heat, his t-shirt was soaked all the way through. Sweat became a constant pain when not even the sun hat he wore could keep it from seeping through into his eyes.

"Let me take over for you Daddy."

"I'm okay sweetpea, I got this one. Come on boy! Come to Papa!"

Anxious to land his prize, seeing it coming so close to the boat, he went against what experience told him and sped up the retrieve for the remaining distance. "Easy... easy..." one of the crewmen even warned him, but he would not have it any other way. When given a brief window of opportunity, the fish was able to break the line and got away.

"Darn it!" he shouted upon it happening, a disappointed look on his face. Like a proper sportsman, Allison naturally took to encourage him, "That's okay Daddy. There's plenty more fish in the sea. You will get the next one."

In turn, he smiled at her. "You couldn't be more right," he said, using the clean towel she proffered to wipe off the sweat on his face. A moment of calm later, he took the chance to hint at her, "You know, that saying applies best when it's not interpreted literally."

She got what he meant.

"Tell me honestly, how are things at home?"

"I love him Daddy."

"That's not what I asked."

"Honestly, we are happier now than a month ago. Of course, we still have problems that need to be solved out, but everything's going in the right direction."

"And, do you think — perhaps — his feelings for you have changed? Diminished?"

"No."

"Are you sure?"

"I'm so sure. Dan loves me, very much. We love each other. So long as we continue to work things out, we will be fine. You and Mom don't have to worry about us."

Elton wanted to say something more but was held back by her continuous reassurance...

"There's no one else I want to be with except for him Daddy, and I mean it in the most sincere, earnest way."

Finally, he nodded in understanding, letting his opinion go. "Then, God forbid that anyone takes him away from you."

29

AFTER SPENDING ALMOST the entire day out at sea, everyone was beat when returning to shore. The complimentary buffet they had for lunch could hardly hold down their hunger anymore, especially to the proud father and daughter who expended most of their stamina waiting for and reeling in fish all afternoon. A short rest back at the hotel later, by the time evening arrived, they all dressed up and went out for dinner in celebration of Allison and Daniel's wedding anniversary at h'ouse — the one upscale, seafood restaurant in the city voted best by both locals and tourists for the past four years running.

The couple that ran this classy place were both New Yorkers. Elton had become quite acquainted with them, as almost every time he visited the Bahamas he would bring company with him there. He came — like many other habitués — originally admiring its reputation for good food and their first-rate service. A wide range of food critics had acclaimed Chef Maya even before she moved to Nassau with her longtime companion and restaurateur, Benjamin Norris. While she was busy in charge of the kitchen, Mr. Norris took great pleasure in taking care of customers out front. Notwithstanding having a full house of fancy-schmancy guests, like tonight, he never fell short of his exceptional greeting to ensure each one of them felt welcome.

"Good evening Elton! Welcome back to Nassau," he greeted cheerily, a grin on his face.

The two had a warm shake of hands, and then Elton introduced the rest of the family. "You already know my wife Brenda, and this is my lovely daughter Allison and son-in-law Daniel."

"How do you do Ben?" Brenda greeted him, extending her hand with the palm facing downward. He then bowed towards it, holding it close to his lips, kissing it symbolically before letting go.

"It's nice to see you again Brenda. And you two, what a beautiful couple, happy wedding anniversary."

"Thank you," Daniel replied politely with a nod of his head.

"It's nice to meet you Mr. Norris," said Allison.

"Just call me Ben, and the pleasure's all mine."

Afterwards, he personally guided the family to their reserved table on a shaded, floating dock next to a grand view of the Atlantic Ocean. It was a small, square, linen-covered table with four beautifully crafted, vintage chairs tucked on each side. It had just started to sprinkle as they sat down. The gentle sea breezes blowing just so kept the torrid heat at bay.

"Is the rain going to be a problem?" he asked them considerately.

"Not to me," said Brenda.

"I actually feel quite comfortable," said Allison.

"You heard the ladies," Elton replied to him.

"Excellent. Azarel here will be your server for the evening. In the case that you need me, just give me a wave, I won't be too far away," he told everyone and then excused himself.

Looking briefly at the set menu, they each made their selections right off the bat. Minutes later, the cocktail waitress came by with a bottle of Dom Pérignon as requested from Elton. She went around to fill everyone's glass and then set aside the remaining bottle in an ice bucket.

"To Allison and Daniel, happy belated anniversary," Elton toasted to the couple and while at it, leaning to his side to give Allison an endearing peck on the cheek.

Brenda also raised her glass. "I wish you both health, wealth, and as merry as the day is long. Cheers!"

"Cheers!" they said to one another, clinking their glasses together and drinking away.

"Thank you Mom, and Dad. This day's been great. I honestly couldn't have hoped for more fun with you guys on this trip."

"Just wait till tomorrow," said Brenda.

"What's tomorrow?" Allison asked.

"Shopping of course! You can't travel and not shop."

"Right."

"You will be coming with me while these two men go browse around for guy things."

"Dan and I are actually planning to go ourselves. We've already visited the tourists' market around here once."

"When did you?"

"Yesterday. We had a little time before dinner. We saw this exotic mask for sale at one of the stands. Dan would like to get it before we leave to add to his den's collection."

"Then Danny can go with your father. There's no need for you to be there."

"But I want to go with him. We haven't spent much time just the two of us this whole trip."

"What about me?! Don't you care to spend some time with your mother, whom you haven't seen for such a long time?"

Sensing this conversation could easily turn into another argument between the two, Daniel decided to step in and suggested, "Don't we have another full day tomorrow? Our flight is not until nine in the evening."

"So?" asked Brenda.

"So, why don't we all go together? Like you said before, 'a family that travels together should stick together'. Or, if you prefer, Allie can always hang out with me for half the day and then the other half she can spend with you. Ultimately of course, if that's okay with her."

"I like that idea," said Allison eagerly, and then turned towards her mother. "What do you think Mom?"

Brenda looked at her chirpy face and then at Daniel sitting to her left and smiled at him, for his sensibleness in putting her daughter first. "Thank you Danny. All right. We will do as you wish for once."

In making this a special night, Elton had organized a little surprise for the young couple. As the others talked over the plan for tomorrow, he had locked eyes with Benjamin from across the room, giving him a go-signal. One moment the local jazz band was still playing music indoors, the next they stopped and marched onto the deck, all the while jamming a swing classic — "For Eternity" by Walter Feigel — led by the saxophonist.

Soon as the band came near their table, Allison's face lit up having recognized the melody of her own first-dance song. "Daddy, did you arrange this?" asked she in astonishment. When the vocalist began singing the first verse, automatically, she started lip-synching along:

What is life when there's no love
What is love and is love enough
When you find that someone
Never letting go of that someone
For eternity...

"Why don't you two love birds dance a little?" Brenda proposed.

Allison looked over at Daniel, who then asked her, "You want to?" She confirmed with a nod. Therefore without delay, he came around the table to take her by the hand and brought her out to an open space not far away. Following the music, he led her body into adoring, rhythmic alignment with his own. From side to side they swayed in close unison while others watched on with hearty smiles.

His fingers interlocked with hers; meanwhile, her eyes melted into his. A time came when his hand on her back held her closer, as little as was that impulse of affection, Allison felt ecstatic and her cheeks blushed. His gaze shifted to her lips just then. As he bent slowly his head forward to kiss her, she closed her eyes and titled her chin upward in anticipation. When their lips finally touched, she was almost close to tears.

Gently, Daniel pulled away. Noticing her misty eyes, he inquired softly, "Still doing okay?"

"Yes, I'm fine," she assured him, smiling from the heart. "It's just... I haven't been this happy for a long time. I don't want this day to end." Wrapping her arms around his back, she pressed her ear against his chest and rested there till the end of the song. As she did so, he kissed her again, this time on the top of her head. She was just listening to his tender heartbeat then, feeling over the moon.

The band received much applause for their wonderful performance. When the two got back to their table, the starters were just being served.

"Are you alright? You look flushed," Brenda asked her.

"I'm okay. I think I'm gonna run to the ladies' room to freshen up a little."

"Want me to come with you? I know where it is."

"No. I will find it myself but thank you Mom. Excuse me everyone, and please start eating without me."

The men stood up respectfully as she got up to leave the table.

30

THE RESTROOM WAS empty of people when Allison got to it. She went in, lightly touched up the makeup around her eyes and proceeded into the middle of the three stalls. Upon closing the door, she heard someone else walk in and into one of the other ones. All the while sitting on the toilet, she spotted that person's feet through the rather large gap at the bottom of their adjoining wall. She did a double take and then held her gaze at the pair of white tennis shoes.

It was odd enough to find a woman not wearing heels at such a high-end restaurant due to its strict dress code, but that was hardly what invoked her attention here. It was the shoes in and of themselves: round tops, rubber soles, and upper canvas linings intertwined with laces, fairly ordinary and inexpensive in appearance. *Where have I seen them before?* She became strangely absorbed in thinking, and did not take her eyes off them until the person moved on out of the stall and then so did she.

As it turned out, it was a petite woman wearing them, who also had on a causal tee and skinny jeans with long, black hair halfway down her back. She was washing her hands in one of the two sinks when Allison walked up next to her and stood before the otherwise available sink, in which a big, black paper bag was occupying.

"Oops. Sorry," said the woman and removed the bag, tucking it between her legs before returning to put on lipstick. "You would think they would have considered building a larger bathroom for all these snobby guests that they planned on serving, but nope..."

As usual around strangers, Allison just kept to herself; meanwhile began washing her hands. At one point, curiosity had her lifting her eyes and taking a glance at the woman's face reflecting in the mirror. Instantaneously, she reacted in a gasp of horror.

"What?" the woman asked her, having noticed her staring open-mouthed.

"Noth...nothing," she barely managed to respond, looking back down at her hands and focusing wholly on washing them.

There was not anything wrong with the woman's face. As in fact she was an attractive lady with eyes as big and wondrous as the full moon and lips as plump. The only thing contributing to Allison's strong reaction was that she looked like Megan in an awfully unsettling way as if they were one person. Even that birthmark on her right cheek was uncanny and exactly where Megan had hers.

"Is that comfortable?" the woman spoke to her again all of a sudden, looking at her in the mirror.

"What is?" Allison asked her back, still feeling awkward.

"Your dress. It's pretty."

"Oh. Thank you."

"I like that asymmetrical hemline, how the skirt dips in the back. I can never wear a dress like that."

"Why not?"

"I'm only five one. The stores never have anything this pretty in my size. Tall girls like you are just so lucky."

"Oh... That's too bad."

"I can't imagine wearing it for the whole night though. I could hardly breathe in mine. That's why I took it off the first chance I got."

"Is that what's in your bag?"

"Yup."

"Mine actually isn't that bad."

"No? It just looks so fancy and fitted at the torso. Must have cost you a fortune."

"I'm not so sure about the price since someone else got it for me."

"Did Daniel?"

"What..." She gulped. "What did you just say?"

The woman looked at herself in the mirror, taking time to rub her lips together to smooth out the lipstick she just applied before giving Allison the once-over again. "I asked you if your husband bought you the dress."

"Oh... no... my parents... my mother... did. It's hardly new."

Allison was ready to get out of there. Trying her best to remain composed, she walked past behind the woman to a dispenser affixed to the wall to retrieve a paper towel for her wet hands, but was beaten to it as they both reached for it at the same time.

"So — do you think he cares?"

"What do you mean?"

The woman used it to blot her lips and crinkled it up right after, tossed it into a trash bin nearby and looked distastefully at her. "I'm just saying, some men aren't into the spoiled, rich type of women. So no matter how you doll yourself up, do you really think he cares?"

Allison was not prepared for this. "That was way harsh. I don't even know you."

"Humph. This is hardly a time to act dumb so save your charade for someone else. The fact is — Daniel loves me, and that's never going to change."

What is this? None of this is making sense. Megan's dead... she reminded herself, running her eyes repeatedly over the woman's facial features to try to prove she was not *her* but failed in doing so.

"What?" the woman urged.

"His feelings for you don't matter to me, anymore."

"Right, because the only thing in question is, whether he loves you more than he loves me."

"I have no doubt in him."

"Good. Because me either. He once told me after we had sex that he wished he wasn't married. He then went on to say that I was everything he ever wanted in a woman. Did he ever say that to you?"

"You are a liar."

"If you would rather I lie to you, sure, believe whatever you want to believe."

"You are dead. *Dead!*"

"To you, maybe, but to Daniel — *never*. There was much more that happened between us than he will ever tell you himself. And the only way to find out what he's really thinking is by asking. That is, of course, if you have the guts to just ask him."

Allison swallowed hard, wanting to counter back yet momentarily speechless. The woman was not about to wait around, thus headed for the door, talking as she went. "Think on what I said. The truth may be ugly, but it's always better knowing it than living a lie —"

A lie?

"— don't you think?"

A lie?!

31

A LLISON HAD DECIDED to mention nothing about what went on in the restroom. As she sat back down at the table, the appetizing main course came in good time to aid her false display of contentment by stealing everyone's attention, so neither Daniel nor her parents suspected anything.

"Anything else I may get you, sir?" Azarel asked Elton in his Bahamian accent.

"Not at the moment. Everything looks marvelous. Please give Chef Maya my best regards."

"Certainly," he said, and gave a little bow before re-treating into the background.

The family then held hands in prayer. During which time, everyone else kept their eyes closed as Elton asked for blessings of their union except Allison, looking across at Daniel, who gradually opened his as well halfway through the intercession to sneak a peek at her. The two ended up exchanging a soft smile.

After the brief ritual, they dug into their food steaming with enchanting aromas. Brenda bragged about her smoked oysters and Elton his perfectly seasoned lobster tails. For every ingredient was so faultlessly executed with great balance of flavors, even Daniel, the only person among them who was not too fond of seafood to begin with, enjoyed his shrimp scampi. Following one satisfying meal, they ate their desserts with equal delight. The champagne never stopped flowing; meanwhile, they drank, chattered and laughed about all sorts of trivial matters.

"Talking about India, it reminds me of this Sikh man that your father and I ran into on the streets of New Delhi."

"Which man?" asked Elton and then drank from his glass.

"Remember that guy with an outrageously long beard? I swear kids, it was the longest I've ever seen. It went all the way down to his knees as I recall, if not farther."

"Oh yes. Now I remember him. Exactly why do women fancy men in beards anyway?"

"Uh. I don't think he grew his beard out to attract women," Allison pointed out.

"I know that, but I mean just men mainly in the whole western world. You hear attractive women on TV raving about leading men in movies and their bushy facial hair. But in reality, whenever we lean in to kiss our ladies, most of you would scream about the tiny bristles on our jawline scraping against your fair skin after the damage is done."

"I don't do that."

"Ahem. Yes you do," Daniel chimed in. "Just maybe not every time."

"Okay... that may be so, but I honestly don't hate it, really. Men's beards are symbolic of knowledge and manhood. They best exemplify masculinity and majesty which women of the world are adapted to admire and adore ever since Adam and Eve."

"Even a goatee?" Elton teased her.

"Sure —"

"Hehe!"

"I'm just saying they mean more than just a trend hipsters follow these days."

Daniel was not falling for her ideology. "Going back to your lecture just now, where did you get all that?"

"I once had a similar discussion in my literature class back at the university."

"That's quite an exaggeration, don't you think?"

"No, there are actual facts about it written in the textbook."

"By textbook you mean a women's magazine."

She just rolled her eyes.

"It just sounds more like some made-up fantasy instead of ideas based off of legitimate facts. I would like to see this textbook of yours when we get home."

"Whatever."

"Perhaps — all this masculinity talk describes male genitals better than it does beards..." Elton added to his remark, barely holding down a chuckle.

While the two men broke into a good laugh at their own witty comments, Brenda intended to interrupt them. "I agree with Allie though. I mean beards do naturally make a man look manlier, that's just the way it is. And we women are inherently attracted to manly men with which I see nothing wrong. Who's a good example... ah, like that actor starring in the popular TV series *Hurricanes* in the eighties. What's his name again?"

"Tom Skye," Elton filled her in.

"Yeah him. My father used to maintain a handsome mustache like Tom's that my mother just *absolutely* adored. During the period he had it, he got praise from both men and women. So, just as long as you gentlemen are willing to take the time to give your rough stubble a nice comb and shampoo every once in a while, you are more than welcome to let it grow out. Otherwise, if you leave it be, after a while it's just ew!"

"Geez. It is only hair after all, you don't have to be so obsessed about it like you are with shoes," Daniel joked around continuously, upon which Elton again burst into laughter.

She frowned, not seriously but rather as a protest. "Alright. I've had it with the sarcasm. Can't we move on to talk about something more productive?"

Right then, Elton beckoned Azarel over so as to order himself a Scotch neat.

"Daddy, haven't you had enough to drink?" Allison reminded him, once again concerned for his health.

"Everyone's still having a good time, why spoil the moment? Danny, would you care for one too? Or do you prefer a shot of something else?"

"Thank you for the offer sir, but I'm good."

"Save it Allie. I have warned your father about a million times. He's just going to do what he wants to do," asserted Brenda, shooting her husband a stare.

Wanting to deviate his drinking habit from being the subject of discussion, Elton, out of the blue, asked Daniel about his family. "So, Danny, how are your folks doing up north?"

"Uh... I suppose they are doing okay. Haven't really gotten a chance to talk to them since the funeral."

"Whose funeral?"

Knowing how drastically things could go south when it came to her parents, and that was to say nothing of the influence of alcohol, Allison was immediately cautious, jumping in to speak on Daniel's behalf. "Dan's sister's funeral. I left Mom a message a few weeks ago to tell her about it. Thought she might have mentioned it to you."

"Oh yeah, so I've heard. How did that go?"

"It was fine. Everything went accordingly. There was a memorial held for her, a small but nice one."

"It's Margaret right? Sorry that we couldn't be there. Give your folks my best," he said, half looking at Daniel and half behind him at Azarel who was returning with his glass of Scotch on a tray.

"It's actually Megan, sir." Daniel found the need to correct him. "But I will."

Brenda just then gave them each a glance and went on to comment deliberately ruthlessly, "Margaret or Megan, po-ta-to or po-tah-to, they are all the same." Straight after, she picked up her glass of champagne, slowly sipping on it till it was gone, in the meantime observing her son-in-law's reaction.

Daniel was more or less bothered by her ignorant remark but had decided to ignore it. Elton on the other hand, did not seem to mind walking on thin ice. In part, it was really the booze talking. "Didn't we meet her at your place last Thanksgiving? She was the young lady who came with a special, little boy. What was the kid's name again?"

"Karl."

"Yes Karl. Anyway, when I first saw them, initially I thought he was her son. Until she approached us and did a little introduction —"

"She approached us? I don't remember that," Brenda argued.

"Oh… right. You were off powdering your nose or something I believe when they arrived. Anyhow, to be quite honest, I was a bit put off by her referring to the boy as her 'soul mate'. Even if she meant it jokingly, I found it rather inappropriate given the circumstances, and in front of strangers she had never met. The conversation quickly got awkward from there and I never pursued further their relation. As I recall, later on, the two just kept to themselves most of the time over dinner when everyone else was having a blast chitchatting, getting to know one another. I could understand she felt obligated to entertain the kid, still, she was an adult, and should know to behave adequately instead of putting up a do-not-talk-to-me attitude. After all, she was a guest at someone else's house."

"She was just being shy. Since we don't have a lot of relatives, every big holiday we used to only spend with our immediate family," Daniel explained to him.

"Really?"

"Yes sir."

"Well, in any case, I thought it was still sort of… rude, if I may say, for them to leave right after they had their meals, claiming that they had to attend some kind of a… uh —"

"A rehearsal."

"Yes! That. It would only have been courteous to the host for them to stick around a bit longer."

"She would have if it wasn't for the church performance upcoming that Sunday. They had to rehearse for it early the very next morning. Because it was such a long drive back, she was only being thoughtful so that Karl could make it back before his bedtime."

"Is that so?"

"Very much. She was working for a non-profit organization back in Blue Port at the time, as a teacher for children with learning disabilities. Karl was just one of the many kids she cared for a great deal."

"That's an interesting career for a young lady," Elton remarked and then gulped down a big mouthful of his Scotch whisky.

"Rewarding, as she would have said," Daniel added, a smile flew over his face. Meanwhile, Brenda was tired of sitting back and listening to him glorifying the woman with whom he once had a fling, and so, set out to strip him of that pleasure.

"I happen to feel bad for the kids," she interjected, acting as though speaking casually, "It wasn't like those children had a choice of who should be their teacher. Personally if I had any little ones, I wouldn't let her come near them."

Much as Daniel would like to keep pretending his in-laws' opinions did not matter, whenever somebody, anybody, chose to speak poorly of his "Meg", it was like attacking him with flying darts coming at high speed that each time pierced through his heart without miss. There were only so many of those he could take.

Allison sensed the tension uprising between him and her mother and knew that it was now or never to settle the fight before it ever began. "Must we continue to talk about her? Can't we change the subject? Daddy?"

Unconcerned, Elton shrugged his shoulders in neglecting his daughter's signal for help. "I got nothing sweetpea," he told her and then kept on drinking from his glass till it was empty.

"Well then… it's getting late anyway, Dan and I should probably —"

"Whatever do you mean Brenda?" Daniel cut in suddenly, destructing her mission for peace, looking for trouble.

"Pardon me?"

"Meg was a kind and loving person. She was very good at what she did, and I can guarantee that you won't find another caregiver who is as devoted as she was to her job."

"Humph. I seriously doubt that."

"Mom, please."

"What? I do. Is that really so hard to believe?"

Agitated by her condescending attitude, Daniel aimed to wipe that smirk off her face once and for all. "Then, out with it, give me one good reason that makes you think otherwise. Go ahead."

It was a bad idea, since his acrid tone of voice did not intimidate Brenda in the least. In turn, she moved in closer to stare him straight in the face, rising her eyebrows and chin slightly in disdain, and let the ugliness fly out of her mouth —

"Because, I don't trust a *whore* to do anything, period."

Her derogatory utterance, momentarily, shut up the three of them and the few guests at the next table who happened to overhear it and turned their heads. Allison looked over at Daniel getting bent out of shape. For the first time, she honestly thought had the comment come from someone else, he might have punched that person in the face by now; but even so, as rude as was her mother, neither she, nor her father was willing to step in to correct what had been said. For they both knew perfectly well her basis for labeling Megan with such a disgraceful title, in absolute truth, they both thought her audacious judgment was bold but just.

The lethal silence maintained for a half minute until Daniel eventually managed to ease up just a bit. "Excuse me," he muttered to everyone upon standing up abruptly from his chair, and made his sharp exit out of the restaurant all before Allison could think up something to help the situation.

"Thanks guys. Couldn't have done it without you," she said sarcastically to her parents afterwards, grabbing her clutch and hurrying off after him.

32

SINCE THE BITTERSWEET end to the night, Allison got back to the hotel room alone, only to find Daniel sitting in bed, fully engrossed in his laptop.

Quietly, she went to sit by him. "My mother obviously had too much champagne. You can't possibly take her seriously —"

"I'm flying back to Minneapolis first thing tomorrow," he right out told her, his eyes remained glued to the computer screen.

"You are not serious."

"I've just purchased a return ticket for 8 a.m."

"You are doing this all because of what she said?"

He did not snap back nor admit to it, a look of determination on his face.

Allison quickly perceived that nothing she said was going to change his mind — not that she wanted him to anyway. The good times basically ended here, as she knew it.

"I'm coming with you then," she told him earnestly.

"I think it's best that you stay."

"Why?"

"Because you don't have to leave just because I do."

"I know, but I want to. There's really no reason for me to spend another day here if you aren't going to be here."

His eyes shifted off the screen considering for a few seconds, and then finally, looked at her. "Fine. Do whatever you want," he said in an irritated tone, slamming shut his laptop, and went to start packing.

The rest of the night, they did not speak.

DAY 22 | SEPT 27 SUNDAY

33

NEVER WOULD ALLISON have foreseen such a dreadful end to the vacation, but when reality hit her, there was no denying it. While most of the hotel guests were still having their sweet dreams before sunrise, the sulky couple was dragging their suitcase down the grand hallway, leaving this supposed paradise for good. When passing by her parent's room, she casually slipped a note under their door, informing them of the early departure.

From the moment they woke to boarding plane after plane, Daniel had not once faltered his resentment and would only speak to her when absolutely necessary. As far as she understood it, he had chosen to stay buried in his own miasma of depression all because of the moronic dispute he had with her mother. Knowing him, she was unbelieving at first that he would resort to such an extraordinary measure of leaving halfway through the trip, but he did. The level of which he still cared for Megan had since become quite clear to her, which was just the very thing she needed to summon up her insecurity about their marriage once more.

As a result of their last-moment decision, flight options were scarce, and due to which their layover time doubled what it should have been. By the time they got back to Minneapolis, it was already mid-afternoon. Daniel's iciness had not thawed if not hardened even more however — not a word out of him from getting off the plane, not a word all the way home in the taxicab. "Did you have a good trip?" the driver asked them at one point.

That sort of typical, feel-good question felt almost like mockery now. *A vacation is supposed to be fun and relaxing for God's sake*, she thought, and the more she dwelt on Daniel's reactions to it all, the deeper she plunged down a cliff of loathing.

First thing arriving home, Daniel left the suitcase in the foyer and dashed downstairs towards his den. She honestly had not seen him acting this rashly and hotheadedly before, thus ended her pretense of everything was just fine and went after him. "Would you like to talk about what's bothering you?" Despite her good intention, he never slowed down. Soon into his den he proceeded, slamming the door on her as she was just catching up. Having made up her mind to get to the bottom of his problem, she held in her own anger and entered.

"What's going on?" she asked upon seeing him pacing back and forth near his desk in obvious exasperation.

"Leave me alone," he said.

"Why can't we talk about this?"

"There's nothing to talk about."

"Do you think I believe that even just a little bit?"

"Allie! Now!" he demanded of her.

"This is crazy. This isn't you. What happened to your rationality?"

"I told you to stay behind. You are the one who insisted on coming along."

"So you would have gotten a few extra hours alone to think things over, do you really expect us to never talk about this again?"

"Yes. That's how we've always done it."

"And look at where we are now. Why can't we do things differently for a change?"

"*Allison!* I'm telling you, out!"

Sick and tired of his constant rebuff, she blurted out the one question that had been stuck in her head since falling out with her parents: "Do you really love her this much?" Which, consequently, stopped his frustrated pacing.

"What?"

"You know what I mean — do you love Megan more than you do me?"

"This is ridiculous. I'm not having this discussion right now."

"Humph. You can't even give me a straight answer."

"*Because I'm not going to dignify it with an answer!*"

"At least we can both safely assume that you love her enough to yell at me like this. How can you let her jeopardize our marriage even after she died?!"

"She has *nothing* to do with how our marriage is."

"Oh really —"

"We had many problems of our own long before she came into the picture."

"Is that supposed to make me feel better? Or was it just a lame excuse for you to sleep with her in the first place?!" she hissed, holding nothing back anymore. Even knowing she might have overstepped the mark there, she had not felt more liberated now that the elephant in the room was finally going to be addressed, or so she thought.

Daniel walked up to her, his face scorching red. "Okay... okay. You want to talk about it?"

"Yes I do —"

"Ed Ramsey." His nose flared.

"What about him?"

"Wasn't he your high school boyfriend?"

"Yes. So? He has nothing to do with anything —"

"You two *slept* together a few months ago did you not?!" His nose flared again as he gritted his teeth to somewhat hold down his fury.

Bewildered by the accusation, Allison narrowed her eyes at him, her brows furrowing. "Who told you that?"

"Who do you think? He called and bragged to me about it a week after you got back from your trip. '*I fucked her... I fucking fucked your wife in Vegas.*' That was what he said to me, word-for-word. So tell me, how do you expect me to feel about that?"

She kept shaking her head. "No. That is a lie."

"Ha! A lie."

"Yes!!! How can you believe something like that just because he said so?!"

"Your best friend doesn't deny it."

"What?"

"I called Sara."

"How did you —"

"Get her number? I copied it from your phone the day I found out from him, but don't you *dare* change the subject just because it's convenient to you."

"I wasn't going to — but they lied."

"They both lied?"

"Yes!"

"Humph. I'm not playing this game."

"What game?"

"*Your game!* For weeks coming up to your trip, all I heard was your singing his praises, raving about how *great* this Ed was to you back when you were dating blah, blah, blah. I could pretend to not mind but that still hurt."

"You mean your ego was bruised. Gosh, you may be a smart man Dan, but you can be so *dense* when it comes to our relationship. We've been married for four years and you still haven't learned *anything* about me. I only said all those things because I wanted you to care."

"So then you went and slept with him to make me care?!"

"For the last time, I did *NOT* sleep with him. And don't you use that to justify your own action. You are the one who slept with that slut!"

Daniel's temper just went deeper into the dark. "Just leave Meg out of this alright?" he cautioned her, but she was all too beside herself to care.

"How? You decided to leave in the middle of our vacation all because of what my mother said about her."

"That's not entirely true. And don't even get me start-ed about your mother. She is by far the most condescend-ing, demeaning person I've ever known."

"That's not fair. She has always liked you. She's never said *one thing* bad about you —"

"I don't believe that for a second, nor that I care."

"I know… I know. It's because she called her a 'whore' is that it? Well?! *Can you really blame her?!*"

Right then, his fingers closed into hard fists. His body fidgeted like a raging bull ready to be let loose. "Don't call her that," he commanded her, his voice taut almost like a threat.

Allison could see it in his glowering eyes his festering desire to take revenge for his deceased sister, or to be more accurately phrased, his ex-lover. It was as though Megan's spirit had truly lived on beyond the grave, taking the form of his wrath that cursed and mocked her. There was not much more she could stomach of this humiliation.

"Go on. Hit me. I have no sympathy for her and never will. Nothing… nothing can ever make me change my mind about that *cunt* —"

She just barely finished that last word, the very word that prompted Daniel to raise his hand and slap her across the face. The next thing she realized was the ringing in her ear that momentarily knocked her out of reality. When she finally oriented herself with what had happened, a glistening tear rolled down her throbbing cheek. She fought to resist the emotions choking up her throat. "That wasn't so hard, was it?"

Having the upper hand, Daniel was not exactly danc-ing with joy. If anything, he was just as shocked at his own outburst of violence. After that, he staggered a few steps back, dropped to the floor, and simultaneously buried his face in his hands. In shame certainly he was for hitting his wife, but somehow even more so for his own failure to shield Megan from further ignominy after her death.

"I owe her Allie. I owe her just that much."

"You don't owe her anything."

"Yes I do."

"No you don't —"

"*Will you just listen to me!!*" he howled, shooting his moist eyes up at her, clasping his forehead in agony and his face contorted as if in great pain.

Allison never thought her seemingly always-judicious husband was capable of coming undone like this, as she had, quite frankly, never seen this side of him before. His look of anguish at which she was looking now, made aware to her just what she believed was the whole of the story could in fact be the tip of the iceberg.

What he went on to say confirmed it.

"I've always known Meg was murdered. I knew with great certainty that she'd never have killed herself, but I just... I just kept my mouth shut in front of the police and let them assume so."

"What are you talking about? — What?"

"The police contacted me the very afternoon I got back from Virginia. They came looking for me at my desk when I was just in to wrap up a few things at the office. They somehow suspected that I had something to do with Meg's death."

"But you weren't even in town when they found her."

"I know, I told them that wholeheartedly, but for some reason they didn't buy it and would not stop drilling me with all these questions. At one point they asked if I noticed anything out of the ordinary the last time I saw her, I just lied and said that she had been depressed for some time."

"So she wasn't depressed?"

"Right. I was in a panic when I told them just so I could get myself out of trouble. They never got in touch with me again after the hour-long chat at the police station. Shortly after that, they declared her case a suicide when it most certainly shouldn't have been..."

"What makes you so sure she was murdered?"

"Because… because she was pregnant. I was with her the Monday morning before flying out to Virginia. We found out together."

They found her that Tuesday… No, no way. "This just can't be —"

"It's the truth. I swear my life on it."

"How come you've never told me any of this before?"

"I'm telling you now."

"Well I don't believe you —"

"The truth will stay true whether you want to believe me or not! I called her a couple times later that afternoon but she never answered the phone. It was so unlike her. I don't know what but something… something terrible must have happened during that short period of time…"

Despite the significance of his assertion, Allison was not at all interested in solving the proposed mystery. There was, however, one thing she wished to make clear of. "How many more times did you sneak over to see her that I don't know about?"

Daniel stopped what he was saying to reply, "Does that even matter now?"

"I asked didn't I? So tell me as it is."

"I don't know," he answered, looking away. "I don't remember."

She took a step towards him, insisting, "Let me rephrase then… how many times did you actually sleep with her?"

In turn, he said nothing back, and that alone scared her.

"So it was more than just the one time you confessed. Am I right?"

"Don't do this Allie —"

"Then deny it. Can't you?"

He looked away from her a second time. His avoidance of her eye contact itself pretty much said it all.

"How… how could you… how could you do this to me… you… YOU FUCKING PIG!!!" Allison lashed out, hitting and shoving him till she stumbled onto the ground in desolation. Then, something even worse occurred to her. "Oh my god..." she gasped, hands over her mouth, "Her baby... was it yours?!" While he continued to keep silent, instead of tolerating it any longer, she roared at him, yanking his shirt repeatedly to get him to speak, "WAS THE BABY YOURS JUST ANSWER TO THAT!!!!"

All at once, he broke out in a startling mix of woe, anger, and frustration, screaming back at her, "YES! YES IT WAS MINE! THE BABY WAS MINE!!" Hot tears that had been welling up in his flaming eyes spontaneously came rushing down his cheeks with no way to stop them. His voice cracked into pieces and just then, he began to sob. "There... sat-satisfied?"

Allison literally felt like being stabbed in the chest to watch him cry over what he had done and be punished by his own inner demon that was his guilty conscience. Rather than releasing her pain, she just sat there, numb.

I must get out of here... I need to get out of here. Right when she was thinking that, by sheer coincidence, Sara called. Immediately getting up off the floor, she left the room before answering her phone.

"Finally! Where have you been for the past two days?!"

Her friend's voice at that moment sounded to her like a godsend. Disguising her heartbreak, she replied, "I told you about the Bahamas trip. We just got back about an hour ago."

"I guess you were having such a good time that you didn't even bother to check your phone. I left you messages like five different times."

"I'm sorry —"

"Hold on a minute, if you did go, I thought you wouldn't be back till late?"

"We decided to cut the trip short."

"'We' as in everybody or just you and Daniel?"

She paused for a second before telling her. "Just me and him."

"Oh?"

"So — what's going on with you?"

"Me? Well, I'm just out buying more beers. Just thought I might bug you one last time to see if you would stop by some time tonight."

"You are having a party?"

"Uh, hello? It's the housewarming I've been stressing you about. Ethan and Reese are staying at my parents' for the night. They've already left so it's just going to be us adults. I sure hope this weather will hold so more people show up —"

"Is Ed going to be there?" she inquired, hopefully.

"I believe so. Is that going to be a problem?"

"No. I was just checking. I'll be there in a bit."

"You mean it?"

"Yes."

"Alright! Let's see... it's five-thirty now. The party's will start in half an hour but just come over whenever."

"Okay."

"Oh goody! I can hardly wait!"

34

A T SUNDOWN, THUNDER started to roar. By the time Allison arrived at Sara's house some twenty minutes later, rain was coming down hard. As the eventual outcome of this massive downpour, some of the guests left early; the good thirty of them that remained were then forced to cramp in the living room of this average-sized, two-story dwelling. The poor weather did not ruin the least bit the mood of these party animals however, nor was the overcrowdedness much of an issue to them so long as the alcohol was free. No one was complaining about the stifling atmosphere being too stuffy, or the ear-splitting music being too loud, for they were all here to have a good night of fun before the long week ahead.

While this place might seem like a presumed nirvana to most people, Allison would have normally had second thoughts by now, and quite possibly had turned around and left as she was not accustomed to this sort of party per se; but having just gone through emotional hell, this place suddenly suited her well. Cutting through the wild crowd, soon she found Sara standing among a group of men in their early twenties and flirting with them.

"… I also had one for a while on my lower back of my ex's name. It was just recently that I had it reworked into a butterfly."

"*Into-a-what?*" one of the men, Mike, asked her in a yell.

"*A butt-er-fly.*" With the music booming in the background, everyone had to enunciate loudly and constantly just to properly communicate. "It's tiny… *it is tiny in comparison to yours of course!*"

"*Maybe you can show it to me one of these days!*"

She smirked in a kittenish manner, replying, "Maybe I will."

Just then, having spotted Allison approaching from behind her newly met friends, she broke off the conversation and went up to greet her with a welcoming hug. The guys just watched them.

"Hey girl, you made it! Is Daniel with you?"

Allison shook her head lightly and causally deferred talking about her personal issues in front of a bunch of strangers. "I got you a gift from the Bahamas but I accidentally forgot to bring it."

"It's okay. You can give it to me some other time. I'd show you around the house but you've already been here before, so —"

"Hey Sara, who is this lovely friend of yours?"

"Oops! My bad. This is my best friend Allison everyone. Allie, this is Jeremy, Mike, Paul and AUR-ELI-ANO. Did I say your name correctly?"

"Sí."

"Excuse me?"

"*Yes, yes you did!*" Aureliano replied aloud with a thick Spanish accent, which made Sara giggle.

She then returned to tell Allison, "Mike was just showing me one of his awesome tattoos," keeping the while an eyeful of him.

"Are you from this neighborhood as well Allison?" asked Jeremy with a grin, his eyes dreamy, showing a genuine interest in her.

Allison in turn just stood there, not knowing whether to respond.

Sara automatically jumped in to end her suffering. "Hands off guys, this beautiful girl here is taken. Now if you'd excuse us, we are going to go get some beer. Be back in a sec."

Grabbing Allison along, she led her through the party people to get to a slightly quieter corner — the kitchen, where she then babbled on continuously in high regard about those four young men as if they were made of gold. "What do you think? Aren't they just gorgeous? And they are forming a rock band! A rock band! I haven't been with anyone who's into music since Kent Connor from high school. Oh my gosh, I still can't believe they only live a block away from me…"

While seemingly listening, Allison had in fact long wandered off course, drifting back to the pain and distress that initially brought her here. When handed a plastic cup of beer filled to the brim, she took and drank it all in one go. Her helpful friend was quick to keep her hands busy, at least at first. As she chugged down one cup after another like it was water, the abnormality of her behavior eventually alarmed Sara that something was up.

"Alright. Spill."

Slamming another empty cup onto the kitchen island, Allison gave her mouth a wipe. "Pardon?"

"Just tell me Allie. What is wrong?"

"Did I say something was wrong?"

"Oh come on. You can cut the bullshit with me. Did something happen in the Bahamas?"

"That trip was a total disaster."

"Uh-huh! I *knew* it. Daniel was being a drag wasn't he?"

Sitting down on one of the stools, Allison reached for another cup of beer and started drinking it. So as to uplift her spirit, Sara took to shaking her body rhythmically as a new song came on, encouraging enthusiastically, "Gosh, I just love this music! You want to dance? Come on let's go dance a little."

Despite her avidity, Allison remained seated, not moving an inch. "No," she refused, "I think I might just stay a while and head on home."

"And then what?"

She did not say anything more, finishing off her beer, again.

Sara was not about to let her be down in the dumps all night, thereby moving on to offer her a few words of *wisdom*. "Allie, listen to me for once. I mean, look around you. You are at a party! Everybody's having a good time and so can you. As a matter of fact — drink this instead." Next, she went to take out a bottle of vodka from the freezer and poured some into two shot glasses. "You will feel much better if you would just let loose," she prompted, handing Allison one of the glasses and gulping down the other herself.

The devil's drink was every bit appealing to Allison at a time like this. Without question, she grasped the little glass and swallowed the hard stuff down her throat. While the bitter taste still lingered in her mouth, she had by then guzzled another mouthful straight from the bottle, counting on the burning sensation to *cleanse* her from the persistent feeling of gloom.

It just so happened that Ed emerged from the crowd at that precise moment. Tagging along behind him was an attractive brunette, tall and slender. As thrilled as he was to see Allison, ever so subtly he disguised it in front of his date. "When did you get here?" he asked her.

Not saying a word, Allison instead rested her elbow upon the countertop and her head her palm, studying the unexpected couple. Eventually, Sara filled him in for her. "She got here half an hour ago."

"Is that vodka?"

"Yes?"

"Humph. You are giving her hard liquor even knowing she can't drink."

"She's fine. It's not like she's a child. Plus she's only had a little."

"A little?!"

She just rolled her eyes at him.

"Aren't you going to introduce me?" said the brunette to Ed, all the while holding onto his masculine arm as if for dear life.

Awkwardly, he proceeded. "Of course. Kate, this is my good friend Allie. And Allie, I've told you about Kate a while back."

"Nice to meet you Allie. I've heard a lot of good things about you already."

Allison looked her up and down and smiled disparagingly. She then reversed her focus onto Ed, who had only been standing there staring back at her as though trying to read her reaction. Right that instant, she got up and approached him, a coquettish look on her face. "Come Teddy," she purred, pulling him smoothly along by the hands until reaching the dancing crowd. "I feel like dancing. Don't you want to dance with me Teddy?"

Astounded by her flirtation, Ed stood gaping at her raising her arms up in the air and jiggling her hips in a seductive manner, completely captivated. Though within the minute, she began to feel light-headed due to the poor ventilation and her feet heavier. On one silly misstep, she would have certainly collapsed onto the floor if it were not for his alertness to catch her in his arms just in time.

"I think we need to get you some water," he told her in all seriousness.

"No. Stay with me like this for a little longer."

Seeing her insistence, he did as she asked. Her arms hugged around his neck, and his hands naturally held around her waist. The two went on to slow-dance to the fast beats, neglecting completely their surroundings. Every inch of their intimacy therefore made Kate green with envy. She could only watch from a distance yet was powerless to stop them.

"I've always thought you would only date blonds," Allison causally commented.

"You are talking about Kate," Ed replied.

"She's pretty. Are you in love with her?"

"No."

"Then — why are you still with her," she said with ever so little jealousy in her tone, which was enough to make him feel elated on the inside.

"I think you know why."

"What is it? Is it because of her small nose, her soft hair —"

"Hehe."

"— or is it because she's tall?"

"What kind of a man would date a woman just because of her hair?"

"It was only a guess."

"Heh. No, no, and no."

"What then?"

"You really don't know?"

"Tell me," she urged him.

"It's because she's good in bed. So I figured, why not?"

She let out a titter, knowing he was just joking around. "You are terrible."

"Didn't I tell you what she does for a living?"

"Some lab assistant at the university?"

"Yes, and an occasional yoga instructor for their summer classes. From that you can imagine how her skill set contributes to our overall sex life."

Her laughter just got louder.

"All jokes aside though, she's a great girl, very bright and easygoing. Just give her some time to warm up to you, you will too begin to like her."

"I'm sure."

Leaning forward on her toes, she held her chin over his shoulder and just rested there for a moment. During which time he looked over at Kate, suddenly feeling obliged to get back to her.

"I should probably check on her," he said, pulling away gently. "She's not used to the party scene. She needs me."

"And you think I don't?" Allison in turn retorted.

Not expecting her to put up a protest, he looked fixedly at her puppy-dog eyes and pouty lips for a second, almost not believing them. At last though, he decided to stick close to his *angel*, rolling with the punches. "Do you honestly know of any man who would date a woman because of her hair?"

"Sure. At least one."

"Who?"

"You."

"Me?"

"Yes. Didn't you used to say that it was the first thing about me that caught your eye?"

"Right. But you had to have known that was not the main reason why I fell for you."

"What was the main reason then?"

"Well —" He looked away briefly and then back at her again, telling her half-casually, "You know me. I was such a high-strung kid back in high school. When we were together... you just knew how to keep me grounded, keep me in line."

"So I was like your guardian angel."

"I suppose... yeah. I enjoyed very much each day that we spent together. Even if it was spent doing things I would not otherwise do by myself, or at all."

"Like riding a roller coaster till you threw up?"

"Still frightens me whenever I think of that time."

"Haha."

"To put it the lamest way possible — I had always felt complete when I was with you... Heh. Can't believe I'm telling you this now."

Smiling a little, she disagreed. "That's not lame at all."

"You don't think so?"

"No. It's just... unfortunately, having a relationship with someone isn't usually as simple as it should be."

"I know what you mean. Anyway — do you realize you were just calling me 'Teddy' again?"

"Yes. Is that okay?"

"Of course. I kinda prefer it to be honest. It makes me feel closer to you."

"You hated it in the beginning remember? You said it wasn't macho enough."

"Did I? Heh. I thought it was cute when you just did it."

"Then I will be sure to call you 'Teddy' more often from now on."

Everything happening tonight so far had been beyond Ed's wildest dream, though much as he would like to deny it, the alcohol, the dance, and the dallying chatter combined all too mirrored their last night together in Vegas for his comfort. Instinctively, he presumed Daniel again had something to do with her stunning affection, thereby asking her when a brief chance came up, "Did something happen with your husband?"

She was surprised that he asked. "What do you mean?"

"Well, I was only asking because you seem... different."

"Good different?"

"Well... yeah, but... would you like to talk about it?"

Instead of venting about her problems, purposefully, Allison sidestepped his question by calling him out for spying on their lovemaking a few days back. "I saw you Teddy. I knew you were watching the whole time behind the railing."

Mortified at being caught, he was temporarily unable to work out what to say. As embarrassment flushed his cheeks, before he would go on to give her a full-blown apology, she staggered him further by asking, "So, how was I? I sure hope you were watching me and not him."

As shocked as he was relieved, he answered truthfully, "You were better than most just doing what you do. Always have been."

"Even better than Kate?"

Swallowing his nervousness, he replied bravely, "She's matchless to you. So is every woman I've ever known and dated."

"Now you are just laying it on thick."

"No. I mean it. I do," he stressed.

Just then, her lips curled into a suggestive grin and receded slightly. "I'm glad to know how much I still mean to you, how much you still want me..."

Spurred on by her prurient talk, little by little, he slunk his hands below her waistline, holding the curve of her bottom when they got to it. As if seeking some sort of consent to go ahead, he gazed at her nervously and gulped. While she gave him that come-hither look in her eyes, he angled his head just right to venture a kiss around her neck.

Allison's mind went blank upon his lips brushing against her skin so tenderly, again and again. The warmth of his breath breathing on her brought her memory back to those passionate days when she and Ed were still an item, how they absolutely could not keep their hands off each other, how she used to sneak out at night to fool around in the back seat of his pick-up truck. Every bit of her craved this reckless moment of excitement, of release. It was like a destiny that was fated to happen to her, that she eagerly accepted. Part of her wanted to just give in to his willing and able arms of embrace once and for all, but then... but then something deep inside her felt really, appallingly, wrong.

"What's wrong?" Ed asked her upon being pushed away precipitously.

"I gotta go," she replied to him, harshly yet determinedly.

Agitated by her sudden disengagement, he was not ready to desist from the madness, but grabbed a firm hold of her, telling her, "I don't understand."

Getting caught up in the emotion of it all, rather than giving him an explanation right then and there, she fought with all her might and yelled in his face, "LET GO OF ME!"

So, he did.

35

DESPITE DARKNESS, ALLISON went outside in haste by the kitchen back door and into the backyard. Ed followed after her, and soon, caught her by the shoulder in the middle of a rainstorm.

"What the *hell* is going on?!"

"I don't know Teddy. I don't know what's wrong with me okay?" she told him in aggravation mainly with herself, and then carried on clomping across aimlessly the wet lawn before her.

Coming around to block her path, he stalled her a second time. "You've been giving me the cold shoulder, and now this... what do you want from me Allie?!"

"I... I ... Please just leave me alone will you?"

As she continued walking on stubbornly towards nothingness, in a blurt of desperation, he yelled out after her, "You can't keep doing this to me!!"

Having heard him, she immediately stopped in place.

All hyped up on adrenaline, with a deep breath, Ed inhaled his pride, came right up to face her, and, without second-guessing himself, went out on a limb in suggesting, "Do you want us?"

"Excuse me?"

"I said — *do you want us?!*"

"There can't be an 'us'!"

"Why not!"

"Why not?! Because I'm married to Dan and I love him. *I love him!*"

"I can't do this anymore... what about me huh? What about me!"

"What about you?"

"Am I just another friend to you?"

Shaking her head, she replied hopelessly, "I *can't* love you. Don't you get it?"

"Then why are you here tonight? Why do you act all jealous of Kate, and why do you care if I'm in love with her?"

"I... I don't know. I'd been drinking earlier so I probably wasn't thinking straight when I —"

"*You are not that drunk,*" he cut right through her defense, his look bleak and unyielding. "I deserve an answer Allie. Explain it to me. *Pleeease.*"

Looking away, she got quiet suddenly. Her body trembled in the whipping wind as the brutal rain hit her constantly in torrents. The two stood there for a whole minute, both panting and drenched in frustration. He especially was anxious to hear her say something again. Eventually —

"I... I just... I just hate to see you with anyone else," she revealed, her eyes crept upward to check his expression before continuing, "I know I'm only thinking about myself, and in some such way, I'm obviously exploiting you in doing so but... but I can't help how I feel..."

Her confession might sound the most self-centered, but it was just what he had hoped for. "Do you mean that? Do you mean what you just said?"

"Every word... I mean every word. I feel awful. And I can't help needing you when I feel awful."

His glum face eventually broke out into a smile.

"I'm sorry... I really don't know what else to say."

Closing the gap between them, he reached out to rub her cheek gently with his thumb and run his fingers smoothly along her jawline. "Then, don't speak. You don't have to say anything more," he whispered to her. Lifting and holding her chin still, he moved in to seal her worries with a serious yet oh-so desirous kiss. Unlike what happened earlier on the dance floor, this time she neither shoved nor yelled but stayed perfectly at ease with her eyes closed, taking it all in. When their lips finally parted, he declared upon her translucent, sparkling green eyes reopening to look at him. Even with minimal light gleaming from the street lamp, they ensnared him with their shine. "If only you knew the effect you have on me just by looking at me like this."

"I'm so sorry Teddy. I really am. It's just... I don't want to lose you —"

"Who said you were going to? This changes nothing, nothing you hear me? You are my girl. You will always be my girl no matter what."

His reassurance granted her great relief, and in return, he put a smile on her face. Though that smile did not last for long owing to her quickly declining physical state. Any moment now, she would have toppled over from overexertion if he were not there to somewhat maintain her. Her body had literally gone stiff from being so cold. Naturally, he removed his leather jacket to wrap it around her and then — like there was nothing to it — scooped her off her feet and carried her back inside the house.

Away from the party scene, all the way he headed upstairs aiming for Sara's bedroom. Thinking that she had zonked out in his arms during the process, quietly and carefully, he nudged open the door, walked over to the bed and laid her down onto it.

He was just turning to leave the room when he caught her muffled sob and wherefore returned to her bedside to switch on the table lamp. Underneath the dim light, he looked down at her lying there with tears down both sides of her cheeks and neck, feeling genuinely concerned.

"Tell me," he said.

Allison shot her eyes at him. Half weeping, half stammering her words, she confided in him in a burst of sheer hatred. "He hit... hit me Teddy. He s-slapped me for that... that whore."

He knew right away to whom she was referring and at that moment, everything about her infatuation tonight pieced together like one complete jigsaw puzzle. Regardless of Daniel's side of the story, he was absolutely undoubting of her and manifestly outraged.

"When did this happen?"

"This afternoon. We were having a big fight —"

"*That son of a bitch!* He's going to pay for what he did!"

Sensing his rising rage, she grabbed his hand and told him, "Don't. Hurting him won't solve anything."

"How can you still be so protective of him?!"

She answered nothing, her shoulders still shaking from shedding tears, tears that never stopped rolling down from the corners of her eyes.

Holding onto her hand endearingly, Ed got down next to her. "Divorce him. *Please,*" he begged in his sternest voice, "I *swear* I would never treat you the way he did. I would do everything I could to take care of you and make you happy. I would be the best that I could be, a good husband to you."

"Teddy —"

"Please hear me out Allie." He took a deep breath before letting it all hang out. "I love you. I always have and I always will. My feelings for you have not changed in the past so many years and I've hoped and dreamt every day that I'd be so lucky to have you back with me. I'm asking you to *please*, leave him and marry me instead."

A smile broke through her clouded eyes just then. She sniffled and blinked away her tears. "You are too good to me you know that? But it's not going to work."

"It will! I promise it will! I promise I would do whatever it takes to make our relationship work. I would let you win all the fights, I would be the most understanding, really."

"I have no doubt that you would do all that for me, but there's just one problem."

"What is it?"

"We are two fools in love with the wrong person."

"Don't say that —"

"It's true," she insisted. "I appreciate everything that you are offering me, but —"

"But you just don't love me anymore," Ed finished her sentence. His face elongated with controlled sorrow.

"It's not like that."

"Then what is it like?"

"I had *loved* you, and in fact I still do, but just not in the same way anymore. Friends are all that we are now and can ever be. It's like I've told you before, if I weren't with Dan, things could certainly be different between us, but I am, and I'm never going to leave him."

Allison might not realize it, but her forthright honesty rocked him a great deal. In the next moment, he got up off the floor and had to walk away for a couple seconds, rubbing the while his face to sort of calm down his indignation. When turning back around to look at her, he was every bit bitter in denial.

"You don't mean that."

"But I do." She sat up in bed to plead with him. "Please Teddy, please don't be like this."

"Then you've got to explain to me. Because I just don't see it."

"Don't see what?"

"What's so special about him. Because from what've you told me, the guy's a total prick."

"Stop it."

"Then tell me. Am I not noble enough for you? Not high and mighty enough?!"

"Stop —"

"What's he done for you? I've skipped work to be at your beck and call. I requested a transfer from work to Arbington and moved there just to be near you. What about him huh?! *Nothing!!* That fucker."

"I said stop this!"

"*I will not!!* He's never been that nice to you. He's cheated on you who knows how many times and now that he's hit you —"

"Is that why you made up that lie?" she snapped at last, and incidentally, he got cautious about what she meant.

"What lie..."

"You know what lie. Even if my marriage were to fail, I would still just want it to be between Dan and me. I could really do without the added drama."

Speechless, Ed gave in. Feeling indignant about how everything he believed in so strongly for such a long time was falling apart entirely out of his control, he lumbered over to the window and looked out into the street for a moment to try and cool down his anger — if it ever worked — before he could begin to pull himself together and speak to her again. "How can you do it? How can you still love him after all he's put you through?!"

"Of all people, I thought you would understand."

"How could I?"

"Don't they say love is blind? I never really believed it until Dan cheated on me, until I came to a crossroads one day having to choose between staying in the marriage or leaving to start over. Considering how you and I ended back then, you still love me for me to this day —"

"I regret... I regret ever letting you slip away from me."

"It's not your fault. It was never your fault."

Getting choked up at the thought of their emotional breakup, he swallowed hard, tried moving on but his heart would not let him. As his mood deepened in blues, Allison dragged her fatigued body out of bed and came to fold her arms around him. Despite the hurt that was tormenting him on the inside, he turned to accept her into his.

"You must grant me this one favor, Teddy."

"What... what is it?"

"Please, cherish what we still have with each other and be satisfied with it."

"Be satisfied with it?"

"Yes. You must."

All the while spaced out in deep thought, he squeezed her against his own chest and held her tightly for a minute, smelling the crown of her head, rubbing his cheek across it several times as though she was his most prized possession that he was not about to just give away. "Do you truly believe he loves you?" he asked her.

"If I don't believe it myself, what can I believe in?"

"And... you are happy?"

She hesitated for a second, though eventually admitted: "Yes. Yes I am."

He nodded his head a few times before releasing her gently, telling her with an asserting, straight face, "Okay."

"Okay?"

"I'll be satisfied."

"Really?" Allison queried, slightly in disbelief.

In turn, he affirmed her, "Yes. Really," ever so prudently stowing away his resentment in the meantime to advise her, "But you ought to get some rest now. Look at you. You can barely stand on your own anymore. Come on."

He held her hand and brought her back to bed. Once lying down, she asked in her selfish little way, "Stay with me, will you?" And like always, he did as she wished, promising her devotedly, "I will be here. I won't go anywhere."

Upon his commitment, Allison's anxious mind gradually grew hazy and eyelids leaden until she let out a long weary sigh and slowly closed them. While she lay there drifting off peacefully, Ed pulled up a chair next to her and sat down into it.

His heart, still heavy with the fresh trauma of her revelation, found itself brutally played. Even so, he was in too deep to quit her, to dash his hope of ever having a future with his *angel* and he knew it so very well. The many hours to come, he thought hard between love and hate, his doomed fate and free will. Like Allison, he too had come to a crossroads, a time to decide what to do with that torn-up feeling inside him at long last or risk living it indefinitely.

In the very end, he made a rash decision.

DAY 23 | SEPT 28 MONDAY

36

"**W**AKE UP ALLIE, wake up!"
                Reluctantly, Allison turned over on her
                side, her eyes still noticeably puffy from all
of the crying before. Seeing her mother, she was quickly
reminded of the shameful thing she had done earlier in
the afternoon and as such, what she had told the police.

"Please, go away," she told her, sniffling a little as she
turned her body back the other way.

"It's Adrian on the phone. The police have arrested
him two hours ago..."

She was slow in assimilating the appalling news, unwilling really, and just lied there frozen, not moving a
muscle.

"... He said he tried your cell a couple times but it
never went through. Anyway — he wants to speak to
you."

"I... I can't."

"It's his only chance to call... but if you are sure, I will
gladly make up an excuse for you. Is that what you want
me to do?"

After a moment to fully grasp the gravity of the situation, she came around. "No," she told her mother, turning
to lie flat on her back.

"Are you sure?"

She sighed and gave a firm nod.

Her mother then set the phone down on the
nightstand. "Take as long as you need to," she told her and
then left the room.

Soon sitting upright, Allison tucked herself into a ball of anxiety. Next, she reached for the phone and held it close to her ear. "Hel-hello," she uttered into the speaker, barely.

"Hi Allie, how are you?"

Her brother's usual, delightful voice only brought her to tears. "Not good at all Adrian. How can you still talk to me after what I've done to you..."

Her sniveling immediately called forth his sympathy. "Don't cry. There's nothing worth crying for here."

"I didn't want to tell them anything I swear, but Mom... she —"

"She made you. Pah! Why am I not surprised?"

"I'm sorry."

"What are you saying sorry for? It's not your fault."

"But it is. Even though I regretted it right away, I couldn't save you... I can't bring you back..."

"Shh... stop crying. That's just what Mother wants. For years she's prayed for me to be put away, I just won't give her that satisfaction — not this time either."

"What do you mean?"

"I have a plan."

"What are you going to do?"

At first, there was a brief pause, and then all of a sudden, he talked in a serious whisper, sounding contrarily calm and confident being in his circumstance. "Don't you worry Allie, I've already figured a way out of this. Unfortunately, I can't tell you the details over the phone you see, since I'm under close watch. But you must trust me on this. Do you trust your big brother?"

"Of course I do."

"Good. It will all be over before you know it. Things will go back to normal again you'll see, and it's going to be beautiful..."

I believe him, and I will never stop believing in him.

Right then —

BOOOOOOOOOOMBLAAAAAAAM!

"What was that?? Adrian? Did you hear that?"
He never responded again.
"Hello? Are you still there? HELLO?!..."

Upon a second bigger and stronger boom went off in the background, it crackled in the midnight sky, waking many sleeping souls. Amongst all, Allison woke up in a rush of panic, throwing herself conveniently into Ed's arms for every bit of solace that he could offer.

"You're okay. It's just thunder," he said to her.

After realizing all that remorse she felt was merely a bad dream, slowly, she pulled away. This was possibly the first time in a long time that she dreamt a dream without Megan in it, and that alone was a load off her mind. Looking down at her clothing, she noticed she was wearing sweats instead of the eyelet blouse and blue jeans she wore when leaving home.

To stop any unnecessary speculation from escalating, Ed quickly elucidated the matter. "Your clothes were soaked. I was afraid you would catch a cold so I got Sara up here to change them out for dry ones. It was all her doing I swear."

"I know." She smiled at his unneeded jitter. Apart from having a slight migraine, she felt well enough to get out of bed and did so swiftly.

"You should try to sleep some more. It's just past midnight."

"How long was I out?"

"Three, four hours."

"No. I should really go home. I'm surprised I fell asleep at all, but for sure I know I won't be able to again without my pills. It's sad, but that's also the truth," she told him, grabbing her moist clothes and soggy shoes from the bathroom and stepping out.

Having no more reason to stay, he followed her out the bedroom and down the stairs. On one hand, they were astounded to descend into one big chaotic mess, but not

so on the other given that it was indeed one of Sara's parties — never was it quite an ordinary housewarming to
begin with. After a long night of carousing, the smell of
alcohol filled the air as a result of plastic cups, empty and
half-full, being carelessly discarded everywhere in the living room. Those guests who had stayed behind for the
night either crashed on the couch or on the carpeted floor
in their own filth, together snoring a chorus.

Towards the front door, the two tiptoed across the
room with their eyes to the floor intending not to accidentally wake anyone by stepping on them. In the middle
of their maneuvers, they stumbled upon Sara passed out
topless next to the fireplace, surrounded by cards and two
fresh-faced males, both of whom looked pathetically
wasted. "It must have been one lousy round of strip poker," Ed mocked them. Meanwhile, Allison covered her
friend's exposed chest with a blanket lying around before
leaving.

The hefty grey clouds had since moved past the sky
above them. The streets were now calm and quiet, making
apparent the chirping sound of crickets awakened after
the heavy shower. He walked her to her car parked across
the road. When it came time to part, he was in every way
considerate of her in light of Daniel's recent ferocity.

"Are you sure you don't want me to escort you?"

"Yes I'm sure," she assured him. His thoughtfulness
just so reminded her of Kate. "What happened to your
date by the way?"

"Honestly, I don't really know. I'm guessing she got
pissed off and left the party long ago."

"Oh Teddy —"

"Nah, with this handsome face, another girl will come
along soon enough..."

Although he said it with a sense of humor, it nonetheless did not lessen her guilt. "Is there maybe something I
can do to make it up to you?"

He happened to have an idea in mind. "Since you asked — I would really like you to go out to dinner with me tonight. There's this supposedly famous Italian restaurant in Uptown. I called and made a reservation last week for Kate and me, but judging by how I ditched her earlier, I really doubt she's going to show."

"Are you talking about Ottimo Cibo?"

"How did you know?"

"Just a wild guess. Dan and I have actually been there a couple times. It's one of his favorite restaurants."

"Right. Well, I'll be off at 5 p.m. today. I can meet you there at six o'clock, just need to go home and change into something more proper for the upscale place. What do you think?"

"Are you sure about this?"

"Am I sure? It would be my pleasure to take you out," he prompted, looking at her with hopeful eyes, yearning for a "yes".

"If that's really what you want then, I guess it's the least that I can do," she affirmed and sealed the deal with a smile.

Ed was more than glad. His bliss was short-lived after all, as by the time he headed back to his own vehicle after seeing her off, it had already subsided and his cheerful disguise melted away. All the way oppressed by burdening thoughts, he drove home.

37

THE VERY MINUTE Ed got back to his house, he marched into his bedroom, opened his sock drawer and reached to its bottom for the little bottle of liquid substance that he had been saving for the right moment. Securely in his hand, he went and grabbed a clean towel to wrap it within before shoving it into the glove compartment of his car for later use. He then proceeded back inside to pack a suitcase full of clothes and daily necessities, returned to load it into the car trunk and shut it up tight.

After shower, he headed to bed but not to sleep. For the rest of the night, he laid there staring at the ceiling fan, all the while self-justifying his own wicked thought that was his *plan*. On occasion, a conceited smirk would emerge on his face as he envisioned Allison's admiring gaze for his courage to finally carry out his ill-willed scheme heartened by a sick mind. Fearing that courage — his audacity — would leave him the second he relaxed, he worked to keep himself wide-awake and prickly till six hours later, when dawn broke.

Despite having no rest at all, he was by then up and driven to get the next thing off his chest. He got to the police station particularly early in order to give himself time for a visit at his superior's office prior to the start of his shift.

"Good morning sir. Is this a bad time?"

Sergeant Taylor was not pleased to see him at his door, nor did he try to appear otherwise but nonetheless, waved him in.

"How are you sir?"

"I'm well. But I sure can't say the same about you," said he, having noticed Ed's bloodshot eyes at first glance. "Late night?"

"Yes, unfortunately," Ed replied, rubbing the bridge of his nose. Meanwhile, he took a peek through the gap between his fingers at Sergeant Taylor, whose grim expression had not slightly changed and looked as though he utterly could not care less.

Therefore, he flat out came to the point. "I need to take some time off sir."

"Oh? What is it for this time?"

"I've just received news last night of my mother's passing."

Sergeant Taylor paused to think briefly. "Didn't someone else in your family pass away just a few months ago?"

"Yes, my grandmother."

He nodded. "That sounds legitimate enough."

Ed felt a small relief. "Thank you sir."

"When do you need your leave? And for how long?"

"The funeral is in three days. I plan on driving down early tomorrow morning and staying there for the week."

"Down where?"

"Michigan sir. Most of my relatives still live there."

Sergeant Taylor nodded his head again but said nothing this time. So, Ed continued, "I do understand it's sort of short notice —"

"Yes it is."

He could not help gulp nervously.

"But — I am a reasonable man, so long as you are honest with me."

He could sense Sergeant Taylor's high-minded eyes scanning him in doubt even without looking at them directly, upon which he gulped a second time and replied, "Yes sir," along with a humble bow.

"Very well then. Just write me a note about it and drop it off in my box. Consider this my official approval."

"Thank you sir for your flexibility," he said and took a look at the clock hanging on the wall. "I should return to my duty. My shift will be starting soon."

He was just turning to go when Sergeant Taylor stopped him. "Not so fast Ramsey. I've been meaning to talk to you."

Worriedly, he turned back around.

"Where were you during your shift on the 17th?"

"I believe I was patrolling as usual sir."

"You sure?"

"I'm positive."

"Then explain to me, why would I receive reports about your radio being turned off that day from 1 to 2 p.m.? Well?"

Naturally ecstatic about the images of Allison in the backseat of his patrol car that just came rushing back to him, he was almost smiling at the remembrance of touching her, kissing her mouth, neck and bosom, and how he nearly went so far as raping her that afternoon. Of course, he mentioned none of the occurrence and right away put up his guard. "There must have been a misunderstanding."

"Oh? How about last month on the 18th? And the 31st? Were those times just a 'misunderstanding' too?"

He pretended to give it a long, hard reflection before responding, "I'm afraid I don't have an explanation sir, but I certainly wasn't trying to avoid calls."

"Is that true?"

"Yes sir."

Sergeant Taylor was only half believing him after all. "If there's something wrong with your radio, get that replaced immediately you hear? Otherwise — you'd better watch your back. Because one of these days, your lies might just come back to bite you in the ass, and I'm not obligated to keep you around..."

Typically, Ed would consider being more self-disciplinary henceforth or at the minimum until the heat died down on him, but not today. Sergeant Taylor's warning felt more to him like a wave of babble to his ears that just floated in one side and out the other. After getting dismissed, he moved right on with his day like it never even happened.

Much like the calm before a storm, the entire morning went by relatively peacefully. With few calls for service to respond to, his restless brain only wandered and wondered about things, things that centered on grudging against Daniel Skala for the loser he made him out to be for years. By lunchtime, he had come to park at an empty lot where he sat in his car to continuously reinforce that animosity implanted by hate and jealousy. Little by little, he became less of himself without realizing it. In a few minutes, Tony, a fellow officer, also pulled up at this spot for a breather. "Hey man, what's for lunch?" he asked him cheerfully, nosy as ever.

"I uh... I didn't bring any," Ed replied, sort of caught unawares.

Sticking his head out the window, Tony looked at him more closely. "Man you look terrible! Hang over?"

To save himself the trouble of explaining, Ed simply uttered, "Yeah."

"Really? That's unlike you. Well, you want some of my lunch?" offered he, meanwhile splitting his vegetarian sandwich and handing over a half of it. Out of respect, Ed accepted it and thanked him.

"Now, I can't guarantee the taste. Chrissie's been try-ing out some new recipes lately. You know, to 'help' me stay thin she said. Like I would ask for that kind of help from her in the first place."

Ed somehow pitied his wife. "She probably just wants you to be healthy."

"I've only gained four pounds since we got married a year ago. She can't seem to ever let that go."

"I'm sure she's just worried."

"It's not like I'm physically unfit. I mean do I look *at all* out of shape to you?"

"No."

"There you go! It's not even her body to begin with! Can you imagine if it were?! Women."

"It's only because she gives a shit. Trust me. You could do a whole lot worse without her taking care of you."

Tony just then looked at him funny. "Christ, you are really unbelievable. How you are still not married is total-ly beyond me." Chomping away on his sandwich, he continued, "Anyway — speaking of Chrissie, I do have a favor to ask you."

"What is it?"

"Are you up for working this Thursday? I sort of need someone to cover my ass."

"Why? What did you do?"

"It's not really what I *did* but more of what I *didn't* do. You see, she had told me weeks in advance to take the day off for our wedding anniversary, but somehow... somewhere... it just slipped my mind. So if you are available, whichever date you want to switch for, you got it."

"I would do it for you buddy. It's just that I will be out of town."

"Since when? I never heard you mention anything."

"It's all unexpected."

"What is?"

"It's my mother... she passed away yesterday. So I'll be leaving for Michigan tomorrow and staying there for the rest of the week. I've just gotten it approved this morning."

"I thought your folks are both Minnesotans?"

"No, just my stepmom, and I wasn't talking about her."

"So you are talking about your birth mom."

"Correct."

"B-bwahahaHAHA!" Tony suddenly burst out laughing.

"What's so funny?"

"Is that what you told Taylor?" he asked him, half suppressing his laughter. Though his laughter was not the least bit amusing to Ed, who immediately broke into a cold sweat, fearing that his fabrication might somehow be easily exposed.

"Is that a problem?" he asked Tony back.

"Not to me. It's just that I know your mother died when you were what? Ten or eleven?"

"How did you know?"

"Just a guess... Haha no. You told me that yourself when you first transferred to the precinct. You don't remember?"

"No, I do not... Well, since you know it's a lie, keep your mouth shut about it will you?"

"Relax. I'm no snitch. Your secret is safe with me. Are you really going out of town though?"

"Yes."

"I suppose you are not going alone. Can I assume you are finally patching things up with Lady Allie?"

Feeling genuinely content at the thought of Allison, Ed could not help a smile.

"I told you she would come around if you gave her a day or two! Not that you did anything wrong as her boyfriend to begin with. Chrissie would have been thrilled for an opportunity to screw around in the backseat of this bad boy..." While it was all just one big fat fiction built upon false hopes and lies of many levels, Tony had been listening for months to Ed talking about the romance, the ups and the downs about his relationship with Allison as if they had never broken up, ever. Since he had no other sources to validate its factuality, he found no reason to doubt and certainly believed every bit of his commitment to his *angel*.

"I'm not going to *fuck* it up again this time," Ed swore sternly to himself.

"Take it easy man. It's just a girl thing they do, getting mad at us whenever things don't go their way."

"But she's not just any girl. She's *it* to me. I want to marry her and start a family with her."

"Go for it man. Haven't you been dating for the past... what? Ten years? It's about time. I bet she's secretly expecting a proposal anyway. Women are so weird about that kind of thing."

Like he needed anymore pep talk on this.

38

L ATER, UPON RECEIVING a radio call regarding two young men engaged in a gruesome fistfight at a nearby neighborhood, both Ed and Tony responded to it and drove off to the location indicated by the dispatcher. When they got there, two of their colleagues had already arrived, taking care of things.

Paul, who had just finished reporting back an update of the scene, turned to the guys and told them, "A young lady has been shot dead just minutes ago. An ambulance is on its way."

"Where's the body?" Ed asked him, all the while watching Cody handcuff the suspect and throw him into the back of his car.

"Over there," informed Paul, pointing at the cul-de-sac about twenty feet away.

"Let's go check it out," Tony suggested, and hence Ed followed along.

Over half way to where the violence initially took place, they encountered a young man sitting on the sidewalk, whose face was covered in fresh bruises and hands smeared with blood that likely was not his own. While his buddy went on ahead, Ed decided to stop by for a conversation.

"What's your name?" he asked the young man, who at first did not respond.

"Are you related to the young lady?"

Slowly, he lifted his head to look up at Ed, his eyes adrift. "She's... she's my fiancé," he told him, his voice shaking from having just gone through the whole ordeal.

"Tell me what happened."

"He... he and I were fight-fighting... and then out of nowhere... he took out a gun and flashed it at me. Before I had a chance to even react, he... he had shot her twice in the chest. I cou-couldn't stop the bleeding no matter... no matter what I did..."

Right then, the young man broke down in a fit of tears, burying his face in his ensanguined hands. Leaving him to his grief, Ed marched on. Tony happened to be heading back at the moment, causally warning him as they passed each other. "It looks brutal man. Be ready for it."

"It's not my first time," asserted Ed, confidently. Since picking up his pace, he gradually noticed spots of blood alongside his path, all the way from scattered dots leading him to a puddle of red where the young lady's body lay. Blood was still seeping from the two holes in her chest and soaking through the layers of her clothing. Such a re-volting sight alone was enough to gag a maggot, not to mention the tinny smell lingering in the air that could po-tentially faint a cow, but he managed to keep himself in check, looking down at her still face and leaning so his shadow shaded completely her open eyes from the sun.

Those almond eyes of hers — their shape, color, and just the way they set deep in their sockets — strangely to him bore an odd resemblance to those of Allison's. The green pigment of their irises was darkened having faded slightly from the blockage of light, yet still all in all re-tained a semitransparent shine. The longer he riveted on her blank stare, the more spellbound he became. Finding it hard to disengage, slowly, he was sinking, sinking into his own unrested mind that began to play tricks on him.

"Teddy!" Suddenly, the dead lady was thought to be calling out to him.

This can't be.

"Why aren't you talking to me?"

"Allie?" he replied finally to his own delusion, imagin-ing *her* to be Allison.

"Let it go Teddy."

"What?"

"Your plan, forget it."

"How do you know about my plan?"

"I've known it for a while now. Since I've been living and breathing in your innermost thoughts, I know everything there is to know about it."

Swallowing back his nerves, he asked her courageously, "Well — why should I?"

"Because it's no use. It won't change anything no matter what you do."

"You don't know that —"

"I do know. You have to listen to me. This will ruin you."

"I will be okay. I will be cautious."

"No, you will not. You are purely acting on impulse."

"I have to try, for *us*."

"But there's never been an 'us' to begin with. Dan is my husband, and I'm in love with him. You and I are friends, and that is as far as we can ever be. I thought I've made my point clear to you last night."

"I don't care anymore. I just know that I won't go down without a fight."

"You and I both know it's far more than a fight, and not a fair one."

"But I'm determined, and I will make you love me again if I have to."

She paused for a moment to smirk, and then warned him, "Then — just don't end up killing me."

"I'd *never* — *never* let that happen."

"Well, it happened to her didn't it? Do you think this was all planned?"

"Who?"

"Heh. You are really delusional. I mean, look at me closely, it's not a pretty picture now, is it?"

He therefore shifted his focus from her face down to her busted chest. Almost instantly, his stomach sank to his toes as if flipped inside out, and his sturdiness from before dissolved away. His breathing quickened and began to rattle in his throat. One moment a rush of saliva gathered up in his mouth, the next he was bending over and puking on the side of the road. At one point, the hurling somewhat subsided. While panting deeply, he turned his head slightly to venture another look at *her* — the corpse — from the corner of his eye. Upon that happening, like a chain reaction, vomit came spewing out of him over again.

Clumsily, he backed away from the horrific scene, almost tripping over his own feet as John Cooper, a homicide detective, caught him by the elbow just in time to save him from falling.

"Boy, you don't look good," said John forthrightly, looking him in the face which had gone from pale to entirely white.

"I'm alright," insisted Ed, pulling away from his grip.

"It's okay son. Every policeman has his first. You will smarten up next time, believe me. I've been there and done that many years ago," John lectured him, thinking he was a newbie. "Now, move your ass and get some rest would you? No offense, but you look dead."

The paramedics had also arrived just then, attending to the victims. Soon as John moved on with his work, Ed as well floundered his way back to his vehicle, all the while still hanging on loosely to his own bizarre hallucination. On passing Cody's patrol car, he approached the suspect sitting defenseless in the backseat, deciding to interrogate him.

"Why did you do it?!"

His fellow colleagues saw and together awaited the suspect's reaction. While the young man did not respond right away, single-minded in his thirst for truth, Ed restated impatiently, "Why did you kill her huh? Answer me."

The guy still said nothing.

"Don't waste your time buddy. I say leave it to Homicide to deal with him," said Paul in an attempt to put his ambition to rest, giving him a pat on the shoulder.

Ignoring Paul and his advice altogether, all at once without thinking, Ed moved to yank at the guy's collar, yelling furiously at him, "ANSWER ME I SAID!"

Despite having just committed manslaughter, the young man appeared uncaring of his own forthcoming predicament and calmly broke his silence. "I meant to shoot him, not her. I love her. I just can't help her if she so chose to take the bullet for that bastard."

In shock at his response, Ed's mouth subsequently gaped open. "Enough already Ramsey. Let him go," Paul tried to intervene again but failed to get him to give way. Meanwhile, Ed pushed on.

"If it's like you said, why would you fire at her twice?"

The young man continued to tell it as it was. "Because I was upset... I was upset that she would go so far as dying for him. She belonged with me! That *bitch*."

"And how is that worth it huh? Now that she's dead, DEAD! You killed her. It's all over —"

"MmmwwahahahaHAHAHA!" the young man suddenly broke out into an evil laugh, and then the next second, a lurid smile flashed across his face and his eyes stared Ed intensely in the face. It was a look as chilling and forbidding as a demon coming straight from hell, perhaps the only thing missing was the blood from that young lady whom he claimed to love on his teeth. "That might be," he went on to say, "but it is so worth every bit of it. She's mine and mine alone. If she's not going to be with me then — to *hell* with her..."

His candid confession might sound mad and hopelessly pessimistic to the others who had heard it, in the oddest sense however, Ed understood him perfectly as he saw a reflection of his own dark side in this cold-blooded, amateur murderer. Be that as it might, the outcome would have been different had it been him in the same do-or-die situation. That was to say, things would have been in his control and no one would have to die in vain — or so he kept convincing himself.

Paul eventually managed to pull him off the guy.

"Get off me!" Ed in turn swung his arms at him to break away and then hurried forthwith into his car.

'To hell with her...' No. No way. Not gonna happen.

Not waiting to catch his breath, he grabbed his phone and made a quick call to Allison in reminding her of their agreed-upon meeting.

"The reservation is at six."

"I know, I remember," she told him.

"You should probably leave home extra early. Since the traffic can be unpredictable by then."

"I do plan to leave by five. That should give me plenty of time to make it there."

"Good... good."

"What's going on Teddy?"

"What do you mean?"

"You sound a little rushed."

"It's nothing... I just... I just can't wait to see you is all."

"Likewise... Don't worry. I won't bail out on you at the last minute," she joked.

"Good... good."

"Are you sure you are okay?"

"Yes, absolutely. I'll meet you at the restaurant in four hours then."

"Right."

"Good... well, bye."

39

S HORTLY AFTER GETTING off the phone with Ed, Allison laid her head back down onto the pillow. She had yet to find the will to get out of bed since this morning, when she heard Daniel leave for work without so much as stepping foot into their bedroom. Last night, she returned home in low spirits, only to discover him asleep in the guest room. It came as no surprise to her that he wanted to be left alone after their clash from yesterday afternoon, as she herself too needed time to get over yet another deception that fell upon her made worse by his self-condemnation.

Coming to think of those colorful days they used to cherish only further augmented her gloom. One thing that continually left her in a daze was exactly when did this whole nightmare originate, hence when did their marriage start to slide downhill in Daniel's perspective. And, if she were to pinpoint a specific cause to it, she would surely hold Megan responsible. Even if he were to disagree, she knew he would not deny at the least that Megan complicated things between them by providing him a tempting escape from their marital problems.

Of course, clearly his relationship with Megan was beyond *just* an affair. There was love, love above that sibling bond they shared that Allison had only just noticed during last Thanksgiving when they reunited after so many years of separation. It might not have been too obvious then, but those desiring gazes that he threw at Megan with a smile shining over the dinner table could not fool her. Every bit of their strange vibe implied there was something more to the supposed brother and sister that she did not dare neither comprehend nor want to at the time.

Perhaps she should have at least spoken up about her concern after everyone had gone home that night as opposed to burying it deep inside her for so long. She did the same later when she heard Megan was moving down to the Twin Cities, and again when Daniel first repented to her his infidelity. Now thinking of all those incidents, she realized they had never really sat down to talk over any of them in a rational manner. As normally after quarreling, they would be hurrying to recover from the unpleasantness of ever bringing an issue up in the first place.

If only their issues could self-resolve with time instead of each one being piled on and shoved aside after the initial anger mellowed into sadness. Like a ticking time bomb, it was doomed to blow up sooner or later and when it did, the situation had already progressed so far beyond repair. What happened yesterday sure felt that way to Allison without exaggeration, yet, regrets healed no wounds, and it really took two to change a relationship. For she and Daniel were both stupidly stubborn people, judging by how things went in the past, she expected the next couple of days to wind up a prolonged silent treatment.

Even after she took great effort to finally get out of that comforting bed of hers three hours later to get ready, Daniel remained a constant bother in her head. Makeup seemed useless, as the mascara she applied on did little to brighten her downcast eyes and the lovely pink blush her sad cheeks. The red lipstick was meant for that final touch to a perfect look but it hardly covered up her dull mood. Even that sophisticated, little black dress she put on looked dreary on her for once. Her heart just was not there, and the meeting with Ed grew to be more of an obligation than anything else as time passed.

This steady weight hanging on her chest as she ruminated on everything of her depressing marriage and the work needed to mend it never went away. When five o'clock came around, she was basically sulking about going but grabbed her purse anyway and headed for the door, until something totally unexpected took place that stopped her in her tracks. It was an incoming call from Daniel that hit her like a miracle. Seeing his name on her phone's screen, right away she felt a fresh charge of energy rushing through her and was infused with hope once more.

After a few rings, she cleared her throat and answered it.

"Hello?"

"Hey."

No one spoke for a moment, and then, Daniel continued, "How are you?"

"Could be better... You?"

"Same."

There went another break. Hearing his voice did temporarily lift her despair, although she was not about to pour her heart out to him like that over the phone.

"Allie?"

"Yeah?"

"What's going on? What are you doing?"

"I was just about to go out for dinner with Sara." She just could not bring herself to mention Ed.

"I see. But you are still home?"

"Yes. Where are you? What's all that noise in the background?"

"I'm on the highway. Listen — I'm sorry. I've been thinking a lot about everything that happened."

She almost did not believe her ears. "You mean yesterday?"

"Yesterday and also, the past couple of months. The thing is — we need to talk."

"About what?"

"About us of course. Don't you think we should talk over our situation, solve things between us once and for all?"

"Right. I agree."

"Good. Well, I'm on my way home right now. I should be there in about fifteen minutes. Just calling to give you a heads-up."

"Okay. I'll be here."

"You don't have to wait for me. We can do this after you get back from your dinner."

"I know but, I really would like to see you before I go."

He went silent for a few seconds, and then, "Alright. As long as that's fine with you, I'll see you soon…"

Daniel's initiative to break the vicious cycle of their blame game no doubt felt tremendous to her. Upset though she might still be, she sensed it diminishing. Going along with his endeavor, for what it was worth, she planned on being completely honest with him this time, and wherefore telling him just how she had been dealing with the whole Megan catastrophe. Although, above all else, she wanted most to let him know how much she loved him regardless of their past and as such, if he was willing to start over, she would be all for the idea.

Sitting by the windows, she looked out for his car to start emerging from a far-off road junction leading to their house; however, there was yet no sight of him ten, fifteen, and twenty minutes later. As a further matter, she had not forgotten her promise to Ed, but in no way was she going to detain her husband's keenness to reconcile for that reason. Even if it meant she could end up running late, ultimately she was eager to keep waiting and expected Ed to understand. Fortunately, minutes apart from sending him a courtesy text, she saw Daniel's car approaching the driveway.

Having been looking forward to his arrival, she went outside and waved at him from the front porch. Just then, Daniel got out of his car carrying a brown envelope in one hand and shut the door with the other. The moment he looked up at her, he smiled a smile that brought her pure joy, making what formerly enraged her at that instant seem insignificant. All she wanted was to be wrapped in his arms and breathe every breath of his that would restore and bring true peace to her soul, like she once was whole, again.

Down the doorsteps she went. When she was just about getting to him, suddenly, there was a loud report — an explosion — snapping through the air. Every bit startled by it, she stood motionless looking at Daniel, whose smile had simultaneously faded and in the next split second, he let out a cough with blood to follow, splattering as he careened face first onto the ground. Prior to her awareness even catching up, around the corner came Ed, stony-faced, bearing a gun in his hand. Determinedly, he came to Daniel's inert body, pointed the gun directly above his head and fired two more times. Right then and there, a trail of blood leaked out from underneath him, tracing across the concrete pavement.

All that evilness occurred in a mere minute, during which time some of Allison's jolliest memories spent with Daniel flashed before her eyes, and some sad ones, then some dark ones, really dark ones, involving Megan, and her death... there was Adrian and more... till the fiendish sequence of her husband's murder eventually sunk in, she screamed in sheer terror. It was then, and only then, did Ed notice her standing there, who thus automatically rushed over in panic, hoping to quiet her down.

Seeing him coming near, Allison quickly turned around up the steps for the door; though it was far too late as he snatched her from around the waist, pulled her back roughly and pinned her down to the ground by force. "*Shh! Shh! It's okay. It's going to be okay...*" he told her repeatedly, covering the while her mouth with his mighty hand still attached to the murder weapon. Her fingernails naturally began to dig deep into his skin as she pinched and scratched relentlessly his hand, exerting desperately to rid it off her face. Since restrained under his control, she could only swing her legs like an maniac and kick her heels against his back to try getting him off but never succeeded.

What was worse, her aggression only threw Ed deeper into his swivet. His face now all fired up, losing altogether his sanity by the time he hit her twice in the back of her head with his gun intending to knock her out. Her scalp bled immediately and throbbed sharply as a result of that savage blow. Subsequently, her struggle died down and then stopped completely. "*I'm sorry Allie, but you made me do it!*" he said to her, half pissed-off, half delirious. Straightforwardly, he picked her up off the ground, threw her over his shoulder and strode towards his car parked about fifty feet down the road.

Allison looked down at the ground from over his shoulder. Half-awake, half-blacking out, all that she saw was his feet moving further away from her home and further into peril. Scared and helpless, in the midst of the chaos she could only pray that someone — anyone — would come in time to her rescue. She held onto that last glimpse of hope until before long hearing faintly the police sirens blaring in a distance. Her heart felt the calm that it needed at that moment. Everything in her surroundings went blank thereupon as she gradually let herself slip into shock.

Whatever happened from then on, only time could tell her fate…

PART TWO

THE LESSER EVIL

40

FTER DANIEL MET his death in the driveway of his house, two homicide detectives and a team of CSI agents were sent there shortly to evaluate the crime scene. The street adjacent to the property was blocked off temporarily as the technicians combed the area to collect evidence. An hour later, Sydney, one of the supervising technicians, approached Detective John Cooper about wrapping up their work.

"Just hang on a minute. Martin's on his way," John said to her.

"It's been well over half an hour. He's either here now or he won't show."

"He said he's coming so he will. We're just gonna have to be more patient with him."

"Can't he just watch the tape later? Why should we all work according to his schedule?"

"Come on Sydney. It's not your first day working with him."

"Right. I forgot he thinks he's all that and then some."

"What's gotten into you?" He looked off to the side of the road for a second where a car just pulled up. "See, there he is."

Soon, its door popped open, and then out came a tall, lean man with a cigarette in his mouth, his hands tucked inside the pockets of his black blazer worn over a fitted white tee and black jeans.

"Hey Martin!"

He looked in John's direction upon being called, shutting the door with a backward kick of his foot and walking up to meet with him.

"So, did the guy confess? Is the Boyle case a wrap?"

He took a deep drag on his cigarette, holding in the smoke for a moment before exalting into the cool night air and then pulled it away from his mouth. "You bet," he replied, plainly, turning to lock eyes with Sydney standing near.

"Hey Sue," he called her.

This whole time, Sydney was really trying hard to overlook their personal issue so as to not let it get in the way of work, but upon his deliberately inadequate greeting, she just lost it.

"You bastard!" she cussed at him, slapping him across the face and walking off in a huff.

"Ouch," he reacted a few seconds later, giving his cheek a symbolic rub down.

John was initially shocked by Sydney's comeback, but then his surprised look quickly wore off. "What did you do this time? Besides calling her by the wrong name, again."

"It was a joke," Martin argued, moving on.

John followed him. "Yeah, but it wasn't funny. What else could you have possibly done to tick her off this much?"

"Nothing worth mentioning."

"Right. You really shouldn't play with a woman's heart you know that?"

"I didn't. It was more about her not being able to accept what she was told."

"Which was?"

"That she's not my type."

"No kidding! You told her that? You don't tell a woman that."

"I was just being honest. Was I not supposed to?"

"Don't play dumb with me."

"Heh."

"If you keep building more enemies, sooner or later, no one's gonna want to work with you except me."

"And that is so bad because?"

John just shook his head. "All I'm trying to say is, can't you at least go easy on the ladies? Especially ones you have to work closely with. I'm not telling you to be their friend, but it wouldn't kill you to be a tad more sensitive with them..."

While half hearing his nagging, Martin was having an eyeful of the aftermath of the homicide situating before him. Just then, he stopped where he was.

"Are you listening to me?"

"Sure," he replied to John, casually, and then took time inhaling his last drag before flicking the cigarette butt onto the floor and crushing it with his foot. Straightaway, he walked on ahead to do a thorough walkthrough of the crime scene at hand, prompting John to drop the idle talk and jump back on track.

All the while accompanying Martin to aid in mapping the trail of crime, he filled him in with more immediate information. "Victim's name, Daniel Skala, 28, married, Caucasian. Shot once in the upper back, twice in the back of the head. His neighbor next door heard a few gunshots and initially called 911. A suspect, named Ed Ramsey, has been arrested shortly after and taken into custody —"

"Any witnesses?"

"Er yes. His wife was believed to be present at the time he got shot. The neighbor also claimed to have seen, out of her window, what looked to be an 'attempted kidnapping' as Mrs. Skala struggled to free herself from the suspect before our men showed up."

"An attempt to kidnap?"

"Yes. She said she heard Mrs. Skala scream, and despite the odd angle from her living room, she vaguely saw them wrestling on the ground near Daniel's fallen body until they went out of her view."

"How long did she suppose the struggle took?"

"Five minutes tops according to her."

"Five minutes… Where was he caught eventually?"

"Right over there." John pointed at a barricaded car parked in the distance. "He was only steps away from his own vehicle."

"I suppose the weapon was still in his hand at the time."

"Yup, we got it. All the while he was carrying Mrs. Skala over his shoulder."

"Did he put up a fight?"

"Not that I know of. I was told he was very much shaken up and looked to be under the influence of alcohol at the time of voluntary surrender. We've found a half-empty bottle of whisky in the passenger seat of his car which might have explained his intoxication."

Martin nodded his head. He then came to get down in front of the marker where Daniel eventually fell dead, and a different marker highlighting a bloodstained envelope lying next to it, studying them.

By the look of things, John remarked, "This should be an easy one to press charges."

"Where is Mrs. Skala?"

"At Lemley County Hospital."

"Have you spoken to her yet?"

"No. She was unconscious when they transported her onto the ambulance about forty-five minutes ago."

Not wasting another minute, Martin got up off the floor and strictly headed for his car. John caught up to him as he was just getting into it. "Her name is Allison, Allison Skala. Thought it might be helpful to know."

"Thanks John. I'll meet you back at the station."

"Actually —"

"Yeah?"

"If it's nothing too urgent, I would like to take a rain check tonight. I sort of promised Carol to be there for Jaden's first birthday. Her relatives are over at the house as we speak... But hey, I will see you first thing tomorrow. I will even come in early. How does that sound?"

"Humph. Figures."

Despite their big age gap, the two had worked side-by-side to solve crimes for years. Things were only different since John started his own family two years back at fifty. Being an old father and all of two little ones, unlike Martin, who was still relatively young and a known workaholic among staff of their department, he had gradually became more laid-back in that sense and seldom pulled unnecessary all-nighters for cases like he used to anymore.

"You won't be able to understand my position until one day you too tie the knot. It changes you, believe me."

"Don't bet on it," Martin retorted.

"Oh you will kid, just you see. Fifteen years ago when I was your age, I was like you, totally high on the bachelor's life. I held pretty much the same attitude about marriage as you do now back then, so, never say never."

"Are you sure about that?"

"About which part?"

"Never mind. What about Jake, give him a call for me will you?"

"He didn't tell you? He's been transferred out today."

"What?"

"Yeah. Both Smith's team and Clark's had been kicking up a fuss about his 'misconduct' for weeks. They eventually wrote out an official report to the Internal Affairs complaining about him and his 'SOP violations', yadda yadda yadda. But most people know that's just their excuse to remove him."

"Why would they do that?"

"Let's just say, there's a more conservative bunch amongst us cops who are less accepting of others' sexual nature if you know what I mean. They just don't want to work with a queer, period."

"Can't he counter complain against them?"

"You expect Jake — a fresh rookie — to take the stand all by himself against a group of trusted officers? Everything's too subjective when it comes to discrimination anyway, hence he will likely never find solid proof to make a case of them. Besides, the committee isn't firing him, so it's probably for the best. The only sad thing is, I know you've grown to like working with him —"

"Who said?"

"Well —"

"Jake's a hard worker with good instincts for his job. Anyone who would let anything blind them from seeing his potential is an idiot."

"*That* I do agree. I mean, who am I fooling? Even I was starting to like the kid. Not that way... but you know."

"Regardless — you said early, I'll take your word for it."

"You betcha boss! Just try not to break your back too much. Remember, there's always tomorrow."

41

SIX-FOOT-TWO AND SET apart from most men by his rugged good looks, many of the female staff recognized Martin as he was coming through the automatic entrance into the hospital. The front desk personnel, especially the young ones, had generally developed a liking for him on a first-impression basis all due to his mysterious, bad-boy charm. One example of which was Anna whom he had briefly talked to just once before. Solely the sight of his coming was enough to perk her up instantly.

He stopped in front of her two colleagues at the desk, inquiring of them. "I'm looking for Allison Skala. She should have been admitted about an hour ago."

"Let's see —"

"Allison Skala you said?" Anna cut in almost immediately, jumping at the chance to talk to him. "Yes, she's here."

Martin therefore slid along to stand before her counter. "What room number?" he asked.

She did a quick search on her computer and then directed her sparkling eyes back at him. "She's up in 208... second floor to your left..." she informed with her intentionally alluring voice, visually tracing from his bristly eyebrows to his well-defined cheekbones and strong jawline before returning to meet his prideful gaze dazzling with wonder.

"Thank you Sue."

"It's actually Anna... but that's okay!"

"I'm sorry. I meant to say Anna."

"Like I said, don't worry about it," she assured him, her smile had not receded in the least.

"Alright."

"Is there — ahem."

"Hmm?"

"Is there anything else I can do for you Officer Blake? Anything else that you need?" she asked him tactfully, her lips somewhat protruding to look more attractive as though hinting that she was ever so willing to give herself away. While her colleagues could only look on, they were slightly disgusted yet slightly envious.

Martin got her signal, but even knowing her overfriendliness would have certainly put him at an advantage, he did not bother wasting more time with her. "No. You've been very helpful. Thanks a lot," he replied bluntly, and then walked away towards the elevator without hesitation, leaving her all caught up in her own embarrassment.

Upon which, business was resumed. A little time later, he located Allison in Room 208. She was by then awake, pale-faced, reclining in bed with her forehead wrapped in gauze and her arm hooked up to an IV. Her parents were there as well, standing by her as he walked in to present himself.

"Detective Blake from Homicide," announced he, flashing his identification badge at them. "I would like to speak to Mrs. Skala for a moment regarding the shooting that happened earlier."

Looking at him in disbelief, Brenda rebuked him sharply for his ill-judged request. "She literally just regained consciousness. You really think this is appropriate?!"

In support of his wife, Elton approached and tried to persuade him to leave. "I'm afraid she is right, Officer...?"

"Blake."

"Right. Perhaps you can come back at a later time?"

Just then, Allison spoke out, her voice quiet and scratchy. "Daddy... Daddy."

"Yes sweetpea?"

"It's fine. He can talk to me now."

"Are you sure? I was just gonna give Clarkson a call and he would be on his way."

"I really don't need a lawyer for this Daddy. You are just making it harder than it needs to be."

Out of concern for her daughter's overall well being, Brenda continued to oppose the idea. "Oh darling, why push yourself? You need rest. She needs her rest."

"It's okay Mom. I can handle this."

"But —"

"Can you guys give us some time alone please?"

Sensing how determined she was, Elton could only give in. "Alright. Come on Bren."

And, so did Brenda, very much unwillingly. "We'll just wait outside then. Give us a holler if you need anything," she told her and gave her a quick peck on the cheek before leaving.

Soon as her parents left the room, Allison adjusted herself to a more comfortable position for conversations. Martin too drew near now to help her with the pillow, saying to her, "I apologize for coming at such a bad time Mrs. Skala, but I'd like to get a head start on your husband's case."

Allison looked at him once, her face unemotional, and then stared out the window about four feet away. She sat there silent for half a minute, spurring him to offer her a few words of comfort. "I'm very sorry for your loss. I understand this isn't easy —"

"What's your name again?"

"I'm Detective Blake from the Homicide Department."

"Does everyone call you that?"

"Eh, no miss. My first name is Martin."

"Martin..." She paused briefly, turning her head to look out the window again. "Have you ever lost a loved one Martin?"

"You are asking me?" Martin was feeling a bit awkward then, since being a rather private individual, seldom did he get asked a personal question such as that, not to mention from a stranger. He nonetheless answered her, "As a matter of fact — yes. Yes I have."

That sort of regained her attention. "Who?" she continued.

"Both of my parents. They died when I was little."

"How little?"

"I was ten or maybe eleven years old at the time. I don't remember exactly."

"So — back when people said all sorts of things to try to make you feel better, did it ever work, or did you feel like hell either way?"

He gave what she said genuine thought. "No miss. It didn't do anything for me. I honestly didn't think there was anything anyone could say to take away my grief."

"Good… good…" Allison mumbled back and then sat quietly for another few seconds, not looking at anything in particular. Even though her calm countenance continued to give little away, Martin never took his eyes off her this whole time, at least not till she looked right at him in the next instant, telling him sharply, "Then — just cut the bullshit with me. Ask what you came here to ask, and then leave me the hell alone."

Without further ado, he got to work. He took out a small voice recorder from his back pocket, set it down on the overbed table and pressed the "REC" button.

"September 28th, 2009, 7:08 p.m. I am with Allison Skala at Lemley County Hospital. Mrs. Skala, did you see your husband get shot?"

She nodded and took a deep breath.

"Can you describe to me how that came about?"

"I was coming down from the porch to get to him. All of a sudden, I heard a loud bang. I stopped where I was and just looked at him. The next thing I knew, his face hit the ground. Then… then I saw Ed coming from around the corner. He approached Dan's body holding a gun in his hand… and… and then he finished him."

"Do you remember how many times he fired at him, and where?"

She took another deep breath. "Once at his back when he was standing, and then two more times at the back of his head after he had collapsed."

"Did you call for help?"

"If you count screaming calling for help."

"Did you at any point struggle with the suspect?"

"You mean with Ed?"

"Yes."

"Did you catch him?"

Martin nodded at her, and thus, she returned to his question. "Yes. I did. But I don't remember exactly how it happened. I just know that he came at me and grabbed me from behind as I was trying to run for the door. He took me down easily and wanted me quiet but I wouldn't obey. So, he hit me in the head with his gun."

"Can I assume that you know this man personally?"

"He is one of my closest friends. Well, was."

"And Dan?"

"What about him?"

"Can I also assume that he knew him?"

"Yes... and no. The guys had never been formally introduced."

"So, they had never officially met?"

"From what I know, that's right."

"Are you saying, the only reason they knew of each other, was through what you told them?"

"I guess you can say that... What is your point?"

"I'm only trying to understand your situation. Do you have any idea as to why he wanted to kill your husband?"

Suddenly, Allison lost her courage to continue as that question, specifically, unnerved her. Of course, she had her suspicion of why Ed did what he did. Thinking about it now after the fact, she could hardly own up to the possibility that she might be the trigger to his barbaric action. She was definitely aware that saying all those cold-hearted things to him last night would ultimately spin him deeper into a negative spiral, but she did not care at the time. Because, in her opinion, even if Ed knew his faithful devotion could only ever result in her rejection, she still never would have expected him — a good, honorable man in her eyes — to have the guts to actually murder somebody, and she certainly would not have predicted such an apocalyptic end to their nothing but toxic love triangle.

"Are you alright?" Martin interrupted her thoughts temporarily but failed to get her to open up again. Seeing this was leading nowhere, he decided to wrap up the interview. "Thank you for your time Mrs. Skala," he told her, retrieving the recorder. "Should I need more of your assistance, I'll be in touch. In the mean time, I'll leave you to rest."

Allison did not respond, nor look up at him. It was as if she had just shut herself down completely and altogether withdrawn from the world around her along with her palpable sense of loss. There was no amount of sympathetic words that could erase that emptiness within her — the newly bereaved. Martin understood that, therefore offered none and left her be.

42

'*H*AVE YOU EVER *lost a loved one Martin?'*
    '*As a matter of fact — yes. Yes I have.'*
    '*Who?'*
'*Both of my parents. They died when I was little...'*
The conversation with Allison, a brief part of it, took Martin back to a depressing past; a past about a tragedy that took place a long time ago that every now and again, raised only ghastly memories to his mind. They were memories of a vivid nightmare, so to speak, which had been relentlessly hovering above his head since he left Room 208, the elevator, and then the hospital. First thing back inside his car, he lit a cigarette and let it dangle between his lips as he steered out of there. On his way returning to the police station, he decided to call someone.

"Hello. This is Levi... Hello?"

"Are you looking at this moon?"

"The moon? Let me get to a window... ah, there it is, a beautiful crescent."

"Do you think they are having a good time up there?"

"In heaven you mean. And who?"

"My parents."

Levi paused for a second. "Marty."

"Yeah?"

"You don't even know who your father is. And besides, I thought you were a committed atheist."

Martin said nothing for a moment, and so, Levi continued, "But, possibly. Perhaps they met and made up in heaven."

"Heh. There's a nice story if I ever heard one."

"Well, you asked for it."

"But you are probably right."

"Oh yeah?"

"He's probably suffering the fire and brimstone of hell while she looks down at him, all smiles."

"For someone who doesn't believe in the existence of any gods, you sure seem to know an awful lot about how the afterlife works —"

"Hehe."

"In any case, that's not at all close to what I said or meant. Did something happen at work?"

"Just a few homicides happened here and there. Nothing too out of the ordinary."

"You are not much of a funny man Marty."

"Hehe."

"Just come off it already and tell me what's bugging you so much that you've decided to call me to talk about the moon."

Just then stopping at a traffic light, Martin took a long drag on his cigarette before replying, slightly uneasily, "I was just feeling a little... moody. That's all."

"Moody? Ha! Now that's funny to hear you talk about your vulnerability out loud you big tough guy."

He was not joking after all, and Levi quickly sensed it.

"Just remember, if it wasn't for what happened, you wouldn't have become who you are today. You wouldn't have joined the law enforcement and been in it for eighteen years, even though nothing so far has come easy for you. It's life. Shit happens. The best thing you can do is to learn from it and move on..."

Martin had heard those same heartening words being said to him numerous times from Levi and also his former therapist — the only two people in whom he confided. Much as he was indebted to their verbal consolation that had been providing him a sense of perspective for all these years, that pain that he once felt, ultimately, was something no one else other than himself could fully comprehend.

The night the tragedy happened, Martin was just a ten-year-old boy. Together with his brother and their mom, they were living at a trailer home belonging to her then boyfriend, Gary, who was an ex-pimp of hers with a serious gambling addiction among other abuses. For days before the murder, a local bookie sent by the mafia had been dropping in to try by threat to collect money Gary had borrowed from them and lost. Martin recalled just one of the mornings, word-for-word what that man warned Gary after giving him a proper beating:

'... I'm just gonna need a bit more time to gather the money.'

'You know Gar. Most people who owe us as much as you do would have lost all of their fingers by now.'

'I... I swear you will have it soon.'

'You swear?'

'Ye-yesss.'

'Humph. You know who I hate more than useless dirtbags like you? Liars. Don't swear it unless you really mean it.'

'I... I do mean it.'

'Then go get the money! I don't care what you do, but I will give you till midnight to come up with the fifty grand. If you still don't have it by then, I can assure you, there will be hell to pay...'

Later that afternoon, Gary left home for the store but never returned again. That night, shortly after the clock stuck twelve, two thugs showed up at the trailer intending to cause some serious violence. Martin happened to be asleep in his bedroom when the terror arrived, until the frantic scream of his mother coming from the next room over woke him. Through the thin wall, he heard her cry and beg desperately for mercy to the men who, only in return, held her up to ridicule:

'Please... I really don't know where he is... please... just let me go...'

'Please please just let me go! HAHAHA! Can you believe this bitch? Ach-tooey! You disgusting whore!'

They dragged her out to the living room as the humiliation continued for minutes longer. A gunshot was then fired and that marked the last time Martin would hear her voice. What followed was the chanting and groaning of the two sick criminals. Curious as to what they were doing to his mother after having murdered her in cold blood, Martin risked sneaking behind his bedroom door and taking a peek through its hinged gap. To this day, he had not been able to tell anyone the horror of what he witnessed with his own eyes at that moment — he saw one of the men sitting on the floor, fondling her nude, limp torso while the other had her legs spread far apart, performing sexual intercourse to her corpse stimulated by his own villainous, masturbatory fantasy.

Martin was beyond mad; so would anyone in sound mind be. He wanted so badly to rush out there to her side and kill those two heartless monsters in her name. His wishful thinking consequently led him to his escape. Using the headboard as a stepping-stone, he moved quickly to climb out of the tiny window above his bed. As luck would have it, he got out safely without getting noticed. Putting all faith in the justice system, he ran across to the next-door trailer to inform the neighbor of what happened and had her called 911. Sadly, when the police arrived, the two murderers had already left and the search was called off a couple hours later despite never having caught them.

The remembrance of his mother's brutal death that forever scarred him, ironically, came to be his initial calling to become a policeman. Ever since he was one, work had been taking priority over all else happening in his life. Though still, he could allow himself an exception or two on occasion.

"Marty?" called Levi, having not heard him for a while.

"I'm here. We should get together sometime soon."

"That's more of your problem isn't it? I work the same hours pretty much every day."

"How about now?" he purposed.

"Now? You sure?"

"Meet me at my place in half an hour."

43

I N FRONT OF her parents, Allison worked to put on a brave face; soon as they took off for the night, she was left by herself in her hospital room, brooding over her own cruel twist of fate, self-suffocating in the process with the never ending thoughts of the would-have-been and never-will-be. She wanted to scream but had no strength. She was tired yet could not sleep. Staring blindly at the vacant bed next to hers, she laid there zoned out listening to the muffled pop songs being played from the adjoining ward. Instead of bringing cheer, the high-spirited music brought tears to her eyes. Like a prisoner doing time in her cell, minutes now felt like hours and hours like days. Just when she began doubting survival of the night alone, Adrian dropped by.

"Is this a bad time?"

Having heard him, Allison looked up at the doorway where his head was sticking out at an angle, instantly overwhelmed. When he approached to offer her a hug, her deadpan expression thawed naturally and she broke down crying in his arms. Her body trembled like it had never done before. Her voice hysterical as she vented to him her despair in great gasping sobs — something about not wanting to live anymore and a lot of self-blaming, foolish talk. Even her favorite person in the world was having a hard time reasoning with her.

"... I'm fin-finished. Now that Dan is gone, my life is o-over for good."

"Shh. Everything will turn out okay."

"No it won't. It's too late... ev-everything is. I did everything... everything I could to save my marriage, I really did, but in the end... I only made things worse."

"Had I known sooner this Ed Ramsey was going to be a problem, I would have taken care of him for you myself. But there's really nothing you can do about it now. What's done is done. I'm still proud that you did your best —"

"But I'm not!! Not one bit."

"I'm just saying, what happened to Daniel was entirely out of your control."

"That's not true. I killed him... I practically killed him. He died all because of me..."

Just then, Adrian grabbed her by the arms and pulled her away from himself in a somewhat forceful manner, looking her straight in the eyes, his face serious, almost a bit mad. "Stop," he told her firmly, "Stop this nonsense right now. You can't bring him back no matter what you do, and damning yourself is just plain pathetic —"

He's right. I am pathetic.

"It won't make things any easier for you, do you get it?"

He's right.

Her body felt like sand that would not maintain itself, and her limbs attached to it useless. She could no longer manage to hold herself up if it was not for her brother being there to keep her going. Grief and sorrow were just free flowing down her cheeks in the form of unending streams of tears. She let out a short mournful squall and then another till he cradled her close again, soothing her with gentle rubbing up and down her back. She had to mentally make herself not think about Daniel for a while, or at least try for as long as she could help it, and just focus on the warmth of Adrian's chest where she buried her face to weep and weep and weep some more.

The moment she calmed down, Adrian let go slowly, allowing her to sit up in bed on her own reclaimed strength.

"Feeling better?" he asked her, sitting down on a chair at her bedside.

"I don't know... How did you find out I'm here?"

"Dad contacted me."

"How did he?"

"You know he always gets what he needs through his army of servants."

"I see," she muttered, almost losing her voice due to all the crying.

"Would you like some water?" Right then, his eyes rolled down her needled arm and he sighed. "I see they've gotten you all hooked up. You are stronger than that Allie. You are a fighter."

"I've always wished to be half as strong as you, but in reality, I'm nowhere close. Deep down inside me I feel sick. So sick that I'm afraid I'm slowly losing it."

"Stop being so negative —"

"No. I mean it." Suddenly, she looked at him nervously, wanting to ask him something badly yet ever so slightly hesitating. "Adrian?"

"Yeah?"

"You would never lie to me, would you?"

"Of course not."

"So, if I were to ask you something, anything, you would tell me the truth."

"If I know the answer, I don't see why not. Why?"

"I was just wondering — what exactly was in that black box?"

"What black box?"

"You know... the one that you hid underneath the bed, the one you told me to get rid of a while ago."

"Oh... that. That's nothing you need to worry about."

"Right. Everyone's trying to keep their secrets from me, now you too."

"It's not like that."

"Then why can't you be honest with me?"

"I'm *always* honest with you. Why are you asking me this now anyway? It's so out of the blue."

"I eh... I'm just curious."

"Just curious? Riiight. You know Allie, if you want someone to open up to you, you can't keep a closed-door yourself. Although, I would almost rather tell you anything else but that."

"Alright. Then tell me, did you kill Megan?"

Adrian literally froze on the spot for a couple seconds. "What did you say?"

One moment Allison realized what she had said impulsively, the next she wished to take it back. "Forget it."

"No! You tell me and you tell me good."

"It was a stupid thing I said, and I really don't feel like getting to the bottom of why I said it. Okay?"

"No, that's not it." Her breaking away from his distrustful gaze scarcely fooled him before he started to question her back. "You've figured it out for a while, haven't you?" She was not responding to him then and pretty soon, a sly grin began to form on his mouth, stretching with excitement.

"How long have you remembered?" he urged on.

"I really would rather not talk about her."

"Allie! This is a time where I need you to be completely upfront with me. Again — how long have you remembered?"

"I don't know..."

"Oh yes you do know!" he persisted, jumping off his chair to grab at her. "Think. I need you to think hard."

"I just… they just all sort of flashed before me right when Dan got shot."

"What flashed before you?"

"Images."

"What images? Tell me exactly."

"This is crazy —"

"I SAID TELL ME!"

"There… there were images of you, and her… struggling in a tub…"

"Uh-huh, uh-huh. And?"

"And… I'm not sure."

"Come on, spit it out!"

"And… and then later… she was dead and there was blood spilled everywhere —"

"BLINGO!" he yelled out in sudden triumph, throwing his fists up in the air as if winning an immense bet. "I knew it would all come back to you one of these days! Tell that to Dad, he might just have another heart attack."

"I don't get it. What's there to be happy about?"

His grin just grew wider. All the while looking so very proud, he blurted out to her, "I killed her Allie — I murdered that *bitch* for you."

"No. She killed herself."

"Did she? HA! You are only contradicting yourself sister."

"I can't always tell what is real and what isn't anymore. I feel… I feel like I'm about to go crazy —"

"Then, let me assure you, what you saw in your head is as real as you and me. And you most certainly aren't going crazy."

"That still doesn't explain much. If what you say is true, I couldn't possibly recall all that detail so vividly without actually being there, seeing the incident firsthand… I mean…"

He saw her confused face start to connect the dots. "I think you've just answered your own question."

"I… I don't understand."

"I think you understand perfectly. It's just a matter of whether or not you want to believe what you already knew all along."

"I couldn't have been there… no."

"Stop doubting yourself so much Allie. All that money our desperate mother spent to have you brainwashed is for this one reason only — she wanted you to forget all about it."

"This doesn't make any sense."

"Give yourself a little more time, everything will come together nicely, and when the right moment arrives, tell the cops the truth and everything leading up to it."

"How is doing that going to help with anything?"

"It's your only way to salvation I'm afraid," he told her in definite terms and moved to hop onto the empty bed to lie down. "Don't you get it? Your insomnia, your physical aches and mental distress, where do you think they came from? Your conscience is slowly eating you up inside and out don't you see? The good thing is, all that can go away, and you will start afresh just as soon as you let the past go."

"You want me to turn you in?" Allison asked to make sure she understood him.

"For your own sake, yes."

"It's beyond ridiculous what you are asking of me you know that? I won't do it."

"But you will, eventually."

"How can you say that about me?"

"Because I know you Allie. I've said it many times before and I will say it again — you are not a very good liar. They will find out you remember everything soon enough and then pressure you into confessing."

"Who are they?"

"Who do you think? Mother for sure will, since she's done it before so don't act surprised. And Carter. Even Dad has to give that manipulative con man the time of day. It's just sickening."

"No."

"No?"

"It's different this time. It has to be. Mom hated that woman."

"That still doesn't change how bad she wants me cut out of your life. Any chance she gets to take you away from me, believe me, she will take it. Why do you think she turned to Carter for help in the first place?"

"Maybe… maybe she was trying to protect the both of us."

"Are you listening to yourself?" Getting up from the bed, he slid to sit at its edge and continued to speak without a hint of equivocation. "I have no doubt she did what she did to protect you. As for me, pah! Don't make me laugh. She had long deserted me like I did her. As soon as she finds out their pitiful tactic failed, I can guarantee she will not hesitate to mess with you again. And it won't take long for them to come to conclude that the only way to save you is to make you turn against me. While I couldn't agree more, I only want you to make use of the opportunity — do it while you are in control of the situation and not forced."

"How can you say it so lightly?"

"Say what so lightly?"

"You want me to turn you in! Have you seriously thought about the consequences of that? It's madness!"

"Haha! Have I? I think you've underestimated me my dear sweet Allie. You should know by now that like Dad, I also know my way around the system. Otherwise, how else would I still be here talking to you? That's proof in itself that everything turned out okay the last time like I said it would."

"I had that dream again... The dream where you called me from the police station and then I lost contact with you forever."

"That's not going to happen."

"You don't know that! And besides, how do you know for certain this will help me? I feel nauseous just thinking about it."

"You are right. I don't. But I'm hopeful, and so should you. Don't you think once the secret's out, you will be able to rest better? Perhaps not at first, but you will, eventually."

Allison might never admit it, but inwardly, a part of her secretly agreed with him; although, when it really came down to it, this was still nothing but a choice between the lesser of two evils. Exactly how to arrive at that decision, she did not know, nor did she dare put any thought into it at this point.

"You have to trust me. Things might seem rough right now but it's only temporary. When this is all over, everything will go back to normal again you'll see, and it's going to be beautiful..."

DAY 24 | SEPT 29 TUESDAY

44

ARLY MORNING BEFORE work, Martin set out to mail off a care package he had put together thoughtfully the night before. Its recipient was his brother, Sean, an inmate serving life without parole at the Federal Medical Prison down in Narthwich, Minnesota. Every now and again he did this as sort of a way to keep in contact with him, though it was not to be deceived into thinking otherwise, given his occupation on which he greatly prided himself, that he was most discomfited by their association, and to say nothing of having to share the same face with a serial killer.

Although twins they might be, the brothers had never been the typical image of twins with an exceptional bond. Born with a dreadful stammer, growing up, Sean was a quiet, timid child burdened by a mild learning disability. As he fell victim to teases and mockeries sparked off by mean peers, Martin, despite being normal and able, was not exempt from them due to their likeness of appearance. Since their mother's precarious lifestyle left them neglected often, they commonly needed to fight their own battles. It was not easy to steer clear of gangs and that culture wherever the family came to settle in but Martin did, thankfully, contrary to Sean, who was not so righteously driven after countless incidents of harassment that belittled him.

At ten years old, Sean began to hang around with the street delinquents, following them doing god-knows-what, sometimes for days on end. Including the night of their mother's murder, he was nowhere to be seen. The coming morning, Martin saw her for the last time at a morgue down in the basement of a local hospital, alone. Prior to being placed into foster care, he even went on to scour the streets for Sean but never found him. The next couple of years that followed, they had completely lost touch. Martin became a police officer shortly after completing college and then a SWAT officer. It was not till about ten years ago, when he saw a face resemble his own on the front page of every local newspaper that he started to wonder his whereabouts again.

The media at the time was heavily covering two criminals at large — one of which being Sean — for planting homemade pipe bombs into random daycare centers and killing five children already from two separate bombing incidents. After having caused a statewide panic, their arrests came two days later. In the wake of his brother's infamous trial, Martin braced himself for ignominy while struggling whether to reach out for connection. Eventually, he wrote Sean a short letter in the first year of his imprisonment. Even though theirs had always been a distant relationship, behind that shiny police badge and his job title, he could not help care for his only blood-bound family.

This unchanging fact nonetheless did not lessen his conscious shame regarding what Sean had done. For that reason, all these years he had been avoiding a visit upon invitation after invitation, or talking about him for that matter. Such was also why he intended to keep discreet his task at the post office.

"Ma'tin! Our first customer! I am not surprised," exclaimed Yuen, the postal clerk, directly from his service counter.

"Hi Yuen. How's it going?"

"Goo' goo'! You always right on time when we open. Another parcel to Narthwich I suppose?"

Martin gave him a nod, handing over the package. Just then, a few other early birds also came in and queued up behind him.

"How is that brother of yours doin'?"

"He's... fine."

"Is he getting out any time soon?"

He took a subtle glance over his shoulder before replying, "Not a chance."

"Oh really? That's too bad. In any case, ten years you've been doin' this, he's very lucky to have you as a brother."

He smiled back, pulling down the brim of his baseball cap so as to steer clear of attention.

Meanwhile, Yuen just rambled on. "If it were my brother instead, ooohh I would have cut him out of my life so fast. *Woosh!* Don't even talk to me about fo'giveness. Did I ever tell you? One time when we were little, my younger brother stole something from convenience store, a chocolate bar of some sort I believe it was, anyway, I don't talk to him for weeks after that —"

"Yuen —"

"And then there's this other time. We were just little toddlers, babies —"

"Yuen... Yuen!"

"Ah, yes?"

"Ahem. I'm sorry to interrupt you, but can we actually be quite quick? I need to head to work straight after this."

"Oh sure, sure. The usual way?"

"Please."

"You the boss!" Yuen thus stamped and processed the package accordingly. "That comes to... twelve dollar even."

Quickly, Martin paid up.

As he was walking away, Yuen called out after him, "Take it easy Ma'tin! See you again real soon!"

He never turned his head.

His obsessive disquiet was only markedly adjusted when he recouped inner peace back at work. As always, his busy daily routine provided him comfort like no other, and the many case files piling up on his desk were just the distraction he needed to keep from wandering off to the shadows of his own past. While he organized them, John just so brought over the physical evidence collected last night from the crime scene of Daniel's murder. "The son of a bitch still won't talk," he spoke of Ed, having returned from questioning him. "Strangely enough, I happen to recognize him."

"Oh yeah?" responded Martin.

So, the know-it-all that John was, went to a great extent to explain how basing on their short encounter yesterday, he *knew* something fishy was going on even prior to the shooting. Although seemingly listening, Martin was in fact more curious about the evidence being laid out before him. At first glance, the bloodstained envelope caught his eyes. He removed it carefully from the evidence bag, opened it and took out the small stack of papers from inside. As it turned out, it was a divorce petition. He causally flipped through the pages till John finished his story and processed to ask about the hospital visit with Allison.

"It went okay. She looked pretty downhearted as you can imagine, but nonetheless was able to recount the shooting in great detail. Here's Daniel's autopsy report."

John looked over the written notes and remarked, "That bastard wanted him dead."

"It is obvious, but why?"

"Have we ruled out provocation?"

"Not yet. The tricky part is, the two men hardly knew each other."

"Is that what she told you?"

Martin nodded. "She also claimed the suspect was a friend."

"A friend? Humph. What the hell kind of a friend is that?"

"She should have no reason to lie about that."

"Honesty though, considering the violent nature of the crime, you would think there was a long-standing feud of some sort between those two."

"You are right. She could be not telling me the whole story."

"There was an unread text message found on Ramsey's phone, apparently sent from her briefly before the murder took place."

"What does it say?"

"'I might be running a little late.' Do you think she might somehow be behind it?"

"Unlikely, unless she's an exceptional actor, I believe very much she loved her husband. In order for your point to be valid it would also have to go against the neighbor's words. Her head injury too argues for it to be a contradiction."

"I took a look into Ramsey's internal records earlier. It's all clear, no mention of previous psychopathic behavior. He however, was recently granted a week off, starting today in fact."

Once more, Martin revisited the evidence. This time, he drew his attention to the small bottle containing some form of liquid. He picked it up and looked at its label closely, enunciating, "Chloroform."

"We found that inside the glove box of his car."

Suddenly, a theory occurred to him. "He was planning to run away with her," he muttered, mainly to himself, as he went over and expanded his mental map.

"There indeed was a packed suitcase in the trunk. Are you by any chance suggesting a love affair?"

"Either that or — even more likely perhaps — just an old lover who was unwilling to let things go after having been exploited in a selfish manner. Presumably Ed Ramsey was her ex..."

"Exploited?"

"... That would certainly explain her struggle to free herself from him. As for the text message, she was obviously referring to a meeting, or better yet, a dishonest scheme if you will, that he somehow managed to trick her into, assuming she knew nothing about it. His entire goal was to get her as far away from the possible crime scene that he perceived might end up being her house... this is good."

"Hold on a minute. How did this speculation come about?"

Just then, he looked up at John, half still brainstorming as he showed him the divorce papers of which he had uncovered moments ago. "This. If Ed Ramsey is in fact one of her best friends like she said so herself, it's very likely that she had been turning to him for sympathy in terms of her marital problems. And, if this so-called friendship turns out to be more of a codependent relationship, doing so would mean exploiting him for her own benefit while he was counting on getting back together with her. Whether it was done knowingly or unknowingly that doesn't matter, what matters is that he realized, or was made aware just recently, that he could get nothing more out of this dead-end relationship... yes, that's right. This is good John."

"So it seems... but everything you are saying could only pan out if they are really more than friends."

"Tell me. How many friends of yours from college were female?"

"That's thirty years ago but let me think... there was Katie, Jen —"

"Any of them you considered best friends?"

"Nah. Nope."

"Any of them you weren't attracted to?"

"They were attractive girls, but I wouldn't say I was attracted to them like that —"

"But if any of them were to offer you sex, you wouldn't say no?"

"Prrrobably... not. This just makes me sound like an asshole. What is your point kid?"

"My point is, it's very unlikely for a man and a woman to stay friends without both parties making an effort, especially when one of them is married. I'm sure you haven't talked to any of those girls and will not again unless your marriage is about over."

"I see what you mean. But still, how sure are you about all of this?"

"That depends on how much of an addict he is to Allison Skala. Even if he's like how a drug addict is dependent on heroin, it will still depend on the level of which she had been psychologically dependent on him to give him the motivation to kill."

John nodded in understanding, taking in his opinion seriously. "Did she mention a recent fight or argument she had with Ramsey when you met with her? That might bring us some more clues."

"I didn't have a chance to go far with my questions, but I wouldn't be surprised if there was," said Martin, standing up from his chair immediately. "In that case, I'm going to go gather some more facts." As he swung around his blazer to put it on, John went swiftly to make a photocopy of the divorce documents to keep for later use, and then handed the original back to Martin.

"In the meantime, I'll count on you to deal with Ed Ramsey. Get him to talk, one way or another."

"I'm on it."

The two got to work.

45

T HE SKALAS' RESIDENCE was a three-story, single family home situated on a knoll on King's Lane, with a sizable, fenced backyard in line with other similar lakeside properties. Nobody would have expected crimes of any sort to happen here — such a lovely, serene corner of an upper-middle-class neighborhood — and certainly not of the magnitude of a murder. The police tape surrounding the house's private driveway however, did nothing to conceal the fact that just yesterday afternoon, a homicide had happened at this very spot, where there were still precise bloodstains on the ground in front of the garage.

Martin parked his car near its sidewalk, got out and marched on towards the front porch. Self-convinced that Allison had already been discharged from the hospital for her relatively minor injury, he headed straight here despite knowing that most people under her circumstance would have found temporary accommodations elsewhere. His instinct was correct. After an initial ring of the doorbell, almost simultaneously, the door opened and out came Allison wearing a welcoming smile in disguise. She had on a loose-fitting, long-sleeve, floral tunic dress, which added a pinch of color to her pale, makeup-free face. Her forehead was no longer bandaged given that the swelling had somewhat, if not totally, subsided.

"Hello Detective Blake. Didn't expect to see you again so soon." Her attitude also appeared much improved from their last meeting. Martin had noticed it right when she started talking, and if she was still in mourning for her husband, she hid it well.

"Good morning Mrs. Skala. Heading out?"

"Actually, I just got back from the hospital not long ago."

"May I come in for a conversation?"

"Of course. Come on in."

Soon as Martin came through the door, she closed it gently behind them, guiding him into the living room. "Do you like tea Martin? Eh… I mean Mr. Blake… or may I call you by your first name?"

"I'm more of a coffee person," he replied. "And yes, just call me Martin."

"I can make some coffee too. I'm assuming regular's okay?"

"No need to bother Mrs. Skala, really —"

"But I insist. Don't worry. I won't take too long. In the meantime, please make yourself at home."

The moment she hurried off, he yelled out after her, "Black!" consequently causing her to stop her pace in the middle of it and turn her head.

"Pardon?"

"This is kinda embarrassing… but I'm lactose intolerant. So I can only drink coffee black."

All the while still having on that awkward, intentionally friendly smile, she replied, "Right… I'll be right back," and then moved right along.

Not known to Martin, her hastiness was wholly attributed to Adrian, who had been hanging in the kitchen this entire time, spying on them through a tiny gap between the blinds. He had not left Allison since last night, partially helping her piece back together the bits and parts of her once lost memory and a lot of nagging her about confessing the truth. While she prepared the coffee, he seized the opportunity to pressure her some more.

"So the cop is here. What are you waiting for?"

"Keep it down will you? He doesn't know you are here. I have enough going through my mind at the moment so please leave. And take your friend with you," she rasped, shifting her eyes onto Justin sitting on the opposite end of the countertop. With a big smile on, he had been watching them argue all morning like watching a real-life soap opera.

"Then just go out there and tell him everything. You can solve the problem right here and now," Adrian insisted.

"It's that easy huh?"

"Yes! Nothing complicated about it."

"For the last time, I'm not going to turn you in!"

"Hehe. She's a sweet one bro, let me tell you that," Justin remarked, chiming in occasionally to their drama.

Adrian turned back to look at Allison. "Why not?" he asked her, solemnly.

"How can you even ask such a question?"

"I just want you to be okay that's all. There's no one else in the world that I care for more than you, and it pains me... it pains me every time to see you hurt."

In an attempt to settle his worry once and for all, Allison looked him straight in the face, seriously assuring him, "I'm fine. Okay? I've had a good cry and now I'm fine. I just need you to do me a favor, leave before the detective finds out you are here —"

"How do you explain the broken mirror in the bathroom then?" interjected Justin, putting her in a fix.

"What are you talking about?" she asked him back, pretending to be oblivious.

"I was just in there. You thought you could just wrap up the broken pieces in toilet paper and throw them into the trash so your brother won't notice what you've been doing to yourself."

"Is this true?" Adrian inquired forthright, looking concerned.

Allison's face flared upon being called out. While trying to hold herself together, she sneered back at him in rationalization of her own destructive behavior. "What's the big deal? I'm only doing what you'd have done in my situation. I've watched you do that to yourself since I was six years old."

"You are going down the wrong path Allie. Hurting yourself does not help you in the least."

"And you are the one to judge?!"

"I know this stuff better than anyone wouldn't you say?"

Her eyes were mad at first, and then, they softened. "Just... just leave me alone."

Adrian only shook his head, not about to drop the subject. "Please Allie. Think about this sensibly. It's not like I'm asking you to lie. Everyone has to come to terms with the truth in the end. That's just —"

"The way of life? I know. You've been telling me. But have you ever stopped to think for a second what I'm going to do if you leave me too?"

"She's got a point," Justin again butted in with his thoughts, but it was a big mistake this time.

"Like I said before, you will start your life afresh once you let out the secret. This big, fat burden you've been carrying on your shoulders is the origin of everything that you've felt wrong about lately —"

"Now, that's not necessarily true —"

"SHUT THE FUCK UP JUSTIN! Will you just let me talk?!" Adrian looked daggers at his friend for a moment before returning to Allison to continue where he left off. "Yes. I might not be around for a while, but it's not forever, and that's what's important."

"How can you guarantee that? How do I know for sure you will be okay like you say you will?"

"Is that what you're worried about?" He understood her demand. What Allison was looking for was a well-thought-out plan of escape, which he simply could not give her. For his scheme had always been taking things as they came, all that he could offer at the moment was really just his half-witted confidence. "You just have to trust me on this."

"You say that every time. One of these days, something bad is going to happen to you and I will be the last one to find out about it."

"It's not going to be like that."

"Ahem —"

"Right."

"I can't believe you have so little faith in me."

"Faith? This hardly has anything to do with faith —"

"Ahem!" All at once, the two heated siblings looked over at Justin. "Allow me to propose an idea," he then said.

"What?" Adrian asked.

"I know this guy from Moscow who lives downtown. I've been dealing business with him for years, and I know he's helped people get out of the States a couple times. If you want, I can try to work something out with him. He's pretty easygoing as far as I know and he works fast. That way, you can lay low for a while until this whole thing blows over."

"Are you talking about Anton Harris?"

"That's the name he goes by, yes. I think his real last name is Savinkov or something fancy like that."

"I know that guy. I used to deal with him too."

"There you go."

"See Allie? This will work out."

"But... how will I ever see you again?"

"Of course there are always ways silly. So long as you'd allow me, I'll *always, always* find my way back to you."

Allison was not entirely for the idea however, thus taking a step back as he reached out to caress her cheek. "No... I can't let you risk it all for me."

"So how much longer do you plan on keeping this to yourself?"

"I don't know... and I don't care."

"Do you really want to wait till Mother finds out and then forces you to turn your back on me? Why you would ever let her get her way is beyond me."

"What's the difference? You are forcing me now aren't you?"

Adrian went quiet for a second, his face going hard and bitter. "So, you are just going to let her win?"

Allison did not answer him and just wiped her eyes with the back of her hand, sticking to the original plan that was to get them out of there as soon as possible.

"Please... just go, the both of you. I really can't take any-more distractions." As she returned to brewing the coffee, Justin too slipped down from the countertop, preparing to sneak out. Her brother on the other hand, had enough of her dancing around the issue and eventually, felt pro-pelled to take the last resort.

"Okay... okay then. I will just go and confess to the cop myself," he declared recklessly, straight away picking up his feet. In turn, she shouted after him in a brisk whis-per, "STOP!" standing in his way just before he could step out into the foyer. Quickly, she took a peek around the doorframe at Martin to ensure he had not heard her sud-den outcry and thereupon, resumed to speak to Adrian in a harsh, warning tone. "Don't be foolish!"

"I'd rather turn myself in than let her play you like that!"

"This is not a joke! Listen to me, they can lock you up for life for a murder!"

"You think I don't know that? It was never a joke to begin with. I killed that bitch for your sake, same with what I'm going to do for you now..." he countered back as though it all made perfect sense, shoving his way out of the room with his pumped-up chest. "Come on, it will all be over in minutes."

"Wait! What makes you think he will believe you?"

"I'll make him. He'd be an idiot to not take me seri-ously."

"No!"

"Get out of my way Allie —"

"Please! WAIT!" she absolutely begged of him.

Finally, he stopped to stare down at her hopeless ex-pression, holding in his sense of victory just that much longer as he knew he was about to get his way.

Allison knew very well her brother's temperament. Even though she felt like nothing but a ball being kicked back and forth between him and their mother, it was be-yond her control. In a moment she closed her eyes and sighed deeply, could not believe what she was about to say herself.

"On one condition — I'll tell him everything myself on one condition."

"Alright. I'm listening."

Temporarily putting aside her devastation, she inquired of him, gravely, "Is it true what you said about this Russian person? He's not just someone you've made up off the top of your head just to make me feel better, is he?"

"No. I mean yes. I do know him."

"Justin?"

"Huh? Oh yes. He's real and all. As a matter of fact I've just spoken to him yesterday, and it won't be difficult for me to get in touch with him again to make some sort of arrangement like we've just discussed."

"And he's reliable?"

"He sure seems that way to me."

"Seems?"

"Where are you going with this Allie?"

Looking Adrian grimly in the face, she replied sternly, "You must go now, and arrange to get out by tonight, can you do that?"

"Is that your bargain?"

"Yes."

Adrian could no longer contain a smirk.

"Promise me, will you? I need to know it's a promise or else I don't know how I can possibly do this —"

When she was least expected, he folded his arms around her and squeezed her in tightly, pledging into her ear, "I promise you, and I swear it." While they locked in embrace, she cried a silent river.

Bearing a dash of irreversible pain, eventually, she let him go. Her heart bled as she watched him and his friend slip out through the back door. Just then, Adrian turned his head to look at her one last time. "Don't forget your promise either." The instant he finished saying it, tears came rolling down her cheeks and once more blurred her vision. The moment she wiped clear her eyes, he was gone, disappeared around the corner taking a part of her with him.

46

URING WHICH TIME the heartrending farewell took place in the kitchen, Martin was browsing through the framed photos of the married couple displayed on top of the fireplace mantel. When finally Allison brought out the coffee wearing her poker face, engulfed by the lovely aroma, he gathered around the center table and settled down into the couch.

"Sorry for the wait. I accidentally poured creamer into the first batch so I had to start over, force of habit, forgive me. I'm so used to mixing everything in for Dan."

"That's okay. You two made quite the good looking couple," commented he casually on the photographs.

"You are too kind Martin. Although, I must admit that we were great together. Certainly we had our ups and downs, but so do all normal couples..."

Bending forward slightly, she stood serving him a hot cup of coffee. As she tilted the pot just enough for the liquid to start pouring, the steam consequently took off and soon dissipated in midair. Right the moment, her sleeve was fleetingly pulled back, revealing a fresh cut wound on her forearm. Martin caught a glimpse of it within the vapor but did not say anything. Acting indifferent, Allison went on to set the pot back down and subtly covered the wound back up.

"Would you like some sugar in it?" she asked him with deceiving ease.

"None will be alright," he replied, studying her the while.

In a state of nervousness, she held steady the cup with both hands and handed it over to him. In return, he thanked her.

"I want to apologize for how I behaved before," she began, rather abruptly, taking a seat on the adjoining section of the couch perpendicular to Martin. "You see I wasn't... I wasn't quite myself yesterday."

He blew on his coffee and then lowered the cup just above his lap. "I very much understand. Grieving can be a long, distressing process."

She smiled mildly, looking down briefly and then back up at him. "I suppose you are here to ask me more questions."

"Yes, unfortunately."

"Well, here I am. So, fire away."

Reaching his one free hand behind him, he took out his voice recorder, set it up to record and then down on the table he put it. "Allow me to be straightforward with you then Mrs. Skala. What were you doing before you walked out and saw your husband get shot in the driveway?"

"I was right here in the living room, just sitting and waiting for him. I wanted to see him before heading off to have dinner with a friend."

"With Ed Ramsey?"

She nodded.

"You mentioned previously that he was a close friend of yours."

"That's right."

"Was he at one point more than just a friend?"

"We used to date back in high school, which was years ago."

"Did you two hang out often since then?"

"No. Only occasionally, and usually with a mutual friend of ours."

"How about recently? Did you see each other in the past week?"

"Yes. Two days ago."

"And — do you perhaps recall getting into a fight or an argument with him?"

"We did have a silly quarrel at our friend's party that night, but it was nothing serious or too out of the ordinary in my point of view."

"Mind if you elaborate on that?"

"Sure. You see, Ed's always been sort of... what's the word... I guess you can say *obsessed* with me, ever since we broke up."

"How did that come about?"

"His obsession?"

"Yes."

"Heh, I'm afraid you'd have to ask him that yourself Martin. I'm just as clueless as you are. But I gotta say, that kind of crazy behavior from him towards me certainly isn't new."

"It sounds to me you are suggesting he was the one who started the argument."

"He did."

"What was it about if you don't mind me asking?"

She let out a deep sigh before answering the question, heavy-heartedly, "He wanted me to leave Dan, and I basically told him no."

"Was it the first time he made such a request?"

"I suppose so. I never paid much attention to it if he did before."

"The party, was Daniel invited?"

"He was."

"But you didn't go with him."

"No. He's not exactly the party type of guy if you know what I mean?"

"Sure. Or maybe — you two had a big fight just before the party, and so you went to it knowing your friend Ed would be there."

Martin blew on his coffee again and this time took a sip at it; meanwhile, he had his eyes hooked on Allison, patiently awaiting her response. While taken aback by his bold speculation that somewhat offended her, she none-theless managed to maintain her poise.

"Why would I do that?" she countered.

"Perhaps to seek comfort from him for your marital problems. After all, he's an eager ex-lover."

She gulped, starting to get defensive. "Are you saying that I intended to cheat on my husband?"

"That's not necessarily what I meant —"

"Then may I know the reasoning behind your theory? I just don't see how you can assume that we had fought before the party based on what I've told you, let alone think that we were going through problems in our mar-riage."

Per her request, Martin thereby set the cup down on a coaster, reached inside his blazer to take out the divorce petition and handed it to her. As she unfolded the papers and looked them over, her eyes immediately puzzled and brows furrowed in confusion, questioning very much its authenticity.

"Where did you get this?"

"Do you remember Daniel carrying a brown envelope in his hand before he was shot?"

"Yeah?"

"That's what was in it."

"I don't believe you."

"It's dated a month ago, at the end of August, which means something had to have spurred him on between then and now that finally pushed him to want to deliver this to you."

"No. This just... this just can't be..."

"It's filed under his name —"

"This just can't be real..."

"— with your name stated as the respondent."

"*Enough!!*" she howled suddenly, throwing the papers onto the table and walking off to the window.

Martin gave her a moment to process the information before continuing. "It seems like you had no idea that this was coming at all. Am I right Mrs. Skala?"

All the while trying hard to quiet down that consternation rattling in her mind, she admitted finally, "We did have a few major issues... but he had not once hinted at the idea of divorce."

"Perhaps something provoked him to come to that decision?"

Tracing her memory back to the Bahamas trip, Allison went on to tell Martin, in short, the far-reaching dispute at the dinner table. "He just wouldn't have it," she spoke of Daniel's reaction to her mother's spiteful remark regarding Megan. "We fought over it again the minute we got home. Honestly, I was quite shocked to see him so angry. He had always been a levelheaded guy. Anyway, my friend Sara called later that afternoon to remind me of her party. I only went to clear my head."

"What exactly did your mom say about Megan?"

"Does it matter?"

"I suppose not."

"She called her a whore."

Martin's eyes widened. "And you agreed with her?"

"It's only the perfect description of her. She slept with Dan while I was on a vacation with friends, and then a couple more times after that."

"How did you find out?"

"He told me. He also didn't cover his tracks very well."

"Perhaps there were traces of him being unfaithful to you this last week?"

"What? What are you getting at?"

"It's just a question."

"I love my husband regardless of his affair with that slut. If you even think for a second that I'm involved in his murder, you are wrong."

"Just answer the question Mrs. Skala."

"My answer is *no*. Okay? Besides — huh — she died, a month ago, committed suicide in her own apartment."

In turn, Martin felt obligated to soften up a little. "I'm sorry to hear that."

But then, "Don't —" she insisted back, breaking out in a sweat of hatred, "don't feel sorry for her. She's the one reason why my marriage fell apart. Everything was just fine before she came into the picture... she... she deserved everything that happened to her... that sleazy *bitch* deserved to die."

A warranted silence washed over them after such a venomous remark erupted out of Allison, an innocent woman by all appearances and most of all a deceived wife. Martin could understand her grudge, and further, her look of evil as it gradually surfaced on the face of an angel. Supposedly, it would be unfair to ask her to feel any sort of empathy for Megan, but be that as it might, he also took caution with her words. For vengeance was only human nature, his experience warned him that sometimes those above suspicion could very well end up being the cause of great wars. Meanwhile, he perceived he must steer the investigation back on track before it went totally off course.

"Let us get back to Ed Ramsey. I've only a few questions left to ask you —"

"No."

"Excuse me?"

Ever since Megan was first mentioned in this so very straining conversation, Allison had started to hear her brother's voice murmuring in the background, pestering her persistently.

Tell him Allie. Only the truth can set you free...

As she held tight to her lie, the deeper she was to get entangled in her own war of nerves and the further she got pulled away from reality.

"Mrs. Skala..."

Just then, she could see Martin's mouth moving but hear no sound coming out of him like he had been muted. The occurrence incidentally made her all the more scared of what was happening to herself. On the contrary, Adrian's voice just grew more intense and louder each time till it was speaking-directly-into-her-ear loud. She was breathing heavier gradually and soon gasping as her body tensed up, exerting relentlessly to pull together her senses.

All that mental effort only led her astray in the end.

"No... NO... STOOOOOOOP!!!!!" she yelled with all her might like that of a person experiencing severe pain, simultaneously dropping to the floor as hyperventilation kicked in. Her hands went, of necessity, for her ears as she sealed tight her eyes hoping to subconsciously shut out all that *noise* in her head.

Concerned, Martin rushed to her. Getting down to her level, he grabbed her gently by the wrists, every bit careful not to startle her. She freaked out anyway at the touch of his hands.

"Easy... easy now," he told her right then, face-to-face and eye-to-eye, holding her with a sense of power and calmness. Slowly, she was letting him remove her stiff, trembling hands from her ears.

"Look at me Allison. Look at me."

And she did, still very much fighting for breath.

"Focus your eyes on me and do as I tell you: take your next breath deep in through your nose —"

GASP *GASP* *GASP* ...

"Hold it in for a second before you exhale —"

GASP *GASP* *GASP* ...

"Come on you can do it. Let's do this together, one step at a time..."

At first, she could scarcely follow his directions.

"You are doing great. Again... steady..."

But his profound encouragement eventually pulled her through.

Afterwards, he assisted her back to the couch, settled her down into it before perching himself on the edge of the center table just opposite her.

"Feeling better?" he asked her sincerely and she nodded. "I'm sorry for grabbing you on your wound earlier."

"What wound?"

"That cut on your wrist."

"Oh... that."

"It shouldn't leave too bad of a scar if you take good care of it from now on."

"I know."

"Does it still hurt?"

"No. I could barely feel it this whole time."

"Just as I thought."

"Huh?"

"Since all pain does pass overtime, all wounds do eventually heal."

Allison looked right at him and smiled. "Thank you for helping me."

"Don't mention it. If my questions were making you uncomfortable, you should have said something."

"No. It's not that."

"What is it then?"

"It's... it's just..."

The truth was hanging on the tip of her tongue ready to be spat out any given second. Just this moment, she looked away deliberately from his virtuous gaze shining brightly at her, feeling partly ashamed of her own flaw to cave in under pressure like her brother had predicted.

Her hesitancy naturally brought about Martin's suspicion. "Is there something you wish to tell me?" prompted he, and as she continued to look away, continued to resist, it made him even more so determined to find out the truth behind those shameful eyes.

"Look at me please."

Timidly, she looked up at him.

"I promise you, whatever it is, I won't judge, and I'll listen."

"But it has nothing to do with my husband's case."

"That's fine."

Soon absorbed in his soft words, Allison felt her vast lie crumbling. Swallowing her last ounce of will to safeguard Adrian, she took a deep breath and blurted out. "Megan didn't kill herself. Even though the police concluded that was the case."

"Are you saying she was murdered?"

She nodded.

Martin paused briefly to think. "And I suppose you have an idea who did it."

She nodded again.

"Who?"

Here we go Adrian. This is what you wanted, no way of turning back now...

"Well?"

You've won... you've officially won...

Martin saw a dark light enter her vision and sparkle ever so much with pride. She was almost going to smile and had she really, he knew it would have been a cruel sneer of sorts completely devoid of joy. It was a vile charge of energy, one filled with hate, sorrow and strife, going through her, one that Allison had been bottling up for far too long that she was ready to finally release off her chest.

47

"IT WAS MY brother, Adrian. He was the one who killed that evil woman, that disgraceful whore..."

As Allison unleashed once again her fury at the thought of Megan, God only knew it was just the beginning of a sad tale. Not taking lightly her allegation, Martin sat and listened eagerly to her telling all...

"A few weeks ago, Dan was scheduled to go on a weeklong business trip to Virginia. His flight wasn't until the afternoon, but he was in a hurry to leave home just after dawn, saying he had an important meeting to attend at the office. I was foolish enough to believe him. Twenty minutes after he had left, I came across his portfolio sitting on the kitchen counter. Thinking that he might have carelessly forgotten it, I tried to reach his cell hoping to catch him before he arrived at work. Since once, twice, and a third time he didn't answer, I tried his work number.

'Good morning, Keith McCoy speaking.'

'Hi Mr. McCoy, is Dan in yet?'

'Nope. Who am I speaking to?'

'It's his wife.'

'Well hello there Mrs. Skala. What can I do you for?'

'Eh... nothing really. Dan left his portfolio at home. I thought he might need it for the eight o' clock meeting,' I told him wholeheartedly, only to find out another one of my husband's deceptions.

'He's not in that meeting I'm afraid.'

'I'm pretty sure he is, since he's leading it.'

'He isn't leading that meeting. I am.'

'There must have been a mistake. He told me it was with the board of directors — perhaps there is another meeting that also starts around eight?'

'Yes, there is. But it has nothing to do with your husband either. He's supposed to be flying down to Virginia later today, but of course I shouldn't have to be the one who tells you that.'

'Yes, I already knew that.'

'He told you that but he didn't tell you he is taking the morning off?'

My heart just sunk.

'*What can Skala possibly be up to? He didn't even tell his own wife about his time off...*' I overheard him tell the others. A man laughed in the background and another man commented sarcastically, '*Probably out fucking some other woman.*'

Had I not had that idea already in my head, I would have normally taken offense by such a cruel, thoughtless remark. I hung up right then. Dan called back in a little while and incidentally, confirmed his lie.

'Hey, just realized you called. What's up?'

'You forgot your portfolio, just thought you needed it for your presentation.'

Sticking to his fabrication, he said to me without the slightest humming and hawing, 'Yeah, I found out after getting to my desk. Thank goodness I have copies on my flash drive so I'm good to go. Actually, the meeting is about to start here, is there anything else?'

I was speechless.

'Allie?'

'Ahem... Yeah. I can't think of anything else.'

'All right, I'll see you when I get back...'

Despite lacking proof, my intuition told me he was with *her* at that very moment. Though I could have said something then, I didn't, and let him go instead.

Soon as I got off the phone, Adrian dropped by. Right away I cried to him and told him everything. He was furious, in a way even more so than I was.

'I'm going to beat that bastard to death!'

'No! Don't.'

'You are not going to let it go this time Allie. I won't let you.'

'What can I do? If I accuse him... I might just lose him... and that's the last thing I want...' I was miserable. I was sobbing so hard that I could barely catch my breath. I didn't think there was a way out of this noxious relationship in which I got my heart so broken until my brother suggested to me:

'Then, confront that woman.'

'Confront her?'

'That's what I said.'

'I... can't.'

At first, I wasn't at all fond of his idea. Had he not continued to pressure me into it, I was just going to — like I had always done — shrug off what had happened and possibly be forever in denial of it. Thank God that he did.

'Allie. Please don't tell me you are going to forget about it. How many more times can you tolerate this before you drive yourself completely mad?'

'Just let me think about it some more —'

'There's nothing more to think about! Each day you let her walk all over you is one more day you have to condone their affair. Is that what you want?'

'Is that what I want? If only this is about what I want.'

'But it is! Ultimately. Only if you'd start to take matters into your own hands.'

'It's not that easy —'

'Stop this useless attitude! Find the strength within yourself and conquer it. That's what you should do. Otherwise, you will end up hating yourself, and if worst comes to worst, losing the one person you care about the most...'

At that moment, Dan was my only thought. The idea of losing him was unthinkable and no doubt getting to me quickly. Eventually —

'Look. Let me come with you. I can be your moral support.'

'Are you sure about this?'

'Of course! I'd do anything for you, anything. Don't you doubt that now.'

I never did doubt him. I only wished things weren't this complicated. I wished when Dan promised me 'happily ever after', he meant it.

I don't remember much about the ride to her apartment building, but I do waiting in the car just outside for a long time. I still wasn't totally convinced of the importance of what I had gone there so rashly to do until the bitter truth hit me — when I saw Dan walk out of the front entrance with my own eyes. I was apoplectic, needless to say, but broken-hearted mainly, whereas Adrian was completely and utterly infuriated. '*That pathetic whore is gonna have to pay!*'

I didn't know then he had a plan all his own, as he had only kept it to himself for the time being, and also because I was too busy worrying about my own part to pay much attention to him. I recall taking long, deep breaths, saying to myself repeatedly, 'Okay, I'm just gonna go and tell her off... I'm just gonna tell her to stay away from my husband...' It all sounded straightforward enough to do, but to actually go through with it was a different story entirely.

Initially, Adrian was to wait in the hall while I talked to her. Though as we got to her apartment unit, things took a radical turn.

In her bathrobe, Megan opened the door and greeted me with a forced smile. 'Hi Allie. What a pleasant surprise.' I was secretly disgusted to see her standing there putting on a friendly act, but nonetheless stood by my prepped line, 'I eh... I was just in the area. I thought I might stop by for a chat...' All the while speaking, I took a subtle glance at my brother bearing a look of disapproval by the door, as if telling me, 'This just won't do sister.'

She couldn't have noticed my disquiet or him being there, and if she did, she didn't say anything about it.

'May I come in?' I asked her.

'Of course,' she said, leading the way, 'I was just going to take a bath. Let me go turn off the faucet and then we can talk.'

One moment I was watching her march into the bathroom, the next, Adrian was running in through the front door after her like a flash. It all happened so fast that I barely had time to react. Following a scream and then a splash, I too went in to find out what was going on.

I couldn't believe my eyes when I saw him have her by the neck, crouching over her petite body lying inside the overflowing bathtub. Her legs sticking out in the back from underneath him swung and kicked the wall ceaselessly as she fought fiercely for her life.

'AHHHAAG... AHHAHAGA... AAAAHHH...'

She tried screaming for help, but her voice broke between times where her head was forced to stay submerged and when it strove to stay afloat. I was almost reluctant to step in to stop him, but I did, eventually.

'ADRIAN! STOP!'

As I tried earnestly to break loose his grip on her, in turn, he pushed me onto the floor with one hand while at all times his other hand remained fastened about her throat, relentless about keeping her under.

'DIE BITCH! DIE!' he yelled at one point, having been totally caught up in his act. She was gradually suffocating, and within moments, her struggle subsided. After the violence had ceased, I crawled my way over to the tub, stuck my head outward just enough to see her still face flowing beneath the water and I gasped.

Just then, Adrian came out of the water and knelt down beside me.

'I have to call an ambulance,' I told him, panicking.

'You will not,' he said, plainly.

'We have to do something!'

'What's there to do? She's dead Allie! DEAD!'

'She's not. Not yet. If help gets here quick enough, she can still be saved...' Swiftly, I took out my cell phone and began to dial. Just before my shaky hands could put in all the numbers, however, he seized it from me.

'You can't do that!'

'We've got to do something to save her!'

'Come on Allie! Stay focused! That woman deserved to die remember?'

'No... That was never the plan.'

'Listen to me —'

'I won't! That was never the plan!!'

'Would you just consider this for a second?! Now that she's out of the picture, Daniel is all yours! No more bullshit drama to deal with, think about that!'

I was desperate, desperate to save my marriage. The way he twisted the matter — making the severity of the murder seem less severe — definitely had a depraved effect on me. Though I was not about to overlook my moral judgment just like that, at least not until he spotted a positive pregnancy test discarded in the sink and showed it to me.

'Look. Look at this.'

She had to have taken it just that morning.

I could deal with Dan's cheats and lies, but not him being the father of her child, never. My incision pretty much went out the window after that.

'What makes you think you can get out of this?' I asked him, and he assured me, 'I have a brilliant plan. All I need is your trust. Let me handle the rest.'

Spurred to action, Adrian stripped her naked and laid her down beneath the water again with her back touching the hard tub floor and her knees bent so as to fit her legs within the tight space. The moment he took out a pair of latex gloves from his jeans pocket and slipped them on, I only knew then he had all along come prepared. Before I was even aware of his next procedure, acting like a pro, he held up her arm half way out of the water and slit her wrist with a knife taken from her kitchen. Straight after that, he flung her arm back into the water, not forgetting to plant the knife in her hand before we packed up and left the apartment..."

Upon the compelling story coming to a close, Allison felt mildly pacified. Though as persuasive as it seemed, Martin remained professionally dubious in order to resist jumping to a conclusion too soon. "So, this happened last month?" he asked her.

"Correct," she answered, and he nodded.

"You do understand what you are telling me?"

"Yes."

"And do you stand by the truth?"

Again, she affirmed him.

"Very well. Now, do you have anything that can back it up?"

"Back it up?"

"Evidence, is what I meant."

Instantly, she got quiet, averting her eyes to avoid looking directly at him.

He sensed her withdrawal and therefore told her honestly, "We are dealing with so many cases at once nowadays, it's impossible to reopen a closed case without supporting evidence, and even then, it's still difficult."

"I understand. But as far as evidence goes, I'm afraid I can't be of help."

"Are you sure about that?"

Their eyes locked once again, steadily on one another for a couple seconds till she was able to break away consequent to a phone call coming through Martin's phone. It was John, calling to inform him of Ed's confession. When told of his guilty plea regarding Daniel's death, Allison was notably apathetic about it rather than pleased. "I guess that's good," she said with little emotion in acknowledgment of the news and just left it at that.

Given that Ed's motive to kill was no longer in question, Martin's job was technically done here. Since their conversation ran dry, out of respect, he finished his cold cup of coffee in one big gulp before standing up. "I should get going." Grabbing his voice recorder and tucking it back inside his pocket, he took out his card from his blazer and gave it to her. "If you decide to change your mind, don't hesitate to give me a call." Allison accepted it without saying anything more and led him on his way.

It almost seemed wrong by Martin the Detective's standard to walk away from curiosity and leave a perfectly good suspense up in the air; owing to his highly demanding schedule however, for now, he knew he must go. Although, much as he strove to suppress his naturally inquiring mind, there was one question he simply could not shove aside.

Just about stepping out of the house, he turned around to ask her, "Where is he?"

"Pardon?"

"You are his sister. You must have an idea."

"I don't know where he is, but even if I do know, what makes you think I'd tell you?"

"Because it's the right thing to do."

"Is it?"

"Your conscience seems to think so. Or why else would you tell me all that?"

"Don't get me wrong Martin. If it were up to me, I never would have told you any of it."

"So, who made you?"

Allison's throat choked up once more as the remembrance of parting with Adrian tumbled over her. "He did... my brother did, all for the benefit of me."

"He made you turn against himself?"

"Right."

"I eh... I'm not understanding you."

"Which part?"

"What you are telling me isn't exactly conventional."

"Humph. You policemen really are a bunch of hypocrites."

Narrowing his eyes, he inquired further. "Whatever do you mean?"

"It's only natural to want to do whatever it takes to protect your loved ones. If you were my brother, you would have been tempted to do the same."

"You mean if I were never a cop."

"No. I mean it would only be easier for you to make that decision since you are part of the law."

"I hope you are not implying the decision to kill."

"But I am. You see, sometimes, some things are just much more important than being morally correct, wouldn't you agree?"

Martin paused for a moment, his thought cautious, zeroing in on a good sense of right and wrong. "I can see the compassion you two share. But with all due respect, if you've been telling the truth, who should have compassion for Megan when she needed it?"

"HA! Talk about compassion for a whore!"

"And respect for a murderer?"

His cutting riposte, incidentally, stripped away the little color on Allison's face, leaving her stone cold. "I have to go. You can see yourself out," she told him rudely, and then turned to walk back inside.

48

BACK AT THE police station, John had set aside on his desk Ed's confession statement, waiting keenly for Martin's return. That might be one case down, but many more to go. Meanwhile, the off-putting stack of pending folders sitting on the other end was a constant motor force telling him just how urgently he needed a cig-arette break.

Like he really needed another excuse to smoke. His nicotine withdrawal had been trying to lure him out for some *fresh* air all morning. With a ciggy in between lips and a lighter in hand, he finally gave up resisting and de-cided to step outside for a bit. He was just heading for the back entrance when Crystal called after him.

He stopped immediately, removing the cigarette from his mouth to greet her. "Hey Ms. Jones. How's it going?"

"Busy. Noth finally put me in charge of this juvie case. Been trying to gather everything for the preliminary hear-ing next week."

The two began walking side by side.

"Good for you. I heard you are adjusting well at his of-fice."

"Did he tell you that?"

"He didn't need to tell me. I know. The last ADA who worked for him quit after six months. The one before that asked for a transfer after eight, couldn't deal with him. He had, for a while, a hard time filling your position until you came along."

"Ah-ha. I must be special then."

"You must be. I've worked with many of you throughout my career and never have I known anyone else who has as impressive of a scholastic background as yours."

"To be fair, most people graduating from Harvard Law School would have opted to work at big law firms."

"Exactly my point. I also heard that you were quite an outspoken leader among your sex back in your academic years."

"Do you mean to say I'm a feminist?"

"Well..."

"I was actually a semi full-time LGBT rights activist for five years after grad school but that's old news. Here I am now and I love my job. I agree that Noth is stern but for good reason, and I never find him difficult to work with."

"Sounds like he's finally gotten it right this time then. Good for him. Anyhow, I'm just gonna get a quick smoke in before my 'boss' comes back."

"Shaw's out?"

"No, Martin, my other boss."

"I see."

"He's always keeping me up to my neck in something. I barely have time to take a deep breath whenever he's around."

She smiled and said, "I actually could take a breather myself too. Mind if I join you?"

"Feel free. It's always nice to have a beautiful woman's company."

"Don't go hitting on me now. You don't know how a feminist like me might interpret it."

"HAHA!"

They headed out where it was sunny, and stood next to the entryway of the building facing the employee parking lot to continue their chat.

"Whew! Finally we are getting some sun. The weather's really been crap lately," John remarked aloud, offering her a cigarette straight from his pack.

She rejected instead of taking it.

"Quitting huh?"

"No. I never did pick that up."

"Oh. I was assuming that you smoke since you were so eager to come out here with me. Mind if I have one?"

"Nope. Go ahead."

Crystal might be one strong-minded woman, young yet decisively independent, but when it came to the dating game, she was just your average girl next door. Despite Martin's notoriously poor reputation recognized among co-workers and in particular the females, since joining the District Attorney's Office at the start of the year, she had been looking forward to working with him. Occasionally when they passed each other in the hall, every time their eyes collided, she felt her attraction for him growing and all those rumors regarding his halfhearted sentiment towards romantic relationships — or just any relationship in general — would fade away as if nonexistent.

"So I presumed you've already heard of the many stories of Sue," said John out of the blue.

"Huh?"

"You can't fool me. You are here to ask about Martin."

Feeling slightly embarrassed, she suddenly did not know what to respond.

"Haha. Don't worry, I pick up the buzzes but I don't gossip about them. And to tell the truth, you aren't the first lady who's approached me about him, so there's really no need to feel bad."

"Okay. You caught me. But it's not like what you think."

"I'm sure, but I'll tell you straight from my perspective anyway. Martin might act all cool and tough on the outside, but the man sure got a big heart and a half for justice. I can honestly say I've never met anyone who's as hardworking and devoted to their job as he is. He takes great pride in what he does and that really shows. The guy's really smart too, but I'm sure you've already heard."

"I haven't heard that. In fact, most of what I hear people talking about him tends to be negative."

"Even from Pamela?"

"Is she supposed to have good things to say?"

"Well... I suppose not. Those two have worked on many cases together in the past. Rumor has it that they dated for a while and things were going just fine until he said something terribly insolent to upset her."

"What did he say?"

"No idea, nor did he admit that they were ever together together, and I never asked him further regarding their relationship."

"Why not?"

"Because unlike you women, we don't like to talk about lovey-dovey things, and I like to respect his privacy if he intends to keep it that way. Besides, you probably shouldn't believe everything you hear, as the word on the street is often far from being the whole truth if it's at all true."

"Is it true that he was in a SWAT team before he became a detective?"

"Now that is true. He quit five years ago."

"Why did he?"

"Stress. At least that's what the guy told me himself, but I'm tempted to think there was more to the story. I mean, I'm sure it's stressful and all working for the SWAT, but being a homicide detective isn't any better in my point of view. As I see him jump from one case to the next without taking a second of break, I just can't imagine stress bothers him that much at the end of the day…"

Having just learnt all of these good qualities about Martin from his closest colleague, Crystal was feeling even more smitten with him than before. "So, who's this Sue? His girlfriend?"

"Nobody I presume, probably just a name he came up with off the top of his head one day that he thought would be funny as hell to use as a tease. I wouldn't take that too seriously, but I also wouldn't get too engaged with him if I were you."

Her smile was held off. "Why?"

"Let's just say, he might look like the perfect package, but he's not your ideal guy."

"How so?"

"What do you think of a man who's always put work above all else, and marriage is likely the last thing on his mind?" While she took a moment to digest his words, John saw someone from the corner of his eye approaching in the distance. "Speak of the devil," he said, and then both of them looked ahead.

Crystal's heart was naturally pounding faster then. When Martin finally reached them, he removed the cigarette from John's mouth and put it in his own. She stared in amazement as it happened, fascinated to see what he would do next. John, on the other hand, was hardly amused.

"That's disgusting you know that?"

Martin took a few good drags out of it before putting it out on an ash receptacle nearby. "I thought you were quitting for your kids."

"Yeah, I thought you were quitting too but then you picked it right up the next day."

"Defensive."

Crystal let out a small giggle as a result of his quick-wittedness, due to which Martin looked right at her for a second. She was just about to say something to him when he looked off behind her, his hand reached for the door handle and pulled at it.

"I'll be at my desk," he said to John, and then entered the building without acknowledging Crystal at all.

John felt obliged to explain his lack of manners for him. "Don't take that personally. He's like that with pretty much everyone."

"I'm okay," said Crystal, not taking offense.

"Good. Well, I better get back to work. Thanks for the chat."

49

ANXIOUS TO WRAP up Daniel's case, John hurried after Martin and soon, caught up to him.

"How did it go with Allison Skala?"

"It went fine," Martin replied plainly and just kept on walking. "So, Ed Ramsey confessed?"

"Yup."

"What made him do it?"

"It's like you have suspected — his obsession."

"Go on."

"He claimed to have been in love with her ever since high school. According to him, they used to date until Daniel came between them and broke them up. That was many years ago, but the guy never stopped worshipping her like some kind of 'angel sent from heaven' and believe it or not, those were his exact words. He had planned the murder a long time ago, but when he actually executed it, to put it mildly, he was shitty at it."

"What did he say about the chloroform?"

"He got it from an ex-girlfriend who works at a laboratory, and like you've suggested before, he had intended to use it on Allison in an attempt to kidnap her and then flee south across the border into Mexico. They were supposed to meet up shortly after he stopped by her house and conveniently murdered her husband —"

"I assume she was not supposed to be at the scene. Seeing her there, he panicked, and so it rendered his kidnapping scheme impossible."

"Exactly."

"Did he mention how he knew Daniel would be home by then?"

"Evidently, he knew where he worked and what car he drove. He simply waited at his corporate office's parking lot for two hours straight and then followed him home. He said he's done that on two other occasions in the past month alone. Nothing short of what a stalker would do if you ask me."

"A stalker."

"Yup. He also said that he would have shot him down on the spot had there not been people around. How he thought this whole plan would ever work out to be a happy ending in the first place is beyond me. I mean, how likely is it really for a woman to fall in love with a man who kills her other half just to be with her? Old lovers or not, I don't think he thought it all the way through…"

Arriving at his desk, Martin settled into his chair. "How did you eventually get him to talk?"

Upon being asked, John smiled with pride, no longer refrained from boasting, "It was all based on a good instinct. Going along with your theory, I figured if there was even a slight chance that he was driven by jealousy, showing him the divorce petition might just break his silence. I was dead on."

"Nicely done."

"Thank you. Now we just gotta put together the report to get the case off our hands. Do you know who from the prosecution team to hand it off to?"

"No, but you can easily find that out, can't you?"

"Sure."

"Good. Because I'm counting on you to take over the case from here on."

Sensing that Martin was not his typical self, he double-checked with him. "Not a problem. So, everything went well on your end?"

"Yes… and no."

"Yes and no? Why the hell no?"

When informed of Allison's bizarre allegation against her own brother, John was not the least bit persuaded. "Anyone can make up stories like that. Remember that Bob Marlin case? And how about that one case where the crippled mother made up that alibi to try to steer us into believing she was out of town when her son was murdered? It was also very convincing at first, but we all know how that one turned out in the end."

"Why would she fabricate a story this severe that may very well get herself in trouble? She would have to be pretty crazy to lie about something like that to a police officer, don't you think?"

"I don't know. There's just something far-fetched about it. On the same day you went asking her for information about her husband's murder, she confessed to you something entirely else."

"She wasn't planning to tell me all that."

"Then why did she?"

"She claimed that her brother pressured her."

"What? No way."

"That's what she told me."

"That's total horseshit then. She told you her brother — the criminal himself — asked to be turned in? Haw! Where is he then?"

"She wouldn't say. She didn't know she said."

"Allow me to be cynical for a second Martin, but nobody does that okay? Nobody. You should know that for a fact of all people."

"I know it sounds bad, but you should have seen her, the sheer struggle she had to go through just to open her mouth about it."

"She's a good actor then, which we have seen plenty of doing what we do. I'm pretty sure she's got you hooked on some tricky manipulation out of self-interest, but no matter the reason, you must pull yourself out. We really haven't the time to dance around a closed case..."

Given the abundant workload they currently had on hand, John's advice should have been well understood and well received. Except when Martin decided to put on his blinders and flick on his focus mode, everything anyone said instantaneously became less than important to him. Having learnt to read him quite well over the years, judging by his prolonged silence, John knew he would not easily give in to this without considerable measure. Therefore, agreeing to disagree, he went on to do a quick lookup on his computer, merely to find out the corresponding detective responsible for Megan's case. When the information showed up on his screen, almost immediately, he smelled trouble.

"Jefferson handled this case."

"So?"

"So, how about I stop by his desk and have a chat with him later in the day? It wouldn't hurt to see what the old man has to say before you dive deeper into this mess," he suggested, out of precaution for his colleagues' mutual enmity.

Despite his goodwill, Martin found the proposal awfully unsettling. All the while feigning indifference, ever so slightly, he exposed his animosity through his tone. "That won't be necessary. I don't need that cocky old mule's approval to look into a case, nor do I need your help speaking to him."

John disagreed. "To the best of my knowledge, I'm afraid yes, and yes you do," he argued, shaking his head at Martin's juvenile stubbornness. "Sometimes you ought to know yourself better. Remember the last time you spoke to the man about a different case huh? I mean here I thought, just a chat like you said, no biggie. You know, like regular people talking to each other, calmly. But then no, no, no... there you went and gave him a black eye —"

"A well-deserved black eye," Martin countered. Even with his inherently placid disposition, when the time came to deal with the stiff-necked senior, there had been incidents where he failed to keep his cool facade in place and just lost it.

"Was it worth getting suspended though?"

"You would have to ask Shaw —"

"And *that* was only three months ago. Seriously, I don't mean to get in the middle of your issues, but why go looking for trouble for nothing?"

"Are you finished?"

Subsequently, John backed off.

50

BRENDA SHOWED UP at her daughter's house an hour after Martin had left. Nervously, she walked up to the porch and stood before the door for a minute, dithering about what she had come here to do. Accompanying her was a silver-haired man dressed in his usual crisp, stripped suit, as befitted his prime status of his profession, well in his fifties. He sensed her perturbation, and so resolved to remind her of what they had agreed upon prior to leaving his office.

"You are doing this because you love her. She will learn to appreciate that. Remember, we are only here to talk to her so that we can help her, and I'll do most of the explaining so do not worry."

His reassurance gave her courage to carry on with her task. She mustered a smile of gratitude and then reached out to ring the doorbell. They waited. A minute later, she rang it again. Though after repeated ringing and knocking on the door, there was still no sign of Allison's coming.

"ALLIE!" howled Brenda. As the uncertainty ruffled what could have been a good start, her friend logically sought verification from her to make certain everything done beforehand was according to plan.

"Are you absolutely sure she is home?"

"Yes. As soon as I saw the detective walk out the front door, I gave her a call like you told me over the phone. She has to know I am coming over. I don't get it."

"I assume you did not mention I was coming?"

"Uh-uh. I wouldn't dare," she said with intensity. "Let me give her a quick call here."

While she did that, her friend had decided on a different approach. Following the cedar fence dividing this property and the next, he came through the stoned pathway towards the backyard to investigate. Around the corner he went and stopped, having found Allison standing barefoot in the middle of the lawn some ten feet away, a dirty box hugged against her chest.

The second Allison saw him, a rush of cold sweat swept across her body. Her skin crawled at a series of horrific flashbacks brought on by his presence. She was in fear, great fear. With nothing to defend herself but a small garden trowel in her hand, she swung it violently in his direction, yelling at him desperately, "You! Stay away from me!"

The man paid no heed to her warning, and instead, looked about her with exceeding enthusiasm. "I found her!" he called out to notify Brenda and then proceeded onward one slow step at a time. "It's good to see you again Allison," he spoke in a peaceful voice, with an undertone of objectification in it and a superior, almost cunning smirk on his face, "You mother's been updating me about your condition, and judging by the way you are reacting towards me, I presume she is right. Nothing fascinates me more than you right now and you should know what that means for you. I promise I'm not going to hurt you, but that is, of course, if you behave and quit fighting. Then we can all sit and discuss merrily about what we are going to do about you next."

In spite of his ostensibly bargaining overture, Allison ignored it, picking up her feet without delay, sprinting and aiming for the deck. Once making it there, she slipped through the sliding door into the living room, threw the two things in her hands onto the carpeted floor and then turned back around speedily to shut and lock it up tight. As she watched the man taking his time strutting up the flight of stairs, meanwhile, her mother was running past from behind him and eventually arrived outside the door. Knocking repeatedly on its glass surface, she demanded her to open it. Allison of course refused and, furthermore, started to back away.

Seeing that the situation had already gone slightly out of hand, Brenda quickly redialed her daughter's number, looking to reconcile with her while there was still chance.

"I'm very sorry darling. We didn't mean to catch you by surprise," she said as soon as Allison picked up.

"Why... why is he here?!"

"Calm down —"

"I will not calm down! I said, why is he here!"

Barely composing herself, she glanced over her shoulder at her friend standing inches away, who was for now saying nothing and advising nothing, before returning to reply to Allison. "You mean Dr. Carter? He's just here to... uh... explain a couple of things. He only means well darling."

"I don't want him here."

"Come on now Allie —"

"I want him gone. NOW!"

Just then, as if looking for reinforcement, she took another glance at Dr. Carter. All the while keeping his sangfroid, he shot her a firm, heartening nod and like that, she persevered with improved confidence.

"You know you are acting ridiculous Allie. Quit belly-aching and let us in at once."

"I'm not nine years old anymore, which means you guys can no longer control me," Allison snapped back.

"*Nobody* is trying to control you. We are here to help you get better. We only want the best for you."

"Who do you think you are fooling Mom? I won't fall for your lie anymore so save it."

"Lie? What lie?! And don't you talk back to me like that young lady! I won't allow it! Open the door this instant!"

"Not in my lifetime I won't."

Feeling utterly embarrassed, Brenda was losing her patience quickly. Her hot-tempered nature certainly did not help the situation, and as their feud intensified, little by little, she was losing her ground as well. Since noticing this, it had become clear to Dr. Carter that blind persistency simply would not do. He was not about to let obstacles waver his ambition however, even if it meant having to go to an unsavory extent just to get Allison to cooperate. Therefore, purposely, he cut in on the mother-daughter dispute in the next available pause, saying to Brenda, "Let me speak to her instead."

Having overheard him in the background, Allison immediately yelled "NO," but that did not delay her mother from handing Dr. Carter the phone. Right when he held it up against his ear, she saw and screamed precisely into the speaker, telling him with eyes grudging, "GO-TO-HELL!"

Faced with such hostility, Dr. Carter managed to maintain his unflinching attitude nonetheless and moved up to stand closer to the sliding door where Allison could see him most clearly, looking right at her.

"He isn't real Allison," he told her with blunt simplicity, "Adrian isn't real."

Allison was not at all expecting to hear a statement so completely confounding and opposed to logic in the middle of this sudden invasion, but the commitment in his tone somehow made it difficult to not take what he said seriously.

"If he was real, I assure you he would have been right there in the room with you, telling us off himself. Don't you think?"

For a moment, Allison's mouth opened, wanting to retaliate but no words would come out. She was so prepared to fight just then, yet now, she could hardly mutter back.

"He... he is real."

"Then, if you don't' mind, prove it to me. Point him out, is he sitting over there by the table or standing near you?"

"He isn't here right now."

"No? Are you absolutely certain?"

"I saw him leave with my own eyes this morning."

"Did you? And I suppose if you need him bad enough, he will just come right back to you."

"What? —"

"Allie! Don't listen to him!"

Upon hearing her brother's voice, Allison felt a shiver down her spine. Immediately, she turned to see him standing behind her, could not believe any of this was actually happening. Her throat twitched as emotion began to choke up inside her all over again, feeling as though it was about to close up for good.

"I couldn't go Allie," he told her, "I couldn't just leave you knowing this was coming."

"But... but you promised. I... I confessed."

"I know —"

"Ah, there we are," remarked Dr. Carter, with a sly leer, telling her firmly, "Allison, what you are seeing is only in your head..."

"Why are you still listening to this yahoo?" Adrian interrupted him in the interim. "I've warned you about this remember? He's just trying to mess with you so don't fall for it."

"I... I..." Allison was stammering to reply then. "I don't know... I don't know what to think."

"You are not doubting me because of what he said, are you? They are only here to tear us apart any chance they get, like they've done many times in the past. Are you really going to just let them this time?"

"I... I thought you left... like we talked about. I don't understand..."

Seeing her look of perplexity, Adrian was getting anxious himself. As anger gradually took its toll on him, his true colors also began to unveil. "I've already told you why I'm here. What more do you need to understand?"

At the same time, Dr. Carter was just as relentless as ever, pushing on regardless of cost. Soon, it became a battle between the two men, each seeking to convince Allison of their own stance.

"You do eventually have to face up to reality no matter how difficult. To do that, you must first forgive yourself, and to forgive yourself, you will need our help —"

"Hang up the phone Allie! I can explain everything to you soon as this fucker leaves us alone."

"You want to get better Allison. I know you do. Deep down, you are a smart girl. So it should be a no-brainer for you to figure out that you *absolutely* can't do this alone..."

"This is bullshit... Allie!"

"You also know that nobody can help you now but us, not you yourself and obviously, humph, not Adrian."

"Are you really listening to him?! He wants me ripped out of your life. How can you just stand there and do nothing?!"

"It's not too late —"

"I don't believe this..."

"— to take that step."

"ALLIE! SHUT-HIM-UP!"

"Let us in —"

"SHUT THIS FUCKER UP NOW!!!"

"— and we can talk."

"SHUT UP!! SHUT THE FUCK UP YOU FUCKING OLD PRICK!!!" All at once, Allison bellowed out in all her fury, her voice taken over briefly by that of Adrian as she turned to confront Dr. Carter head-on with a face burning hot, throwing her phone fiercely at the door in his direction. As a result to that smash, it fell and hit the steel track, cracking its screen.

No matter how she put on a brave front, Dr. Carter was unshaken; Brenda on the other hand, could not have been more stressed by her daughter's latest outbreak of aggression that crushed her to pieces. Her vulnerability came punctually to aid his continuous tactic of psychological manipulation as he rushed to console her with an embrace, asserting loudly so as to make himself heard through the dividing door. "Look how you are hurting your mother with your behavior. You don't have to feel the way you do if you would just let us help you."

Doubts surged up within her corrupted mind like a constant whirlwind to which Allison had absolutely no control. Lost, she dropped to the floor in total agony, lashing out a second time and in real tears: "LEAVE ME THE HELL ALONE!!"

Dr. Carter had no desire to back down however, as in fact he was quite pleased by his own deliberate mind game that eventually broke her spirit. Such a troubled state of soul was just what he had hoped for Allison, as it generally made easier what was set to happen in due time. Until then, he knew time had come to retreat, but not before making certain that she expected his return.

"I won't give up on you child, you can mark my words. Till we meet again, I bid you a good night of rest. Believe me, you are going to need it."

Her body shuddered a little as she sat hugging her legs up to her chest and cried burying her dejected face in her knees. Despite her obvious misery, a sense of victory washed over Adrian. Right after Dr. Carter and their mother had left her yielding to defeat. Straight away, he approached to try to pull her out of her depression.

"Screw them Allie! You don't need them."

"Go away Adrian. Go... away."

"Don't let them get to you like this. We can work this out together, just like before."

Slowly, she raised her head to look up at him. "Just for once... will you do as I say?!" At that moment, he noticed her watering eyes were a different vibe than the sadness he had expected to see, a vibe that spoke acrimony. A sniffle later, she scrubbed away her tears and looked up at him again. Her expression had by then changed from vexed to numb.

"I'm done with you," she told him, hard-heartedly, "I never — ever — want to see you again."

He heard what she said, and was dumbstruck at first, feeling like someone had literally taken a hammer and bust apart their everlasting bond right in front of him yet he could do nothing to save it.

"So, this is it?"

"I think so."

He nodded at her, bitterly. "Fine... Do whatever you want," he rasped, and then removed himself from her sight.

51

"MS. ALLEN, WILL you come in here for a moment?" Dr. Carter spoke over the intercom.

A few seconds later, there was a knock on the door. "Yes, Doc?"

"Have you rescheduled my 8 p.m. appointment?"

"Yes. I've moved it to the same time next Thursday."

"I'm afraid that won't do."

"Oh..."

"I need you to move it to the week after that, and do the same for all other appointments for the rest of this week and the next. Pardon me for not being more specific before."

"That's okay, not a problem."

"Just let the parents and guardians know something urgent has come up for which I must go out of town. If any of them have questions, take down their numbers and I will give them each a call personally tonight."

"I will do that. And, Mrs. Wright called back while you were away, about half an hour ago."

"Did she leave a message?"

"Yes, I have it right here."

"Thank you. Just leave it to me. Anything else?"

"Mrs. Conner is on line two, sounding kind of jittery. She said it's about her son."

"Tell her I'm with a client and I'll call her back soon."

"Yes, Doc."

"Also, would you fix some tea and bring it in for Mrs. Crawford?"

"Certainly." Then, off she went, closing the door on her way.

One moment Dr. Carter finished speaking to his secretary, the next he looked over at Brenda sitting opposite him at his desk in his office, self-possessed as he usually was, observing her. She had been quiet in dejection since calming down from her earlier bout of hysteria for witnessing the mental state Allison was in; hence he decided to break the silence by sympathizing with her.

"I'm sorry you had to see her that way. I'm sure it's hard for you, a caring mother, to have to watch your children sabotage themselves like that."

She finally lifted her face to look at him. "It was hardly my first time — as you know — but somehow, each incident that happened still feels new to me."

"It's only understandable. I don't believe this is something you would ever want to get used to."

"Jo."

"Yes?"

"Be honest with me. How bad is she? Is there really still hope to be had?"

"I'm not gonna lie. Allison's case is indeed a special one. Currently, I don't have any record of patients who've undergone the same procedure she did, yet still managed to remember so much of the event that traumatized them in the first place. Then again, all my other patients have to go through mandatory follow-up treatments right after the surgery, which in contrast, your daughter was exempt from because of the exigency of the situation at the time."

"It's my fault. I should have kept you current about her condition like I promised. It's just — so many things that happened this month were beyond El's and my control, least of all Daniel's passing."

"Daniel? Are you referring to your son-in-law?"

"Yes. He was shot just outside their house."

"When was this?"

"Yesterday afternoon. Allie apparently saw everything. El and I rushed to the hospital shortly after receiving a call from the police saying that she had collapsed at the scene."

"I see. That is very valuable information right there…"

Just then, Ms. Allen brought in a pot of tea and some apple scones on a plate. She set everything down on the desk and left quietly. Dr. Carter moved to pour some hot tea into a teacup and offered it to Brenda.

"Thank you."

"You should try a scone. They are fresh from this morning. I get them at a good little bakery just down the street," he recommended, half-leaning, half-sitting on a corner of the desk diagonal to her.

"Thanks for the offer, but I'll pass. Haven't had much of an appetite these days."

"I understand. But eating is important, because without energy, you can neither think, nor act straight."

"I know." She blew on her tea to cool it and then took a sip. "You are not having some?"

"It's made for you, so drink as much as you like."

She managed to give a grateful smile, but before long, that smile shifted into a frown again.

"What is it Bren? Go ahead and tell me your concerns."

"About my son… there seems to have been no real improvement on that part either."

"As I recall explaining to you, there's no guarantee she will forget about him completely —"

"That's never what I wanted, for her to completely forget him. They were once a strongly bonded pair. I don't want her to ever forget that. It's the bad things... the bad memories that she can do without."

"That is exactly what I meant too. But like I have stated from the beginning, we went into this knowing it was an experiment, a test."

"Don't tell me that again. It makes me sick just hearing it..."

"Desperate times call for desperate measures. There's nothing wrong with that."

"I know, but the desperate time has now passed, we've taken care of that, and our priority hasn't changed — we want her to get well and lead a normal life instead of wasting time daydreaming about her dead brother as if he's still alive."

"I wouldn't despair just yet, as her chance at a full recovery hasn't simply changed because of this minor setback."

"But... how likely is the same procedure really going to work on her the second time around if it didn't work before?"

"Is that what the issue is? You are doubting my decision."

Dr. Carter read her mind totally. Feeling abashed, she sat tight in her chair and waited for him to continue but suddenly, he got up and walked to stand before the window behind his desk with his back turned to her. Even just for a moment, she got more anxious in that dead-air time till he finally spoke again.

"It was many years ago, but I still remember vividly the first time you brought Allison into my office. She must have been eight or nine years old at the time."

"Nine. She was in fourth grade when Adrian had his first 'accident'."

"Right," he replied, solemnly, turning back around to face her. His expression then was of apparent sorrow and almost, out of character. "I had never seen such a sweet, well-mannered little girl. Despite her troubled brother and his misfortune, I couldn't imagine anything bad happening to her. Unfortunately, things don't always turn out the way they should. Seeing what she's become over the course of many years pains my heart no less than yours. I suppose, what I'm trying to say so inarticulately is that, although I am not of blood relation to your family, I too only want the best for your daughter. In the same way that I cared for your son when I was treating him way back when..."

All the while listening to his heartfelt speech, Brenda tried hard to stifle her emotion but failed miserably in the end.

"I'm sorry. I didn't mean to upset you," he apologized to her upon her bursting into tears.

"No... It's not you... I should be the one who's sorry. My husband and I have always had immense faith in you. I don't know what's come over me..."

"Well, I do. You are just sick and tired of having to deal with one sick child after another. It's my shortcoming for not being able to do more for your family. Forgive me."

"That's alright... *SNIFFLE* ... excuse me..."

Swiftly, he lent her his handkerchief, moving behind her while she finished what she was intending to say.

"We know you are a busy man, and we do appreciate every effort you've made to help us."

"And I appreciate your continuous trust in me." He gave her a gentle squeeze on the shoulders as a gesture of comfort, asserting confidently a moment later when she gazed up at him, "Don't worry, she's in good hands with me and my team. I will make sure that we give a hundred and ten percent this time around to cure her — once and for all — for her sake. I promise you that with all my heart."

With that, Brenda smiled a genuine smile filled with hope, a smile that would seal pretty much any deal henceforth, in the name of Allison, put forth by her doctor friend who had been playing his cards right and predicted this all along.

He returned to sit down in his leather chair. "Now, going back to our plan. I suggest that we act soon or risk losing more precious time, in view of the fact that the longer she is to linger in her delusion, the longer she is to needlessly suffer."

"El will be home tomorrow night. He's flown to Washington this morning to take care of some business for the company. He might have better luck talking her into cooperating than I could if we wait till then."

"I'm actually thinking sooner than that."

"Sooner? I suppose we can try again later tonight."

"No. In fact, I need her to rest tonight."

"So, tomorrow morning then?"

"Haha. That's not what I have in mind either."

"Oh?"

Occasionally crafting his words in his favor, right then, Dr. Carter proposed to her ardently exactly what he had in mind. Much like a hungry salesman to a desperate customer, it did not take much convincing to get her to go along with his idea.

"'That's no problem. Just give me the consent form to sign now, and I will talk with El as soon as I leave here. He will make arrangements to accommodate your needs."

"Perfect." He was satisfied then. "There is still one last thing."

"What is it?"

"I know I'm in no position to speak about this, but please be warned, from the video you presented me earlier, something about his attitude tells me he won't simply give up the case."

"He? You mean the detective."

"That's right. Like I said, just be warned."

She took his forewarning to heart.

52

AFTER SPEAKING TO her husband over the phone, Brenda acquired Martin's personal phone number from a reliable source. According to direction given to her, she tried to get in touch with him. Martin was just leaving work the very moment his cell phone rang. It was by then midnight, and there was hardly anyone else left at the police station.

This late hour generally put him in a contemplative mood. He would usually think about many things, work-related things mainly, and tonight, it was mostly about his meeting with Allison.

'You policemen really are a bunch of hypocrites…'

Hypocrites…

Having been so caught up in thought, he had missed the call yet did not even bother to check whom it was from.

Meanwhile, another diligent worker had also just called it a night. The minute she stepped out from one of the conference rooms into the long corridor leading to the back exit, it was totally by chance that she saw Martin walking by ahead of her.

Not shying away this time, she called out after him, "Detective Blake!"

Martin heard her, and so turned his head briefly to see Crystal coming his direction and then looked straight ahead again, never slowing down.

"You know, it is rude to keep on walking when some-one's trying to speak to you."

He was absolutely unconcerned about her opinion. "We aren't working a case together. So if it's a 'hi and bye' sort of ritual, you can save that for someone else."

Crystal had every right to be annoyed by his haughty attitude but she was not — not even close in fact — as she found herself smiling at it. Right then, she quit bugging him and only walked at her own pace, until seeing him eventually come to a stop just outside she did quicken to catch up to him.

Once out the door however, she regretted it.

"Look. Who's this beautiful lady? Is she the girlfriend you've been hiding from everyone?" said to Martin, the good-looking man with short blonde hair standing near, a cupcake in his hand with a lit candle on top.

"I'm sorry. I didn't know you are having company," she said to Martin.

The man went on to introduce himself, extending his hand towards her. "Hi. Name's Levi. Nice to meet you."

Awkwardly, she shook it, clarifying, "My name's Crystal... We are just collogues."

"Ah."

In the next instant, he looked mindfully back at Martin, who was perfectly irritated and strictly repeated what he had asked him before Crystal showed up and interrupted them: "What are you doing here?"

"I've come to surprise you of course," replied Levi, and then turned to tell Crystal, "It's his birthday today," trying hard to lighten up the atmosphere.

"Oh. Happy birthday —"

"It's not my birthday."

"Except that it is. Don't mind him Cris, he's in a very bad mood for no apparent reason."

Sensing the tension between them, Crystal barely managed to smile. "It's very nice to meet you, but I'd better get going since it's getting quite late. I still have loads of paperwork to do tomorrow morning so... I'll see you tomorrow, Detective."

Martin was, as usual, unresponsive, and so she proceeded down the road to her car. As soon as she had left, the quarrel between the two men immediately resumed.

"You have her call you 'Detective'?"

"*Don't change the subject.* I told you not to come here."

"I didn't think you would be walking out with somebody."

"You didn't think... I never asked you to put on a show."

"I don't mind. Just thought you could learn to appreciate it somehow. I even closed the shop early to —"

"Well I don't... I *don't* appreciate any of it."

As a direct reaction to his rigidly harsh words, Levi blew out the candle of his cupcake and chucked the whole thing into a trash receptacle near by, no longer maintaining his happy-go-lucky posture. "You know... a part of me thought you might say that."

"So can you just quit it for good?"

He responded with a few sour nods. "Sure. Consider that done. But just so we understand each other, I'm not the one who has a problem with us being seen together..."

Upon Levi's walking off, Martin's anger was only then markedly assuaged. He was about to go after him when his cell phone rang a second time. Strange enough as it was for him to receive calls this late at night and not from John, it was anonymous.

He picked up the call anyway.

"Hello."

"Is this Detective Martin Blake?"

"Yes, this is he. Whom am I speaking with?"

"This is Brenda... Brenda Crawford to be exact, Allison Skala's mother. We've met once yesterday at the hospital."

He was taken aback. "Yes... I remember you Mrs. Crawford. If you don't mind my asking, how did you get my number?"

"I'm afraid I can't tell you that Detective. You see... you see the reason that I called... I would like to have a chat with you in regard to my daughter's behavior earlier today."

"What behavior are you referring to?"

"It's about the story she told you... about Megan Skala... about her death."

It was definitely unusual for a mother to speak on her grown-up daughter's behalf in such an unorthodox — almost sneaky — way. Martin noted that, and was forthwith transfixed by the mystery of it all.

"Okay. You have my attention," he said to Brenda, but only to have her refuse to discuss the matter remotely.

"I would much prefer a face-to-face conversation if that's alright with you?"

"Of course. You can come by the station tomorrow morning and ask for me —"

"Actually, is it possible for us to meet in private? You can name the time and place that is most convenient for you and I'll be there. It shouldn't take up too much of your time."

Without a pause for consideration, he gave her the information.

DAY 25 | SEPT 30 WEDNESDAY

53

D AWN HAD BARELY broken. The sky was just changing from purple to red when Allison left home in her car to hurry off somewhere. She still had on that tunic she wore all of yesterday with a men's jacket — Daniel's jacket — over it, and the baseball cap he used to wear often when they went on dates.

At that precise time, Martin arrived at a small café called Gezellig nearby work. Levi, its owner, could not refrain a soft smile from behind the cash register seeing him walk in, considering their little quarrel from last night.

He could never stay mad at him for long. "You didn't say you were coming in this early."

"Work."

The shop was still fairly empty. Brenda, who had been waiting anxiously for Martin's arrival at a back corner table next to the window, was really the only sit-in customer there as yet for the day.

Levi looked briefly in her direction. "Gotcha. I'll bring over your espresso." Thereupon, he went on to prepare it.

Martin moved his way to Brenda's table. Contrary to his serene state of mind, she had been quivering on the inside even since seeing him at the door. Intending very much to smooth that over, soon as he sat down in the chair from across her, she began the meeting with idle talk.

"This is a nice little shop. Do you come here often?"

"When I feel the need for a break, I come here," he replied.

She smiled faintly, looking out to the street. "I don't recall the last time I was in the area, but I do remember this drive-in theater just down the street from here back when I was attending university. That was a long time ago."

"Was there one?"

"Oh yes, I believe it was called 'Pennington's Drive-In'. It was quite a popular place at one point for the collegians to hang out and bring their dates. I've never actually been in it, my father was always against this sort of bargain place, but opera houses I've been to plenty... How old are you, Detective, if you don't mind me asking?"

"Thirty-seven."

"Thirty-seven years old... you must have grown up in the 80s?"

"Yes ma'am."

"Well then, I'm not surprised you haven't heard of it. New things are constantly replacing the old. The same goes for this kind of old-fashioned coffee shop. Nowadays, Brews and Eriksson's Coffee are everywhere, young folks like yourself would rather go to them instead."

"Most people visit Brews to hang out with friends and whatnot, as opposed to me, I just want peace and quiet for a change, and a moment to clear my mind, really."

"I suppose, being a detective, you must have quite a hectic agenda every day."

Martin nodded at her remark.

Levi just so brought over his coffee at that moment. He set it down in front of him on the table and left without a word, knowing best not to disturb their conversation. Right then, Martin took a simultaneous glance at the big wooden clock fixed on the back wall that just ticked over to seven-twenty. He decided to not waste time further. "So, Mrs. Crawford, here we are per your request. What is it that you want to talk about?"

Upon his forthrightness, Brenda's heart shivered. She picked up her cup of tea and slurped up the warm liquid in a few mouthfuls hoping to soothe her stomach jittering with nerves. It only helped a little. When she set the cup back down onto the saucer, she looked up at him bravely and too cut to the chase. "I'm going to be frank with you then. The truth is — my daughter is very ill. Everything she told you about Megan Skala's death was merely from her imagination."

"Is that so?"

"Yes, you mustn't believe her."

Regarding Allison's allegation, Martin indeed still held doubts, but in spite of that, he had chosen to act as though he was definite about it for the time being with purpose to dig down deeper. "But I do," he insisted, "As a matter of fact, I find it difficult *not* to believe her."

"Why?"

"For one thing, she was the one who initiated the allegation, which I fail to find a legitimate reason for anyone to lie about something of such severity to a policeman."

Shaking her head, Brenda urged on. "But you mustn't believe *any* of it."

"Well — have you any proof that I shouldn't?"

Just then, her brows furrowed into knots and eyes appeared unwilling. Though for the sake of her daughter, Brenda knew no alternative than to show him what he asked for. She had actually come prepared for this part, thus reaching into her handbag and taking out her phone. Its screen had been preset to showcase an eight-minute surveillance clip recorded and dated just one day earlier, titled "KITCHEN_CAM2_092909". Handing it over to him, she instructed, "Just hit play. It should change your point of view about the whole thing."

While she fell back into stiff silence, Martin did as directed. Right from the get-go, he recognized Allison's kitchen even at the strange angle from which the clip was taken, despite the fact that he never did step foot into it yesterday. Before long, he saw himself passing by its doorway in view. Following behind him was Allison, who reappeared on camera a minute later, walking into the kitchen to prepare the coffee. According to his memory about their meeting, nothing was out of the ordinary thus far, but it was what he did not see behind the scene at that time that went unpredictably odd.

His eyes narrowed in suspicion as he watched Allison pacing from one side of the countertop to the other, talking to herself strangely quietly the while. He had to turn up the volume just to hear some of the bizarre dialogue being communicated. All at the same time, she was behaving as though she was having a quarrel with her brother who was — most certainly — not there. Furthermore, at the height of *their* argument, he saw her peek apprehensively around the doorway. From there, the conversation quickly crumbled into a mournful farewell that eventually ended with her opening and closing the back door, by then looking terribly wretched.

Her seemingly deranged behavior surely looked perplexing to Martin, but he was even more so shocked that it all happened in the presence of him underneath the same roof. As he returned the phone to Brenda after watching the clip in its entirety, questions started to pop up in his head like mad, thirsting for answers.

"Mrs. Crawford, this is one very interesting, surprising if you will, corroboration for your claim. But first of all, I'm curious, just how long have you been spying on your daughter?"

"I wouldn't exactly call it spying, Detective. It's not like I watch her through a lens every moment of the day. As a matter of fact, we've only just recently tightened our surveillance again."

"How many of them are there?"

"The cameras?"

"Yes."

"Ten in total. One of my husband's closest friends is a realtor who helped her and my son-in-law find their home soon after they got married. We had those secretly installed a week before they moved into the house."

"Of course you did."

"Knowing how stubborn she is, we could only execute without her knowledge —"

"Or her consent."

"My husband and I are not proud of it, but we really haven't a choice."

"Are they really necessary?"

"Oh, absolutely," Brenda asserted. "That is the only way for us to monitor her condition properly I'm afraid..."

"So, Adrian is her brother, that I know. Who is this Justin?"

"If I were to guess, she was probably referring to Justin Maverick, one of our old neighbor's sons back in Victoria Avenue. He was a chaotic kid as I recall, but a good friend to Adrian nonetheless up until he passed away from a drug overdose a couple years ago. Allie sometimes hung out with them together, but I'm not so sure why she's thinking him up too."

"I presume this is hardly the first time you've caught her behaving like that."

"You are right, but for a long time she was fine up to just recently. Danny had always been her rock before his sister, Megan, came between them."

"What problem by the way, or problems, does your daughter have?"

"Years ago she struggled with depression but made a full recovery from it. Judging by our doctor's latest observation however, it is slowly relapsing."

"Because her marriage was failing?"

"Well, part of it, but, mainly... we believe that she is still very much in denial."

"In denial of?"

Even though it had been years since the tragedy was last called to mind, Brenda still felt every bit of the pain that she went through as a mother like it had all just taken place. Sadly, her sorrow only deepened as she set about explaining that harrowing past to Martin. "One thing you must know, is that my children were a close-knit pair growing up. They loved each other dearly regardless of anything and everything."

"I believe that point has been quite well established from the clip you showed me Mrs. Crawford."

"Yes. The thing is... ever since my son was diagnosed with borderline personality disorder, over the course of many years, he had gotten himself into a lot of trouble with the law stemming from his substance abuse. One of those times... he accidentally killed his girlfriend. Since you've already heard it all from my daughter's own mouth, I will not bore you with it."

"You are saying that, what she told me about Megan's murder, was in fact based off of her brother murdering his own girlfriend?"

"Correct. At the time it happened, Adrian no longer lived with us. My husband and I rarely heard from him, but we knew that he remained close in touch with Allison. It was summer time, about two weeks before her freshman year in college was to start, I found her spending days at home in her room, barely eating anything or talking to any of us. When I confronted her about it, she was telling me nothing at first, but then — in my own motherly way — I was able to eventually pull words out of her. That was when I learnt of the details with regard to the murder. I never used to discourage their relationship but right then, I made her a deal out of rage. I said to her, 'Either you tell the police what happened or I will, but then you will have to forever sever your ties with him.'"

"So she chose to turn him in."

"Right, which directly led to my son's arrest later in the night."

"And she feels responsible for his imprisonment, but at the same time is in denial of it," Martin summed up for her, presuming that was the case. However —

"No. Not quite," she said.

Finding it difficult to continue, Brenda broke briefly to blink away the tears slowly welling up, sniffling as she tried hard to sort of hold in her emotions. Noticing there were not any tissues around, Levi, who had been occasionally observing them from afar, brought over a box of them and handed her some. She accepted and used them to dab the corners of her eyes, all the while being careful not to smudge her mascara.

After Levi left them, a few deep breaths later, she carried on. "It's not so much his captivity that my daughter feels guilty of. She's too good of a person to not feel bad for what happened to that girl... It's what went on after that."

"What happened?" asked Martin.

"Adrian called to speak to her from the police station. Shortly after handing her the phone, I decided to listen in on another line. I can honestly tell you, I never knew words that cruel were possible coming from him to his dearest sister, his most-loved person in the world. He basically accused her of betrayal, saying things like, 'I will never forgive you for what you did', and so forth. I couldn't let the conversation continue for long before I ran back to her room to put an end to it. But... but then..."

"But then?"

A stream of tears trickled down her cheek. Her mouth opened slightly, her lips trembled the moment she spoke out in a brittle voice: "I got a cal-call from the police the following morning. They told me that my son... he... he had hanged himself in his own cell overnight... *SNIFFLE*... Excuse me."

Martin's eyes widened a little upon her dramatic delivery. Sitting back in his chair, he waited for her to recompose herself before asking further, "How long ago was this?"

"It's been seven years. Losing Adrian was devastating to our family as a whole, although it was especially hard on Allison. She was strictly in denial of his death from the beginning. We tried to put her through therapies to help her cope but she'd refuse them. During which time when depression hit her hardest, by day she would be tearful most time, and by night restless due to reoccurring night terrors. At the absolute worst, she would hallucinate about him. We caught her talking to him in her room quite a few times in a similar manner to the video you saw. We were ready to postpose her academic plans but ultimately decided not to."

"How come?"

"Well, as luck would have it, Danny came into her life in the midst of it all. They met shortly after college started. From the day she told me about him, things began to take a turn for the better. She became more cooperative when it came to doctor visits and went regularly, wanting to recover quickly. We saw her condition improve day by day until she came to be normal again. Soon, they got engaged and then married. We could not have been happier for her. But... like I said earlier, Danny had been her rock for all these years. He was the reason she forgave herself for what happened to Adrian. Without him standing by her side now, as much as I hate to admit, I'm afraid... I'm afraid my little girl is drifting back to her delusional self once again..."

Right when she finished talking, tears came pouring and this time, like rivers, no amount of will could stop them. While she sat there sobbing, Martin made use of the time to ponder over everything. After a brief reflection, as convincing as was her revelation — and the added waterworks — he had chosen to remain skeptical, reckoning its biased nature coming from a loving mother.

"You do understand I can easily find out whether you are telling the truth, Mrs. Crawford."

"You think I'm lying to you?"

"No comment."

Frustrated at his incredulous way, Brenda retorted, "I am telling you the truth! You must have to be *blind* to perceive it otherwise. If I could go back and do it over... I swear I would have never given her the idea to turn against her own brother. That is the one regret that I have to live with for the rest of my life..."

"What about the victim then? If it wasn't for your daughter's cooperation, that girl would have died devoid of justice. Have you thought about how her family would have felt?"

"Have I?! Humph! Do you have any children of your own?"

"No ma'am, I do not."

"Then you couldn't possibly know how we parents feel, to have to watch your own children suffer yet can do nothing about it, could you?"

"I suppose not —"

"And you certainly don't understand what it was like for me to catch my son hurting himself on multiple occasions in mourning after some dead friend... I've already lost one child of mine, I'm not about to lose the other, uh-uh..."

Her eyes were ablaze and tone emphatic as she declared her stance, but even then, Martin still failed to be of one mind. "I'm sorry. I know where you are coming from, but I disagree. If everyone starts bending justice, shaping it to fit themselves, it would be the end of law and order. Should it ever come down to that, innocent people are the ones suffering for it. Is that fair then? No."

His lukewarm sentiment continued to worry Brenda. Momentarily, she took to calm down her frustration before pushing on. "Be that as it may, but despite what my daughter told you, she was *not* involved in Megan Skala's death, not in any of that nonsense. I hope I have made myself clear."

"It does seem that way in accordance with everything you've told me, but my opinion ultimately suits no purpose. Like I've already told your daughter, without solid evidence, the case is closed as is," he told her straightfor-wardly, but that fact alone hardly settled her and he no-ticed.

"What can I do for you exactly, Mrs. Crawford?"

Lifting her downcast face, she looked pleadingly at him. "I want you to promise not to pursue the case. Don't forget, she has just lost her husband. I'm asking you to *please*, have mercy on my child. Leave Allison alone."

Her entreaty only served her more harm than good however. Martin had been curious about her real inten-tion since the start of their meeting, but even more so now than before. His instinct told him there was something unnatural about her perseverance in clearing her daugh-ter's name for something she claimed never even hap-pened. All the while holding steady his ground, he shrewdly analyzed her facial expressions as he would a typical suspect, trying to discern whether there was more to the story than he had been told thus far. What only took seconds seemed like an eternity to Brenda when their eyes held during this painfully uncomfortable pause, and then parted as hers started darting about as though searching for an escape route out of his penetrating stare.

All of a sudden, he stood up, finishing his coffee in one shot and leaving the money he owed along with a generous tip on the table.

"Detective?" uttered Brenda, almost in desperation, still yearning for an agreement.

"There really isn't much to pursue solely hinging on what your daughter has disclosed. I *can't* — however — promise you anything. Should there be any evidence that emerges, I will not hesitate to intervene. After all, that is my job. Can you understand that?"

His response left her little peace. Martin could tell, but since receiving not another word from her, he turned around and departed, leaving her sitting there slackening in disappointment.

54

MUCH HAD THE meeting with Brenda stimulated Martin's acquisitive mind. He hastened back to the police station and did, first thing, a quick search in the database of criminals and arrestees for the last name "Crawford". As it turned out, she was not lying. The data indicating the date, location and cause of her son's death clearly and precisely coordinated with her earlier revelation. Digging deeper into Adrian's criminal background, he discovered a long list of offenses and violations varying in severity, and most importantly, information concerning the death of Miranda Holmes — his then girlfriend — at the top of the page. The homicide taking place seven years back to which he had signed a confession, was detailed in a way hauntingly akin to Allison's claim as regards Megan's supposed murder, just like Brenda had specifically pointed out.

"Adrian Crawford," John suddenly read off his computer screen from behind him, which in turn broke his concentration. "Is this the same Adrian you told me about yesterday? Allison Skala's brother?"

"Yup."

"I'll be damned! So he's dead. It can only mean one thing — that woman is sick in the head. Mystery solved!"

Martin spun around in his chair to face him for a moment, taking a long look at the unusually bearded John appearing terribly worn out. His greying hair was messy and shirt untidy as if he had just scrambled out of bed this morning to get here. Adding to his already light complexion, the dark circles beneath his eyes were practically black.

"I overheard you talk to your wife on the phone. Is everything okay?" he asked him, basically feeling obligated to.

"Jaden's got a fever of 101.8. Carol and I were up all night taking care of him."

"Did you bring him to the doctor?"

"She's taking him to the emergency room as we speak. I'm gonna try to get out of here early today if I can help it."

"You should. You don't look too good yourself if I may say so."

Unleashing an enormous yawn, John replied, "Point taken," but as he picked up his feet to return to his desk, Martin stopped him.

"Wait."

"Yes boss?"

"You are a normal guy."

"That depends what you mean by 'normal'."

"You grew up in a regular household, with regular parents and siblings."

"True."

"And you love your children like any good father would."

"Right."

"This is a strictly hypothetical question."

"Just hit me with it."

"I was wondering — would you ever cover for your son, as in make excuses for him in concealing something bad he's done?"

"What sort of bad things?"

"Let's say he's killed somebody at one point in his life."

As always, taking the proposed quandary all too seriously, John gave it genuine consideration before answering, "That's an interesting one Martin, but my definite answer is no. If he's an adult by then, that's a hell no. He should learn to be responsible for himself and his own actions. After all, that's what growing up is all about. Certainly though, I can't help but think that some overprotective parents would answer 'yes' to your question in a heartbeat. You see how many juvie cases we've dealt with in the past involving that same goddamn scenario."

"Very true," Martin agreed wholeheartedly.

"And the rule doesn't only apply to parents."

"How so?"

"Just use yourself as an example. Years ago when your brother was still at large, had you known where he was hiding out, you would not have hesitated to report that information or even arrest him yourself, but not everyone could do that to their kith and kin. All I'm saying is, yes, love is blind blah, blah, blah, and yes, it makes us do crazy shit. That's why sometimes it takes real courage to go for the right judgment. Now, to people like you and me that's fairly easy to do, but to some, being righteous means little to them when it all comes down to it. Make sense?"

"Sure," he muttered back, somehow sounding less self-assured than before.

Just then, Sally from the front desk stopped by to deliver a package wrapped gorgeously in floral-printed paper. It had no sender's address but only a note taped on its surface that said "ATTN: DETECTIVE MARTIN BLAKE" in big black letters.

"This just came for you. A lady dropped it off."

"A gift from a secret admirer. Is Valentine's Day around the corner again?" John teased him, bumping him lightly with his elbow.

"It's only the end of September," said Martin.

"Maybe it's an early Christmas gift then. Ahhh, how I miss those glorious days! You know, girls used to send me flowers on a weekly basis," boasted John, giving Sally a wink while at it. Uninterested in his swaggering way, she rolled her eyes at him and straight away returned to her duties, incidentally making him feel older than he was.

"The younger generations just keep putting me back in my place, how lucky am I to have married Carol..."

Not realizing John was still talking, Martin had long switched on his focus mode, believing the mysterious package contained more than its given notion. With great desire to unveil its secret, right then and there, he tore away the wrapping paper and ripped open the box within to get to a heavily duct-taped, brick-shaped black box.

The oddly constructed object quickly drew both detectives' attention. While Martin checked it closely for possible openings, John brought over a box cutter to help expedite the operation. Holding the box down securely on his desk, Martin traced around its top edges to cut away the tape and down into the cardboard very cautiously so as to not fracture whatever that was hidden inside. When finished with all four sides, he looked over at John and said to him, "Ready?"

"As ever," he replied, prying at the lid with his fingers and removing it in one quick motion. A waft of odor, slightly musty and tinny in its composition, was then simultaneously released into the air. The two looked down at the silky white fabric tucked tightly inside the box. Before digging into it, Martin quickly slid on a pair of disposable gloves to avoid leaving fingerprints. He then shoved his hand downward at a corner and instantly, he felt something enfolded within this seemingly ordinary fabric.

With help from his other hand holding down the box, he pulled out the entire thing in one piece. Examining the fabric closely, he noticed there were spots of old mildew coating all over it. The stains only expanded in scale as he anxiously unrolled it, revealing — ultimately — the most crucial clue to the riddle of Megan's death.

The silky white fabric was in fact a bathrobe. Their mouths literally fell open at the pairs of female tennis shoes and plastic gloves that had long been cloaked within it. Apart from the mold-invaded matter, there were visible bloodstains still encrusted on them. During inspection of the shoes, Martin reached inside and found a positive pregnancy test just lying on one of the insoles. Then, something in him clicked.

"Oh my god — she killed her."

"What?" John asked.

"These were the shoes she wore to Megan's apartment, and these were the gloves she put on before she cut her wrist."

"You are saying Allison Skala is a murderer?"

"YES! She may be sick in the head but she is! Most definitely. That will also thoroughly explain her mother's concern about the case being reopened."

"Wait a second. No one said anything about reopening the case. And besides, why would she drop this off now after having kept it all this time?"

"That's what I'm going to find out."

Stripping off his gloves, Martin ran instantaneously to the front desk asking Sally with vigor the time of which Allison left the station.

Slightly startled by him, Sally asked him back, "Who?"

"The woman who dropped off the box! When did she leave?"

Sensing the urgency, she informed him shortly, "About ten minutes ago. She was wearing a Twins baseball cap and a light, black jacket."

Though the chance might seem slim for him to catch her right then, naturally, Martin rushed outside towards the public parking lot to do a quick walk through just in case she was still in the area. During which his eyes scanned relentlessly the rows of parked cars like laser beams, until he spotted in the distance a woman with the distinctive features Sally provided sitting inside her car with her face buried in the steering wheel. Briskly, he moved to cut through the vehicles, jumped in front of an oncoming one to stop it, determined to get to her before she would drive off.

"Allison Skala!" he yelled out her name as he reached her car, slamming his hands on the driver's side window.

The woman immediately looked up right at him, her eyes still watering from old tears and cheeks crimson, appearing frightened by his jarring stir. On a closer look, much to Martin's surprise, she was not Allison. Though nonetheless, he presented his police badge and gestured her to lower the window for a chat.

"What the *hell* was that?! Just because you are a police officer, doesn't mean you can do whatever you please you know!"

"Are you the person who dropped off a package just now?"

"Yes? Is there a problem?"

"What is your name and who gave it to you?"

"What?"

"*Just answer the goddamn question!!!*"

As she became alert to the seriousness of the situation, she grew to be more cooperative. "My name is Sara Lawson. Here's my driver license if you want to see it. I'm only doing an errand for a friend."

"Who is your friend?"

"Allison Skala. She told me to deliver it to some Detective Martin something — wait a minute — are you him? To be honest, I have no idea what's in that box."

"How long ago were you with her?" Martin continued, brusquely.

"I don't remember exactly... but I'm gonna say about half an hour. I came straight from meeting her at Moonshine. That poor girl... if it wasn't for my constant meddling, she wouldn't have lost her husband, and she definitely wouldn't have to leave —"

"She's leaving? Where is she going?"

"She didn't say, because she didn't know for certain herself. I'm guessing it all depends on her parents.

They've always been pretty controlling of her life from my understanding. Worst case scenario, if they were to take her away right this minute, she would basically have no say."

"Did she mention where she might be heading after your meeting?"

"No, and I didn't ask her either. I only used to pry into her personal life occasionally for a friend… I'm never doing that to her again for sure. If she wants me to know something, she will tell me and that's that — *SNIFFLE* —" Uncrinkling the tissue paper in her hand, she blew her sniffles into it before finishing what she was saying, "I'm sorry I can't be of much help. But if I were to guess, she probably headed home, seeing that she was constantly saying how tired she was during our talk…"

Not chancing another minute, Martin flew right out of there and hastily took off in his car.

55

WHEN MARTIN ARRIVED at Allison's house, he saw most of the police tape ripped and discarded on the front lawn next to the driveway where an empty black van was parked. His alertness was raised another notch soon after he came up to the porch and found the front door ajar. He thereby pulled out his gun and held it downward near his thigh, pushing at the door slightly. The squeaks it made might very well have incidentally announced his presence. Since hearing nothing from the other side, he thrust it open all the way and proceeded inside with caution.

Unlike the previous time he was here, every window was now closed and curtained off, making the interior exceptionally dark. On the assumption that there had been an intrusion, he crept about from wall to wall to check for suspicious characters but ultimately found none hiding in corners of the rooms. Naturally, he moved his way up the stairs.

The floor squeaked as he reached the middle landing where he looked up at the dim, little hallway on top of the staircase before two rooms. The room off to the left had its door shut, whereas the master bedroom straight ahead had its wide open. In a moment, he resumed his pace towards it. Something about the stillness of the house was just too suspenseful for him to take his actions lightly, therefore each time that he lifted his foot, he elevated with a vigilant mind. At one of those steps, his eyes went, unexpectedly, to the ceiling inside of the room from where a noose was hanging off the fan and his heart sank.

Assuming Allison was in the room primed to end her life, he knew he must act smartly in the next few seconds. Luckily, years of training on crisis negotiation had him well prepared for this task.

"Mrs. Skala, it's me, Martin," he spoke up calmly so as to create a distraction, all the while approaching the doorway in steady fashion. "You aren't just gonna have your friend drop off the evidence without giving me official closure now, are you?" When he finally got to it, what caught his eyes next was perhaps even more shocking — Allison lying there on the bed looking seemingly dead.

Very quickly, he moved to scrutinize the room, its closet and bathroom before tucking away his gun. His attention automatically returned to her and straight away, he examined around her neck for marks of constriction but there were none. Despite her unusually — almost sickly — pale face, she was breathing normally. Her pulse also felt to be beating regularly into his touch at her wrist, leaving him mystified by her apparent coma.

"Wake up Allison!" he yelled, grabbing her by the arms and shaking her. In a second's time, a deep, imperative voice replied to him, "You won't be able to rouse her however hard you try." From the corner of his eye, Martin noticed someone standing at the door. He turned his head sharply to see a tall doctor figure in white lab coat and thick spectacles entering the room. His arms, the whole time, crossed in front of his chest to manifest a sense of confidence that was equally intimidating as it was arrogant.

"Who are you?" Martin asked him, reaching into his blazer, ready to draw out his gun. Right that instant, three more men — younger men — all dressed in white lab coats, whose identities were obscured by the medical masks covering their mouths and noses, came forth from behind the doctor, each pointing their guns at him.

"Be wise, Mr. Blake," Dr. Carter advised him, smiling slyly.

In turn, Martin withdrew his hand, turning his body to face him completely. "What did you do to her?"

"I'm afraid that's not your business to mind."

"I don't believe it's in your control whether it is or isn't," he countered, and sneakily activated his voice recorder from his back pocket.

Keeping a steely face, Dr. Carter appeared virtually unshakable. "I suppose I shouldn't expect any less stubbornness from you despite your age. After all, you are only a detective."

"I suggest that you remove your men immediately, and stop whatever operation you've got going on here before things get out of hand."

"And I would have suggested you restrain your curious nature and stay out of this matter, but I reckon in both yours and my case, they are merely silly requests. Wouldn't you agree?"

Ignoring his remark, Martin shifted to glare at the three gunmen instead. "I'll not press charges if you all surrender now. Consider it your last chance. Don't go further than you'd regret —"

"MmmwHAHAHA!!" Suddenly, Dr. Carter burst out into chilling laughter. "I truly admire your perseverance Mr. Blake, but unfortunately, they only answer to me. Since — let's be honest — I'm really the one with the upper hand here." Curling the bottom corner of his lip in contempt, he went on to call on Jonah. The gunman on his right responded by leaving the room and coming back swiftly with a medical syringe attached to a needle in his hand.

"You do know that assaulting a policeman is a serious offense," Martin forewarned him, but Dr. Carter was undeterred. Upon receiving a go-ahead, Jonah progressed towards him, holding the needle upright in a position to inject. As a precaution that Martin made a fight of the commanded procedure, one of the aides stepped forward to assist with his gun aiming at his forehead.

Before all hell could break loose, Martin watched carefully as the gunman advanced within his reach, calculating the perfect time to strike back while it was still possible. Just then, he shifted his head to the side at warp speed out of his firing range, and then seized the opportune confusion to clutch at the barrel of the gun with his left hand, while his right hand came in from the side with a knifehand strike hitting the gunman's wrist, as a result of which, forcing him to turn the gun against his own chest.

Fearing that he might accidentally fire at himself during the tussle, the gunman was about to give way and let go of his weapon. Just in that nick of time however, when Martin was most distracted, Jonah slinked behind and stabbed him in the back of his neck with the needle, injecting the drug from the tube into him. Soon as the instrument was retrieved from his flesh, Martin felt a tingling sensation plunging down his spine. Right on the spot, his legs went weak and he fell paralyzed to the ground just seconds later.

There was nothing he could do to stop the drug from taking him over. His vision gradually blurred, and just before losing consciousness, he saw vaguely Dr. Carter crouch down next to him, looking down upon him like a hawk would his prey. "Do not worry Mr. Blake. You will be awake again soon enough…"

DAY 30 | OCT 5 MONDAY

56

NOTHER COOL AUTUMN day. At a regional park near Lake Marit, a young mother was enjoying a peaceful saunter with her two daughters alongside vibrant fall trees. Not long after they moved on out of the shaded woodland, baby Ruby in the stroller had resorted to squalling to get her attention.

"Let's stop here for a second," she said to little Jane, her courageous three-year-old toddler, who only continued on her own down the paved trail, chasing butterflies as she was repeatedly warned to not go far.

"No em not," little Jane would reply to her mother each time. It seemed the more she was told "no", the more likely she was to do the opposite. So, all the way she ran till the end of the straight path where it diverged into two separate directions. Then, finally, she came to a halt and turned her head to ensure Mom was still in sight.

"You too slow mommy!"

"Don't go up the hill all by yourself Jane! Unless you want to get a boo-boo like the last time!" her mother cried from quite a ways.

"Don' worry I won'!" Though her mouth might promise one thing, her fearless mind was conflicted. As little Jane looked around herself plotting a way to surprise her mother, a light bulb lit up in her head. Hurriedly, she crouched down behind some ragweed along the hillside and hid among them, hoping to jump out at her when the time came. While waiting there, she looked up at the blue sky with scattered white clouds sailing by and squinted at the birds resting remotely on the electric wires, totally fascinated.

Just then, a series of movements coming from the backdrop of a hilled woodland glade caught her hearing. Upon which, she turned around to look across it, thinking, *what could have created such a ruckus? A big rabbit? No no... a fat squirrel maybe...* One moment she was imagining it to be one of those animals she encountered often in the backyard of her home, the next her eyes dashed towards the commotion at the foot a big maple tree surrounded by fallen red foliage and branches, and her legs followed.

It took great effort to go three inches up the slope wearing toddler shoes, but her tenacious will helped her get further. Although, by the time she discovered the cause of all that excitement, it was not quite what she had in mind. As it happened, it had been Martin all along, stirring as he regained consciousness with a sore body and a migraine. His black blazer was badly scuffed and torn from his right arm up with leaves and twigs stuck to it and to his hair; his face grime-smeared, and there was a cut on his left cheek from where a little blood had been shed.

He needed time solely for his brain to snap back into reality. Little Jane, however, was not about to leave him be.

"Hello mister, are u ok?" she asked him politely, goggling at him in astonishment. "My name is Jane. What is your name?" Right that next instant, he heard a woman's voice in the background calling out anxiously for her. Understanding it was the little girl's mother, he scooped her up in his arms and brought her back down to the main trail, only to get shouted at in return.

"Let her go you sick, sick freak!"

Before he had a chance to explain himself, the mother had taken her from him and forthright scurried up the paved hill pushing the stroller along.

It was probably for the best.

With them gone, Martin could at last have his moment of serenity, a crucial moment to quickly gather his thoughts and find out his location. A big relief came when he found his gun still secured in its holster under his blazer. Then his phone and set of keys, both of which were inside the front pockets of his jeans right where he last left them. Perhaps the only thing missing was his voice recorder. He went back shortly to the maple tree to sweep the area for it but was out of luck. Studying the curved landscape, his eyes traced a route up the incline as he gave the "LOCK" button on his key fob a press. What immediately followed was a honk of his car horn coming from high ground as he had suspected intuitively. Going after the clue, he found his car parked on the side of a two-way road — there was only one place in his mind to go.

When he got back to the police station, disappointment awaited him. Despite his thoughtfulness to remove his torn-up jacket and give his mucky appearance a fix before stepping foot into the building, he learned only after, that it would not have made much difference had he not. Literally like dropping in on a rival's party, everyone he passed by gave him a cold stare and some shook their heads. It was this sense of unwelcomeness that led him to feel very odd showing up at work on this particular, normal day, at a normal hour.

Notwithstanding all the idle speculations regarding his disappearance, the one person who had managed to keep their faith in him unaltered was John. Although, after seeing his colleague for the first time in five days, "excited" was hardly the right word to describe his feelings. With Martin gone, he had been left to pick up his slack on top of his own, hence an incredibly disordered past few days for him.

Frustrated in part, he came by Martin's cubicle upon his arrival to have a word with him. "Where have you been? I never thought unannounced absences were your forte."

"How many days was I gone?" inquired back Martin, eying his tidy desk.

"You've been MIA since last Wednesday and today is Monday, so you do the math. I texted and called you countless times and never received a response. Whatever happened to teamwork?"

"Sorry."

"You should be. You could have at least warned me before you ran and did something thoughtless like this. I even went to your apartment early this morning to look for you but you weren't there."

He looked right at John. "You came to my apartment?"

"That's what I said. I rang the doorbell for five minutes until your roommate opened the door and told me."

"My roommate?"

"That's right. What was his name again... Ah, Levi. He told me his name was Levi. It would be rather odd of him to answer the door in his pajamas had he not been your roommate so I just assumed."

"Yes, my roommate. What else did he tell you?"

"Not much else. I had always thought you lived alone to be honest... but screw the idle talk for now and just tell me — where the *hell* were you all this time?"

As if his vanishing was of no consequence, Martin replied, casually, "I was kidnapped."

"What? This is not something to kid around about."

"You know I don't joke," insisted he, taking a quick scan at the few bystanders who appeared to be quite in shock by what he said. "But finding out exactly what happened to me really isn't the most important thing at the moment, or is it?"

Right when he finished speaking, everyone dispersed and returned to their usual work, except John. Having agreed with Martin, he advised him, "You'd better report to Shaw ASAP before he goes totally berserk. He already took it out on me once last Friday for not knowing where my partner had disappeared off to."

"That can wait."

"O...kay. I suppose it's up to you when to get your ass kicked. Then, let me catch you up on what happened these past couple of days..." As he went all out to give a verbal update on their two top-priority cases, Martin, however, was apparently more interested in his own file cabinets, meanwhile pulled out each drawer and dug through them. John had to stop himself in the middle of a sentence to ask him, "What are you looking for?"

"The black box with all the evidence to reopen Megan Skala's case."

He was staggered. "Oh Christ. You've got to be kidding me —"

"Where is it?" asked Martin, turning to focus on him, expecting a straight answer.

Much as John was bugged by his bullheaded dedication to a closed case, somehow he knew this was coming, thus telling him, "I passed it down to Jefferson while you were away."

"You did what?!" hissed Martin, shoving all the drawers shut at once, clearly upset. "You are not serious."

"Well, technically, he came and sort of took it."

"When?"

"The same day we got it really. One of his guys must have overheard our conversation and blown the whistle on us. Since it *is* his case to begin with, I let him."

"I can't believe you John —"

"What am I supposed to do? You tell me."

"What is he going to do about the case then?"

"Well... I wasn't going to tell you this now but, since you asked... I believe he sent the stuff down to Forensics for analysis, but when I checked with him this morning, he insisted that the case remains closed as is. So I assumed the DNA match came back negative. I'm sorry pal."

When John attempted to pat Martin on the shoulder, he swung his arm at him, refusing to accept what he had been told. "I don't believe this."

"Does it ever occur to you that maybe you've been wrong this whole time."

"How so? You know the story. I've played you the whole goddamn recording."

"Yeah, but a story told by a mad person, who also claimed that her dead brother was the murderer. Who knows how many more things she said weren't real?"

"So you think stuff like this just shows up at your door out of the blue for no reason? You are a fool John."

"Am I? I've seen the report Martin. Evidently, there was a suicide note linked to Megan's death."

"What suicide note?"

"The investigating team seized a handwritten note from her nightstand the same day she was found dead in her apartment. I saw it with my own eyes when Jefferson showed me the case file."

"Allison Skala mentioned nothing about a note... What says the autopsy report?"

"There wasn't one."

"What?"

"Stephen must have not thought it was necessary, given that there was enough evidence to determine the cause of her death."

"Stephen, as in Stephen Connelly, Jefferson's side-kick?"

"I don't like where you are going with this. You *can* not agree with them, but both of those guys are honest, honorable men."

"Says who?"

"Says me! And many other police sergeants and offic-ers."

Martin paused to give things a thought, but failed to concur with John after all. Furthermore, all this brand-new information only strengthened his curiosity if not worry. "What was the cause of death then?"

"Severe blood loss from a laceration on her wrist."

"No way."

"Yup."

If Allison Skala was telling me the truth, Megan should have technically died from drowning. The cut on her wrist would have only been a cover-up for the homicide. The autopsy would have certainly indicated fluid in her lungs should that be assumed true, yet Stephen, the coroner for this case, somehow decided one was not needed...

"And she was inside the tub, naked, when they found her?"

"Correct. She was in a sitting position with water up to her chest."

"She was sitting?"

"Yup."

That's not what she told me. Could she have remembered it wrong?

'... I watched him strip her naked and lay her down beneath the water with her back touching the hard tub floor... her knees bended so as to fit her legs within the tight space of the tub...'

Or, could she really have made up the whole story? And if so, what about the bloody shoes and gloves? No... something just isn't adding up.

"Perhaps if we had consulted him like I suggested, you wouldn't have had to go through all that trouble for nothing," John added.

"Consult Jefferson?"

"Yes."

"Pah! The day that I do that would be the last day I have any dignity for myself... you can mark-my-words."

Realizing he had accidentally struck a raw nerve, in an attempt to put down the fire before it could get worse, he urged Martin in his most sincere manner, "Come on kid. Don't loose your cool over this. There are still many more cases waiting for us to solve. Let's just worry about those for now, huh?"

Sadly, it was not up to him should the fire decide to go where it intended.

57

AS MARTIN CONTINUED to hold firm his belief, he only grew increasingly livid talking to John. Instead of arguing with him to no avail, soon he set off like the wind to seek Jefferson out for a confrontation. Seeing he was not at his desk, he stormed from hallway to hallway, conference room to conference room in quest of him.

Meanwhile, Jefferson was meeting with prosecutors regarding a different case in one of the rooms. Disturbed by the commotion in the hall, he approached to close the door for some privacy, only then Martin pushed it back open, almost hitting him in the nose. Startled, he backed away slightly, somewhat managing to compose himself so as to not lose face.

"Oh hello, look who's back from his vacation," mocked he, looking at raging Martin with his head held high.

While paying no attention to his scornful greeting, Martin blurted out, "Allison Skala is the murderer."

"Excuse me?"

"You heard me... What did you do to the evidence huh? Burnt them?"

"I'm sorry to interrupt, but what is going on here? Are we even talking about the same case?" asked Sam, one of the prosecutors sitting in the room, utterly puzzled by his seemingly reckless accusation.

"Humph. Hardly," sneered Jefferson, telling Martin off, "Now if you would take your childish game back out-side, we are in the middle of an important discussion. Un-like you, the rest of us haven't the time to dance around and make a fool of ourselves."

"Then answer my question," Martin persevered, tak-ing a step towards him, "Where is the evidence?"

In turn, Jefferson backed away some more, and as everyone awaited a response from him, a flush of embar-rassment rose to his face. Though he was in no way going to break that easily.

"I have no idea what you are referring to."

"You son of a —"

"*Watch* your tone, Blake."

All in due course, John arrived at the scene. Sensing a chance to escape such an in-your-face humiliation, Jeffer-son said out loud specifically for him to hear. "Can some-one remove this lout? We are all trying to work in here. I can't stand anymore distractions."

Before John could break through the crowd of fasci-nated onlookers plugging up the tight doorway to get to Martin however, the latter had already launched himself at Jefferson, grabbing him by the collar and firing back at his feigned ignorance. "You came and took the box from my desk, I'm only asking for it back. Now for the third time, where is it? Give it back or else —"

"Or else what? Don't think that you can terrorize me kid. I've dealt with a lot worse than your entire career put together. You would be *wrong* to think that I'm even re-motely afraid of you. I said the case is indefinitely closed, period. There is absolutely *nothing* you can do about it," snapped Jefferson, staring deep into his pupils and not blinking. He might be the only one not threatened by Mar-tin's savage way, because to everyone else, the sheer wrath on his face was undoubtedly, ferocious.

His increasing aggression prompted Sam to stand up and give him an ultimatum. "Let him go now or I will report you to Shaw!"

John as well came forth now to try and talk him out of it. "Come on buddy. You've gone far enough. Let it go..." Eventually, he managed to pull him away, but not without work.

While things seemed to be ending on a fortunate note, Jefferson, for one, was not about to dismiss eagerly the ridicule Martin had done him. Nothing at present could possibly satisfy him more than getting him into serious trouble. Due to that fact, he went on to provoke him.

At the precise moment Martin turned for the door, he remarked loudly and deliberately so that everyone heard, all the while fixing his collar, "What a loony. Crazy obviously runs in his family."

There were a few poorly suppressed laughs, but nothing truly bruised Martin's ego except for his own inner vulnerability. Leaving no time for second thoughts, he pushed John aside and swung back around sharply to punch Jefferson across the face. The two thereupon resorted to physical scuffling, tipping chairs and shoving tables as they clashed with one another at close quarters. More of their colleagues hearing the rumpus had come to watch, while some just simply walked on by the doorway shaking their heads, feeling shamed by the two law enforcers' not-so-civil behavior.

The twenty-five-year age gap between the men quickly came as a drawback to Jefferson, who was soon forced to the floor with Martin on top of him and both his arms riveted to the ground. Despite being in a lesser position, his tongue was still as sharp as ever. "*I dare you to hit me again Blake... go ahead you son of a bitch!*"

Gasping for breath, Martin was just about to raise his fist again had Lieutenant Shaw not shown up at the door or yelled "STOP" right the second. Of the onlookers, many had scattered upon his coming; the few that remained made way for him to come through. Upon his entrance, the room immediately went quiet, equivalent to a television on mute.

"Let him go, now!" he ordered Martin.

Bitter as he was, Martin knew very well the consequence if he were to disobey, thus freeing Jefferson from his sturdy grip and getting off of him.

Jefferson then sat up on the floor. While wiping off the little blood from the corner of his lips, he scowled ominously at Martin as if telling him telepathically: *you are going to pay for this*.

"My office, both of you," Shaw commanded.

As Martin turned to stand up, in a sneaking whisper, Jefferson cursed at his back just enough for him to hear. "*Wimp,*" he called him.

Halfway, Martin stopped, his hands turned once again into fists. Sensing a reaction, the provoker finished his kill —

"*What a useless piece of pussy.*"

Just like that, acting completely on impulse, Martin spun back around cocking his fist and drove it unthinkingly into Jefferson's nose. His head was thrust backward momentarily by the impact of that blow, as it returned to its normal position, blood came dripping onto his clean, white shirt.

Every eye in the room was stunned by Martin's bold move and every person considered his action stupid, especially Lieutenant Shaw, who now would have no choice but to punish him accordingly. "*To my office I said,*" he commanded a second time, directed at Martin, giving him a black look.

Despite the physical pain Jefferson must be feeling, he grinned lightly, and spoke up to the commander in a rather insolent tone, "Well Shaw, I trust you to do the right thing this time. Lay down the ground rules for this one, and just make sure they are well understood once and for all."

58

THE BRAWL MIGHT be over, but its aftermath was just starting to take effect. Sam, having been there the whole time, offered to testify as an impartial witness, even though he clearly sided with Jefferson on this occasion. Surely, Lieutenant Shaw had always held Martin's work in high regard, but so much for that, an assault like this was doubtless severe enough to warrant an arrest and should that happen, not even God could save him.

Sitting outside Shaw's office, Martin naturally grew more worried waiting to be called in and not just about what punishment he would receive — but in particular — about what Shaw was going to say this time. The previous, similar incident that happened was barely three months ago. He had been seriously warned then to tone down his "juvenile ego" and should have known better to not let himself go out of whack like that again, especially since the pledge he took in front of him at the end of their one-on-one conversation. Because the last thing he wanted was to lose his job, thoughts as such literally made him sick to his stomach like he was about to vomit his brains out. If only he could do it over, perhaps he would have hesitated with those punches, but just perhaps.

Fifteen minutes later, Jefferson came out after having spoken with Shaw. He said not a word to Martin and just shot him a look of smug satisfaction when going by, as if the bruises on his face were well worth it.

"Come in, Blake!" called Shaw.

It did not help his nerves one bit when Shaw demanded him to shut the door upon his entering the room, in a sense solidifying the gravity of their conversation to come...

"... Disappearing for five days, and then assaulting a colleague on the day of your return. This is not a playground where you can just come and go and do whatever you want. This is work God dammit!"

"I was working as a matter of fact —"

"*Do not bullshit me!* Not only did you embarrass yourself, but you also embarrassed me with your idiotic, *brainless* action. Why you would ever put your career at risk like that, I will never understand."

Martin gulped back his nervousness, could no longer bear looking directly at him. "I was just trying to approach him about a case."

"So you can't be civil huh? Must it result in savagery?!"

"No..."

"*Speak up God dammit!*"

"No sir!"

"You betcha no! There's absolutely no need to turn to physical violence against one another, especially not on my watch. And I don't give a damn for what reason..."

He was feeling quite shamefaced and had decided to keep his mouth shut and let Shaw come down on him like a ton of bricks for the next two minutes. Not wishing to dwell further on the matter, Shaw eventually took a long, deep sigh to sort of mellow his black mood before telling him his verdict in blunt terms.

"Three-day suspension effective immediately. I was gonna go with ten if we weren't so god-damn understaffed. You are in tremendous luck, let me tell you, that Jefferson's decided not to press charges for the bloody nose and swollen cheek you gave him."

Knowing that he had gotten away lucky, Martin thanked him, but that did little to ease Shaw's fury.

"Uh-uh, don't thank me. Whatever feud going on between you two I do not intend to find out, but I warn you,
one more misstep, next time I won't let you off this easily,
nor can I. So I suggest that you spend the next few days
straightening up your act. Do I make myself clear?!"

"Yes sir!"

Prior to his dismissal, Shaw felt much obligated to
give him a pointer or two regarding a little fact of life.
"Learning to respect can go a long way kid. Jefferson's
been with the police force most of his life. It is no doubt
that he's been through and achieved more than you and I
combined. Had he not turned down multiple offers to
move up the hierarchy, he would have certainly been a
major or even a county sheriff by now. His credibility is
pretty much assured you see. Even the chief himself has to
put up with him sometimes and give him some leeway.
You've got to at least recognize that and play along with
the politics. So next time, before you let his senior attitude
get the best of you, think of what I said and be the bigger
person."

Martin could only, at best, force a nod towards him.
Swallowing his pride, shortly, he removed himself from
there holding in a stomach full of bitterness. Since there
was no reason to return to his desk, he headed straight
out.

As if walking blind, he took no notice of whomever he
came to pass in the corridor and almost collided with
Crystal on his way. "Excuse me," he said to her briefly and
moved right on, not bothering to spare a second of his
time. Not everybody could resist the temptation of physical attraction, however.

Upon a brush of his sleeve running by her arm, Crystal's heart raced a little faster. She felt an urge to call out
after him and did so immediately. "Detective Blake! Wait!"

He stopped for her. When she caught up to him, first
thing, she proffered stoutly a bandage she had kept previ-

ously in her wallet, telling him, "Here, take this. For your face."

"My face?"

"Over there, you got a cut on your left cheek."

In consequence of her kindness, Martin felt slight warmth inside him in contrast to the hostility he had been getting from everyone all morning. "Thank you," he said to her after accepting it.

"You are more than welcome. I saw the fight. I was in the conference room where you and Brad were at it with each other."

"I know. I saw you."

Right then, she dimpled into a winsome grin, tucking her beautiful, chocolate-brown hair behind her ears. She was going to continue in good spirits but was abruptly cut short.

"Well, I —"

"Actually, I think I'm better off like this. My face doesn't hurt that bad anyway."

"Oh... okay, no problem." Confused, she retrieved the bandage. But just as he turned his back on her, she came around in front of him, asking openly, "You know, I was just going out to grab some coffee, would you care to join me?"

Certainly without a doubt, Crystal would be an ideal girlfriend in many aspects. Based on their comparative allure and intelligence, she and Martin could very well make a supreme couple with much to be envied, provided that he truly fancied her that way. Noting her notion, part of him felt bad turning her down, but he was not one to tamper with a lady's affection either.

"I think I'll pass. It's just that I uh... I'm busy."

"Oh... right. I've actually spoken to John earlier. He said that you guys have been swamped with work lately so I can understand... My workload's been quite the opposite the last few days on the other hand, so —"

"It won't be necessary."

"Huh? I'm trying to say, if you need assistance with anything, like the case that you mentioned earlier in the conference room, I would be happy to help out in any way I can."

"I know, and my answer stands. Not that I don't appreciate your gesture, but I've got it covered."

"But —"

"If — if somewhere down the line I do need help from the prosecution team, I'll make sure to let you guys know."

"I see... Of course."

"Good. Now, excuse me."

As he resumed walking away, Crystal ran the risk to ask him briskly, "How long have you known?"

That question brought him to a standstill.

Acting on a hunch, she continued, "My dad was a policeman for twenty years. Since day one of joining the force, he had to hide his secret from everyone, even from my mom. He never truly loved her. As a matter of fact, he only got married because his pastor said it would be good for him. They divorced when his secret leaked out and he was fired from his job for it. That caused quite a scandal actually... But, despite all the drama that happened back then, now he leads a happy life living with his partner and their dog in a humble apartment downtown. I think, overall, it was a very brave thing he did for himself. Though in all honesty, I think you are handling it far more considerately. I mean, you give an impression of a lone wolf and maintain this icy image to keep women from getting involved with you... but dare I say, not every woman is like what you think of them. Sometimes, maybe she's just being friendly. We all can use a friend in some way or —"

"I'm not what you think, Crystal," Martin interrupted all of a sudden, turning around to face her. "I don't need friends the way you do. And even if I do need a friend somehow, it would be completely moronic of me to befriend someone who's got me entirely, and utterly, *wrong*, from the start."

"But —"

"I'm sorry for the loneliness you feel I guess, but I don't do charity —"

Crystal would have come back at him had he not stated everything so assuredly and unwaveringly...

"— I'm sure you will find some other men who will lend you a shoulder or two to cry on, but not from me. Do you get the picture, or do I need to say more?"

... Instead, she just stood there, tongue-tied, wishing the ground would swallow her up and end her discomfiture.

Right the next moment, he left her.

59

H AVING NOT COME across a case that excited him to this degree in years, Martin therefore would not simply give it up. The many unknowns heightened his desire to seek out Allison, who was not at her home when he arrived. Considering the state in which he found her last, he was not surprised and in fact suspected that she had been taken against her will that very same day. If his abduction theory proved true, he had everything to believe that her parents were in some way responsible.

Straight after the stop-off, he called John from his car to try and obtain the Crawfords' current address on record. Given that he had just been temporarily suspended from work, John strictly denied his request. "No can do Martin," he told him, appalled at his daring endeavor. "I don't know what you are up to, but don't you think you should at least try to keep your nose clean for a while?"

"Give me the address John. I'm just looking for a chat with them."

"Yeah, just a chat. I believe you."

Adamant about getting his way, Martin resorted to telling him about his conversation with Brenda, in addition to finding Allison lying unconscious, and his collapse resulting from an assault by armed physicians. After hearing him out, John was left aghast.

"Are you sure it wasn't just one of your nightmares you are telling me?"

"Come on John."

"Okay... So, now you are thinking her mother has something to do with it all."

"Allison Skala is missing. People don't just vanish without a trace. If her parents do know all along about the murder she committed —"

"Hold it. We have hardly proven she actually did kill Megan."

"You are right, but *if* that is true, they are doing whatever it takes to protect their daughter, even if it is against Allison's own wish to be saved."

While understanding his rationale, John still could not neglect his apprehension. "Can't you just leave it to our colleagues to handle this? You are on suspension for Christ's sake."

"Leaving it to whom do you suggest? Jefferson? John, I was knocked out cold for five days and dumped under some tree in a park. I'm desperate for an answer."

"And we are going to pay for your curiosity now aren't we both? I have three other mouths to feed have you forgotten? Unlike you, I can't lose my job."

"I think you are over exaggerating it a bit, all I'm asking from you, is their address..."

Knowing that his opinion meant little to Martin at this point, he gave in in the end. "You better know what you are doing, Martin."

"Of course I do, always."

"If you say so... Give me a few minutes here. I will forward you the information. Don't say I never warned you. If you so happen to dig yourself into a hole again, you know the drill."

60

THIRTY MINUTES NORTHEAST of Arbington was a small, historic town called Ship's Haven, famous for its gorgeous riverside view and many hills. The most well known of those hills, on which some of the finest homes in Minnesota were situated, was Hampton Hill. The further up that slope, the grander the houses became; therefore none of those opulent structures befitted royalty quite as well as the handsome, French-inspired chateau standing proudly at its peak, one erected on a land of ten acres, overlooking the utmost breathtaking view of the St. Croix River. Such a magnificent, ivory beauty had been the local crown jewel of luxury properties for many years, and such was also the Crawfords' private residence.

From its ornate swing gate, Martin followed a long, paver driveway sided with vast neon-green lawns for about a minute, till it opened up into a circle with a stone fountain outlined with colorful fall blooms in the middle. Pulling up behind a Rolls Royce parked around the curb just off of the front steps, he got out standing in awe of the majestic mansion and its perfectly manicured landscaping, but was before long interrupted.

"How may I help you sir?" a formally dressed butler called out to him from the front door set between two tall, sculpted columns.

Consequently, Martin walked up to him, presenting his police badge as he spoke, "I'm here to see Mr. and Mrs. Crawford in regard to their daughter Allison Skala."

The butler checked his identification carefully, scanning him up and down, asking, "Is this about her husband's murder?"

"I'm afraid I can't say."

He looked directly at Martin. "I see. One moment please."

After retreating into the mansion for a short period, he returned to officially let him in.

"Would you like to check your coat sir?"

"No, I prefer to have it on."

"Not a problem. Right this way."

Through the arched hallway, Martin followed him to the end of the grand hall where a marble staircase curving up awaited them. Taking into account the aristocratic and regal charm of its exterior, he surely did not expect any less sumptuousness from the interior of this stately home — a place so massive, so architecturally stunning and rich in antiques that just touring it could take up a whole day. Once reaching the second floor, they took a left into the west wing. Every room alongside their way was elegantly appointed, some akin to ones from a royal palace. At last, they stopped in front of a French door all the way down the long corridor.

Perhaps smaller in size, this room was nonetheless still spacious, coffered ceiling, crystal drop chandeliers and all that, well equipped with a mini bar, a high-definition television above the stone fireplace, and posh furnishings at its forefront arranged in a cozy manner.

Turning to Martin, the butler informed him, "Mr. Crawford is finishing up with a guest. He will join you in here shortly. Please help yourself to any books for the time being, or if you prefer, the television."

"What about Mrs. Crawford?"

"Mrs. Crawford is out of town at the moment."

"May I ask where she's headed? And what for?"

"I regret that's not my information to give, sir," he asserted. "I'll have Mrs. Gomez bring up some refresh-
ments." Soon afterwards, he excused himself from the
room.

Not ever had Martin seen such an enormous collection of books peculiar to a single household. Even though
he had never been fond of reading, he felt every bit in-
trigued by the great back wall of potential wonders and
single-mindedly, approached to explore it.

*'Biblical Literatures', 'Biographies of the Greats', 'Sci-
ence Fiction Novels'...*

His fingers traced along the gold-plated labels on the
edge of the bookshelf, eventually, stopped at one that read
"Neuroscience". It was a particularly big section of hardcovers after hardcovers of hundreds of pages on psychiatric research and discoveries. A fat folder sticking out
within them naturally caught his notice. Removing it at
once, he causally flipped through the enclosed stack of
scholarly articles concerning the topic of memory erasure.
When reaching the bottom, he discovered a thick copy of
information explaining an experimental surgery conduct-
ed under the name of Joseph M. Carter, MD-PhD, and began reading it. Upon looking into the two "Consent for
Participation" forms stapled to its end page, he was
astounded to see Allison's name stated as one of the
twelve voluntary subjects for a neuropsychological study.
The first procedure had been done locally early last
month; as for the second, identical procedure, it was
scheduled to take place at a research facility in Sweden in
two weeks.

"Did you find something that strikes your fancy?"
Suddenly, Elton came striding into the room towards the
mini bar completely unannounced. Slightly caught off
guard, Martin silently composed himself, closing and putting back the folder to its original place before turning
around. Mrs. Gomez just so brought in a plate of hors

d'oeuvres in the meantime, along with a pot of freshly brewed coffee and tea.

"Just set the tray down over there," Elton instructed her from the bar counter, flicking his chin at the center table as he yanked off the stopper from the bottle of Scotch in his hand.

Mrs. Gomez did as told and then stepped aside, waiting to be dismissed.

"Please Mr. Blake, do take a seat and help yourself to the food."

"Don't worry about it. I don't plan on staying long," Martin replied straightforwardly.

Elton took a glimpse at him while pouring some whiskey into a tulip-shaped glass and then told Mrs. Gomez, "I'll handle it from here Martha. You may leave us alone now, and close the door for me on your way."

She did so swiftly.

Getting back to Martin, he asked him, "Do you drink by any chance?"

"Not usually, no. Got to keep my head straight doing what I do."

"Is that so? A dear old friend of mine is also a detective. For as long as I've known him, he's always been a hard drinker. That's strictly his favorite thing to do at his leisure, drinking. Well, that and fishing really... How about a cigar? Would you be interested in having one of those?"

"No, but thank you. I'm trying to quit smoking."

"Oh? Are you just starting out?"

"Ah... no. I just haven't done a good job staying on the beam."

"That is difficult to do no doubt. I happen to have been through the whole thing and let me assure you boy, it's going to be a tough journey. But should you succeed, it will be one of the best decisions you ever make in your life, just you see." Coming around the counter with his drink in one hand, he extended his other hand towards the leather settee. "Please Mr. Blake."

At his insistence, Martin moved his way over there and sat down.

"I do apologize for the wait. It's been very busy the past couple of days for me working with my realtor," said Elton, settling himself into the leather armchair nearest Martin.

"Are you selling this place, Mr. Crawford?"

"As a matter of fact, I am. My wife and I have been meaning to for a while now actually. As I'm getting closer to retire from my business in the States, there's really no point in continuing to pour money into maintaining such an expensive estate once we move to Europe."

"You are moving to Europe?"

"Yes, Sweden. We are expecting to some time near the end of this month if everything goes according to plan."

Martin grew mindful of him upon his mentioning "Sweden" but did not show it, casually asking, "Why Sweden?"

Elton was every bit eager to explain. "I've indeed asked myself that same question, considering the number of enchanting places to which Brenda and I have travelled. To put it simply, we've always dreamt of living in a foreign country, and Stockholm just happened to be the one city she fell deeply in love with. I suppose it has something to do with her mother's side of the family being Swedish, so she feels particularly connected to that culture and the people. A few months ago when we were there again, we came across this breathtaking, waterfront villa. The next thing I knew, I had made an offer to purchase it and started planning the move. It's easy telling you now, but the entire process was not without hassle, believe me." He paused to nose his whiskey, and then took a sip from the glass before continuing, "Speaking of real estate, if you don't mind me asking, do you currently own a place, Mr. Blake?"

"I have a condo."

"I figured as much, as do most young police officers. Well, between you and me, just as a thank-you for your excellent, investigative work on my son-in-law's case, if you ever want to buy a house, I'm more than eager to recommend a reliable agent. A close friend of mine who would take your condo off your hands and sell you a nice house free of commission..."

In spite of such generosity, seemingly without strings attached, Martin felt as though it was a bribe in camouflage, an allurement of some sort offered to him to gain his alliance. Whether or not that was true, he was not to be enticed by unwarranted advantages.

"Thank you for the offer, but I'm not interested."

"Don't get me wrong. I wasn't necessarily asking for an answer right this minute."

"I know."

"I'm merely suggesting if you ever wish to own a house —"

"I really have no thought as such."

Elton smiled, patiently insisting, "Perhaps you might change your mind in a year or two."

"I don't think so. My condo is just fine, but thanks for your *selfless* concern, on my account."

Keeping their eyes sharp on one another, the two men sat steadily still, both tried to read the other's guarded expression upon Martin's blunt, ironic delivery; until finally, Elton loosened up. Taking no offense, he leaned back in his chair crossing his legs, saying with a mild smirk, "Very well then. Suit yourself."

Martin took to carry on the conversation from a different aspect. "You have quite the collection of books, Mr. Crawford."

"Yes I do. I suppose that is one of the few things I'm still stuck in time with. Everything's in digital format these days, honestly, who would have thought two decades ago that was even feasible. But by no means am I complaining.

I reckon that you found yourself a good read during the wait?"

"I'm not much of a reader, but I did see that you have a large selection regarding neuroscience, specifically about psychosurgery. I'm just curious, why the interest?"

Elton nodded his head at him. His lips parted slightly to take a deep breath. "I'm not gonna lie, you've indeed touched on a rather sensitive topic of mine. It's like what my wife told you, my daughter, Allison, is still having a bit of a hard time accepting her brother's death, even though it's already been many years since. For the sake of her health, it's just another option into which we are willing to venture in order to get her well again. If that option ever becomes practicable."

"'An option'?"

"Yes, an option to surgically remove some of her bad memories, so to speak. Ones that rid her of her sanity —"

"An option, or a desperation?" Martin hinted back at him forthright, as a result cracking his veneer of composure.

"How do you mean?"

"Tell me — where is she?"

"I'm afraid that information is off limits to you Mr. Blake. I'd ask you to respect my family's privacy —"

"You've sent her away for a quick fix again, haven't you?"

"I'm not understanding you?"

Martin had decided to strike while the iron was hot. "To Sweden. You've sent her away to partake in some surgical experiment that could potentially erase her memories so that she won't remember what she's done. For your own selfishness, you would rather risk her life to keep her from dealing with the consequences of her own careless decision —"

"What careless decision? I hope you are not talking about Megan Skala's death again because it is getting old.

That woman killed herself and that's that. Whatever you have against Allison, you are wrong."

"Except that she *is* the murderer, and you've known it all along."

"ENOUGH! How dare you strip my daughter of her innocence with such a ludicrous indictment! Just who do you think you are?!"

"I'm only doing my job. I have new evidence to prove her guilty —"

"No you do not!!"

The entire room just then went harsh. During the time Elton let his inflamed temper slowly go and made clear his point. "Not that I believe any so-called 'evidence' exists, but if you did have something, wouldn't you have brought that to my attention from the start of this conversation? Why bother wasting all this time digging for clues?"

Martin might still look strong-willed as ever on the surface, but inwardly, he could not have felt more powerless without a single corroboration in hand and only relying on his own gut instinct. To make matters worse, before he had a chance to think up how to advance from here, his opponent was already one step ahead in preparation to take him down by shame.

"Quit it, Detective."

"If you really think I will give up searching for the truth, you are mistaken."

"I was told you are stubborn. After all, it is your steadfast perseverance that got you this far. But, do you really have a choice? Just one phone call, I can have my lawyer file a lawsuit against you for your verbal harassment based on a false assumption. Now — do you really want to go public with your circumstances?

"My circumstances?"

"How do you think the general public would rate a homosexual officer, who had previously, intentionally and

willfully, unhanded a serial killer that sent this nation into
frantic terror?"

Martin's cheeks went flush instantly upon the accusation, his voice much quieter. "You are making that up."

"Am I? Which part? I might be exaggerating it a little,
but you know best who you are and what you did."

As the feeling of pins and needles prickled over him,
he had literally nothing to counter back. "No one... no one
will believe you."

"Humph. I think you've underestimated me, Mr.
Blake. Perhaps — perhaps the name 'Jason Webb' sounds
familiar to you?"

Jason Webb...

That name that still echoed in Martin's head was a direct evocation of a failed SWAT operation he undertook
back when he was still part of the team. Like Elton had
declared with due emphasis, during a close-range pursuit
that could have most certainly been successful, he allowed
his sentiment to overtake his better judgment and deliberately let go of Sean, his serial killer of a brother, from his
grasp. He thought he was careful in that less than a second
of a moment, but apparently not so to dodge his former
teammate's, Jason's, keen sight and most definitely, he
never would have guessed this to come back and bite him
now.

Elton continued with a wry grin. "As much as I want
to be understanding of your situation, I'm afraid others
won't be quite as forgiving once that information is made
known to them. Imagine what your colleagues would
think of you, and whether people in general would consider a person like you fit for enforcing law. If you are
smart, you will not risk your future for this. Even if you
don't care about yourself, think for your boyfriend Levi."

"What do you have against him?"

"He owns a coffee shop, doesn't he? All I'm going to
say is, the media will print anything so long you pay them,
and people will believe anything they read as it is. I can

also add in a story or two about Susie Claire Blake, your drug addicted prostitute of a mother. I have a folder full of her history with men, which, I'm so sure, that she would much rather have rest in peace with her. Everyone loves a scandalous scoop like that and that's a fact you can't change. Certainly though, I can either do all of the above or nothing at all —"

"Is this blackmail?"

"Consider it whatever you like, I'm only asking you to stay out of my family affairs is all. The game is over, as you know it. You have no proof of anything, and it does you *absolutely* no good dwelling on questions to which you will *never* get answers..."

Feeling cornered and very much beaten, Martin was at a loss for words. He knew no matter how he tried to conduce the truth, fundamentally, no evidence meant no conviction. It was hardly up to him anymore when all was said and done.

A short while later, someone knocked on the door.

"Come in," ordered Elton.

It was the butler.

"Yes Thomas?"

"Mr. Davis has arrived and is waiting in the parlor."

"Very well." Elton thus got up from his chair, approached to offer Martin a shake of hands as the final step to close the deal. "Thanks for coming in, Mr. Blake. I sincerely hope we have a mutual understanding on the matter discussed."

In turn, Martin shot a look up at him, and then at the butler standing in the doorway before returning his focus on the hand extending at his eye level. Reluctantly, he grabbed and shook it.

Elton was looking well pleased then. "Good. Now if you'd excuse me, I have some important business to attend to. Thomas —"

"Yes?"

"Please see Mr. Blake out."

PART THREE

CONSCIENCE

THREE YEARS AFTER

61

"IT'S ALMOST STRANGE to see that color on your face," said Levi.

"What? Am I turning red again?"

"Precisely. Are you really that nervous to see him?"

Martin said nothing further, basically too neurotic to speak on the matter lightly. Six in the morning, he was getting dressed up to visit Sean in prison for the very first time. He thought he would be mentally prepared for this day when it finally arrived, but he thought wrong.

"You've got to turn your brain off and stop worrying about what to say to him," Levi took to advise him.

"Easy for you to say."

"I'm just trying to get you to look on the bright side. He should be happy enough to know that you are spending a day off just to visit. What did John have to say about this?"

"About me seeing Sean? I didn't tell him."

"No, about you taking some time off. He must have been surprised as hell. Knowing you, you are the type of person who'd even work on a holiday."

"He's fine with it. We just wrapped up two big cases this last week. He probably couldn't care less had I decided to take a whole week off instead of just two days."

"Until something comes up again and then vacation's over right?"

Martin shot him a serious look. "That's just part of my job, to be available at all times."

Levi just grinned, checking his watch. "I should get going or I will be late to open. Are you coming in later today?"

"I'm not sure yet. Depends if I can make it there and back in one piece... I'll text you."

"You are not much of a funny man Marty. Tell Sean 'happy birthday' for me would you please?"

Keeping his head down, Martin replied a faint "okay" and finished tying his tie. Levi sensed his low spirit and so tried to cheer him with a peck on the cheek and a bit of his usual humor before leaving. "You know, worst-case scenario, if he starts throwing things, at least you know you will only be there for half an hour."

It somewhat worked.

"Riiight. Thanks."

"Haha. Like I said, just relax and you will be fine..."

If being fine meant with the help of nicotine stimuli, Martin would not feel too bad going overboard with the cigarettes on this potentially momentous day, just to be safe. From the moment he got away from the city's bustle onto the expressway, he was never without a ciggy in between his fingers all the way to the federal facility two full hours later. Not letting himself overthink the situation, he came through the visitors' gateway quickly, parked his car at the first spot he saw in the parking lot and got out walking into the building with a care package in his hand.

All right. Here we go.

Given his occupation, this was hardly his first time coming to a penitentiary. Rarely had he ever felt so overwrought being in one, in fact, never. Owing to the special reason that brought him here today, this depressing place of grim loneliness suddenly felt grimmer and much darker.

If nothing else, the check-in process went without too much trouble. Because no physical items were permitted beyond the security checkpoint, he turned in the package prior to going through the metal detector. After that, he was guided to a small meeting room where he would sit tight and wait.

Escorted in handcuffs by a unit staff, Sean arrived at the door ten agonizing minutes later, looking neat in his khaki pants and button-down shirt worn over a white undergarment.

Right that second, Martin stood up.

"Are you twins?" the unit staff asked him out of curiosity, amazed at their parallel images.

"Yes," he responded, his eyes consistently locked on Sean.

"You don't say! That's certainly a first."

As they were talking, Sean had aimed for the closest chair and moved to sit down into it before Martin could officially initiate a greeting.

He then too lowered into his seat again.

Joined by a table between them, the brothers might be palpably within reach but deep down they were miles apart. Granted, they had never sat face-to-face like this for a chat ever before, therefore the awkwardness was simply inevitable. Staring idly at the grey floor, Sean uttered no word and only shook his leg constantly in a nervous manner. Martin wanted to be the most understanding for the next thirty minutes, but exactly how to break his brother out of his withdrawn self was truly exceeding his comprehension.

Upon the door closed, he began. "How are you?"

Seconds later, Sean replied in brief, "Good."

"Good... Did they —"

"How a-aa-about you?"

"I'm sorry?"

"How about you?"

"Oh, I'm doing fine. Thank you for asking."

There went a moment of silence until Sean resumed the conversation, all the while trying his best to keep his stammer under control. "Wha...what were you saying?"

"What was that?"

"You said somm-mm...something. Then I stopped you."

"Oh, right. I was just going to uh... compliment your hair. It's short and nicely trimmed. Did they ahem... did they cut it for you?" Martin only realized how ridiculous his question was halfway through his sentence. Before he would be soaked up in embarrassment, he noticed a half-suppressed smile sneaking across Sean's lips and his eyes slowly creeping upward to look at him. That little gesture by itself alleviated the dispensable dread amidst them.

"How are they treating you?" Martin continued with much ease.

"I get my ow...own cell and am fed every day. The only baaa...bad thing is when they force those pills down your throat at night whether you li...like it or not."

"I'm sorry."

"Nah. N-nooot...not your fault. You work?"

"Yes. I'm a police detective."

"A real one?"

He nodded.

"That'ssss impressive."

"Thank you —"

"You u-u-u-used to dream of one day becoming a cop so you could teaaa...teach those bad guys who took advantage of Mom a lesson. Like that fucker Gary."

"That was a long time ago. I'm surprised you remember what I said."

"I don't remember much else. We weren't thhhh...that close as kids. Except occasionally sharing the same bed, we di-d-didn't talk."

"Right."

"Have you vvvi...visited her?"

A wave of grief just then crashed over Martin. "She..." He almost held back breaking him the bad news. "She passed away, Sean. Thirty years ago."

"I know."

"You know?"

"I ssssaw her at the hospital. Mrs. Belinsky, Ji...Jimmy's Mom, took me. You remember Jimmy?"

"Um... no, not really. But you did see Mom down at the morgue?"

"Yes."

Sean's affirmation was — quite literally — a weight off Martin's chest. He sighed with deep solace and added, "She was cremated three days later. I took her ashes and scattered them into the Mississippi River from behind the children's playground she used to bring us to all the time —"

"How did it happen? Who k-k-ki...killed her?"

Wanting to spare his brother the violent details, he had decided on somewhat of a white lie. "There was a burglary at the trailer. They shot her."

"And Gar-rr-gary?"

"Yes. They got him too."

"Good..."

Sean nodded his head a few times in recognition, rubbing his tongue against the ridges of his back teeth to sort of restrain his lips from trembling, and blinking to keep his eyes from watering. Reckoning it was probably best to stick to lighter subjects, Martin did so henceforth. "I got you another package. I've left it to the officers to deliver to you. Honestly it isn't much. I can only hope that you like to read —"

"I like to read," Sean replied frankly. "They thought I couldn't fu-fucking read, man I proved them wrong."

"Yeah? Do you prefer magazines or books?"

"Novels."

"Right."

"I finished all the ones you sent and wen...went to borrow from the library."

"I heard the library is decent here. You can even get new editions sometimes."

"Egh. It's alright."

"So, what kind of novels? As in what genre?"

Slouching against the back of his chair, Sean tilted his head back to think deeply for a moment, eyes at the ceiling. "I like that Stephen guy."

"Stephen... Stephen King you mean? That's like horror stories then."

"I like them gory. It can't be tha...that good of a book if it doesn't involve some sort of bloodshed."

"Is that right."

"Mm-hmm. There's this one book I'm reading. I've actually b-b-br-brought it here to show you... HEY! YOU!!!" he shouted out of the blue, looking off to the unit staff standing in a corner. "GIVE ME MY FUUU-FUCKING BOOK BACK!!!!"

Subsequently, Martin turned to his side where he was then given a paperback novel. Taking a look at its cover, he was surprised to see a familiar name — the author's name — printed just below the title of the book, namely, *Erase.*

Allison Skala... It can't be the same person, can it?

It appeared to be a fairly new release, published just last year in May.

"They said I'm not allowed to give it to you myself. A bunch of aa-a-assholes! They are doing it to get me worked up."

"They are just following the standard procedure. I'm sure they have nothing against you. Why don't you tell me about this book."

"It's about a m-murr..."

"Murder?"

"Yup. If you are curious, you can pick up where I left off. I'm at a g-g-good part too. Read it out if you want."

Therefore, Martin flipped to where a comb was kept to bookmark page 225. One last glance at Sean anticipating his start, he went on to narrate the plot, line by line from the top:

"... I almost puked as a result of that laceration, whereas my mother kept a cold face the entire time, flinging Maggie's arm back into the tub. Turning to me next, she demanded, 'Take those bloody shoes off. I don't want you leaving smears everywhere.' As I did so, she had gone and brought back a shoebox lying around the apartment. Since I was all too overcome with horror to be of much help in terms of wrapping up the mess, she sent me to the living room to cool off and act as lookout. Not long after I went, she came out of the bathroom talking in a hurry.

'Let's go. Brad will be here shortly to take care of the rest.'

'Who's Brad?'

'Uncle Brad.'

'He knows about this?'

'He will as soon as I inform your father. What? You think I would have us risk going to jail for this? If only I had the patience to wait till the guys sort out their plan, I wouldn't even need to kill her myself... I can tell you more about it later, but let's get a move on before the neighbors become alert.'

Leading the way, she safeguarded the shoebox against her chest before stepping out with me following after. One moment she closed the door stealthily behind us, the next we were aiming for the stairwell, hastening towards it. Just about reaching the end of the narrow hallway, a man emerged from around the corner with his pit bull walking in our direction.

Things got a bit problematic then.

'Excuse me,' she said to him as they were coming to pass one another. It was at that moment his dog suddenly went mad and launched its mouth at the shoebox in one quick jump. It only just missed it but nevertheless wounded her on the arm as a consequence. During the terror, the box slipped from her care by accident. I moved swiftly to pick it back up from the floor just before the ferocious creature could come at it again.

WOOF — WOOF —!

Yanking at its leash, the man yelled, 'No Rocky! Stop!' barely able to get it under his control. 'Sorry. He's still new to the hood, not listenin' to nobody. A real pain in the ass really. All his shots are up to date I swear. So please do me a favor, don' call the cops.'

'It's... it's okay. It's only a scratch,' she told him, still in a bit of shock.

'So we cool? Cool. You know, my apartment ain't far down this hall. I can get dat cut taken care of fo' ya. I've got gauze and bandages —"

'That's not necessary.'

'You sure? It won' take very long —'

'No! I mean yes, I'm sure. We're hurrying to get somewhere. So please, excuse us.'

Before he could stall us further, we had picked up our feet and hustled away.

Down the stairs we sprinted. We did not stop until reaching the ground level when my mother heard voices coming from the lobby. She was careful to spy on the people talking before we would move out of the shaft to head for the entrance. On that first peek, her heart just plummeted to the floor.

'You've got to be kidding.'

'What's going on?'

'Policemen, two of them.'

'Should we wait till they leave?'

'No. Absolutely not.' She thought for a minute, and then turned to say to me, 'I have an idea. You are going to get out through the back exit. I'll meet you at home. And take the box with you.'

'Why don't we go together?'

'I want to keep an eye on them. Just do as I say. We haven't got time to waste.'..."

Much as Martin would like to keep on reading, he stopped after reciting two whole pages, thinking he had come to chat with his brother instead of poring over some mystery novel.

"This is a very interesting book," he commented and closed it.

"So?"

"So...?"

"Did she l-l-l-leave by herself?" Sean asked him en-thusiastically, apparently just as hooked to the story and wanting to know what happened next.

"You want me to continue?"

"YES!"

Therefore, Martin picked the book right back up.

"… Nothing else could have sent me deeper into a cold sweat than seeing a police car parked in the driveway the moment I got home; but before I would shut down in panic, Ned came out of the vehicle. It was a major relief. Propping the shoebox securely against myself, I too got out.

'What happened to your shoes?' he approached and asked me.

'What do you mean?'

'I mean why are you barefoot?'

I left no explanation and just kept on walking, heading for the door.

'Are you not talking to me anymore?'

'What do you want Ned?'

'Well — I was just stopping over to see if you'd like to hang out this weekend.'

'You couldn't just text me about it?'

'I was going to, but then…'

'But then?'

'But then you would just blow me off like you've been doing lately.'

'I'm sorry, but I've been busy.'

'Even this weekend?'

'Why not?'

'I thought your husband won't be back for a week?'

Surprised that he knew about that, I stopped to question him, 'Who told you?' Though just before he could act ignorant, I figured it had to have been Sally's doing. 'Right, don't answer.' I was looking quite pissed then, mostly deliberately hoping to drive him away, but he was persistent about following me.

'I'm sorry if I've upset you.'

'No. It's fine.'

'But you don't look fine... Is something wrong?'

Arriving at the door at last, I opened it and went inside. 'I've got to go Ned.'

'So this is it. You aren't even going to invite me in? Come on Alice,' he said almost in a begging tone, his hand casually cupping over mine that was holding the side of the door. Knowing he would not just quit for quitting's sake, I gave in and let him come in. When he did, I made up an excuse to step away for a moment. 'I'm going to go get changed.'

'You need help with that?'

I decided to say nothing.

Seeing I was not amused, he apologized, 'I'm sorry. I was entirely joking.'

'Just wait for me in the living room. I'll be right back.'

While he headed there, I went and grabbed a roll of duct tape from the kitchen drawer and straightaway proceeded upstairs into the guest bedroom and locked the door. Not knowing exactly what I was doing, I spent minimal time taping the shoebox around and around for several times until it turned solid black before I would hide it underneath the bed for the time being. As I crouched down to shove it into the tiny space from the side of the bed, unexpectedly, I freaked out seeing at its opposite end a pair of eyes staring back at me. I gasped and withdrew myself, trying to hold down a shriek while scooting all the way backward till my back bashed the closet door.

My heart had never pounded faster. I was so scared and confused then suddenly, there came a familiar fit of giggles.

'Adrian? Is that you?'

'He-hahHHA! Hi Alice,' he responded, coming to me from around the bed. 'Sorry to make you jump like that.'

'Thank God it was just you!'

'Who else did you think it was?'

'Nobody. I didn't expect to see anyone in here.'

'That was the whole point!'

'Shh! Keep it down. We are not alone.'

'I know. That Ned guy is here. I was watching you two through the windows. I'm surprised you let him in the house at all. A bit of a risk taker aren't you sis?'

'You know… you know about the murder?'

'Of course. I gave my input where I saw fit.'

'You and Mom talked?'

'Don't act so shocked —'

But I really was.

'— Who do you think gave her the idea in the first place?'

Meanwhile, Ned was calling for me. 'ALICEEE!'

Shit.

'There's a lot more things going on that you don't know about, but this is hardly the time to dish them out. You've got to get rid of him.'

'But the box —' I barely got my words out before he took out a lighter from his pocket and lit it on fire.

'What are you doing?!'

'Just go! I can handle this from here.'…

… The doorbell rang just seconds after Ned had left. I opened the door to see my mother, standing looking disturbed. 'What was that about?' she asked me.

'What?'

'That policeman, what was he doing here?'

'Relax Mom. He's a friend of mine.'

'Did you —'

'Of course not. I didn't tell him anything.'

'Good… good. Let's get inside.'

Soon as I closed the door, she was looking for the shoebox. 'Where is it?'

'I uh… I got rid of it.'

'What do you mean you got rid of it?'

Right then, there was a bang coming from the ceiling above us. 'Adrian's upstairs.' I informed her.

It was as if she had misheard me cursing her or something, first she stared, and then she glared at me as I walked past her towards the living room to get the fist-aid kit for her arm.

'Stop right there.'

I did, and turned to look at her.

'What did you just say to me?'

'I said Adrian is upstairs.'

'Why are you talking like this?'

'Like how?'

'Are you doing this to upset me?!'

'What? No.'

'How long have you been talking to him?'

'I don't understand —'

'Answer me!'

I don't understand why she finds the need to start yelling at me. 'I...'

'Actually, don't tell me. Because you have to be mistaken young lady, mistaken you hear!!'

It was to the least of my expectation to have to argue with my mother over whether I talked to my brother at a crucial time like this, but despite absurdity, I could see it in her face and hear it in her voice that she did not intend to just let it go.

'In any case, he's here, probably still in the guest room,' I told her, calmly, calling out to my brother, 'Adrian! Come down!'

In the next half a second, she grabbed at me roughly, hissing in my face. 'Stop this nonsense and listen to me. The Adrian you see isn't real.'

'Why would you say that?'

'Because your brother is dead — he's dead!'

I was totally muddled at best. 'What are you talking about?'

'Listen —'

'I just saw him a moment ago...'

'LISTEN TO ME I SAID!!!!' she bellowed, slapping me across the face for no reason. Her flaming eyes directing at me looked as though they were about to pop out of their sockets from pure rage. 'I'll only ask you to do this once, so *don't* get further on my nerves. Now repeat what I say: Adrian isn't real.'

'You are acting crazy again Mother —'

She slapped me again. 'I said — Adrian isn't real. Say it!'

'No —'

'Say it! He's not real! SAY IT! *SLAP* SAY IT!!!!'

'STOP IT MOTHER! STOP THIS!'
'SAY IT! *SLAP* SAY ITTTT!!!!!!!'
'OKAY HE'S NOT REAL! HE'S NOT REAL!!!!!!!'

Finally, she let go of me and I dropped to the floor instantaneously, hopeless and tearing up. 'Why... why you are doing this to me...'

All that physical torment apparently scarcely satisfied her. In a moment, she looked down at me and declared, 'You are coming with me now. We are going to the doctor.'

'No... NO! You can't make me!'

'Really? We'll see about that.' Startlingly, she pulled me by the arm down the basement stairs without care. I tried fighting her grip and succeeded, climbed back up a few steps but then was dragged back down again. Reasoning with her was like talking to a brick wall, useless. Ignoring my screaming pleas, once getting to the storage room, she pushed me in and locked me up inside.

'Let me out Mom! LET ME OUT!' I howled, pounding the door violently but ultimately, it did nothing to change her mind.

'Let's hope... let's hope Joseph has something... anything to fix you this time.'..."

THE NEXT DAY

62

MEDICAL DAILY: A newly developed neurosurgery is on its way to potentially become the most efficient cure for severe depression. Its pioneer, Dr. Joseph Carter, joined us earlier in the week to discuss his marked success of the procedure...

"I don't care how much they praise it, no way am I going under the knife for anything. I'd much rather be a slave to pills for life if I have to," one man commented while watching the broadcast.

"Well, you wouldn't be so sure if you were me," a second man responded to his remark. "I'm almost down for anything that would help me forget about what happened with my ex-wife."

"What happened to her?"

"She used to threaten to kill herself when I had to leave home for work. She was depressed both during and after her pregnancy and I was always too busy to be there for her so it was really my fault. Anyway, one evening I came home, she was right there standing with a knife to her throat. Before I could get to her, she had done it. I rushed her to the hospital but the doctors couldn't revive her."

"Oh my... I'm sorry."

"Yup. I've been to tons of therapy sessions since and group counseling every week for a year just to be able to speak about it. Even after all that, the nightmares still won't go away. For months, I had only three hours of sleep on average each night and I couldn't focus at work during the day. I almost got fired. With the medication I'm taking now, my condition is improving but the progress is slow. I just don't want it ever relapsing you know."

"Now I see why you sounded so desperate."

"That, and besides, Dr. Carter is supposed to be this world-renowned physician. He must know what he's doing. If anything, I'm more concerned about how much he charges, since he's known to only attend to the wealthy and famous. I've heard appointments are by connection only."

"Is that right? That's one high and mighty man then if you ask me —"

"Mr. Dixon!" called Laura, from the reception desk.

"Well, that's me," said the second man. "Back to the daily grind I guess. Nice talking to you." As he headed up there, the first man scanned the deserted room and decided to make conversation with the only other person left sitting at the end of the couch holding a small bouquet of red roses — Martin.

"So, what brings you here?" he asked him inquisitively, but Martin was too occupied to speak, his eyes fixated on the television the whole time as he recognized Dr. Carter on its screen, talking arrogantly about his leading-edge treatment in a prerecorded interview:

INTERVIEWER: This is groundbreaking news. So Doctor, can you explain briefly how it's achieved on a prospective patient?

DR. CARTER: Certainly. As we human beings do naturally repress traumatic memories, the procedure will simply obstruct part of the neural pathways in the brain to aid this specific process. If successful, it should block the patient's recall after he or she is exposed to trauma triggers to prevent negative emotions from occurring.

INTERVIEWER: So what happens to the traumatic memories? Are they really permanently erased?

DR. CARTER: Not in the sense most people think of it, as in fact they will remain perfectly intact in the brain. The only difference is they are now — essentially — locked up in perpetuity. The patient will no longer be able to connect the dots between themselves and the trauma even when reminded, and hence it's like it has been permanently erased from their memory.

INTERVIEWER: This sounds like a rather impactful surgery.

DR. CARTER: It is, but it's also a minimally invasive one that can be done in under an hour through a small incision in the skull and the assistance of advanced robotic instruments.

INTERVIEWER: That's what I've heard. But nonetheless, many experts in the field, particularly ones in the States, still are concerned about its risks and potential complications. From my understanding, there have been heated, ethical debates since you first theorized the idea some four years ago. Is it true that you've relocated your research studies to Sweden so as to avoid being under fire by criticism?

DR. CARTER: Humph. Do you think it's true Ms. Pickett?

INTERVIEWER: Only you can answer that question, Doctor, but hopefully not?

DR. CARTER: Well, I can give you a definite no if that does anything. Bear in mind that people, experts or not, will always be critical of new things, but that never once deterred me from wanting to invent new methods to improve lives and perhaps never will. I'm extremely proud of how far my team and I have come in terms of finding a cure for the millions that are suffering right now. The fact is, of all the patients who've gone through the treatment, most have shown an immediate reduction in their symptoms right after the surgery...

"Mr. Hansen." Just then, Dr. Cooke came out of the therapy room, approaching the man who attempted to talk to Martin earlier. "Thank you for taking the time to come in today."

"Nah. I appreciate you catching this early, or else I might have had to end up paying everything out of pocket."

"It's always a good idea to keep your insurance information up to date."

"I couldn't agree more."

"Good. Well, when Laura's done with the paperwork you can be on your way. I will see you back here in two weeks to check on your progress."

"Thanks Doctor."

"Don't mention it." She then moved along to speak to Martin, who had by then gotten up and was ready to be greeted.

"And you, Mr. Blake."

Straightforwardly, he leaned in to kiss her on the cheek. "It's been a while Lisa."

"I said you didn't have to come up."

"I know. I was early."

She smiled, looking to the flowers. "Are those for me?"

"Happy birthday," he told her and handed her the bouquet.

"Thank you," she said happily, giving the roses a sniff. "Ready to go? I have exactly two hours before my next appointment."

"I am if you are."

"Have you thought about where you would like to go eat?"

"I don't care where. As long as they don't only serve seafood."

"Heh. You and your 'seafood allergy'."

"I just can't deal with the smell."

"Alright, don't worry. I know the right place to go..."

The two eventually came to a nice little bar-and-grill about ten minutes away on foot from Lisa's office to have lunch together. The last time the siblings gathered was briefly at her wedding reception six years ago. This was priceless time when compared to the occasional phone call they exchanged to stay in touch with one another. Despite it was mostly she who did the talking, conversations flowed naturally between them over the table along with plenty of laughter. Martin, mainly, just enjoyed her company.

"So, what did you do on your own birthday?" she asked him.

"I went to Narthwich to visit Sean."

"Really. How is he doing?"

"Fine. Still as thin as I remembered him."

"I heard from Levi that you were planning to go, but I wasn't sure if you really did come through this time. Good for you."

"When did you talk?"

"I'd say... about a month ago. He calls me up from time to time to keep me posted about my little brother, and to remind me of his 'freakishly dicey' temper."

"He still talks about that night at the police station?"

"I don't think he would let that one go for a very long time," teased she and took a sip of her drink. "Did you at least let him celebrate with you this year? Your big fortieth?"

"I stopped by the shop in the afternoon to see him."

"And?"

"And... and then I left and went home."

"That's it? He told me he had this whole thing planned. Candlelit dinner and all."

"Maybe he did, but I was too tired to do anything after the long drive so..."

"Oh Marty..."

"What?"

"You know what."

"I'm never into that sort of gesture. He should know that about me by now."

"Yes, but it's never really about how big the cake is or what gift he got you. It's the effort that courts."

"I never asked him for that kind of effort."

"You never asked for anything, that's true, but he had good intentions, the least you could do is be courteous."

"All right. If it matters to you this much, I'll call and apologize to him later. I just don't see why it's such a big deal."

"I'm sure that's what he wants…"

Martin just so caught her saying that sort of discreetly. "What is it now?"

Since he asked, Lisa had decided to take the chance to exercise her sisterly privilege and give him a little heart-to-heart. "How long have you guys been going out? Five years?"

"Six next month."

"You know a lot has changed since you first got together."

"Like what?"

"Like society, what most people think of a same-sex relationship —"

"Lisa…"

"They are even talking about same-sex marriage now."

"He's behind this, isn't it?"

"No."

"Lisa."

"Right… maybe a little bit. But I can understand where he's coming from. He told me his college roommate is eloping to get married in Iowa —"

"Then you don't understand where I'm coming from."

Crossing her arms, she sat back and let Martin put up his defenses.

"I don't mean it in a psychological sense. It's just… that is just something I have to forfeit for my career."

"By 'that' you mean marriage?"

"That whole concept, yes, and I couldn't care less about what others do in their own circumstances."

"Does he know how you feel about this?"

"We've gone over the subject many times, he just needs to get that out of his system and move on."

"You know, it's one thing to be self-conscious, it is totally another to end up losing someone you love so dear because of it."

"Stop trying to analyze me Lisa, *please*. I don't need you to do that... anymore."

There went a brief pause before she would drop the sensitive topic and continue, "So, what then? You went home and took a nap?"

"No. I read a book."

"You read a book? Here I thought you hated reading. Or was it a book for work?"

"Yes and... no."

"This sounds interesting."

"It was... but you know what, enough about me. Let's talk about something else."

"Okay... Ah, I'm hosting Mom's seventieth birthday in three months. Just giving you a heads-up before I forget."

"A heads-up for?"

"The party. I'm sure she would want to see you. It's going to be at my house on a weekend so everyone can come —"

"I'm not going."

"Marty —"

"He's going to be there isn't he?"

"Yes... Dad will be there."

"Then I'm definitely not going."

Half-battling a grin, Lisa shook her head. "It's funny how much you and him are alike, considering you aren't even related by blood. To tell the truth though, he's mellowed out quite a lot with age, not that he was ever really mad at you in the first place. Mom told me that he's wanted to reconcile with you since the day he kicked you out of the house. He really regrets it."

"He regrets it?"

"Yes, as difficult as it is for a stubborn, old, Catholic man to admit that he was wrong, he does."

"Okay. I hear you."

"So you will come?"

"No."

"Why not?"

"Because whether he regrets anything is the least of my concerns. I just... I just don't feel like seeing them —"

"Ever again?"

He said nothing.

Meanwhile, she added, "I understand you may never feel the same way for them as you do for your birth mother, but I know they did and do still love you very much like you are their own son."

"That's exactly why I can't bring myself to go see them. I just... can't be who they want me to be anymore."

"Is that what you're worried about? They don't care about that."

"Yeah right."

"I mean it. You are who you are and they've accepted that. I bet they would even want to meet Levi if you'd bring him along. They just miss you is all and are desperate to see you. They are certainly not getting younger so any day could be their last, especially with Mom's heart condition."

The thought of their old age and mortality incidentally softened his stance. Martin could not help ponder over what she said for a moment. "You should have been a salesman you know that. You would have made millions by now with that smartass mouth of yours."

"Nobody can persuade someone to do something they don't have the will to do anyhow. I just want you to seriously contemplate the idea, for their sake and your own."

"And I will," he concluded and let out a deep sigh. "Have you decided on a date? In case I do make an appearance."

A spontaneous smile lit up Lisa's face upon his change of heart. "Let me take a look at my calendar," she said and then reached into her handbag for her planner. During the process, she also pulled out a paperback novel for the pen used to bookmark the pages. Instantaneously Martin's eyes shifted to it, almost got weirded out seeing it was that same novel by Allison Skala, the one he had gone out to buy after meeting with Sean yesterday and finished reading last night.

"What is it?" asked Lisa, having caught him staring at it.

"That book."

"This? One of my patients gave it to me last year as a gift. I just got around to reading it. She wrote it as a matter of fact."

"Allison Skala. She's your patient?"

"Yes. For three years now. Do you know her personally?"

"More or less. When was the last time you saw her?"

"A few weeks ago, but hold on a minute. Why you are so curious about her?"

"She was once related to a case."

"You are referring to her sister-in-law's death."

"She told you?"

"I'm her psychiatrist."

"Right. You said she's been your patient for three years."

"Yeah?"

"Is it possible she didn't go to Sweden for treatment then?"

"Let me stop you before you start fishing for answers from me. You do know that I'm not obligated to tell you what we talk about during counseling, as in fact that information is strictly confidential and therefore I won't simply give it to you just because."

"I was afraid you'd say that."

"Besides, it's only a fiction."

"What is?"

"The murder in the book. I assumed you've read it."

"Right. Is that what she said it was? Something she dreamt up?"

"Come on Marty. I shouldn't need to tell you this, but think about it logically. How many times are murders written in mystery novels real? They can be based off of real-life events but they aren't really what they seem. If it makes you feel any better, I was the one who encouraged her to write that book."

"You did?"

"Yes. I thought it would help her move on from her past and it did. She's been making good progress towards recovery since. Although I must still suggest you to leave her alone for the time being if you can help it."

"Who said I was going to contact her?"

"I know you Marty. You are good at what you do for a reason."

"Sure, but honestly, there's nothing I can do about that case. I mean I tried, but it's been closed and done since the start."

"I see. Then why are you still wondering?"

"That's a long story for another day… Anyway, let's get back on track here. The date for the party?"

"Okay. Let me see…"

THREE MONTHS LATER

63

THREE IN THE afternoon, business was decently
streaming in at Gezellig on this particularly snowy,
January day. After a long morning running around
town slaving away at two back-to-back homicide investi-
gations, Martin too stopped by the shop briefly to bring a
touch of humanity back into himself.

Originally, he had come for a cup of espresso and
perhaps a little chitchat with Levi about his cold, hectic
day, but upon his sitting down on one of the stools at the
counter, someone tapped him on the shoulder. The moment he turned his head to look, he almost did not believe
who it was.

It was Allison with her hair in a low twisted bun, at-
tired in a wool trench coat and a scarf around her neck,
looking cheerful. "Detective Blake," she said to him, "I
thought I might run into you one of these days. I heard
that you hang out here sometimes."

Astounded to see her, Martin was temporarily struggling to formulate a response. Meanwhile, she worked to
summon up his memory. "It's me, Allison Skala. You were
in charge of my husband's murder case three years ago
around the end of September."

"I remember you," he replied, finally. "How are you?"

"I'm good. May I?"

He gave her a nod, and so she settled onto the stool
next to him. Her mood got more serious then, and possibly a little sad. "I would like to apologize to you formally
for all the trouble that was brought unto you by me and

my family. While there's no excuse, I want you to know that I'm deeply sorry."

"It's no problem, just part of my job."

"You see the thing is... I hadn't been well for a long time."

He had decided to ask her bluntly. "Did you go to Sweden?"

"Excuse me?"

"Did you go to Sweden for treatment?"

"I'm sorry. I heard you the first time. I just didn't expect you to know about that. But to answer your question — I didn't go."

"Oh?"

"I mean I did go, but I didn't go ahead with the surgery. It did, nevertheless, take me some real courage to get out of it, but that's beside the point. As in fact, shortly after arriving in Stockholm, I came back to take care of my husband's burial and never did return like I promised my parents. I've moved and changed my address since just to stay under their radar. It was working well for a while... forgive me for going off topic like that."

"It's okay."

"Anyway, I go to therapy here, locally."

"Why didn't you go through with the surgery? What changed your mind?"

"That's another long story. Let's just say that I discovered something my parents had slyly done for the longest time, which incidentally awakened me to the full scheme of decisions being made behind my back, and moreover, the severity of my condition. I suppose in the end, nothing explained to me better than watching myself loss grip of reality..."

The whole time she was telling him, Martin patiently listened. Even just from the little bit she confided, he could tell she had been through a lot the past few years to get to where she was today. Now he understood why Lisa insisted he leave her alone.

"I suppose the truth will always set you free. Whether good or bad, you are entitled to know."

She smiled at his reassurance. "I agree... It feels sort of inappropriate telling you this, but you remind me an awful lot of someone every time we talk."

"I hope that's a good thing."

"It certainly is for me. I'm usually bad at talking about myself with people I hardly know, but somehow it seems easier with you. In any case — there's just one more thing." Right then, she reached inside her shoulder bag and took out a USB thumb drive. "Here, I've been meaning to give this to you."

He accepted it.

"You will find out what it's about as soon as you open the file, and you have full rights as to what to do with it afterwards." Looking off briefly to the big wooden clock, she started to stand up. "I'd better get going. I'm meeting with my editor in half an hour across town. I don't have my car with me so I can't miss this bus."

"Let me walk you out." He too stood up.

"You don't have to, really, the stop is just outside —"

"I don't mind."

In turn, she smiled with gratitude. "Alright then."

Actually, Martin did not plan to be nice just for nice's sake. There had been a question — a rather unseemly one — stuck in his head that he had longed to ask since seeing Allison again. During the wait at the bus booth, he made an effort to bring it up.

"I didn't know you are a writer."

"I guess I never did tell you. Did you happen to see one of my novels at the bookstore?"

"I actually read one a few months ago."

"Really? Which one?" asked she, delighted to find out.

"I believe it's called, *Erase*."

"Ah. I wrote that two years ago. My psychiatrist urged me to get back to writing as she considered doing so to be highly cathartic. It's actually my first ever mystery fiction.

My two other published works before it are more of the romance genre... So, tell me honestly, what did you think of it?"

"I'm no critic in that area, really."

"Still, I would like to know your opinion."

"Well, it's a rather fascinating story filled with interesting characters and twisted plots," he told her candidly. At the same moment, a bus had come to a halt at the stop where a few of the people waiting for it started to queue up to get on.

"Thank you. I'm actually quite proud of how it turned out. I just hope that my next novel can live up to the same potential. Anyway, this is my bus." Swiftly, she moved to get in line and Martin followed. Since knowing no better time than now to ask his question, he did, briskly.

"Mrs. Skala."

"Just call me Allison."

"Did your mother kill her?"

Allison surely heard him. While she did not react strangely upon being put on the spot to address such a delicate yet almost ridiculous inquiry, she also did not turn around to reply to him until reaching the bus door a few seconds later. "Well, what would you have said?"

"Pardon?"

"What would your answer be if you were me?"

All of a sudden, he felt utterly naive to have asked a question with such an obvious answer.

"I love my mother, Martin. As unreasonable as she can be sometimes, I do. I made a mistake three years ago that I will never be able to go back and correct, but not again, never again in fact. So, can you understand there's only one possible answer to your question on my part?"

From her resolute gaze, Martin perceived a shared flicker of understanding that he was not able to fully grasp till now.

"Miss, are you getting on?" prompted the bus driver.

"Yes," Allison said to him, and then to Martin, "Take care." Like that, he watched her off. The bus went down towards the lighted intersection and before long receded from his view as it turned the corner.

Returning to his desk at work, Martin dug out the piece of audio about Allison's allegation of Megan's death from his own archive folder and listened to it again — for the last time — and then deleted it from his record permanently. His mind too, slowly but surely, learnt to let it go. Next, he opened the file inside the USB drive given to him. A surveillance video started playing, showing the attack that happened to him years ago at the Skalas' residence and the moments after he lost consciousness:

"... Do not worry Mr. Blake. You will be awake again soon enough." He heard Dr. Carter speak and watched him turn to talk to his men. "This should buy the Crawfords some time. Give him another dose of thiopental. I want him gone for the next couple of days." ...

64

A S THE BUS turned the corner out of Martin's view, Allison, standing gripping the handhold, breathed a deep relief to regain her composure, but was soon distracted by someone calling her.

"Ms. Allie."

She turned her head to look up at a familiar face staring back at her. *Of course,* she thought immediately, and replied in a tone of quiet annoyance, "Father sent you."

"Where are you going?" the man asked.

"Why don't you ask one of his other slaves? They seem to have been doing a good job following me around lately. I hope they are getting rewarded as promised."

"Your parents want to see you. They are worried."

"They are worried about their reputation."

"You know that's not it —"

"So now they've ordered you to come get me. How typical."

"They wouldn't have to if you'd just cooperate."

"Humph, cooperate."

"Yes —"

"You can *save* it! Thomas."

Her abrupt raise of volume lifted a few heads, but only for a short while before they would return to their own business on their electronic gadgets.

"This is not a time to be stubborn."

"So I should listen to you too, an all-willing, obedient servant."

Thomas just barely owned up to that mockery. "Call me whatever, but I'm not ashamed like you think I am. I've worked for your father for a long time and I'm loyal to him because of what he did for me many years ago."

"Is that why you are explaining yourself? How pathetic. So you owe him your life now I take it."

"In an abstract sense, yes. If it wasn't for his help, I would surely have spent most of my life behind bars for what I did —"

"And instead of that you are glad to be his lapdog —"

"*Watch your tongue —*"

"What am I saying wrong? He's got you under his thumb all these years by information he keeps against you like he's done to many of you. It's just a part of what he does to get his way. Only that you've developed a sort of Stockholm syndrome to make yourself feel better about the situation. It's either that or you are really *dumb* enough to believe that he cares about you, his so-called right-hand man —"

Having been very much provoked, he impulsively grasped Allison's arm half way through her sarcastic insult, pulling her close and warning her in a harsh, irritated tone, "You don't want to mess with me I tell you. I'm not afraid to break a few bones, which I would have done already had you not been Elton's *precious* little daughter, so just thank your lucky stars that you are. If I were you, rather than being a selfish, inflexible brat, I would have smartened up by now and been grateful for having parents with such power and influence, who are prepared to defend me at all costs whenever I decide to act out of spontaneous rage..."

His petty threat might have been a hollow one, by which Allison was not the least bit intimidated given her bulletproof position she knew he would not dare touch her, but it was, regardless, adequate and relevant enough to shut her up even just for a short period. Meanwhile, the intercom went off announcing the next stop. Utilizing the interruption, she broke free from his grip.

"I'm going to the park, *alone*," she told him firmly, keeping her expression bleak. "When you see my parents again, remind them for me that I'm old enough to fend for myself, and as far as they're concerned... I didn't say anything worth worrying about to the cop this time so try not to lose sleep over it."

The automatic door opened shortly afterwards, and she got off the bus unaccompanied.

It was beginning to snow heavily. Although the wind had let up, the rapid snowfall made it impossible to see far. Following the plowed sidewalk that was once more going white, eventually, she arrived at Oakfield Memorial Park. From the main gate, she entered the cemetery and went up the slope that led her to a big, naked oak tree extending its long, frosty boughs over rows of tombstones.

Carrying certain courage, she located Daniel's and crouched down in front of it. Despite the cold, she removed her leather gloves, devoted to brush off the snow blanketing the stone with her bare hands. Rubbing her fingers tenderly across his name on the marker, she ruminated on the good memories that united them, but not for long before something grisly on her mind intruded those pleasant thoughts. Even though Daniel was long dead and gone, every time she came here, she could still feel Megan's lingering existence attaching to his, reminding her about her death, and sense his grudging. One moment she closed her eyes to clear her silly thinking, breathing in the surrounding peace and silence, the next, she gave a deep, calming sigh and reopened them. Upon which, she spotted an object half-buried in the snow near the base of the headstone.

Curiosity had her reaching out for it, but if serenity was what she came here for, what she discovered was far from that. As it turned out, it was a framed picture of Allison herself, sitting in the nude in a tub of blood with a bruised neck and gashed wrist, looking to have been brutally slain. Shocked by the image, she flung it and her legs moved apace to back away, almost too quickly for her body to catch up. "Who... who did this?!" she shouted in panic, and looked out across the hazy graveyard but saw no one except for the stillness that unnervingly greeted her. Panting in fright, she waited till the frantic heartbeat in her chest calmed a little and worked up the nerve to venture a look to the ground two feet ahead, where she presumed the picture had landed. Oddly enough, it was not there or anywhere around to be seen.

Please God... wake me up from this nightmare...

Again, it was her conscience's doing, messing with her head. She had learnt to recognize it for a fact after all this time, but could not escape it nonetheless.

I only did what I did because I loved him...
I wanted him all to myself, was it really so wrong?

J Y Barris is an author and graphic designer.
She lives in Minnesota with her lovely husband, Sam, and
their two chubby cats. Or was it her chubby husband and
their two lovely cats... ☺

Visit her at jybarris.wixsite.com/erase

23378687R00246

Printed in Great Britain
by Amazon